The turn of the century was an auspicious time for a young Japanese man to embrace a military career. Japan had only begun to embark on the road to fulfilling what it considered its divine destiny. Having only recently industrialized, Japan vitally needed the raw materials and markets of China. In 1895 Japan fought a war with China, only to find its rightful fruits snatched away by the European powers. Not to be undone, Japan simply aspired to more expansion as part of its divine destiny.

The military was the forger of the empire, and as such was held in high esteem by the Japanese people. At the age of fifteen, young Tomoyuki applied to one of the recently opened military academies. Years later, he would be known as General Tomoyuki Yamashita. When asked why he, the son of a doctor, chose a military career, he would answer: *It was perhaps my destiny* . . .

ADVENTURE THROUGH WORLD WAR II

THE SGT. #1: DEATH TRAIL (600, $2.25)
by Gordon Davis
The first in the dynamic World War II series featuring the action crammed exploits of the Sergeant, C.J. Mahoney. With a handful of *maquis*, Mahoney steals an explosive laden train and heads for a fateful rendezvous in a tunnel of death!

THE SGT. #2: HELL HARBOR (623, $2.25)
by Gordon Davis
Tough son-of-a-gun Mahoney leaves a hospital bed to fulfill his assignment: he must break into an impregnable Nazi fortress to disarm the detonators that could blow Cherbourg Harbor—and himself—to doom. . . .

THE SGT. #3: BLOODY BUSH (647, $2.25)
by Gordon Davis
C.J. Mahoney is sent to save an entire company from being torn apart in Normandy's savage Battle of the Hedgerows. And if the vicious panzers don't get him, the vengeful Yank commander will. . . .

IN SEARCH OF EAGLES (913, $2.50)
by Christopher Sloan
The breathtaking drama of World War II dogfights comes back to life when Captain James Sutton undertakes an incredible mission. The chances for survival are minimal, but Sutton is born for the glory of the air!

Available wherever paperbacks are sold, or order direct from the Publisher. Send cover price plus 50¢ per copy for mailing and handling to Zebra Books, 475 Park Avenue South, New York, N.Y. 10016. DO NOT SEND CASH.

THE GREAT COMMANDERS OF WORLD WAR II
VOLUME IV: THE JAPANESE

ZEBRA BOOKS
KENSINGTON PUBLISHING CORP.

ZEBRA BOOKS

are published by

KENSINGTON PUBLISHING CORP.
475 Park Avenue South
New York, N.Y. 10016

Copyright © 1982 by Charles Pfannes and Victor Salamone

All rights reserved. No part of this book may be reproduced in any form or by any means without the prior written consent of the Publisher, excepting brief quotes used in reviews.

Printed in the United States of America

To Susanne Salamone: A woman of unlimited love and dedication who gives this tired writer endless inspiration.

Table of Contents

PREFACE	Page 7
INTRODUCTION	Page 11
CHAPTER ONE GENERAL TOJO	Page 28
CHAPTER TWO ADMIRAL YAMAMOTO	Page 77
CHAPTER THREE ADMIRAL NAGUMO	Page 137
CHAPTER FOUR ADMIRAL TANAKA	Page 188
CHAPTER FIVE GENERAL YAMASHITA	Page 228
CHAPTER SIX ADMIRAL OZAWA and ADMIRAL KURITA	Page 277

Preface

We now come to our fourth volume in the Great Commanders series. Since beginning work on these books we have grown in self-confidence and enthusiasm for this valuable series. Though each volume can stand alone, we hope that when the series is completed it will form a compendium of the entire history of World War II. We are interested not only in personalities; strategy, tactics, logistics, espionage, politics, and scientific discoveries are discussed, as well, and analyzed in relationship to the total history of the war. We hope that this series will be welcomed as a valuable asset by students and enthusiasts of the war, for it represents thousands of hours of painstaking research undertaken in order to present the latest, most up-to-date facts about its every aspect.

In this volume we cover the Japanese commanders. One glance at the table of contents will indicate to the reader that we have not restricted our choices of the Japanese commanders we will discuss to army men. There is a reason for this. First, for Americans, the better part of the war against the Japanese was fought on the sea. It is the names of the Japanese admirals that immediately come to the minds of Americans. Second, the war in the Pacific, except for what action took place on the large Asian mainland, was fought on islands that were either jungle-covered or were too small to accommodate vast numbers of army forces. Consequently, the Japanese war in the Pacific against the Americans was for the most part a naval war. Army forces did take part, of course, but it was toward the naval commanders that American interest turned.

In our introduction we discuss the reasons why the Bataan Death March occurred and why General Homma paid the ultimate price because of it. General Tojo, Japan's wartime prime minister, is examined in our first chapter. Though history has put a cloud over his reputation, we have tried to clarify his position and present the case for understanding him as a Japanese patriot. After Tojo we discuss Admiral Yamamoto, the creator of the Pearl Harbor Operation. Though branded a warmonger by Americans, he was in reality most reluctant to go to war. Admiral Nagumo, the Cautious, is the subject of our next chapter, followed by Admiral Tanaka, who was known as the Tenacious One. In chapter five we examine the career of General Yamashita, the Tiger of Malaya, and in the last chapter we look at the parallel careers of Admiral Ozawa and Kurita. Their paths were to meet in the world's largest naval battle, the Battle of Leyte Gulf.

Again there are many people we would like to thank. We have said it before, but we must say it again: We thank all the people at Zebra. We again want to mention our wives and children, whose smiling faces and endless admiration give their husbands and fathers boundless inspiration. We would particularly like to thank Tom Pfannes for giving us the benefit of his expertise in the subject of Japanese warships.

Victor A Salamone
Poughkeepsie, New York

Charles 'Chuck' Pfannes
Cold Spring, New York

March 17, 1982

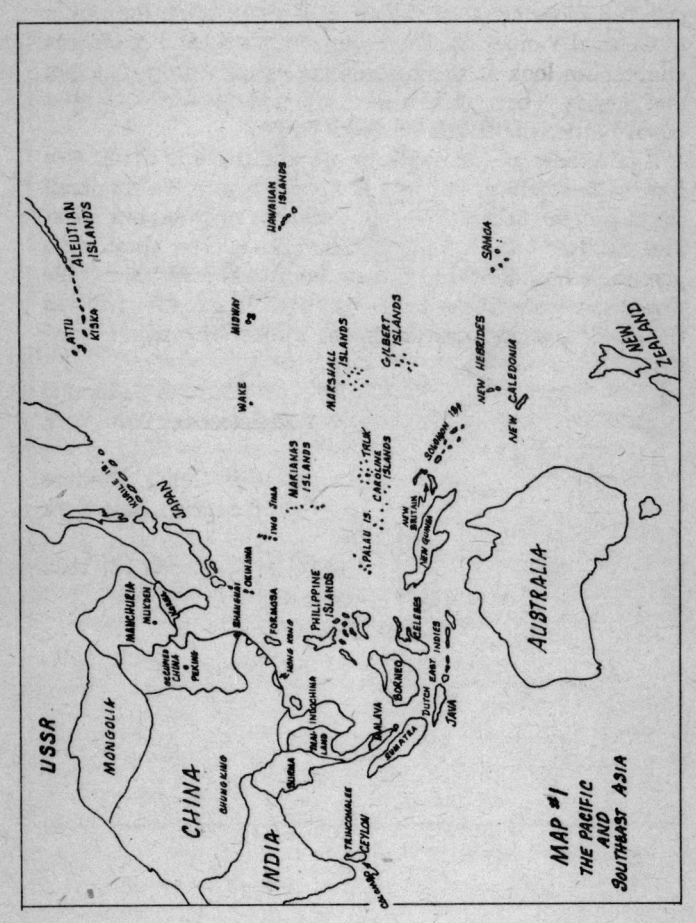

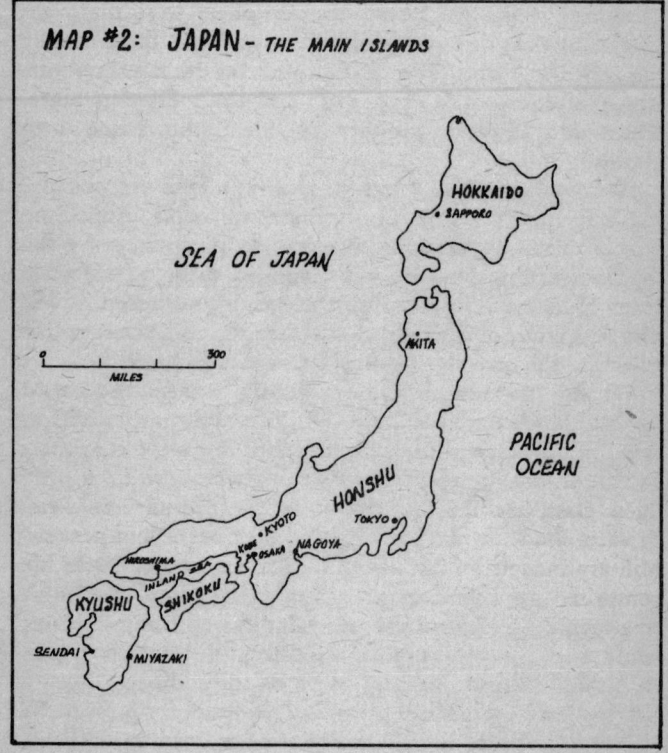

Introduction

The Bataan Death March and General Homma

When many Americans reflect on World War II and their thoughts wander to the Japanese, more often than not they think of the Bataan Death March. There were many incidents of atrocities recorded in the war, but these usually happened to others. The death march on Bataan, however, was exacted against Americans and their Filipino allies. These were American servicemen; men from home town U.S.A.

How could such an event happen? Who was responsible? It is our intention to be as objective as possible. This in no way is meant to be a justification or an apology for the Japanese action. Rather, it is intended to be an objective study of how and why the horrible tragedy occurred. It will also be a study of the man who ultimately paid the supreme price for the atrocity, General Masaharu Homma.

When a Japanese civilian entered the ranks of the armed forces, his life underwent a radical change, particularly in the army. The army's values and discipline were absolutely brutal. In the Japanese Army the officers formed a privliged class. At the bottom were the ordinary soldiers. Privates had no human rights; they were nonpersons. Military indoctrination, training, and routine barracks life comprised an unending stream of humiliation and harsh treatment. Physical abuse of trainees was commonplace, while weapons and vehicles were treated with more care than the recruit. Cruelty towards subordinates was a psychological technique, providing an outlet for pressure by allowing each rank to shift the oppression downward. Thus, the lowest of the low, the recruit, was the recipient of the greatest abuse.

Japanese military leaders believed that stiff discipline was the only way to train troops. Junior officers were cautioned against being lenient, for it was felt that hate directed at an officer could easily be redirected towards the enemy.

> "The skillful commander could, by treating his men with calculated brutality, mold them into a fierce fighting unit against the enemy in time of war."[1]

The inevitable result of this kind of training was the creation of a breed of vicious fighters. Men under pressure of combat express this irrational destructive behavior with acts of inhuman brutality against their enemy. Individuals whose own dignity and manhood had been so cruelly violated would hardly refrain from doing the same to defenseless persons under their control. But this insight represents only one piece of the total picture surrounding the why of the death march.

An Imperial soldier was trained to fight to the death for his emperor. Such sacrifice brought great honor to his family and personal salvation to himself. Perhaps his instruction manual stated it best:

> "Bear in mind the fact that to be captured means not only that you disgrace yourself, but your parents and family will never be able to hold up their heads again. Always save the last bullet for yourself."[2]

Thus, to be taken prisoner was a fate worse than death. A soldier literally ceased to exist, his name expunged from the register of his own village or town. This view left the Japanese soldier ignorant of Western ethics. He regarded all military captives as subhuman, worthy only of the greatest of contempt. Death was better than surrender.

Because of this, the Japanese placed little value on safety devices, since that would be a demonstration of cowardice. For them the only virtue was the acceptance of life-and-death risks. Precautions were unworthy. This attitude found expression in the way the Japanese handled their own sick and wounded. These soldiers were damaged goods; it would be more heroic if they perished. The Japanese Army had no trained rescue teams to remove the wounded under fire. It had no medical system to care for the front line wounded and inadequate ones at best behind the lines. Its attention to medical supplies was minimal, and, in times of crisis, wounded Japanese soldiers were usually simply killed. If this attitude toward "damaged goods" was fundamental in the treatment by the Japanese of their own comrades, it was all the more reflected in their treatment of their prisoners-of-war.

Therefore, since a Japanese was taught never to surrender, he was bound to fight to the death. If the situation was hopeless, he was expected to kill himself with his last bullet or grenade, or, better yet, charge the enemy in a mass suicidal attack.

To the Japanese then, an American, Filipino, British or any other of their foes who had become prisoners of war were disgraced by the mere act of surrender. They were "damaged goods," no longer complete men. The prisoners had suffered the greatest humiliation. The Japanese were always perplexed by the American lack of sense of humiliation upon surrendering. More often than not the Japanese soldier was angered by this attitude.

In order to understand another piece of the puzzle it is necessary to understand this great cultural difference. Many of the harsh orders that American prisoners were forced to obey were simply what most Japanese soldiers themselves were expected to do. The forced marches and closely packed transhipments were commonplace to them. In other words, what was very often seen as atrocious behavoir was in reality a normal callous attitude towards subordinates. However, in the case of the prisoner of war who was even a rung lower, not even fit to be considered human, and who by his very surrender had forfeited his dignity, the treatment was worse yet. The Japanese code of behavior, Bushido, had seen to that.

Having reviewed the cultural reasons for the attitude that made the death march possible, let us now turn to the man who would die because of it, General Homma. Homma was born on November 27, 1887, on Sado Island off the northwest coast of Japan. At age fifteen he chose the army as a career and subsequently entered the military academy. After graduating at the head of his class, he was assigned to an infantry regiment with the rank of 2nd lieutenant. After a successful tour of duty he was posted as military attaché to Prince Chichibu, the youngest brother of the emperor. In 1914 Homma attended the staff college, from which he graduated with honors. From there he was assigned, in 1918, to a British Army unit, where he observed firsthand the horrors of trench warfare. When the First World War ended he was assigned to the 1st Battalion of the British Army's East Lancashire Regiment. From there he went on to the general staff of the British East Indian Army in India. Finally, Homma returned to Japan in December 1925, attaining the rank of major. There he was assigned to the Imperial Army Headquarters.

Homma quickly earned a reputation as a military genius, thus assuring his future. In the early 1930s he found himself once more in London. In 1933 he returned to Tokyo and an appointment as regimental commander of the 1st Infantry Regiment. Two years later he was promoted to major general and made head of the Army Propaganda Department.

Homma soon became known as a moderate who opposed war with the United States and Great Britain. This pro-Western leaning led to his making a number of important enemies, among them, General Hideki Tojo. Though he attempted to steer clear of political intrigue, Homma's high position in the army thrust him into the camp of the pro-Anglo faction. He violently opposed the choice of Tojo as vice war minister because he knew of the latter's anti-Western attitude.

This opposition to Tojo drove Homma out of Tokyo to a posting in China. The Sino-Japanese war was already in full swing when he took command of the 27th Division. While a divisional commander he cemented his reputation as a brilliant and courageous leader. However, the antagonism of the army leaders toward him resulted in his remaining in China.

In December 1940 Homma was transferred to Formosa as

the head of the Japanese forces there. During his time on that island his subordinates began to sense a negative trait developing in their commander. More and more he isolated himself from his juniors while drawing deeper and deeper into his own private world. He left the daily running of his command to subordinate officers and became oblivious to the reality of what was actually happening in his own command.

Events moved in rapid succession and Japan found itself moving closer to war. On November 2, 1941, Homma and General Tomoyuki Yamashita were ushered into the office of General Sugiyama, army chief of staff. Sugiyama informed them that Japan would soon be at war with the United States and Great Britian. The chief of staff eyed Homma to see his reaction, knowing full well the latter's pro-Western attitude. In fact, Sugiyama disliked Homma, but he knew that he was one of Japan's most brilliant strategists. Sugiyama explained the army strategy and then told Homma that he was to command the Fourteenth Army, whose objective was the conquest of the Philippines.

Homma asked why the Fourteenth was being allotted only two divisions with which to carry out its task and why he was expected to accomplish his mission in only fifty days. He stated that he had too few men and too short a time. Sugiyama was upset that Homma had questioned his authority. He shot back, saying,

> "The fifty day period is an integral part of the strategic pattern for the entire Pacific campaign. The figure is firm and you will have to accept it."[3]

Unconvinced, Homma continued to question his superior. Both Yamashita and another general who was present confided to Homma after the meeting that the fifty days and the small allotment of troops were unrealistic. Sugiyama, however, was boiling with rage. He would not forget the heated debate.

Back at his headquarters in Formosa, Homma fumed. His staff informed him that if MacArthur decided to make a stand in the Bataan Peninsula, the allotted forces would be insufficient for the task. Homma sent a message to Sugiyama emphasizing his staff's appreciation. In response he received this curt reply.

> "The main purpose of the attack on the Philippines is the occupation of Manila, which is not only the political capital but a place of military importance. The troops opposed to you are third class and unworthy to face in battle. If therefore they retreat to Bataan, there is no reason why you should not blockade them there."[4]

After the attack on Pearl Harbor on December 7, 1941, Homma's forces were loaded aboard transports and dispatched to the Philippines. With his two divisions, approximately 60,000 men, he faced the task of assaulting the mountainous island of Luzon. Nevertheless, thanks to the ill-trained Filipino troops, Homma gained a beachhead on Lingayen Gulf on December 22, 1941 (*see Map 3*).

MacArthur was soon forced to implement War Plan Orange,* ordering his forces into the highly defensible Bataan Peninsula. This was the very thing Homma feared. Unhappily for the defenders, MacArthur's hesitation in ordering the strategic retreat resulted in no food being stored in Bataan. This added another piece to the story of the death march.

MacArthur was able successfully to conduct a retreat into Bataan thanks to Imperial Headquarters which, as we have already seen, ordered Homma to take Manila. If the general could have diverted his forces to Bataan he might have cut off the retreat, thereby sealing the fate of MacArthur's forces. With Manila in his hands, Homma realized that the city was useless without the strategic positions on Bataan and the island of Corregidor. Both of these could be successfully utilized to deny access to Manila Bay.

The fighting on Bataan proved brutal. Homma

---

*See Volume III, *The Americans*, Chapter 6.

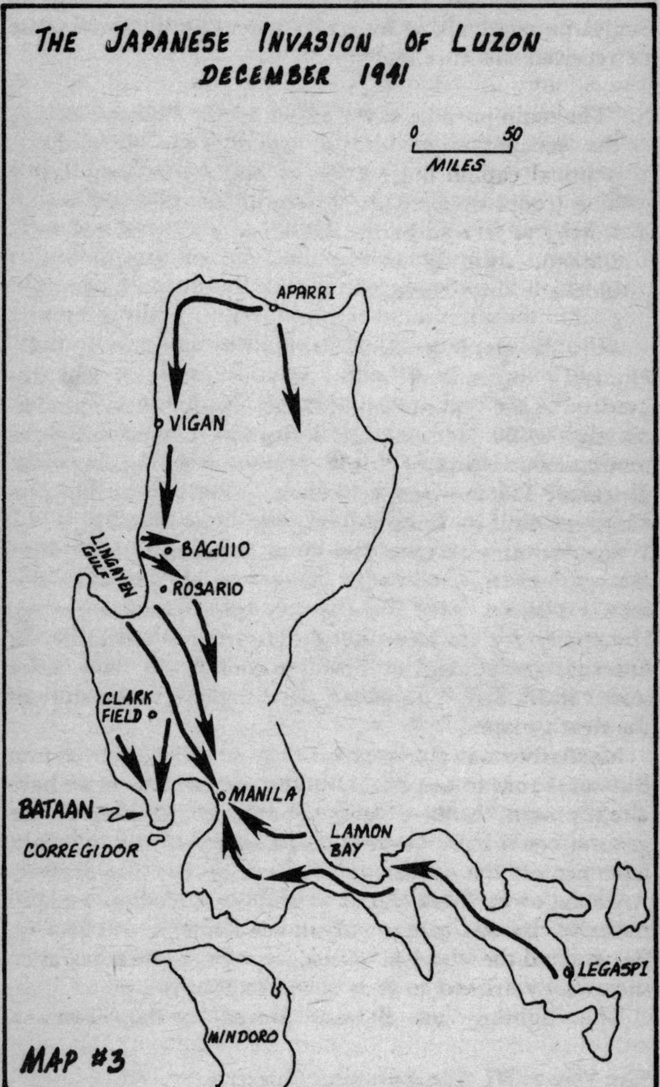
THE JAPANESE INVASION OF LUZON
DECEMBER 1941
0
50
MILES
APARRI
VIGAN
LINGAYEN GULF
BAGUIO
ROSARIO
CLARK FIELD
MANILA
BATAAN
CORREGIDOR
LAMON BAY
LEGASPI
MINDORO
MAP #3

underestimated the strength of his defenders, believing that they had only twenty-five thousand troops. In reality, he faced a combined force of seventy-eight thousand men. Sugiyama pressured Homma to clear the peninsula, even threatening to remove him if the task were not accomplished in short order. Homma remained, but his forces were depleted. It was incredible that General Headquarters pressured him to clear Bataan but refused to provide him with the forces to do so. Homma's low estimate of the number of troops on Bataan might have convinced Sugiyama that his field commander did not have that much with which to contend. Instead, Homma found himself facing three times the number of soldiers originally estimated. And these were entrenched in excellent defensive terrain.

The blow came to Homma on February 8, when he received a message from Imperial Headquarters. His chief of staff found him at his desk in tears holding a message stating that the emperor was very concerned at the lack of progress. This was the most humiliating thing a Japanese officer could hear. Homma knew, however, that it was Sugiyama who had sent the message, using the emperor's name. It was this knowledge that caused him not to commit suicide. He also knew that this message was Sugiyama's way of covering up his own strategic error by ordering Homma to take Manila instead of slamming shut the gates to Bataan. Now that a stalemate had resulted, Sugiyama was anxious to pass the buck.

Homma dictated a letter to Imperial Headquarters questioning the necessity of continuing the attack on Bataan. Sugiyama burst into a fit of rage upon receipt of the letter. He quickly called a meeting of the General Staff and urged Homma's recall. The General Staff presented arguments against this rash decision and the meeting ended in a compromise. Homma was to remain in command, but his chief of staff would be replaced. In the latter's place Sugiyama was directed to appoint a "more aggressive" man, Major General Takaji Wachi, a personal friend of Sugiyama's. In addition, Homma's antagonist sent Colonel Masanobu

Tsuji, a noted fanatic, who was responsible for numerous atrocities in China and Malaya. Now Sugiyama had two spies on Homma's staff.

Despite all this there was one ray of hope for Homma. Reinforcements were also dispatched. Homma looked aghast at these reinforcements when they reached the Philippines. They were units of misfits, poorly trained and equipped. Once more Homma vented his rage at the man out to sabotage his career.

Nevertheless, Homma began preparations for the attack. In his appreciation of the enemy he constantly made two glaring errors. He underestimated the strength of his enemy and overrated their physical condition.

"They are never allowed to go hungry."[5]

This conception was entirely erroneous: At that very time the men of Bataan were starving, and many of their number were suffering from some sort of tropical ailment.

On April 3, Good Friday, the final attack began, ending in a huge success a week later. Major General King, though under orders from his superior General Jonathan Wainwright not to surrender, realized that further resistance was suicidal. Food was nearly exhausted and the troops barely able to continue. King took it upon himself to surrender, and at 3:30 on the morning of April 9, 1942, he sent two staff officers under a flag of truce to make contact with the Japanese commander.

Unfortunately, King was not to meet Homma. Instead, he met the general's representative, Colonel Moto Nukayama. King found himself in a difficult position, for Nukayama demonstrated an obvious contempt for him. In fact, Nukayama thought King was actually Wainwright, there to surrender all of the Philippines. King had a difficult time trying to convince the Japanese that he was simply the commander of Bataan and as such could only surrender that area. Nukayama was visibly annoyed and refused to listen to any terms King proposed, particularly those regarding the treatment of prisoners of war. General

King did all he could, but was unable to secure a pledge from the Japanese that any prisoners would be well treated.

Homma had, however, already made plans for the disposition of the prisoners. He was not a savage beast out to vent his vengeance. In fact, he wished to stick very closely to the Geneva Convention guidelines regarding the conduct towards prisoners of war, something he wasn't obliged to do, since Japan was not a signer of the convention. Nevertheless, Homma wanted the prisoners treated properly. As early as March, a few weeks prior to the April 3 offensive, Homma had held a conference where he brought up the topic of future prisoners of war before the assembled officers. He anticipated the need to evacuate any prisoners as quickly as possible so that the Japanese could concentrate on the campaign. He assigned five officers to the task of planning for the movement.

On March 23, the five officers completed their plans and submitted them to Homma. The plans were relatively simple. They divided the chore into two phases, the first covering the assembling of all the captives, the second the actual journey to the prison camp (*see Map 4*). Balanga in the east of Bataan was selected as the assembly point for all prisoners. From there they were to proceed to the prison camp. For the first phase no provision was made for transportation, because most of the distances to be traveled were short, the longest being twenty-five miles. The Japanese Army did not pamper its soldiers in any way. Vehicles and fuel were much too precious commodities to waste on men who were capable of walking. The Japanese soldier was used to marching, it was a daily routine in his training. Thus the relatively short distances the prisoners would have to walk to Balanga were not considered excessive by Japanese standards. At any rate, the prisoners would have little choice. Balanga was the food depot; if the prisoners wanted to eat, they would have to walk to Balanga.

Colonel Takatsu was given command of this first phase and General Kawane was responsible for the second. It was the latter's job to feed the prisoners, care for the sick and

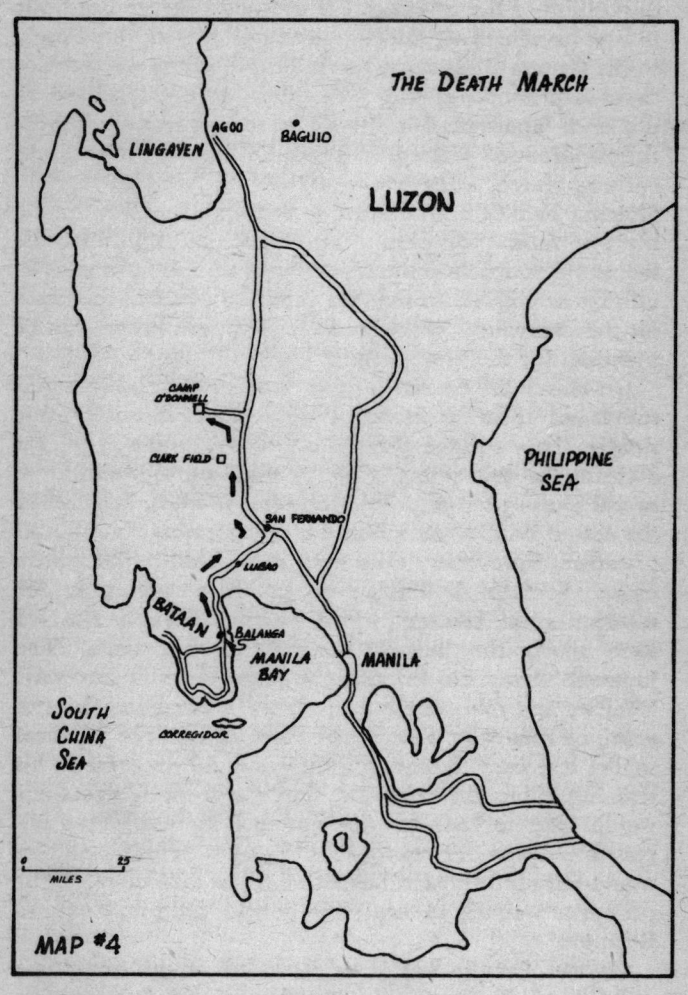

wounded, and provide transportation to the permanent prisoner-of-war camp. Kawane had planned to issue the prisoners the same quality and quantity of food issued to his own troops. Even before the fall of Bataan he designated four towns along the anticipated route and assembled rations there. Balanga was the first of these towns. From there it was sixty-five miles to the final destination, through Orani, then along Route 7 to Lubao in central Luzon, where again the prisoners would be fed. They would then push on to San Fernando where they were to receive their final meal before reaching the internment camp, Camp O'Donnell, a short train ride northward. Kawane even planned to establish field hospitals along the way to care for the sick and wounded. Ideally it was hoped that all would be transported in vehicles, but given the fact that the Japanese Army was not highly motorized, it was expected that large numbers would have to be marched. However, there would be enough food for the marchers.

This then was the plan submitted to Homma and the one he accepted. He added an order that the captives were to be treated with a friendly spirit. Tragically, neither the plan nor the order were carried out. Why?

A number of fatal errors turned the march into one of World War II's great atrocitites. The two phases were under the command of two different individuals. No one person was responsible for coordinating the entire operation. Second, there was the fatal miscalculation regarding the number of prisoners. The Japanese had estimated the potential number of prisoners to be somewhere between twenty-five and forty-five thousand. They never anticipated that the total would exceed seventy-five thousand. They compounded this error by underestimating the physical condition of the defenders of Bataan. The Japanese labored under the misconception that the enemy was adaquately fed and in decent health. They never expected what they eventually found.

Another serious underestimation was of the length of time the defenders would hold out after the launching of the April 3 offensive. When the capitulation came sooner than expected, Colonel Takatsu and General Kawane found themselves not yet ready to deal with the prisoners. The fall of Bataan in less than one week after the beginning of the offensive took them completely by surprise. They now were faced with double the anticipated number of prisoners, already underfed and sick, and the preparations for moving them were not complete.

Since Homma's offensive was considered secondary to the main drives in Malaya and the Dutch East Indies, he was given a lower priority in troops, supplies, and equipment. He had barely enough transportation and supplies to accommodate his own troops, let alone a horde of the enemy. His men suffered food shortages. Even medical supplies were in short supply, and many Japanese soldiers died needlessly for lack of proper medical attention. Many thousands suffered from malaria and other tropical illnesses. Suddenly responsible for over a hundred thousand civilians, Filipino and American troops, the Japanese found themselves overwhelmingly burdened.

For days after General King's surrender the prisoners poured into Balanga. Some, the lucky ones, came by truck, but for the most part they were on foot. Along the path to Balanga no food was provided. After all, why should it be? The longest one might have to travel was twenty-five miles. That was not impossible, of course, if one were healthy. Because of the state of the men, however, the trip to Balanga was a horror. It took some groups over two days. Water and food became an obsession, particularly the water. The first phase proved a complete failure. It was totally disorganized, uncoordinated, inadequately supervised and excessively brutal, as the merciless Japanese soldiers vented their vengeance and hatred on their captive foe. They looked upon the prisoners as something less than human and treated them as such. Thousands of individual horror stories could be recounted. The brutal behavior, however, seemed arbitrary, almost at the whim of the group leader. Some Japanese were rather benign to the captives, but many were just the opposite. Slowly then, the POWs made their way to Balanga.

Once at Balanga, the second phase of the Japanese plan was scheduled to take place. Transportation was supposed to be provided for one quarter of the prisoners. The remainder were expected to walk, but were also scheduled to rest along the route. Unfortunately, like phase one, this part of the plan was also a failure. It culminated in the tragedy that became known a the infamous Bataan Death March.

When the prisoners assembled at Balanga, the area became a cesspool of filth.

". . . a quagmire of filth and corruption, the smell and stain of diseased human waste covered the area like a fetid mist and hastened the spread of dysentery germs."[6]

Then they marched away from Balanga. A number of the prisoners were allowed to ride on trucks. Regrettably, because of the underestimate of prisoners expected, many more walked than was originally anticipated. Once more brutality was the rule of thumb. At times a compassionate Japanese mitigated the tragedy, but cruelty prevailed. By the time the horror was over, nearly 650 Americans and almost ten thousand Filipinos had needlessly perished.

When Americans found out about the death march nearly two years later, they viewed it as a deliberate Japanese policy of torture and murder. In fact, the death march was not an organized policy, nor was it consciously and maliciously directed.

". . . it was, rather, the confused result of a tragic combination of circumstances, attitudes and events."[7]

Most of the atrocities were perpetrated by relatively junior officers or private soldiers, not the generals.

We can now tie all the pieces together and see how and why this tragedy occurred.

The phase plan was not sufficiently modified or corrected to fit the reality of the situation. Leadership was absent.

Where was Homma? He had a more important problem to deal with—the assault on Corregidor. The pressure from Sugiyama to end the campaign was foremost in his mind. The disposition of the American and Filipino troops captured on Bataan was low on his list of priorities. Besides, he felt that adequate preparations had been made, and he had no reason to suspect that the plan was not being carried out. He didn't feel this way because he was not concerned, but rather because he had a job to do. The very fact that he ordered a plan organized for the disposition of the captives proved that he was concerned. How could he know the outcome? In fact, Colonel Glattly, a medical officer, has said,

> "The so-called death march would have been nothing more than discomfort for those who were in good physical condition."[8]

Unfortunately, the captives were anything but healthy, and Homma was never informed of the weak physical condition of the Bataan forces. Even at his trial he claimed that he knew nothing of the death march.

Granted, the weak physical condition of the prisoners coupled with inadequate means of transporting them contributed to the disaster, but that in itself could not entirely have caused the horror. The real horror was the

> ". . . results of hundreds of years of violence, treachery, and superstition, of a difficult competitive existence in a crowded land where human life was the cheapest of commodities, and of a deliberate indoctrination."[9]

That and the code of Bushido, which looked down on prisoners. To be a prisoner was to be disgraced. This code, in combination with the training of the brutal army system produced a soldier who was prone to ignore the sufferings of others, who was totally unfeeling. The fact that the POWs on Bataan were not ashamed for having surrendered was difficult for the Japanese to understand and infuriated many of them. They looked down on the prisoners with utter contempt.

Then, of course, we cannot neglect the desire for revenge. Most of the Japanese had suffered themselves throughout the Bataan campaign. Friends had been lost because of the enemy. This made the Japanese vengeful and they readily vented it on the pitiful ragged prisoners.

It's obvious that the great cultural gulf between the Americans and Japanese contributed to the horror. Language and custom differences made for misunderstandings. The fact that Americans freely questioned orders, something a Japanese would never do, was hard for the latter to comprehend. The first reaction when an American questioned an order was to strike the impertinent prisoner. Furthermore, the Japanese soldiers frequently acted out of emotion. Not accustomed to thinking for themselves, they were lost when faced with a difficult situation. For instance, a Japanese soldier was told that no prisoner was to escape. But what if a prisoner fell from exhaustion? What then was a Japanese guard to do? If he stayed behind with the prisoner, he risked the escape of the others. If he went ahead then the fallen prisoner would probably escape as soon as he had recovered. Faced with this dilemma, the Japanese soldier frequently became hysterical, and in his frenzy, kicked, slapped, or more often than not killed the prisoner. That solved his problem very neatly. Now no one escaped.

Thus the causes for the death march can be broken down into five major categories: the deteriorated physical state of the defenders; the Japanese unpreparedness to receive so many prisoners in such weakened condition; the cultural background of the Japanese soldier who, by training, was taught to be cruel particularly to those no longer worthy to be treated as human; the desire for revenge; and finally, the failure of the Japanese leadership to adequately supervise and restrain the hostility towards the prisoners. Thus was one of the potential horrors of World War II allowed to become a reality.

As for Homma, after the fall of Corregidor he was recalled to Japan in a state of disgrace, thanks to the machinations of Sugiyama. In 1945 he was returned to Manila and put on trials for crimes against humanity, crimes he never committed nor ordered committed, and he was found guilty. MacArthur refused to consider commutation of the death sentence. In the spring of 1946, General Homma met his end by firing squad.

Tojo

Chapter I

Tojo! Was he Japan's Hitler? When Americans hear the name Tojo they immediately conjure up the image of a short, bucktoothed, sword-waving, arch criminal who typified the Japanese warmonger. During the war years Tojo was the butt of most of the American's war hatred. V-mail airogrammes had printed on them such statements as "Tojo is a bum."[1] Was he, though, the smirking Japanese villain, totally treacherous and devious, or was he instead a scapegoat who took the blame for the war on his own shoulders in order not to implicate the National Essence, *i.e.*, the Imperial Emperor, Hirohito? Was Tojo the architect of the Pacific War, or was he instead a Japanese patriot who believed strongly in the righteousness of Japan's cause?

This chapter will attempt to shed some light on those most difficult questions. They are difficult indeed, for the sources can be very confusing. The authors, however, have attempted to analyze the endless piles of information and come up with an accurate image of the real Hideki Tojo.

Tojo was born in Tokyo on December 30, 1884, one of eleven children. His father, Hidenori Tojo, was a career soldier in the Imperial Japanese Army. Entering the army as an enlisted man, Hidenori rose in the ranks and had attained the exalted rank of lieutenant general by the time of his retirement at the age of fifty-three. Young Hideki thrived on the exploits of his father and with the premature death of his two older brothers, was pushed into the honored position of number one son. This meant that he was expected to carry on the profession of his father and become a soldier. To most Japanese, the army was the embodiment of all that was good in the past, for the soldiers were the inheritors of the ancient samurai code of

Bushido.*

Hideki's stature was not great, but his spirit was strong. He was fearless and tenacious, which caused his classmates to nickname him the roughneck. He was imbued with the love of the military life and its important place in the service of the emperor. He was eleven years old when Japan embarked on an imperialist war against China. As an emerging industrial nation, Japan desperately needed areas in which to expand. Raw materials and markets are the bread and butter of any industrial nation. As a result of the 1895 Sino-Japanese War, Japan received Formosa and the Chinese were expelled from Korea. Unfortunately for Japan, however, they also learned a harsh lesson in international diplomacy.

During the war against the decrepit Manchus, the Japanese had invaded Manchuria. The Chinese government, in no position to oppose the superior Japanese forces, ceded southern Manchuria to Japan. There was immediate opposition from Germany, France, and Russia, who did not want the Japanese presence in Manchuria. The politicians of the Meiji government had no option but to back down in the face of this foreign threat. The resulting loss of face sent a rage through the army, who accused the politicians of knuckling under to foreign pressure. An important lesson was learned, however. If Japan was going to hold its head high among other nations of the world, its military might had to grow along with the nation. She therefore set out to become a power to be reckoned with. With that, the army and navy ministers took on greater stature within the government. The long-term effect of this was the erosion of civilian control as the generals and admirals appropriated more and more control of the government.

For the young Hideki, as for other Japanese males of the time, life was an experience of contrasts, with the extremes of overindulgence at home and strict discipline at school. Because he was the eldest son, and in Japanese society the eldest son held a revered position, Hideki was catered to.

---

*Bushido literally means "the way of the warrior."

Consequently, he demonstrated many of the traits Americans would label as those of a spoiled brat. As a student he was opinionated, obstinate, and quick to get into a fight. Though considered an average student, he held his own in the highly competitive Japanese schools. At the age of fifteen, Hideki entered a military preparatory school. Because of his small stature, many were surprised that he was able to keep pace with his fellow students. He quickly realized that hard work would be required if he was to keep up with or excel over his peers. Tojo diligently applied himself with a driving intensity. In the military academy that he attended following preparatory school he ranked tenth in a class of three hundred and sixty-three. He once remarked about his accomplishment,

> "I am just an ordinary man possessing no shining talents. Anything I have achieved I owe to my capacity for hard work and never giving up."[2]

While Tojo was a student at the military academy the international situation again boiled over and Japan found itself embroiled in a conflict with Czarist Russia. The *causi belli* was Korea. The Koreans were unhappy with the Japanese protectorate and called for autonomy. In the meantime, Russian troops moved down from their Manchurian bases into the northern part of Korea under the pretext of protecting a forestry concession granted them by the Korean government.

After the humiliation of having to back down in 1895, Japan was not about to do so again. Instead, without any declaration of war, on February 8, 1904, the Japanese Battlefleet struck the Russian Pacific squadron, which lay at anchor in Port Arthur. The similiarity to the future attack on Pearl Harbor is noteworthy. At that particular time, Japanese diplomats were negotiating in Moscow just as they would be in Washington on December 7, 1941.

The Russo-Japanese War was brilliantly fought both on land and at sea by the Japanese. In Japan itself, the war was enthusiastically accepted. Nowhere was the patriotic fever expressed more ardently than in the military academy where the young cadet, Hideki Tojo, was chomping at the bit, impatiently awaiting the opportunity to fight.

The new 2nd lieutenant, decked out in his infantryman's uniform, a samurai sword hanging from his side, sailed for Manchuria in the spring of 1905. By the time he arrived there, however, Russia's mighty Baltic fleet, which had sailed halfway around the world, was lying in ruins or at the bottom of the sea, thanks to the great Japanese naval victory in Tshushima Straits orchestrated by the legendary Admiral Togo, and its army was near defeat. Though dreaming of glory on the battlefield, the new lieutenant's first assignment was to garrison duty.

Though outwardly appearing enormous, economically the Japanese victory was proving to be a great drain. The Japanese had suffered a great loss of life, so that the victory appeared more pyrrhic than glorious. While Japan's army was bled white, the Meiji government bowed to the inevitable, a negotiated peace. President Theodore Roosevelt of the United States volunteered his services as mediator. When the Treaty of Portsmouth was signed on September 5, 1905, the Japanese people were appalled by the fact that Russia was not required to pay an indemnity. It appeared to the ultranationalists that even though Japan had won a great victory, once more she was getting the short end of the stick. Right-wingers turned their fury against the United States, causing widespread street riots that were quelled only by the declaration of martial law.

Lieutenant Tojo was highly disappointed with the settlement, more so because of his anticipation of glory on the battlefield and the possibility of rapid promotion. Instead, he had to be content with the slow advancement concomitant with peacetime.

Tojo remained in Manchuria until 1906. Three years later he married Katsu Ito, a college student in Tokyo. Though she was emancipated for a Japanese woman, their marriage would prove happy and fruitful, producing seven children. Responsibility for a wife and family made Tojo more than ever anxious to advance. Attempting to emulate his father, who by now had reached the rank of general with service in two wars, the young officer applied himself to duty, working long hours. Obsessed with the desire to be successful, he drove himself to the limits of human endurance. Slowly but surely he moved up in rank. In 1907 he made 1st lieutenant, and six years later reached the rank of captain. In 1914 he was selected to fill a vacancy at the staff college, and he graduated with honors in December, 1915. One of his classmates was Masaharu Homma, the future conqueror of the Philippines.

During World War I, Tojo served in the War Ministry's adjutant general's office. For Japan, this war proved an opportunity to increase its empire at the expense of the Germans. Joining the side of the Allies, Japan occupied the German-held islands in the Caroline and Mariana Groups as well as the German-held Chinese port of Tsingtao. From its newfound position of power, Japan issued a list of demands, known as the twenty-one demands, to the Chinese government. If China accepted them it would literally make her a Japanese protectorate. Protests immediately came forth from Britain and America. Japan was forced to drop the most extreme demands, but it was obvious that she was not yet done with China and more problems were definitely ahead.

For most of the war Tojo held routine staff and regimental posts, with the exception of one short spell in Siberia as part of the Allied interventionist forces directed against the Russian Bolsheviks. His service as a staff officer, however, did not go unnoticed, and the future appeared bright.

In August, 1919, Tojo was sent to Europe. This marked his first exposure to the Western world. He spent two years in Switzerland as assistant military attaché and then, in 1921, moved on to Germany, where he became Japan's military attaché. Thanks to his ability to speak German, Major Tojo's eyes were opened to the horrors of Germany's economic plight. He came to know the people and grew to admire their ability to live under the hardships of the postwar depression. From his stay there he became an ardent Germanophile.

In the latter part of 1921 he was ordered back to Japan. He traveled home by way of the United States, and from this short acquaintance he acquired a lasting impression of that country. Tojo saw the richness of the United States, but he also witnessed the casualness of the people and felt that their interests lay only in material pursuits. He

> "viewed the Americans of the roaring twenties as undisciplined, unmilitary, and unconcerned with anything except pursuit of the jazzy life."[3]

Although America was materially strong, it appeared to Tojo that it lacked spiritual strength. He arrived home to Japan with two distinct impressions, an admiration of the Germans and a criticism of America's superficiality.

In 1922 he was thirty-eight years old, but his appearance made him appear much older than he actually was. Prematurely balding, with his hair close-cropped, he wore a moustache and was always seen with horn-rimmed glasses. This appearance made him seem austere. In fact, he picked up the nickname "Razor Tojo." A compulsive worker, he had no hobbies nor did he participate in sports. His work, he often said, was his hobby. He had few personal indulgences and whatever spare time he did have he preferred to spend with his wife and children. The one weakness he had was for tobacco, frequently smoking up to sixty cigarettes a day. He had few friends—his abrasive personality saw to that. Few people were even admitted into his personal life. His political views were to the right, and he was a firm believer in the oneness of the Japanese state and the unity of the people under the divine emperor. Tojo retained many prejuduces from his youth and added new ones as the years passed. He hated the Russians, and as far as he was concerned, that nation remained the first and last enemy. America he viewed as a intruder in Asian affairs, and one who lacked spiritualness. He particularly despised the latter's racial prejudice towards the Japanese.*

---

*In 1924, The United States passed an immigration law which was particularly harsh toward the Japanese.

The 1920s was a decade of optimism. Nations attempted to outlaw war with paper documents and attempted to limit naval development in order to avoid the pitfalls of the armament races typical of the pre-World War I years. Japan was no exception. In 1922 Japan signed a naval limitation treaty in Washington that limited the Japanese navy to a 5:5:3 ratio of capital ships to that of the United States and Great Britain. Even the army was reduced by four divisions in an attempt by the civilian government to forestall militaristic aggrandisement. There was also talk among the politicians of the prospect of disbanding the costly Kwangtung Army stationed in Northern Korea and Manchuria. In 1929, Prime Minister Hamaguchi initiated a friendship policy with China in hopes of working out an equitable solution of both Chinese and Japanese claims to Manchuria. That attempt, however, met a heated response from both within and outside the military.

Many ultranationalists were up in arms over the prospect of a negotiated compromise, since they firmly believed that it was Japan's right to rule not only Manchuria, but all of Asia. These extremists believed that the country should be purged of weak-kneed civilians and governmental control should instead by placed in the hands of soldier administrators who would then bring Japan to its rightful place in Asia. One radical right-wing group established at that time was the Cherry Society, so called because the cherry blossom falls from its branch at its peak, symbolic of the samurai's traditional dedication to live and die for his duty. Many Army men joined this group and other similiar ones in opposition to the liberal government.

Thus far, Tojo had not joined any of these groups, but his sympathy lay with the right-wing elements. In August, 1929, he was posted to the 1st Infantry Regiment stationed in Tokyo, his first regimental command. His commanding officer, General Mazaki, was greatly impressed by Tojo's performance and aptly described him as a "ball of fire." Two years later, he became chief of the Organization and Mobilization Section of the Army General Staff, also in Tokyo.

In 1929 the Great Depression hit Japan exceptionally hard, causing widespread suffering. Factories were shut down, resulting in high unemployment. Along with the closing of factories came a disastrous crop failure creating widespread famine. Huge numbers of Japanese looked to the left-wing parties such as the Communists for answers to their plight. The solutions proposed by the Communists did not sit well with the right-wing elements who felt that expansion was Japan's answer to the Depression.

Tojo and other members of the army felt that Japan's disaster was the fault of corrupt politicians, businessmen, and of course, America and the other Western nations.

What could solve Japan's woes? To the men of the Kwangtung Army the solution was simple: Manchuria. Its wilderness could be transformed into a civilized and prosperous area. Japan's unemployment problem could be solved there, and those suffering from the effects of overpopulation could find a new home there. This would also guarantee the homeland markets and raw materials. The nation, it was felt, needed Manchuria for survival.

The Depression had unleashed many pent-up hostilities within Japan. One of the victims of this hostility was Prime Minister Hamaguchi, who was struck down by a bullet fired by a right-wing fanatic on November 14, 1930. With him perished any soft approach toward China. The army could not help but benefit by the assassination. It was Hamaguchi who had advocated a reduction in the army's size along with a nonaggressive attitude toward China. At this point, the Kwangtung Army decided it was time for action to assure Japan's place in the sun. Acting unilaterally, as a private legion of General Kanji Ishiwara and Colonel Seishiro Itagaki, this army eliminated the Chinese war lord in Manchuria, Marshall Chang Tso-lin, and, after a contrived incident of a bomb blast on railroad tracks, invaded Manchuria on September 18, 1931, without Tokyo's blessing. Japanese forces quickly attacked a Chinese garrison close to where the explosion had occurred, and another force drove on Mukden, which promptly fell the following morning. The army's unilateral action was without sanction. Any protest or advice from Tokyo was ignored. Claiming that the Chinese had struck first, the army justified its action by stating that the Japanese were simply defending themselves.

Within a few months, the Kwangtung Army reached the Great Wall of China. Manchuria, now renamed Manchukuo, was solidly in Japanese hands. The Kwangtung Army declared the area to be an independent state under Japanese protection. No politician in Japan dared to interfere for fear of assassination.

At the time of the Manchurian incident, Tojo was at staff headquarters in Tokyo. He diligently went about his task without comment on the army's independent action. In 1933 he was promoted to major general and appointed head of the General Affairs Bureau of the War Office. His statements as head of this bureau were in no way original, but they expressed his deep belief that it was the destiny of the Japanese people to rule Asia. He further expressed his jealousy of the United States and condemned the ambitions of the Soviet Union and the obstinacy of the Chinese. Japan, he went on, must rely on her strength and be wary of the West.

Luckily for Japan, the Manchurian incident ended successfully and both the people and the government accepted the army's action as a fait accompli. In addition, there was a great sense of relief that the West did not react in a hostile manner to Japan's action. The denouncement by the League of Nations was ineffectual.

In 1934, Tojo became deputy commander of the Military Academy, but he only held this post for five months, because of his supposed opposition to an ultranationalist faction known as the Imperial Way. There were within the army two divergent factions, the Imperial Way and the Control Clique. The former appealed to the young officers, who joined the Imperial Way Society desiring the elimination of party politics and business. These idealists wanted the establishment of state socialism under military control. To achieve their goal they would stoop to murder, if necessary. Governmental officials who did not conform to their view were intimidated and assassinated. Tojo was not an advocate of the Imperial Way, and it was his supposed action designed to entrap members of this faction that led to his dismissal from his position at the Military Academy. The other faction, the Control Clique, held as its main goal Japan's expansion into China and Southeast Asia.

Early in 1935, Tojo left the Military Affairs Bureau to command a brigade in southern Japan. Though not a member of any ultranationalist group, he sympathized with their objectives. He was considered reliable and efficient and his reputation was on the rise. That October he was assigned to head the gendarmeries of the Manchurian Army, the Kempeitai.

Tojo quickly recognized the potential of his new position and managed the Kempeitai with vigor. One foreign journalist called him "a forerunner of Himmler."*4 His responsibilities were wide, but basically they encompassed all aspects of security. He efficiently compiled dossiers on any person or activity deemed suspect.

While Tojo was serving in Manchuria, Japan's worst wave of political assassinations took place. On February 26, 1936, groups of soldiers of the Imperial Way faction, some from Tojo's former regiment, set out on a murder binge, in an attempt to remove hated members of the government. Assassination squads killed the Lord Privy Seal, the minister of finance, the inspector general of military training, and others. The War Ministry was occupied, as were the prime minister's residence, Police Headquarters, the law courts, the Diet Building, and newspaper offices. The assassins urged the military to join them in purging their country of soft-line parliamentarians and big business interests. They felt that these elements were the stumbling blocks preventing Japan from achieving its divine destiny. They claimed further that these factions were responsible for misleading the emperor, and that it was their duty to cleanse the government of these insincere advisors.

The assassins had hoped that their commanding officers

---

*Himmler was head of Germany's Gestapo.

would join them in the coup they had initiated, but these hopes were soon dashed to the ground. Emperor Hirohito made a rare intervention and openly stated that the young officers were, in reality, rebels who must be crushed. With the emperor's condemnation the extremists could not hope to successfully hold the reins of government. Loyal troops were sent in to crush the rebellion, and by the 29th it was all over. Thirteen of the leaders were quickly placed on trial and executed while others were imprisoned or cashiered from the service. Still others were posted to Manchuria, where they were given a hero's reception by the men of the Kwangtung Army.

During the February 26th assassinations, Tojo was ordered by the commander of the Kwangtung Army to crack down on any action by sympathetic junior officers. The army commander, though in agreement with the ideals of the rebels, was averse to joining the junior officers in what he saw as a half-baked scheme. Knowing that there were some junior officers in the Kwangtung Army who might be persuaded to act independently in conjunction with the rebels, he ordered his security chief, Tojo, to take all action necessary to maintain order. With cold efficiency, the latter pinpointed possible troublemakers and immediately ordered their arrests. Between five and six hundred people were subsequently arrested.

For his loyalty and dedication, Tojo was promoted to lieutenant general and in March, 1937, became chief of staff of the Kwangtung Army. This position thrust him into the public limelight and placed him in contact with diplomats, politicians, and journalists.

Japan, meanwhile, moved one step closer to achieving its destiny. In December 1936, it signed the Anti-Comintern Pact with Germany, directed at the hated Communist regime of the Soviet Union.

Meanwhile, one prime minister after another tried to form a workable government only to be foiled in his attempt. One journalist noted that the job of prime minister was "the most dangerous job in the world."[5] Although there were many factions tearing at Japan, not one of them gave rise to a single strong leader, as in Germany and Italy. There was no equivalent of a Nazi Party nor was there a Hitler or Mussolini waiting in the wings to lead Japan to its destiny.

There was one common denominator that united all the various factions, however, and that was the belief that Japan was destined to rule Asia. Most Japanese, even the moderates, believed that the East Asian Co-Prosperity Sphere was no different from what the British believed their empire to be. If the British could rule so many vast colonies, then why not Japan, as well?

In June, 1937, a man came to the fore who was looked upon by all groups as the right man at the right time. Prince Fuminaro Konoye, a member of an ancient noble family, became prime minister. He seemed to be a good choice. Ultranationalists viewed him as a sympathizer, while liberals considered him an intellectual who would lead Japan to friendship with the West. Within a month of Konoye's assumption of office, on July 7, 1937, a Japanese detachment carrying out night exercises near the Marco Polo Bridge near Peking, China, was allegedly fired on by Chinese troops. Settlement of the issue could have been immediate and swift, but Japanese expansionists considered this an ideal time to further the nation's claims and provide Japanese Manchuria with a buffer against Communist Russia and the Chinese Communists proliferating in the north. The army promised the Konoye government that the war would be swiftly concluded, for Chiang Kai-shek's forces were inferior to those of the Kwangtung Army. Partly to protect the settlers in the northern part of China and believing that the army would conclude the war rapidly, the Konoye government gave its sanction for reinforcements to be sent to China.

Tojo believed that the Chinese threat had to be eliminated so that Japan could prepare herself to face the real enemy, Soviet Russia. The Chinese, however, fought more doggedly than expected and more and more Japanese troops had to be introduced into combat. One of Tojo's goals was Japanese control of Inner Mongolia. Therefore, he personally conducted a blitzkrieg against a Chinese Army of ten thousand men. His ruthless conduct of the campaign was marked by deep raids and relentless pursuit. After two weeks, Tojo felt secure enough to return to army headquarters.

As commander, Tojo demonstrated certain outstanding qualities. He was meticulous about the welfare of his men and took care of the smallest detail. He ate the same food as his men and saw to it that they were properly clothed. As for himself, this foray was psychologically satisfying. In his long military career this was his first experience of command in combat. He could now feel confident that he would never be criticized for being a noncombat-tested general. It has been commented that Tojo's campaign was one of "textbook precision."[6]

The China war dragged on. Japanese troops pushed further and further south as one city after another fell to the ruthless sword of the conquering troops. Shanghai's fall was followed by the horrible rape of Nanking, where over two hundred thousand Chinese civilians were indiscriminately put to death in an orgy of pillage and rape. At home in Japan, the ultranationalists were in their glory, for they felt that Japan was now on its way to fulfillment of its divine destiny.

By 1938 the Konoye government was facing internal difficulties as the China War continued far beyond the date projected. The prime minister considered resigning but instead was persuaded to revamp his cabinet. He replaced his foreign minister with General Ugaki in the hope that this man would be effective in bringing the China conflict to a successful conclusion. As war minister, Konoye chose General Itagaki, a divisional commander from China. A man well versed in Chinese affairs, Itagaki personally desired to localize and quickly end the fighting in China.

In May 1938, Tojo was recalled to Tokyo to assume the position of army vice-minister. He brought with him a wealth of expertise. The war, however, continued to drag on. Rather than giving up after the fall of his capital, Nanking, Chiang Kai-shek moved his government to

Chungking, in China's interior, and there, with American and British support, continued to resist. Tojo not only faced this war situation, but the problem was compounded when Japanese troops clashed with the Russians along the Manchurian border during the summer of 1938. This skirmish ended in a stalemate, but it was only a harbinger of greater problems with the Soviet Union yet to be faced.

In the fall of the same year, Tojo made a speech before a Veterans Association in Tokyo. During the course of this speech he noted the reasons why the solution to the China problem had been delayed. This delay, he said, was caused by

> "Soviet, British, and American assistance to the Chinese Nationalists. Japan must therefore make resolute preparations against the Reds in the North and the Anglo Saxon powers in the South."[7]

The Japanese press made a big news item of Tojo's firebrand speech. The public was disturbed at the prospect of fighting not only the Russians, but the Americans and British as well. Tojo's boss, the war minister, felt that his assistant was overstepping his bounds and harbored thoughts of dismissing him. Tojo, however, had hawkish friends in high places, so no move was made to remove him from office.

Tojo then called together a group of leading industrialists and told them his views on the war situation. He reiterated what he had told the Veterans Association: The Chinese would continue to oppose Japan as long as they were supported by the British and Americans who, deep down, wanted to thwart Japan's ambitions. He went on to say, however, that the real threat was the Soviet Union, whose policy it was to have Japan bled white in China while it prepared for war against Japan. He then went on to warn the industrialists that they must toe the line or suffer the consequences.

The audience was furious at Tojo's treatment of them

and applied pressure to have Tojo removed. In this they were successful. In December 1938, he was quietly transferred to the nonpolitical post of inspector general of the air force, in which position he remained for a year and a half. He significantly increased aircraft production and reorganized the structure of the air force. Great events, however, were taking place in the world.

Another frontier war occurred between the Soviets and Japanese in Mongolia. This time it ended in a Soviet victory as the forces of Marshal Georgi Zhukov crushed the Japanese. The Germans, at that time, also signed a non-aggression pact with Russia. This was followed by Germany's swift conquest of Poland, Norway, Denmark, Holland, Belgium, and France.

Prime Minister Konoye resigned in January 1939, and Baron Hiranuma, an ultranationalist, was chosen to replace him. This government collapsed after the Germans concluded the nonaggression pact with Russia. Hiranuma's government was succeeded by one headed by General Abe. This regime lasted from August until January when it was replaced by yet another government, this time headed by Admiral Yonai, a known moderate.

Yonai's government was doomed from the outset. Ultranationalists resented his position of opposing any alliance with the Axis Powers. Hotheads planned his assassination, but, thanks to a timely warning, the admiral was saved. Under army pressure, however, Yonai was forced to resign in mid-July 1940, and for the second time, Prince Konoye was handed the Imperial Mandate.

As his foreign minister, Konoye chose Yosuke Matsuoka, and for war minister, Army General Hideki Tojo. By this time, the latter had become one of the most powerful individuals in the army bureaucracy, holding important positions on no less than twenty-one different committees.

"Tojo belonged to: the Japan Manchukuo Economic Committee; the Central Air Defense Commission; the Manchukuoan Affairs Board; the Cabinet Information and Cabinet Planning Boards; the Central Price

Committee; the Ship Control; Electric Power, City Planning, Home Industry and Motor Car Manufacturing Committees; the Valuation Commission for Iron Manufactures; The Disabled Soldier's Protection Trust; the Naval Council, the Air Enterprises Investigation Committee, the National General Mobilization Committee; the Education Control Council and the Liquefied Fuel Committee."[8]

This enormous influence eminently qualified him for the prestigious post of war minister.

The prime minister and war minister began their relationship in an affable manner. Both accepted as a primary goal the satisfactory conclusion of the China Incident. In time, however, the working relationship between them became strained, and the war minister began to look upon Konoye with contempt.

The cabinet was officially invested on July 22, 1940. At a series of meetings beginning a few days later, the cabinet reviewed in detail the important issues affecting Japan's future. A draft study was prepared, entitled "Main Principles of Japan's policy for coping with the Situation in Accord with World Developments." In this study, Japan's conflict with China was discussed in broad terms. Basically, the plan considered the escalation of the China conflict into a Greater East Asian war. Both Matsuoka and Tojo were in accord with its contents. Japan, the plan said, faced encirclement unless it could present a firm stand. The European war presented Japan, it went on, with an ideal opportunity to look southward to Indo China and Indonesia. With the European powers preoccupied with their own war, now was the time to strike. Tojo, though not the author of this plan, heartily agreed with its contents.

The foreign minister, meanwhile, was laying the groundwork for bringing Japan closer to the Axis. However, he was only mouthing a sentiment advocated by the Japanese military leaders and hawkish government officials. Germany also desired the treaty, in hopes that Japan could tie the British down in Southeast Asia. Besides, the Germans said, the treaty would restrain the United States.

While the treaty talks went on, Japan forced the impotent government of Vichy France to sign a convention allowing it to occupy northern Indo China. This would give Japan air bases for attacks against China in the south. This move angered the United States, who felt that this Japanese maneuver, besides being imitative of Hitler's bluster, threatened the Burma Road over which America was sending supplies to China. The United States therefore, immediately initiated an embargo of vital materials, scrap iron, and aviation fuel to Japan. The American action and the pressure exerted by pro-German forces finally threw Japan firmly into the Axis camp. On September 27, 1940, it became a reality as the Tripartite Pact was signed. The reaction of the United States was that three gangster nations were out to conquer the world.

In the first article of the Tripartite Pact, Japan recognized the leadership of Germany and Italy in the establishment of a new order in Europe. The second article accorded Japan that same right in Asia. Articles III through VI pledged the Axis partners to assist each other for the next ten years with all the political, economic, and military means each one possessed should one of them be attacked by the United States. Tojo was elated over the signing of the pact, for he believed that the United States had been responsible for hampering Japan's expansion.

As war minister, Tojo was superefficient. He paid a great deal of attention to all aspects of his responsibility and expected others to follow suit. He tried to set an example of how a commander should act and was a firm advocate of commanders' not being tied to their desks. Tojo drove himself tirelessly for endless hours. One objective he was determined to accomplish as war minister was that of gaining control over the independent tendency in the army. He knew that the army's tradition of independent action, as evidenced in Manchuria in 1931 and northern China in 1937, was displeasing to the emperor. Thus, he was bent on maintaining strict order, and he dealt forcefully with insubordination. For example, while negotiations were in progress with the French for the occupation of northern Indo China, army troops, incited by aggressive and impulsive staff officers, twice crossed the border and became needlessly involved with French garrisons on two separate occasions. Tojo immediately ordered the court martials of those responsible officers with the rank of regimental commander and below and either replaced or discharged local staff officers. He justified his actions in the context of the emperor's desire for tighter control of the military.

Meanwhile, the Japanese foreign minister, Matsuoka, made an official state visit to Germany early in 1941. There he participated in a formal ceremony signifying ratification of the Triple Alliance, which had been signed the previous September. En route home, Matsuoka stopped over in Russia, where the Treaty of Neutrality was signed with Stalin's government. This treaty was aimed at freeing Japan to expand southward without concern about an attack by the Soviets.

On June 22, 1941, Germany attacked Russia. A shock wave of alarm swept through Japan. She had hoped that Germany's conflict with Britain would dilute British strength in the Far East. Now, free from the threat of a German invasion thanks to Hitler's attack on Russia, England would be more able to defend its interests in the Far East. There was also concern that a quick German victory over Russia might deny Japan a share in the victory and bring the German presence into the Pacific. Matsuoka, who had so recently concluded the neutrality pact with the Russians, advocated an immediate attack into Siberia. However, wiser heads prevailed, and the attack never came off. Instead, Japan's interest was focused in a different direction: south.

Tojo's tenure as war minister was fraught with tension between his nation and the United States. As relations between the two countries deteriorated, Tojo began seriously to contemplate the prospect of a war with America. The United States had already embargoed iron and steel and had threatened to extend this embargo to include oil if Japan persisted in its aggression. What the United States viewed as aggression, however, the Japanese considered a divine mission. Consequently, Japan began more and more to realize that the oil of the East Indies was essential to offset any embargo. Therefore, attempts to negotiate with the Dutch were initiated, but to no avail. Thus plans for a military move into the East Indies were drawn up, but Japan also realized that any aggression in this area would have to include the Philippines and Malaya as well. This would, of course, embroil Japan in a war with the United States and the British Empire.

Already, on May 3, 1941, Tojo had stated that operations against the Indies and Malaya would require bases in Thailand and Indo-China. In order to ensure this he gave his consent for the occupation of the latter. On June 16, he said:

> "If we don't finish the job before year's end, we will have to abandon our policy of establishing the Greater East Asia Co-Prosperity Sphere."[9]

Germany's attack on Russia had left Japan with a host of options. Tojo, however, was against involvement in Russia even though Foreign Minister Matsuoka firmly advocated it. Instead, Tojo was concerned about China and the United States. What would be America's reaction to a move against the Soviets? How could Japan move both northward and to the south simultaneously? Therefore, he said, the movement to the south had to take priority, because Japan urgently needed the vital natural resources of that region.

At an Imperial Conference on July 2, Tojo laid down the policy to be followed. First of all, he said, the Japanese must continue to apply pressure on the Chinese Nationalist regime in order to bring about its overthrow. Second, war preparations must be made in the event of a war against America and Great Britain. Finally, Japan had to place heavy emphasis on Indo-China and Thailand.

The significant point of these recommendations was the fact that Russia was not considered the main threat. Instead, the two Western democracies were viewed as the major enemies. An immediate reaction to the conference was the reinforcement of the Kwangtung Army with an additional three hundred thousand men, bringing its strength up to seven hundred thousand. For Japan the die was cast. The direction of her energies would be to the south.

Before the end of the month, Japan extended its protection to include the rest of Indo-China. The decrepit Vichy government had no choice but to accept the fait accompli. Within forty-eight hours of the Japanese occupation, the United States, Holland, and Great Britain embargoed all trade goods, particularly oil, and froze all Japanese overseas assets. This economic blockade was tantamount to a declaration of war, since its continuation meant a slow strangulation of Japan. Without oil, the latter was doomed. The only option for Japan short of loss of face was for it to seize its own oil supplies in the Dutch East Indies. Tojo and the Army General Staff were irate over the harsh Western reaction. The army gave Konoye until October to resolve the deadlock via diplomatic means. After that, the war machine would swing into action.

Konoye made every attempt to convince the Americans that the occupation of French Indo-China was not a military operation but rather a mutually accepted agreement reached with the Vichy authorities. After a taste of Hitler's methods, the United States refused to buy that reasoning and demanded an immediate Japanese withdrawal.

Although the prime minister did not desire trouble with the United States, the economic boycott was quickly leading to an irrevocable rupture of relations between the two nations. Konoye even went so far as to propose a summit conference with President Roosevelt aimed at reaching some form of an agreement.

Tojo placed little faith in a one-on-one summit if and when it did take place. Roosevelt at first reacted favorably to the proposal but was quickly convinced by Secretary of State Cordell Hull that many prior meetings would be necessary before any such conference could actually take place. Hull was in no mood to appease the Japanese, not after the British failure of appeasement at Munich in 1938.*

The freezing of assets and the oil embargo were the last steps in the encirclement of Japan, a denial of her rightful place as the leader in Asia, and a challenge to her very existence. She was, therefore, determined to take action. At another Imperial conference on September 6, a general plan of national policy was agreed on. Its policy statement read:

> "For the self-defense and self-preservation of our empire, we will complete preparations for war, with the first ten days of October as a tentative deadline, determined, if necessary, to wage war against the United States, Great Britain, and the Netherlands."[10]

Negotiations were to continue, but a deadline had now been set. After that deadline expired, negotiations would cease and Japan would proceed with its last alternative: war. The emperor emphasized that every effort should be made to bring about a diplomatic settlement, in support of which he read a poem composed by his grandfather, Meiji.

> "All the seas, everywhere,
> are brothers one to another,
> Why then do the winds and waves of strife,
> rage so violently through the world?"[11]

Tojo considered the decision reached at the conference to be an Imperial decree. If no breakthrough was made by mid-October, he was ready to proceed with war.

On September 18, an assassination attempt was made on Prime Minister Konoye. Although he was unhurt, the incident left him shaken. The army pressured him to make preparations for war. Konoye in turn reminded Tojo that

---

*Britain allowed Germay to occupy the Sudetenland in Czechoslovakia in return for assurances that Hitler had no additional territorial demands in Europe.

he was still striving to keep negotiations open with the United States. Although Tojo was all for that, he declared that the October 15 deadline must not be violated.

The navy also felt that time was running out for them. Oil was necessary to keep the ships at sea. If the navy did not act soon, it would not have the ability to act in the future, as its oil stocks were being rapidly depleted. Lack of oil would make it incapable of challenging the American fleet, which would be allowed to roam freely. Admiral Nagano, chief of the Naval General Staff, said:

> "We are growing weaker while the enemy is growing stronger. . . . When there is no hope for diplomacy and war cannot be avoided, we must be ready to make up our minds quickly."[12]

Why were the negotiations deadlocked?

China was the crux of the problem. The United States wanted Japan to withdraw completely from China. Japan refused to make such a pledge, except in the vaguest terms. On the other hand, Japan's minimum demands included British and American restraint in interfering with the Japanese in China and the cessation of the aid by the two nations to the Chinese Nationalists. Japan was willing to make one concession, though: not to press beyond Indo-China, except for China, and even to pull its military out of the former French possession after a just peace had been established in the Far East. Beyond that, Japan would do nothing else for the time being. To pull completely out of China would endanger her security and open Asia to the forces of communism, not to mention the loss of face she would suffer if she bowed to the demands of the Western nations. The Japanese considered themselves the bulwark against communism in Asia.

Tojo believed that war with the United States was inevitable. Japan and its empire, he felt, would be placed in a desperate situation unless the United States altered its stance. His country, he reasoned, was being forced to take the ultimate step to war in order to defend itself and assure its preservation. He believed that in making concessions by abandoning a portion of their national policy for the sake of a peace Japan would not placate America. The United States would simply continue to demand more and more until Japan ceased to amount to anything in the world. Japan would therefore find herself a mere puppet subject to the whim of the American government. At least, war offered a fifty-fifty chance of victory. To sit back and do nothing would ony lead to slow strangulation. So Tojo exerted pressure on Konoye to take the steps necessary to accept the risk. America was rich, but she lacked Japan's fighting spirit, he emphasized. The United States would keep the negotiations open, since she realized that her greatest ally was delay, for in time, Japan would not be in any position to resist.

The prime minister continued to press for keeping the negotiations open with no deadline attached, but Tojo reiterated that Japan could not afford to wait much longer before taking action. On September 25, he reemphasized to Konoye that the armed forces chiefs would hold to the Imperial decree of September 6 designating October 15 as the final day to reach a peaceful settlement. As far as Tojo was concerned, the specified deadline was an Imperial decree that could be changed only by the emperor himself. Anything else would be a violation of the emperor's wish. The army, he stated, would not deviate from the agreed-upon stance. If negotiations proved fruitful, fine. If not, then the decision for war would be made at the expiration of the allotted time.

Tojo was becoming highly upset with Konoye's faintheartedness. Imperial decisions could not be made light of. To do so would be to insult the emperor. Tojo expressed his feeling that if Konoye was too weak to stick to a promise (the deadline date), he should resign.

Konoye invited his war minister and the naval minister, Admiral Oikawa, to a special meeting at his residence on October 12 in order to review the diplomatic impasse with the United States. Time was growing short and the prime minister was becoming worried. Konoye said that he could not possibly agree to Japan's being engaged in an even greater war than the one in China. Hostilities against the United States had to be avoided at all cost, even if it meant the temporary evacuation of China. Tojo angrily shot back that if Japan gave in to the Americans now, she would be doomed. He went on to state that, in all good conscience, he could not agree to the evacuation of China. That act would simply demoralize the military, in addition to exposing the country to the dangers previously stated.

Konoye thus found himself in a bind. He had recently asked the commander-in-chief of the Combined Fleet, Admiral Yamamoto, what he thought were the chances for naval victory in a war with Britain and the United States. The reply was disheartening. Yet, at the October 12th meeting, and at another one two days later, Admiral Oikawa, the naval minister, failed to express these sentiments in the presence of Tojo.

At the October 14th cabinet meeting the issues were once again debated. Tojo was the master debater and held center stage. Again he argued the familiar points. To continue with the stalled negotiations in Washington required great confidence in the fact that they would eventually prove successful, he said. Did the foreign minister have such confidence? Admiral Toyoda, who had been foreign minister since the spring, said that the biggest problem still revolved around the issue of China. If Japan evacuated China, then the talks would more than likely be a success. Tojo replied that Japan would not kowtow to the American demands. The long and expensive conflict in China would have been for nothing, Manchukuo and Korea would be jeopardized, and northern China exposed to communism. Morale would also be crippled.

"Withdrawal from China meant dishonorable defeat."[13]

Japan had been willing to compromise, said Tojo, it was the United States who was not. Japan would not capitulate! Tojo forcefully repeated his suggestion of a few days earlier that the cabinet should resign.

Konoye's position was untenable. Tojo had seen to that. The cabinet resigned on the 16th.

Who was to become the next prime minister during this most crucial period? What was obviously needed was someone strong enough to deal with the critical deadlock, yet someone with the ability to make decisions with authority.

Marquis Kido, Lord Privy Seal, and an intimate advisor of the emperor, took it upon himself to find just such a man. On the same day that the cabinet resigned, he summoned Tojo to his private residence and asked him some pertinent questions. Tojo made an excellent impression. He respected the Imperial wishes, and as far as Kido was concerned, that was most important. As a soldier and subject of his majesty, Tojo would comply if the emperor himself changed the decision reached at the September 6th Imperial Conference. Kido felt this to be an important prerequisite in any candidate for prime minister. Personally he did not care for Tojo and felt that other people were more qualified for the position. Prince Higashikuni, an uncle of the emperor, was unquestionably suited to fill the vacancy. In fact, even Tojo favored him. Kido, however, did not wish to involve a member of the Imperial family at such a critical time. If Japan did go to war and lost, it might topple the monarchy if it were concluded that the emperor was responsible for the catastrophe. Therefore, he recommended Tojo, whom he knew to be loyal to the throne, in addition to being a hard-working and dedicated subject. At such a time, on the brink of war, Tojo seemed the logical choice. Thus, for better or worse, the army was given its opportunity to run the country. If the nation went under, it would be the army's responsibility.

After the council of elder statesmen (the *jushin*) accepted Kido's recommendation, Tojo was summoned to the palace on October 17. There, to his great surprise, he was given the Imperial mandate to form a cabinet by the emperor himself. After a brief period in which to ponder this mandate, the fifty-seven-year-old Tojo accepted the post with great humility. After leaving the Imperial residence, he went first to the shrine dedicated to Emperor Meiji, where he offered homage, then to the Admiral Togo memorial, and finally to the Yasukuni Shrine dedicated to Japan's war dead.

The foreign press was quick to judge that Tojo's appointment was a sure sign that war was imminent. Throughout Japan newspapers responded in a positive vein.

> "Tojo's aim was to build Japan into a high degree defense state. . . . Japan was imperiled by the encirclement of hostile powers and General Tojo, the soldier-premier, was a logical choice at such a time."[14]

Tojo was not an adventurer. He has been described in many ways. Americans equated him with Hitler. Yet he was not the founder of a political party. As a soldier, he was authoritarian and believed in his country's divine mission. He accepted the use of force as necessary in order to fulfill that mission. But he was not a political tyrant in the same vein as his Axis allies. Yes, Tojo did have control, but that control could only be exercised as far as the emperor allowed. The best description of Tojo would be that of a nationalist who believed in his duty to his emperor and country.

On October 18 Tojo was promoted to full general, a rank befitting his exalted political position. On the same day he began to staff his cabinet, choosing people whom he felt would provide the backbone for the times ahead. However, he took over the Home and War Ministries himself in order to insure direct control of internal security and military affairs.

That same afternoon Tojo went on the radio and outlined his "determination to contribute to world peace by settling the China affair and establishing the Greater East Asia Co-Prosperity Sphere."[15]

The emperor then acted to rescind the September 6th Imperial Decree. No emperor had ever before rescinded a decision reached at an Imperial Conference. Tojo was ordered to "go to a blank paper."[16]

In America, the State Department viewed the new Japanese cabinet as possibly being workable. Even the Catholic Maryknoll Missionary, Bishop James Walsh, the Superior General of the Maryknoll Order and later a prisoner in Communist China until his release in 1970, reinforced the evaluation in a specially prepared memorandum for Hull, the American secretary of state, dated October 18, 1941. Bishop Walsh considered the cabinet to be a product of the peace faction in the Japanese government. The American Ambassador to Japan, Joseph Grew, noted to Washington that because Tojo was a general he could exert a far greater influence and control over the extremists and the ultranationalist groups within the army itself. U.S. Army intelligence however, differed from the State Department view and concluded that the Tojo government was anti-foreign and highly nationalistic and would probably reflect Axis leanings.

Tojo was now faced with the decision of which way to go. The two military services pressured him for an early decision. The Navy Chief of Staff Admiral Nagano said that the situation was urgent, for the navy was consuming four hundred tons of oil per hour. The army chief of staff added that at the present time the army had enough strength to seize Southeast Asia, but if Japan hesitated, her offensive ability would wane, until gradually, by-mid 1942, the United States would possess too much strength. This would deny Japan the opportunity to strike. Japan would then be completely at the mercy of the United States.

During the trials following the war, one of the crimes attributed to Tojo was the deliberate planning for war from the moment he became prime minister. The evidence, however, does not support this charge. War came not because it was desired, but because there was no other option.

On October 30, a staff study was presented to Tojo showing that the cost of proceeding without war was prohibitive in terms of Japan's long-term power position. Though desiring the success of the negotiations, Tojo would not compromise on any point detrimental to Japan. On the last day of October the new prime minister called his cabinet together and discussed three possible options that the government could take. The first was to suspend all war preparations. The second was to decide on going to war at once. The last was to continue war preparations with a firm decision to embark on war in early December, while still conducting diplomatic negotiations.

The cabinet meetings were characterized by heated debates. Tojo recommended acceptance of the third option. Although it sparked heated exchanges, Tojo said:

> "We are going to undertake both diplomacy and military operations simultaneously; so you must give your word that if diplomacy is successful, we will give up going to war."[17]

As a compromise, however, November 30 was established as the deadline for the negotiations. If by that time no breakthrough had occurred, Japan would go to war.

On November 1 another important Imperial conference was held. There Tojo reiterated to the emperor that negotiations were getting nowhere and it appeared that war would begin soon. The emperor told him to use all means to break the stalemate in Washington. In response to that, Saburo Kurusu, an experienced foreign diplomat, was flown to Washington to assist Ambassador Nomura with the negotiations. At the same time, Tojo told the emperor during another audience that he felt that Japan would be going to war shortly after the 30th of that month. It was after this conference that Admiral Yamamoto ordered the navy to take up battle stations for a surprise attack on the American fleet at Pearl Harbor.

Most evidence seems to point to the fact that Tojo knew nothing of the Pearl Harbor plan until just about that very time. Two weeks later, at a session of the Diet, Tojo broadcast a short but poignant speech to the nation. In it he said that Japan was at the crossroads of her long existence. She was not to be frustrated in the successful conclusion of the China incident by an economic blockade.

Meanwhile the negotiations in Washington continued. Tojo's foreign minister, Togo, attempted to convince the United States that Japan was negotiating in good faith. But the United States refused to accept that. The Japanese diplomatic code, the Purple Code, was broken, thanks to the genius of Colonel William Friedman. The ability to read this code showed the Americans that the Japanese were, in fact, negotiating in bad faith. The Americans might see the Japanese attempting to negotiate, but the breaking of the code revealed that Japan was in reality making preparations for war.

When Kurusu and Nomura presented Japan's final offer to Cordell Hull on November 20, the American secretary of state looked upon it with cynicism. The Japanese offered to withdraw from southern Indochina, but in return they wanted Hull's assurances of free access to the raw materials and oil of the Dutch East Indies, along with the elimination of the United States embargo. The proposal stated that troops would remain in north Indochina and in China itself until the successful conclusion of the China incident.

The United States' reply to the offer was received six days later. It reiterated America's insistence that Japan should not only withdraw from Indochina, but from all of China, as well, including Manchuria. If Japan would consent to these conditions, then the embargo would be lifted. To the Japanese this represented nothing more than an ultimatum. It appeared to them as if America was out for one thing: the strangulation of Japan, and nothing less. They felt that the Americans were unwilling to bargain in good faith. The fact that Manchuria was even mentioned particularly irritated them, since they considered that they had strong claims to that area. Tojo stated that the American response stated in Hull's note showed that the Americans were insincere and not willing to seek reconciliation.

On that same day an extraordinary session of the Diet

was held. The emperor, dressed in full regalia, was seated upon his raised dais. Respectfully Tojo approached the throne, whereupon the emperor read him a brief message that formally empowered the prime minister with the right to pass whatever laws were necessary to meet the crisis. The emperor had sanctioned Tojo's dictatorship. Tojo then spoke out angrily, accusing the Americans, the British, the Dutch, and the Chinese of conspiring to strangle Japan by encirclement. Japan's very existence was at stake, he said.

Even while the Diet was in session, Admiral Chuichi Nagumo's task force, consisting of six carriers, began its historic voyage to Hawaii from the Kurile Islands.

On November 29 a special meeting was held with the emperor and his advisory council, made up of ex-premiers. The emperor remained silent, but the tone of the ex-premiers, particularly Konoye, expressed the emperor's wishes. They questioned Tojo about Japan's ability to fight an extended war. Was war absoutely necessary? Without hesitating Tojo retorted that not only was war necessary, the country's very existence depended on it. She had been challenged and no matter what her military preparedness was she could not back down. War was unavoidable. Using the same logic expressed by Yamamoto, Tojo spoke of the projected knockout blow against the United States Pacific fleet, to be swiftly followed by consolidation of an empire in Southeast Asia, the area that contained all the resources needed to sustain Japan's needs. America might then be forced to concede victory to the Japanese. He did say, however, that if Japan faced a protracted war, there was no other alternative but to fight it.

Who was to blame for the impasse? In the Americans' view the atrocities perpetuated by the Japanese against the Chinese alienated them from any sympathy with the Japanese cause. The latters' obvious disdain for the West, as evidenced by the Panay incident and other similar aggressive moves, and Japan's conspicuous union with the Germans and Italians, caused the typical American to view the menace in the Pacific with disgust.

As for the Japanese, in their opinion they were fighting in China to secure their own future. From that vantage point the United States and others were looked upon as adversaries. It was therefore a matter of life and death. The Americans were not sympathetic to the needs of the Japanese. Unquestionably the Americans, with their harsh exclusion policies, looked upon the Japanase as an inferior race. Thus, from the Japanese perspective, war was not only necessary, it was mandatory. So we come back to the original question. Who was to blame? In reality, both were guilty. As John Toland so ably put it:

> "A war that need not have been fought was about to be fought because of mutual misunderstanding, language difficulties, and mistranslations, as well as Japanese opportunism, irrationality, honor, pride, and fear of American racial prejudice, distrust, ignorance of the Orient, rigidity, self-righteousness, honor, national pride and fear."[18]

On December 1, Tojo made his war speech, which systematically laid down the reasons why war was necessary. The government voted unanimously in favor of war. The emperor gave his sanction. The attack would commence on December 8 (December 7 in Washington).

The next day Yamamoto signaled Nagumo's fleet: "Climb Mount Niitaka." This alerted Nagumo to the fact that hostilities would commence on the agreed-upon day.

Meanwhile, Emperor Hirohito informed Tojo that negotiations with the United States had to be severed before the first act of war took place. Tojo instructed his foreign minister to prepare to break off negotiations half an hour before the scheduled attack on Pearl Harbor. This action was to serve as a declaration of war.

Because they had successfully broken the Japanese diplomatic code, the United States knew something was about to happen. Unfortunately, the Japanese naval code remained unbroken and the United States had no idea that the Japanese fleet was en route to Pearl Harbor. Instead, the Americans thought the fleet was in Southeast Asian waters.

On Saturday, December 6, President Roosevelt sent a note to the American ambassador in Japan with instructions to personally deliver the message to the emperor. Noting the ominous moves of the Japanese military forces in the direction of Thailand and Malaya, Roosevelt wanted the emperor to intervene personally for the sake of peace. When the message reached the central telegraph bureau in Tokyo, its delivery was delayed, on the advice the Army General Staff. The President's message was not sent to Grew until ten hours after its initial reception.

Upon reviewing the message, Grew went to the Japanese foreign minister, Shigenori Togo, and asked for an immediate audience with the emperor. Togo consulted the prime minister, who asked if the message contained any concessions. After being informed that it did not, Tojo said that he had no objection to its being given to the emperor, since it was too late to be of any consequence.

It truly was too late, for at that very moment, Nagumo's fleet was moving into the attack position.

In Washington, the ultimatum was transmitted to the Japanese Embassy on December 6, and simultaneously received by United States Intelligence units. When the unsuspecting Nomura and Kurusu delivered the final message on Sunday, December 7, they were met with an icy reception by Hull, for the attack on Pearl Harbor had already occurred. Owing to inefficency, the message was delivered after the attack, the very thing Emperor Hirohito and Yamamoto wished to avoid. In anger, Hull reproached his visitors.

> "In fifty years of public service I have never seen a document more crowded with infamous falsehoods and distortions so huge that I had never imagined any government on this planet was capable of uttering them."[19]

General Tojo, in full uniform, went to the National Shrines in Tokyo to commune with the spirit of his late father. Japan's die was cast—now it was all or nothing.

On the day of the attack Tojo spoke on the radio. The West, he told the people of Japan, was attempting to dominate the world. They must anticipate, he said, a long war, but the fate of Japan and East Asia was at stake.

"The objective in the Greater East Asia War is founded on the exalted ideals of the founding of the empire and it will enable all the nations and peoples of Greater East Asia to enjoy life and to establish a new order of coexistence and co-prosperity on the basis of justice with Japan as the nucleus."[20]

Subsequently, the Japanese war machine won a spectacular series of whirlwind victories. The forces of Imperial Japan surged southward and eastward in a deluge of devastation. Oil, rubber, rice and glory were their goals. One area after another fell to the might of the Sons of Nippon; Guam, Wake, Manila, Mandalay, Malaya, Hong Kong, Singapore, Sumatra, Bataan, Borneo, Corregidor, New Guinea, Java, New Britain, and the Solomons. Victory after victory filled the Japanese with a feeling of invincibility. Like the Japanese population, Tojo was euphoric during the days of conquest.

Ironically, Japan's rapid and brilliant series of victories brought dissension instead of unity to her Supreme Command. The navy wanted to expand towards Australia, Hawaii, and India. On the other hand, the army still felt that the only reasonable course was to make the empire so defensibly secure that America would accept a compromised peace. The navy's plans exceeded the original war plans, calling for Japanese forces to go over to the defensive once the original objectives were met. The Naval General Staff wished to destroy the British Indian Ocean fleet and follow that up by taking Australia. Admiral Yamamoto, dismayed by the incompleteness of the Pearl Harbor operation, recommended a bold strike against Midway Island in order to entice the American fleet into a decisive naval enagagement.

After weeks of debate a compromise was reached between the army and navy. The plan to take Australia was shelved. The army, already heavily extended at other points, felt that to engage in a ground war in Australia would far exceed its capabilities. It did, however, accept a less ambitious plan for assaulting the coastal port city of Port Moresby in Papua, New Guinea, approximately four hundred miles north of Australia. The navy, meanwhile, would proceed down from New Guinea, take the Solomons, Samoa, Fiji, and New Caledonia, thereby effectively isolating Australia. For the moment the Midway proposal was tabled.

On March 13, Tojo and the two chiefs of staff presented their new plan to the emperor using as justification for the plan the need for continuing the offensive in order to completely defeat the United States and Great Britain.

During the postwar trials one of the charges brought against Tojo by the International Tribunal was his sanctioning of the atrocities practiced by the Japanese forces and his not observing international conventions regarding the treatment of prisoners of war. There was plenty of evidence submitted to substantiate these claims. Tojo had indeed made some damning statements early in 1942 that gave credence to his acceptance and even approval of the atrocious behavior of the Japanese forces. He said that his government would not be inhibited by Western concepts of warfare that included the humane treatment of prisoners. In another statement he said:

> "We have our own ideology concerning prisoners of war, which should naturally make their treatment more or less different from that in Europe and America."[21]

ON MARCH [20] OF THAT YEAR TOJO'S NAVY MINISTER OPENLY ANnounced that Japan would not recognize the international convention of 1909 concerning the treatment of prisoners. He justified this statement by stating that the Allies had waged war on the basis of retaliation and hatred.

There was, in fact, a particular reason for this harsh treatment, which the Japanese put to good use. It was a means of destroying the myth of the white man's superiority. It was a simple fact to show off to the Asian people: the sorry plight of the ragged, skinny, white men. The same men who, for over two hundred years, had subjugated the Asian peoples, lording it over them from their position of superiority, were now humbled by an Asian nation. In the process of humiliating the Westerner, however, horrible crimes were committed, the Bataan Death March heading the list.

At his trial Tojo admitted having made the statements he was accused of but concluded his defense by stating that he took it as policy not to interfere when a general was given a task to perform.

It was Tojo also who initiated the policy of utilizing prisoners as a source of labor.

"I hope you will see that they are usefully employed."[22]

This led to such horrible projects as the Death Train.*

After the war a tally of prisoners was made. The Germans had captured 235,473 British and American during the war. Of these, 9,348 died in captivity; 4%. The Japanese on the other hand captured 95,134 British, Australian, American, Canadian, and New Zealand troops. Of these, 27,256 perished, or 28.6%. The statistics speak for themselves.

In April, a daring bombing raid was made on Tokyo led by Lieutenant Colonel James Doolittle, who flew B-25 bombers from the deck of the aircraft carrier *Hornet*. The

---

*The construction of a railroad through the jungles of Thailand in order to support the fighting in Burma. British prisoners were used in this project.

raid caused little damage but had a deep psychological effect. Eight of the flyers were captured. The newpapers called them mass murderers. Tojo came to their defense by pointing out that there were no statutes on the books making it a capital crime for an enemy flyer to bomb Tokyo. Despite this, the eight aviators were condemned to death. Fortunately, Tojo was able to commute the sentences of five of the prisoners to life imprisonment, but the others were executed.

In Tokyo Tojo listened to the news from the various war fronts. After the Battle of the Coral Sea in May 1942, he told the Diet that the Japanese victory had caused the Allies to abandon Australia. He referred to Australia as the "orphan of the Pacific." On June 5, without the knowledge of all the facts surrounding the Battle of Midway, he addressed a delegation of international journalists in Tokyo and informed them that Japan was prepared to fight the enemy until victory was won, even if it took a hundred years. A month later he was informed of the true extent of the Midway debacle.

As the war situation deteriorated following Midway, Tojo found that he had to assume more power. On August 7, 1942, the Americans invaded the island of Guadalcanal in the Solomons, thereby initiating a six-month-long battle on land, sea, and in the air. As the situation began to swing against the Japanese, a crisis occurred in the cabinet. Tojo subsequently dismissed his foreign minister and assumed the position himself. He was now prime minister, war minister, and foreign minister.

Tojo spent much of his time touring industrial and war plants, addressing rallies, and encouraging the population. As victories turned into defeat he attempted to maintain the population's determination to fight to a successful conclusion. On December 28, 1942 he spoke before the Diet. In his speech were noted traces of the protracted struggle facing Japan. Things had temporarily slipped, he said, but eventual victory would still come to the Emperor's people. Nineteen-forty-three, he went on, would be the year of decisive battles.

At the beginning of that year the prime minister suffered a severe cold, but by the end of the month was well enough to address the Diet once more. His mood was defiant as he told them that Japan must be ready for both offensive and defensive warfare. The inclusion of the word *defensive* was a hint that things were not going as well as indicated.

As a war leader, Tojo worked untiringly. He was most attentive to detail and took precise notes on everything. At night he recopied these notes into a notebook. Then he would work on plans, memorandum, prepare drafts of policy, and phone subordinates to give them their orders for future projects. He was keen of mind and could readily answer questions on the spot about virtually any subject in the area of his responsibility. He paid precise attention to the minutest detail. Tojo even took street tours during which he would surprise everyone by peeking into garbage pails to see if food was being wasted. He used the military police as his private force. Tojo carried many grudges and disliked criticism no matter how just it might be. The police were used to quell his critics.

Was this action justified? Tojo claimed that it was for the good of the nation. His defenders assert that his policy stemmed from a fear that critical statements might lead to a loss of morale and a spirit of defeatism. On the other hand, his detractors pointed out that these moves not only spread terror, but were for his own personal aggrandizement. It was these policies and others similar to them that led to his being dubbed the "Hitler of Japan."

As 1943 progressed, one disaster followed another. There was no shortage of bad news. As a means to salvaging the deteriorating situation Tojo began to look with interest at the occupied countries. The harsh Japanese occupation had already nullified much of what he now attempted to do, but he viewed his concept as a necessary policy if Japan was to achieve the military victory it so desperately desired.

Tojo made elaborate promises to the occupied nations, guaranteeing that they would soon become independent countries within the co-prosperity sphere. He announced to the Diet that before the year ended, Burma would become an independent state. In July he traveled to Singapore, where he met Ba Maw, the collaborationist leader of Burma, in order to discuss plans for Burma's independence, which was granted on August 1, followed on October 14 by that of the Philippines. Though mere puppets to Japan, millions of natives viewed this as liberation from the white man's yoke, something they had never known.

In November, 1943, China, Thailand, Manchukuo, the Philippines and Burma sent delegates to Tokyo for the Greater East Asia Conference, at which Ba Maw said:

> "One billion Orientals, one billion people of Greater East Asia, how could they have been dominated, a great portion of them ... by England and America."[23]

Tojo emphasized the common bond between all Asians. His presence dominated the meeting as he presided over the gathered representatives of billions in a paternal manner. A new spirit, he said, was moving in East Asia, the spirit of Pan Asianism.

As 1943 turned into 1944, the Allies pierced the outer defensive ring of Japan's empire. The news from Europe was equally bad. The German army in Russia was in retreat, and in September, Italy surrendered. The Axis was being squeezed from all angles.

At home, Tojo felt the need to apply emergency measures to increase production. The hours of work were increased, age limits eliminated, and more women were added to the work force. Even Geisha and tea houses were, to the chagrin of many, closed. The situation obviously called for harsh action.

By the end of January, 1944, the Americans stood ready to assault the Marshall Islands and General MacArthur was applying the finishing touches to his isolation of the onetime Japanese bastion of Rabaul.

Meanwhile, the Lord Privy Seal, Marquis Kido, was

beginning to give serious thought to what might happen if Tojo fell from power. Was there a way Japan could make a negotiated peace without any loss of her national essence, *i.e.*, the emperor?

Since the Allies had penetrated the outer defensive ring, Tojo simply proclaimed an inner defensive ring stretching from Burma, through the Andaman Islands, the Philippines, Carolines, Marianas, to the Kuriles.

In February, 1944 the Marshalls were assaulted and fell rapidly. It was apparent to everyone that the inner defensive ring would soon be put to the test. On February 18, Hirohito summoned Tojo to his presence and authorized the prime minister to request the resignations of both chiefs of staff. This action was necessary because neither branch of the service seemed able to halt the American advance. The major question in Tojo's mind was who he could get to replace General Sugiyama, the army chief of staff. Then, in direct violation of national policy, the emperor authorized the prime minister himself to assume the position.

The outgoing chief of staff was disappointed at the combination of both the military and civilian governments. Upon leaving office he said:

> "If the war minister and army chief of staff are one and the same person, political considerations will find their way into military decision making, and the entire system of discipline by which orders are accepted in the field may well break down."[24]

That evening, Tojo called a meeting with the outgoing General Sugiyama and other army officers. The general pointed out that Germany's problem was Hitler's interference in staff matters. Tojo replied angrily that Hitler was originally simply a common soldier, whereas he, Tojo, was a Japanese general. A bitter debate ensued, but in the end Tojo won out.

Thus the prime minister assumed even another powerful position. He was a true shogun.*

---

*A military leader who once ruled Japan under the Emperor.

Now that he was military leader, Tojo prepared to meet the common challenge. He ordered an all-out offensive in Burma. The attack began on March 8, but a bitter battle of attrition followed, and under the superb leadership of the British General William Slim, Allied forces halted the Japanese drive at Imphal and Kohima in India.

Behind the scenes a movement developed to dump Tojo. The former prime ministers, the *jushin*, looked upon the prime minister as an autocratic ruler. They blamed him for Japan's current situation and therefore wanted him removed. Konoye and Admiral Okada even went so far as to suggest that Tojo's replacement should be a person who would make immediate peace overtures to the Allies. The time to dump Tojo, however, was not yet ripe, but it was approaching rapidly.

Tojo staked his reputation as chief of staff on defending Japan's inner defensive ring. On June 15, 1944, Admiral Nimitz's Central Pacific force assaulted Saipan in the Marianas. The struggle for the inner defensive ring had begun.

Tojo called for an all-out defense of Saipan. The Imperial Navy attempted to stop the American landings but instead suffered a severe loss at the Battle of the Philippine Sea on June 19 and 20. This battle echoed the death knell of the once proud Japanese carrier force. On land, the American Marines and soldiers fought bitterly against the determined Japanese defenders. The battle was marked by the ferocity characteristic of all the island battles thus far. Near the end of the struggle, the Americans witnessed an orgy of suicides. Unfortunately, the perpetrators this time were not only the military. A pre-war Japanese possession, Saipan contained a sizable Japanese civilian population. During the war years they were repeatedly told of the ferocious Americans who would pillage and rape. Thus, for the greater glory of Japan and for the protection of their own sacredness, and on account of their belief that a Japanese must never surrender, these civilians took their own lives in great numbers.

With Saipan lost and with other islands in the Marianas chain under assault, the time had come for the throne to make a symbolic change in leadership. Tojo had to go. On July 17, 1944, a resolution was adopted by a meeting of ex-premiers recommending that Tojo not continue as prime minister. Despite this vote of no confidence, Tojo was determined to remain and aimed at reforming the government. But all support for him had disappeared. Like the captain of a sinking ship, Tojo found himself alone. On the 18th of the month, the cabinet resigned. Tojo's options were exhausted. He had to follow the cabinet's example.

An embittered prime minister went on national radio and gave his final address to the people. In his message he confirmed the loss of Saipan and outlined his reasons for resigning. Chief among these were his failures and the pain he was causing the emperor. After the address he went to the palace to present his resignation and that of his cabinet. Tojo met Kido there and bitterly attacked the ex-premiers for bringing about his downfall.

In Tojo's place, Kido and the *jushin* desired to nominate a moderate like Admiral Yonai for the office of prime minister, but they held back for fear that the Army would refuse to obey anyone but an army man. Consequently they settled on General Koiso, a former Kwangtung Army commander who at that time was serving as governor general of Korea. As far as the Japanese people were concerned, nothing had changed in regard to general policy.

For Tojo the humiliation was complete when, on July 20, 1944, he was placed on the army retired list. He now faced the boring existence of political oblivion.

In January, 1945, the emperor, on his own accord, summoned all the senior statesmen to the palace to solicit their views on the war situation. As a former prime minister, Tojo was automatically a member of the *jushin*. At a later meeting, in the emperor's presence, he spoke with great candor on the war situation in general. By that time the Japanese empire was unquestionably shrinking. Manila had fallen, the Americans were on Iwo Jima, and the Japanese Navy, for all intents and purposes, was resting on the bottom of the sea. In a speech Tojo denounced the decline of fighting spirit and equated peace with defeatism. He said positively that Japan now was in a better position, because as the enemy approached more closely to the country it incurred longer supply lines, whereas it was just the opposite for the Japanese. He also stated that Germany's defeat mattered more to the Americans than that of Japan. Once that was accomplished, he went on, America would have to worry about the Russians, and this would not allow them to concentrate their efforts on defeating the Japanese. Meanwhile, he said, the strong home army would not allow the homeland to be invaded.

> "Things would get worse, but if the army and navy and the people could be united under the emperor as never before, Japan could hold out."[25]

Tojo was either presenting a strong front because he still believed there was a ray of hope, or he just did not have the ability or desire to comprehend the true situation. He was way off base. His predictions proved all false.

In one respect, however, he was right. The Japanese were indeed fighting to the death for the empire; but no one was optimistic that the war could still be brought to a successful conclusion. He totally denounced the American "unconditional surrender" demand.

On April 4, General Koiso resigned. Tojo was a member of the conference of senior statesmen who met that same day to choose a successor. Tojo and Konoye were once more on opposing sides. Was the new cabinet, Tojo demanded, prepared to perpetuate the war or to surrender? The *jushin* debated the issue and their final choice was former Prime Minister Admiral Suzuki. Although seventy-eight years old, the aged admiral appeared to be the person most suited for the task. The admiral wished to decline the appointment but Emperor Hirohito urged him to accept. Suzuki consented and began immediately to search for some way to make peace. Tojo did not favor Suzuki's appointment but knew that if the emperor approved, there was little he could do about it.

Meanwhile, the military situation went from bad to worse. The Soviet government gave notice that they would not renew their treaty of neutrality with the Japanese. On May 1, the Japanese heard the news of Hitler's suicide followed a week later by Germany's surrender. Japan herself was by then being devastated by round-the-clock bombing. In June, Okinawa fell.

In July the Japanese government attempted to use Russia as a means of opening up negotiations with the Americans. Little did they know, however, that at the Yalta Conference the previous February the Russians had promised the Allies that they would attack Japan three months after the end of the war in Europe. Stalin was eager to share in the spoils. Prolonging the war could only benefit the Russians. Accordingly, the Japanese peace overtures were never forwarded to the Americans.

Meanwhile, at Potsdam, where the final Allied War Conference was being held, the conferees reiterated their strong stance regarding unconditional surrender.

Then, on August 6, 1945, the nuclear nightmare struck Hiroshima. This was followed three days later by another nuclear attack on the city of Nagasaki. On the 8th, the Russians tore up the neutrality pact and crossed into Manchuria.

In the interim, Tojo remained in the capital in the event the emperor required his services. Despite the atomic attacks and the Soviet declaration of war, Tojo still desired to continue the fighting.

The emperor was finally forced to intervene in an effort to halt the destruction. A group of fanatical officers, feeling that the emperor was being ill advised, attempted to assume control of the government by force. One of these officers was Tojo's own son-in-law. The attempt failed, and on August 14, in an unprecedented move, Emperor Hirohito himself announced the surrender on the radio.

That same day Tojo's son-in-law committed *hari-kiri*. It was Tojo who broke the news to his daughter. During the funeral many army officers expressed the opinion that Japan should continue to resist. But Tojo, ever a loyal subject, said that the Imperial will should be followed. In the meantime, he prepared himself for his own personal end.

On September 2, the instrument of surrender was signed on the deck of the battleship *Missouri* in Tokyo Bay. Six days later General MacArthur established his headquarters in Tokyo. In the meantime, Tojo had made his own plans. He knew that the Allies would exact retribution on those who had led Japan and was aware that he was high on the most-wanted list. He went to a neighbor who just happened to be a doctor and asked him exactly where the heart was. Tojo told the doctor to mark the spot on his chest with ink.

Rumor spread that Tojo was contemplating suicide. General Shimomura, the minister of war, summoned Tojo to his office when he heard the rumor and urged the former prime minister to reconsider his action. Shimomura asked Tojo to face trail and accept responsibility for the war, so that the emperor should in no way be implicated.

Tojo had already considered this point. In fact, he had proposed submitting a statement to General MacArthur stating that the war had been forced on Japan and that he was solely responsible for reacting to the American threat, thus absolving the emperor of all blame. But, he told Shimomura, he would not accept being dragged off as a common prisoner. If that transpired, he would be forced to save face by killing himself.

For over a week following the surrender the Allies made no move against Tojo. On September 10 he was interviewed by reporters. During the interview he accepted full respnsibility for the war but emphasized that this did not necessarily make him a war criminal. That night Tojo took a writing brush in hand and wrote his last testament. He offered his profoundest apologies to the emperor and stated that his death would act as an atonement for his own role and his responsibility for the defeat.

After lunch on the 11th, Tojo went into his study. Outside, Mrs. Tojo heard a loud disturbance. Vehicles filled with American M.P.s pulled up in front of the house. She went over to her husband, who ordered her to leave. As she did Tojo told her to take care of herself.

Tojo opened the window and asked the men who had come to arrest him if they had a warrant. The Americans replied in the affirmative. Tojo walked away from the window and closed it. A few moments later a shot was heard. The military policemen forced the door open and found the former prime minister sprawled in his chair bleeding profusely. He had shot himself in the chest, near the heart. Tojo feebly asked for water and drank the profferred cup. He was in a great deal of pain. A doctor was immediately sent for and one of the Americans was overheard to say, "We want this bastard alive."[26]

Tojo was near death. The scene in his study resembled a comic opera. Newsmen and cameramen were falling all over each other trying to record his last words and photograph his death agony. Tojo gasped, "Tell MacArthur I do not want my body to be put on show. Tell him to treat me as a soldier."[27] To his great dismay, the arrival of an American army doctor, who quickly administered transfusions, saved his life. He was taken to a hospital where the bullet, which had just missed his heart, was removed. He would live to face trial.

The bungled suicide attempt caused Tojo to become the brunt of ridicule. Everything about the man was open to criticism. His leadership was censured and he was accused of every type of corruption and even of sexual excess. Tojo was branded a failure. After all, he couldn't even kill himself successfully.

His recovery was rapid. After leaving the hospital he was sent to Sugamo Prison on December 8, 1945, the anniversary of the attack on Pearl Harbor. While in prison he and the other "criminals" were exposed to a spartan existence. Tojo was a model prisoner, a man of forbearance and tolerance. He became an inspiration to all the other prisoners.

Tojo's trial began on May 3, 1946. During the trial there were few who could stand beside "Hitler's gang." Neither the emperor, nor members of his family, nor anyone who could implicate them were to be tried. Tojo was the chief scapegoat.

The head prosecutor was Joseph Keenan, a man whose dislike for the men in the dock was obvious. As the trial proceeded, public interest waned and few people even bothered to attend the sessions. On December 28, Tojo took the stand. That event did serve to arouse some public interest. On his shoulders was placed the blame for all acts of brutality: the Death March on Bataan, the Death Railway, and the treatment of prisoners.

Tojo took four days to prepare his statement. When he presented it he was eloquent. He accepted full responsibility for Japan's decision to go to war. He went on to state that the decision was provoked however by the economic sanctions placed on Japan by the Western powers. The freezing of her assets and the oil embargo had created a critical situation for her economic defense. Tojo apologized for the declaration of war's not being given before the Pearl Harbor attack. It was not, he said, intended to be that way. He then went on to explain the different standards of the Japanese and the Allied soldier, which made the Japanese treatment of prisoners appear unduly harsh to the Westerners. The emperor was left totally blameless.

Japanese public opinion began to swing back in Tojo's favor and away from the contempt heaped on him at the time of his attempted suicide. The final verdict was delivered in November 1948, almost a year after Tojo's defense of himself. The people of Japan and the emperor were found not guilty. The army leaders, the verdict went on, had deliberately lied to the emperor. Prince Konoye, who had committed suicide in December of 1945, was posthumously convicted for signing the Tripartite Pact.

Many of those in the docket were sentenced to life imprisonment, others were given twenty years, and still others were condemned to death. Hideki Tojo was one of the latter. His guilt was for waging aggressive war, for crimes against peace, and for his responsibility for atrocities against prisoners of war.

Tojo was in no way surprised at the sentence. Security measures around those convicted were tightened. The Allies did not want Tojo and the others to cheat the hangman's rope as Goring had done. Intricate searches were made for anything that could be used in a suicide attempt. Tojo regarded these precautions as insulting, for he had accepted the verdict calmly.

While in prison a peace descended upon Tojo, a peace usually accompanied by a deep religious faith. He found great consolation in Buddhism and in its belief of enlightenment.

The execution date was set for December 23, 1948. Tojo was allowed one final meeting with his wife and four daughters. Since he was allowed only five people, he thought his sons would forgive him for not having them present at his last meeting. During the talk with his family he spoke mostly of religion and about how vital it was in one's life.

During his final days Tojo wrote his political testament. Again he apologized to the emperor and the nation for leading them into war. He expressed his deep belief in the Imperial line and criticized the trial, which denounced the men in the docket as war criminals. Tojo also predicted a future war between the United States and the Soviet Union which, he said, would be fought in Asia. He also warned of the dangers of communism.

At 1:00 AM on December 23, the prison guards entered his cell. They found the ex-prime minister composed, fully dressed, and waiting for them. They put handcuffs on him and led him along the corridors toward the prison's Buddhist chapel. There he joined the other condemned prisoners. They prayed, said their farewells, and in a chours cried out, *"Banzai."* The guards then led him out into the courtyard, which was lit up by large floodlights. Near the age of sixty-four, without his glasses and dentures, thin and pale from his months in prison, Tojo, the former prime minister, war minister, foreign minister, chief of staff, the shogun of Japan, looked more like a harmless old man who should be fishing with his grandchildren than a war criminal. He climbed the scaffold steps, the rope was placed around his neck, and the trap door sprung open at 1:30 AM.

MacArthur denied Tojo's widow the right to her husband's remains. Instead the body was cremated and the ashes scattered, for the Americans feared that radical groups would seek to deify the former prime minister. Some of his ashes, however, were reputedly hidden by a Japanese worker at the crematorium and were returned to his widow on April 23, 1955.

How can we understand the man? Tojo was first and foremost a nationalist, whose primary concern was his emperor and country. He was not self-seeking, even though his assumption of so many offices made it appear that way. All the powers he amassed during his rule were for one purpose and one purpose only: to serve his emperor and his country. Granted, he was a firebrand, but he felt that this was justified. His country was in peril, it was slowly being strangled, and for it to survive, the strangulation had to end. War became the only path open, since all other means led to naught. His methods at times were imprudent, and from our perspective, brutal, but a great deal of that was the result of cultural differences. In the Western view, the Japanese felt that a prisoner had forfeited his rights. They expected nothing more and nothing less for their own men who became prisoners of the Allies.

Was Tojo a great man? Perhaps dedicated is the word most appropriate to describe him. But in the eyes of his countrymen, particularly when they were winning great victories, yes, he was a great man. Japan finally recognized his patriotism. On August 17, 1960, a joint tomb was erected in Kasu for the Japanese war criminals who were executed. The inscription on the tomb reads:

"The tomb of the seven martyrs."[28]

Yamamoto

Chapter 2

Yamamoto was a name that inspired fear and loathing in most Americans during World War II. He was considered one of the chief warmongers among the Japanese militarists, but he was, in fact, nothing of the sort. Pressured by ultranationalist fanatics, he did what he felt was best for Japan. The admiral launched the strike against Pearl Harbor not because he was a jingoistic militarist living for the day that the fury of war could be unleashed upon the hated American barbarians; rather, he agreed to attack because he knew that Japan had no chance to win a protracted war against the highly industrialized United States. In fact, his life was more than once threatened by assassination during the 1930s because of his opposition to the militarists. Three months before he launched the Hawaiian operation his own prime minister branded him pro-American and pro-British. In anger he responded, "I am Japanese. As a Japanese I do only what is best for my country."[1]

Yamamoto's entire life can be summed up by that phrase, "for my country." His first priority was always duty to his emperor and his nation. Reluctant to precipitate war, loathing the army militarists, he was, however, honor bound to do his duty and fight the war the only way he knew how. Totally!

The story of Yamamoto began in 1884 in a small village in western Japan. It had been but seventeen years since Japan climbed out of its feudal era, and the nation was only thirty years removed from the time when Commodore Perry forced open the tightly locked doors of the island kingdom. In many ways, however, the Japan that young Isoruku was born into still resembled the Japan steeped in ancient culture.

On April 4, Isoruku, the seventh child of a schoolmaster, was born. He was called Isoruku, meaning fifty-six, because that was the age of his father. The impoverished schoolmaster was a former samurai of the Nagoaka clan and had participated in the Boshin War against the Meiji Restoration. As a member of the Nagoaka Clan he raised his children to love and revere the ancient traditions. Consequently, Isoruku forever held a special place in his heart for his clan and his home town of Nagoaka.

Isoruku Takano's* youth was relatively happy. He played, went to school, and developed into a stout, energetic, athletic young man. At the age of fifteen he put his name down for admission to the Naval Academy.

The academy that young Takano entered was founded in 1873. Originally housed in Tokyo, the school was soon transferred to the island of Etajima near Hiroshima. The navy itself at that time was also relatively new. Though still a fledgling it was growing by leaps and bounds as Japan attempted to shake off centuries of isolation and propel itself into the modern age as a rival to the Western nations. In the midst of this exciting era of growth within the navy, the schoolmaster's son from Nagoaka was accepted into the Naval Academy.

The course of study at the academy lasted four years and consisted of hard work and harsh discipline. Devotion to the emperor and to Japan was the main lesson each cadet learned within the monastic walls of the Naval Academy. During the fourth and final year the cadet was posted to a windjammer where he learned all there was to know about the sea, sailing, and seamanship. Upon graduation each cadet took with him a number of important lessons, chief of which was deep respect for the emperor and the country.

Isoruku graduated seventh in his class. His graduation coincided with Japan's boldest move since its entrance into

---

*Takano was his true family name. Later, as was the custom, he was adopted by a family of means by the name of Yamamoto.

modern history. The country challenged Imperial Russia. The year was 1904 and Japan had boldly insisted that Russia withdraw from Manchuria. When the czar refused, war began in February of that year. Isoruku was posted as an ensign to the cruiser *Nishin*, which was part of the protective screen for the battleship *Mikasa*, flagship of the legendary Admiral Togo.

The Japanese blockade of Port Arthur was correctly construed by the Russians to pose a major threat. They responded by dispatching their fleet from its base in the Baltic Sea. After traveling halfway around the world this fleet was decisively destroyed in a one-day battle in the Straits of Tsushima. The fleet action that destroyed a superior force in such short time was a lesson the young ensign never forgot. During this famous battle, Yamamoto was wounded when an enemy shell hit the *Nishin* and injured his right leg and left hand, resulting in the loss of two fingers. You might say that Yamamoto's career was saved by a finger, since the loss of a third finger would have forced the young man to leave the navy. Though wounded, the future admiral was ecstatic at having taken part in the great naval battle that heaped glory on the Imperial Navy.

After the war, following a period of recuperation from his wounds, Yamamoto spent the next few years pursuing the usual occupation of naval officers in times of peace: cruises, training courses, and more cruises. Shortly before the outbreak of the First World War, his parents died. As was the custom, he was adopted by a prominent Nagoakan family, by the name of Yamamoto. In a special ceremony he renounced his family name of Takano and took the name of his adoptive family. Soon afterward he was posted to Naval Headquarters and promoted to the rank of commander. Shortly thereafter he married a local Nagoakan girl.

Not long after the nuptials Yamamoto was ordered to the United States for a course of language study at Harvard University. He spent only one month at Harvard, and instead devoted his time to studying America and to pursuing his life's passion, gambling. He learned how to play poker during his stay in America and fell completely under the spell of the game. Later on in life he often told his associates that after he retired from the navy he wanted to go to Monaco and spend his remaining days gambling in its glittering casinos. It has been said that he was uncannily lucky and probably would have done rather well raking in the chips. However, he did more than gamble and attend athletic events during his time in the U.S. Yamamoto became fascinated with the study of the economics of oil. As a navy man he knew that oil was necessary for the existence of any modern navy, and so he began to learn every aspect of oil production from the time it was pumped from the ground until the display of the finished product fresh from the refineries. On one vacation trip he hitchiked to Mexico in order to visit that country's oilfields.

In addition to his interest in petroleum, Yamamoto developed a keen interest in aircraft during his stay in America and managed to tour various aircraft factories. By this time he was perceptive enough to realize that future wars would be dominated by air power. His foresight would be vividly corroborated twenty years later at Pearl Harbor. At the time, however, the tried-and-true naval strategy was based on the battleship.

Upon returning to Japan in July 1921, Yamamoto joined the Second Fleet as executive officer of the light cruiser *Kilagami*. In December of the same year he was reassigned to the Naval Staff as an instructor. Promoted to captain, his big opportunity came two years later when he was handed his first independent command as executive officer of a new air training center at Kasumigaura.

During its formative years the air corps was not highly regarded, and as a result usually failed to attract the cream of available recruits. Yamamoto set out to rectify this. His belief that the plane would dominate any future war made him determined to build a powerful naval air force. Working long hours studying various aircraft and their potential, he even went so far as to earn his aviator's wings, although he was now forty years old.

After eighteen months at the air school he was ordered

back to the United States as naval attaché. The Aviation Corps regretted losing their popular commander and gave him a rousing send-off by flying a squadron of aircraft over the ship carrying Yamamoto to America. In the conservative military circles of Japan this event confirmed the deep respect that the aviators held for Yamamoto. His reputation as an advocate of air power was firmly established.

Assuming the position of naval attaché in Washington, D.C., Yamamoto was directed to learn all there was to know about the defense programs of America. He kept a sharp eye on the development of American aviation.

While Yamamoto's career continued to advance, the world of the 1920s was roaring its way forward. It was an optimistic age of international treaties and goodwill. The belief of that generation was that paper treaties and conferences could insure future peace. Perhaps the most famous of the conferences of the era was the Washington Naval Limitation Conference of 1921-22. There it was agreed to halt all new construction and that the United States, England, and Japan would maintain a 5:5:3 ratio regarding the maintenance of all capital ships, *i.e.*, battleships and cruisers. The limiting of Japan to only 60% of the tonnage of Britain and America was not decried in 1922. However, by the end of the decade and far into the 1930s, this treaty was roundly condemned in Japan. Interestingly enough, the limitation was on capital ships but did not apply to aircraft carriers or destroyers. This loophole allowed Japan to work its way around the treaty limitations.

In March of 1928, Yamamoto returned to Japan where he found himself attached to the Naval General Staff for a short period. Shortly thereafter he was given command of the cruiser *Isuzu* and in December was named captain of the aircraft carrier *Akagi*. He remained with this ship almost a year before being posted to the Naval Affairs Bureau of the Navy Ministry. In that position he was sent to the 1930 London Naval Disarmament Conference as an assistant to the Japanese delegation.

Upon his return home, Yamamoto was given command

of the First Air Fleet. During this period Japan's army invaded Manchuria, upsetting the delicate balance of peace established by the League of Nations. Yamamoto, by now a rear admiral, held a key appointment in the technical arm of the navy. This assignment enabled him to insist on the increased production of aircraft. Many of the excellent aircraft that would later wreak havoc on the United States came to their blueprint stage under the prodding of Yamamoto.

By 1934 Japanese militarists and right-wingers had increased their grip on the reins of the government. These groups were highly critical of the naval limitation treaties and actively sought to free Japan from their shackles. Meanwhile, the British requested that another naval conference by scheduled in London during 1935. Because of anticipated difficulties it was decided that preliminary talks be held prior to the commencement of the main conference. On September 7, 1934, Yamamoto, still only a rear admiral, was appointed chief delegate to represent the Japanese at these preliminary talks. During these talks he emerged as a national figure.

There were many in Japan who were puzzled by the selection of Yamamoto as chief delegate. However, there was no question but that he was the most suitable and highly qualified. During the 1930 Limitation Conference he had made a favorable impression on the other countries with his knowledge of modern technology and naval affairs. These nations found him affable, reasonable, and easy to work with.

On September 25 the Yamamoto party sailed from Yokohama harbor and traveled by ship to Seattle where a train carried them across the vast territory of the United States with one short stopover in Chicago. Needless to say, the uneventful train ride was one long round of poker, bridge and *shogi*. When they arrived in New York the Japanese delegation boarded a British liner for passage to London.

As we have already seen, the question of naval disarmament dated back to the Washington Conference of 1921-22 and its 5:5:3 formula. The Japanese subsequently became disenchanted with the ratio, feeling that it placed them at a distinct disadvantage in the event of a war with the United States. The Naval Ministry, however, was satisfied with the conclusion of that initial conference, since the ministry was by and large staffed by level-headed personnel who believed in a nonbelligerent navy. The hawkish elements (the fleet faction) later opposed the treaty and considered it a sign of weakness and subservience to Western imperialism. The most vocal critics were, for the most part, younger officers imbued with the desire for Japanese expansion. This hawkish faction directed their ire toward those in favor of the provisions of the treaty (the treaty element).

By the time of the London Conference, this rebellious faction had gained a great deal of strength and publicly advocated the abrogation of the insulting terms that prevented Japan from becoming a first-rate power. In addition, they felt that the clauses of the treaty were a threat to the nation's defenses. Now it was 1934, and Yamamoto found himself facing these problems once again.

Since attending the London Conference of 1930, Yamamoto had devoted long hours to the study of the entire issue. He was acutely aware that the ratio system would have to go. In fact, when he landed in London, he stated in fluent English that

> "Japan can no longer submit to the ratio system. There is no possibility of compromise by my government on that point."[2]

Although that was his government's official position it may not have been his. From his prior experience in the United States he knew the depth of that nation's industrial base. Any Japanese attempt to become involved in an unrestricted shipbuilding race with the Americans would seriously damage Japan's economy. Whether Japan had seventy percent or the sixty percent demanded by the disarmament conference would make little difference if she became enbroiled in a war with the United States. The latter's industrial capacity would allow it to quickly surpass whatever Japan could produce. The sanest course, therefore, was to avoid a conflict between the two nations entirely. This did not necessarily mean that an unfavorable treaty should be concluded, but that compromises must be sought that—while limitations might still be imposed—would also provide for Japan's security. This was Yamamoto's line of thought. In effect, he was walking a tightrope, since his personal feelings differed from those of the fleet faction. The latter was counting on him to put an end to the unequal treaties. Among the Japanese people, the feeling was that the previous treaties should be allowed to lapse so that the nation might be free of any limitations.

While in London Yamamoto was promoted to vice admiral in November. As a participant in the conference he made a lasting impression on the delegates from the assembled nations. He proved the equal of any man there and demonstrated his determination to forge a treaty as favorable to Japan as was humanly possible. On one occasion, the Americans argued with him that Japan should not feel threatened by the ratio. He quickly shot back that in that case the Americans should not feel threatened with a 5:5 ratio. Yamamoto found that the British were much easier to deal with than the Americans.

The preliminary talks continued through November and into December, the British constantly attempting to keep the discussions going by avoiding any stumbling blocks to compromise. On December 20, the talks recessed.

The following year the main conference began. Yamamoto's place was taken by Admiral Nagano. The latter was a different sort than his predecessor and the conference in which so much early hope was placed wound down to its inevitable conclusion, the ending of disarmament and all limitations.

Yamamoto, meanwhile, had left London in January and begun the trip home by way of Europe and Asia. There was one brief stopover in Berlin at the request of the Japanese ambassador to Germany. Being revolted by the proposal that the Japanese hotheads and militarists were openly advocating for a Japanese-German alliance, Yamamoto was unenthusiastic about the visit. Had he his own way the stopover would have been avoided completely, but protocol made the detour necessary. Originally he was scheduled to have a private audience with Hitler, Ribbentrop, and the German naval minister. At that time Ribbentrop held no official position but was unofficially wielding the power that would eventually catapult him to the head of the German Foreign Ministry.

The Japanese ambassador, privy to Yamamoto's distaste for Hitler and his cronies, wisely cancelled the scheduled meeting and limited the visit to a courtesy call on Ribbentrop and the naval minister, who both professed a keen interest in the progress of the London talks. The admiral kept his lips sealed regarding the naval discussions, much to the chagrin of Ribbentrop. Following the meeting the Japanese contingent resumed the journey homeward via Poland and Russia, where they managed to visit Moscow. There they boarded the Trans-Siberian Railway, and after gambling their way across Siberia, arrived in Tokyo on February 12.

Following his return Yamamoto sat idly by in Tokyo awaiting an assignment where he could best utilize his talents. Ostracized by the hawkish element, he toyed with retirement, but by the end of the year he was appointed chief of the Aeronautics Department of the Navy Ministry. This department was directly responsible for all matters pertaining to naval aviation. Pleased with this new appointment, Yamamoto soon cast aside any thought of retirement. There was no doubt in Yamamoto's mind about the role aircraft would play in any future wars. Unfortunately, his views were in the minority. The majority of senior naval officers still tended to place their faith in the giant battleship with its big guns. Aircraft to them was secondary.

Now that naval limitations were scrapped, the Japanese began a massive shipbuilding program that included the construction of three massive battleships, the *Yamato*, the

Musashi, and the *Shinano.** Yamamoto openly opposed construction of these monsters, which were designed to carry 18-inch guns and a full load displacement of seventy-two thousand. In contrast, the British battlecruiser *Hood* had a displacement of but forty-two thousand. Yamamoto wanted the main shipbuilding effort concentrated on the construction of aircarft and aircraft carriers. Yamamoto's theory was that no matter how large the battleship, it could never be unsinkable. Aircraft, attacking from above, could destroy a battleship before it ever had the opportunity to fire a gun. Super battleships were therefore destined to become white elephants.

> "They are like elaborate religious scrolls which old people hang in their homes—a matter of faith, not reality. In modern warfare battleships will be as useful to Japan as the samurai sword."[3]

Naturally, the battleship proponents demanded proof of his claims. Unfortunately, he could not provide any at the time. Later, Pearl Harbor, Taranto, and the successful sinking of the *Repulse* and *Prince of Wales* would vindicate him, but for the present, he was unable to argue his point against the orthodox view with any measure of success, and to his chagrin, in July of 1936 the Japanese navy formally decided to construct the proposed battleships.

Meanwhile, in February of that same year, young army right-wingers favoring a hard-line policy toward England and America and desiring a more conservative nationalistic government, set out on an assassination binge against those Japanese officials whom they considered too soft and too pro-West. These included the Lord Privy Seal, the finance minister, the inspector general of Military Education, the Lord Chamberlain and the prime minister himself. Three

---

*In 1940 the *Shinano* plans were changed from those of a battleship to those of an aircraft carrier. It was completed in November 1944 and sunk a few weeks later by an American submarine, never having launched a plane.

of them were killed, while others were seriously wounded. Yamamoto objected to the army's move, but since he held no official position at the time, he could not effectively oppose them. In time, however, he and others of like mind would find themselves in a position to resist the tyranny of these army radicals, and in the name of the Imperial Navy, oppose the right-wing militarist moves.

Following the February 26 incident, Admiral Nagano was appointed navy minister. One of his first moves was to request that Yamamoto become vice minister. The latter was reluctant to accept this political position since he personally did not care for the newly appointed navy minister. It was Nagano who had declared Japan's withdrawal from the London talks in 1935. In addition, it was no secret that Nagano favored the signing of an anti-Comintern pact with Germany. Unfortunately, Yamamoto found himself placed in such a position that he was forced to yield to Nagano's promptings, and to his distaste, to leave the congenial post as head of the Aeronautics Department to become embroiled in the political turmoil that characterized the duties of naval vice minister. On December 1, 1936, the appointment became official, and Yamamoto entered the political scene at a time when the army establishment had increased its hold on the government and was advocating a belligerent attitude towards China and the Western countries.

Soon after assuming his new post, Yamamoto found himself in opposition to the Army faction, which was continuing to strengthen its position within the government.

Nagano was shortly ousted as navy minister, but Yamamoto remained on, feeling a deep sense of responsibility to the political role with which the navy had entrusted him. It was clear to him that if the prevailing situation remained unchecked Japan would find itself headed down the road to eventual ruin. Thus Yamamoto considered it the navy's duty to thwart the autocratic methods of the army.

In order to achieve this he felt that the navy must present a united front against the opposing tactics. Therefore, "navy hawks" had to be eliminated from high naval positions. However, Yamamoto needed a navy minister who was in complete accord with his own position. Luckily, the new minister shared Yamamoto's views. In fact, Mitsumasa Yonai was an old-line member of the treaty faction of the 1920.

In July, 1937, Yamamoto was shocked by news of the incident at the Marco Polo Bridge near Peiping (Peking), which sparked the Sino-Japanese War. This incident might have been settled peacefully since the Chinese were most conciliatory, but the army hotheads were eager for war and did everything possible to insure that the incident was used as a pretext for a full-scale war between the two countries.

Yamamoto's opposition to the war was openly avowed, but to no avail. Japanese troops swept southward and on December 13, the Chinese capital of Nanking fell to the slaughtering swarms of jubilant sons of Nippon. At the same time an American naval gunboat, the *Panay*, was erroneously bombed by Japanese naval air units. This unfortunate event could have ignited a war between the United States and Japan. The Naval Ministry was quick to apologize, since the last thing they desired was to escalate the conflict to include the United States. The Japanese Navy did all that was humanly possible to make amends. A ship was sent up the Yangtze to aid in the rescue and a personal telegram was sent to the President of the United States expressing Japan's deepest regrets. Yamamoto's curt statement regarding the affair reflected his mood.

"The navy can only hang its head."[4]

Two weeks later the *Panay* incident was settled and the crisis past, thanks to the quick acceptance of responsibility by Japan and their obvious regret. Yamamoto vowed that such incidents would not occur in the future.

With the arrival of 1938, Japanese politics turned even more sharply to the right. Yamamoto and the Naval Ministry steadfastly refused to be swept up by this trend. Instead, they remained critical toward the army and the right-wingers and were particularly critical of the hawkish faction within the navy itself. Unfortunately, the Naval Ministry found itself helpless regarding decisions concerning the war in China, since that was the province of the army. The possibility of Japan's concluding a treaty with Germany and Italy though, was another matter entirely. Conclusion of this alliance would directly affect the navy, since such a treaty would make England and America potential enemies. A war with those two powers would throw the entire responsibility on the navy. Yamamoto and Yonai both objected to the proposed pact, claiming that all it could accomplish would be to push forth the possibility of a future war, something the Naval Ministry desired to avoid at all costs. Yamamoto often lamented to his chief that with the way things were going Japan would soon find herself embroiled in a costly war with the United States.

On January 1, 1939, the Japanese Government underwent a drastic change when Prime Minister Konoye resigned. Once more this change failed to affect the makeup of the Naval Ministry. The new government under Prime Minister Hiranuma still wrestled with the problem of signing the Tripartite Pact with Germany and Italy. Yamamoto continued forcefully to oppose the treaty, but as time went by it became increasingly dangerous for him to do so. The right-wing elements exerted enormous pressure on Yamamoto and Yonai to endorse the pact. Threats of assassination and blackmail were used to induce the two naval officers to change their position. Police protection had to be provided to protect them from possible harm.

The Hiranuma government held seventy meetings in all on the question of the Tripartite Pact, but was unable to reach a conclusion since the navy's leaders continued to withhold their endorsement. Consequently, Hiranuma's government collapsed in August following the conclusion of the Nazi-Soviet pact. Ostensibly the Tripartite Pact was designed as an anti-Soviet treaty, but the conclusion of an agreement between Germany and Russia pulled the rug out from under the Japanese government. Under the pretext of the worsening situation in Europe, the cabinet resigned.

With that resignation Yonai and Yamamoto were swept out of office.

Yamamoto was not happy with being forced out and expressed a desire to remain on. Instead he was sent back to the fleet and named commander-in-chief of the Combined Fleet. That move probably saved him from assassination by some radical, since he was now far removed from the political storm.

As war clouds continued to darken over the European sky, and with the right-wing fanatics clamoring for closer ties with the Axis, Yamamoto, now elevated to the rank of full admiral, left behind the tumultuous life of a desk-bound politician. As commander of the fleet his primary duty was the protection of the homeland, and a policy of rigorous training for war was initiated. Heavy emphasis was placed on training the fleet in night maneuvers. It was ironic that the man who opposed war so strenuously should now be preparing the fleet for just the thing he had been trying to avoid for so many years. However, whether he approved of war or not was academic, since Yamamoto felt a strong sense of duty toward his country; if the nation went to war he wanted the fleet ready to accept the challenge. With Germany, England, and France at war, the future boded ill.

In January 1940 the Japanese government underwent still another change. Only four months had elapsed since the previous change. The imperial mandate was now handed to Admiral Yonai, the former naval minister. As we have previously seen, Yonai opposed the Tripartite Pact, so this move was interpreted as a sign that the emperor himself was against the forces of the right. Some, such as the Lord Privy Seal, Yuasa, felt that the Yonai government represented a last chance to check the rise of fascism. According to the History of the Pacific War compiled by the Historgraphical Research Society and published in 1953-54:

". . . the emergence of Yonai was obviously partly the work of pro-U.S., pro-British senior statesmen, and was opposed by both the army and the reformists."[5]

During Yonai's term of office, therefore, there were no more attempts to bring up the subject of the Tripartite Pact. The army hated the new prime minister and did all in their power to topple him, for they considered the appointment of Yonai to be a plot by the emperor's pro-Western advisors. Unfortunately for Japan, less than half a year later the Yonai government resigned and another government was formed under former Prime Minister Fuminaro Konoye. Two months later, on September 27, this government signed the Tripartite Pact.

General Hideki Tojo was chosen by Konoye to be war minister. Tojo was a volatile man and a champion of the Tripartite Pact. Yamamoto held many misgivings about the pact and the new cabinet, for he sensed what was in the making and was convinced that

> "A war between Japan and the United States would be a major calamity for the world, and for Japan it would mean, after several years of war already, acquiring yet another powerful enemy—an extremely perilous matter for the nation."[6]

The official navy view however, had shifted dramatically. The new navy minister was Admiral Oikawa, with Admiral Toyoda as vice minister. Oikawa was not nearly as formidable a character as his predecessor, so, when asked to back the Tripartite Pact, he did so obligingly. When he presented his case to Yamamoto and other naval dignitaries during a conference in Tokyo he said that if the navy openly opposed the pact it would more than likely bring down the second Konoye government, and the naval minister felt strongly that the navy should not allow itself to be responsible for the government's collapse. Most of the naval officers present remained silent. Yamamoto, however, raised an important question. He noted that eighty percent of all materials needed for production came from Great Britain and America. Japan's endorsement of the Tripartite Pact placed shipments of these materials in jeopardy. Could the government compensate for loss of these materials?

Oikawa did not reply to Yamamoto's question. Instead, he asked all present to grant their approval to the signing of the pact. All agreed except Yamamoto, who was enraged.

Shortly thereafter Konoye himself expressed a desire to meet with the commander-in-chief of the Combined Fleet in order to discuss the navy's prospects in the event Japan went to war against the United States and England. Yamamoto answered:

> "If we are told to fight regardless of consequences, we can run wild for six months or a year but after that I have utterly no confidence. I hope you will try to avoid war with America."[7]

Unfortunately not all the naval leaders felt the same way. Yamamoto tried to tell them that

> "if it is necessary to fight, in the first six months to a year of war against the United States and England I will run wild. I will show you an uninterrupted succession of victories. But I must also tell you that if the war be prolonged for two or three years I have no confidence in our ultimate victory."[8]

These prophetic words fell on deaf ears.

Yamamoto now found himself faced with a dilemma. He disagreed with the direction his country was taking and lamented watching Japan rush forward into a war he was sure they could not win, but, as commander-in-chief of the Combined Fleet, he was not in a position to disassociate himself from any war that might break out. The political stance of his country was not his responsibility, since he held firmly to the old navy tradition that only those in the Naval Ministry should be involved in politics. The rest of the navy must submit to the navy minister's authority. Thus, while outwardly gearing the navy for war, inwardly he grieved over the situation.

Tirelessly, he prepared. Keenly aware of Japan's unique position, he knew he must formulate a plan through which

Japan could hope for a victory, even though he knew that there was little hope for any ultimate victory. The United States was simply too great a country, with too deep an economic base. After all, he had been there and seen the industrial potential of that nation. Japan's only hope, he reasoned, was some extraordinary measure that could end the war quickly. It was in this frame of mind that the idea of the Pearl Harbor operation was conceived. If the navy could destroy the American warships as quickly as possible, if the Japanese fleet could strike a severe blow against the American Pacific Fleet and cripple its strength, perhaps Japan could achieve a chance for a negotiated peace.

When the plan was first presented for review, almost all ranking naval commanders disapproved of it. Most naval strategists over the years had accepted what had come to be known as the "orthodox" plan. This called for a Japanese attack on the Philippines. The attack would prompt a response from America and cause her to dispatch its fleet to aid the besieged islands. Meanwhile, from positions of strength in the Marianas, the Japanese fleet could whittle the American fleet down in a campaign of attrition, so that when the decisive sea battle (à la Tsushima Bay) occurred, the Japanese fleet could apply the coup de grace on the remnants of the enemy. Of course, this plan was hypothetical, but over the years, during the course of war games, it became the time-honored program for victory, until any deviation from this plan was considered unwise.

The Hawaiian operation, however, had been germinating in Yamamoto's fertile mind since sometime in 1940. He harbored grave doubts about the orthodox plan, having concluded that an attritional battle was too risky. Japan could ill afford to lose too much, not with the American potential. An attack by aircraft against the American fleet would be less costly.

Early in 1941, around the time he was putting the Pearl Harbor plan into definite shape, Yamamoto began to give serious thought to retirement. After all, most commanders-in-chief only served for two years, and in August that period would be up for him. Though he frequently stated that he looked forward to retirement, he knew that if he were called on to remain at the helm he would gladly do so.

The Pearl Harbor plan was officially drawn up and submitted on January 7, 1941, in a nine-page document. Yamamoto opened the document with the following statement:

> "No one can make any definite predictions concerning the international situation, but it seems obvious that the time has come for the navy, and the Combined Fleet in particular, to go ahead with arming and training itself, and possibly drawing up a plan of operations on the assumption that war with America and England cannot be avoided."[9]

The formulated plan was based on Yamamoto's conviction that victory had to be achieved the first day.

Ironically, just around this time the American ambassador to Japan, Joseph Grew, cabled the State Department stating the the Peruvian minister had managed to find out from various sources that if trouble developed between the United States and Japan, the latter would make a surprise attack against the naval base at Pearl Harbor. Grew went on to say that his informant considered the rumors fantastic, yet considered them important enough to inform his American colleague. This message was transmitted on January 20, 1941, but was disregarded in America. However, an interesting point is that the plan to attack Pearl Harbor had not been accepted by anyone in Japan at that early date. In fact, Yamamoto was a voice crying out in the wilderness. The United States State Department seems to have accepted the news of the strike with the same conviction of its impossibility as most Japanese who had heard of it from Yamamoto.

On the other hand, Yamamoto was convinced that the plan would succeed. As proof of this he pointed to the November 1940 attack by the Royal Navy against the Italian fleet at Taranto. Of this attack he said:

"If the British could sink ships at such a depth,* why not repeat this type of attack on a much bigger scale."[10]

Yamamoto's proposal now made the rounds of those naval units that would have to implement it in the event of hostilities. Furious debates commenced for and against the plan. The opposition included some very powerful personalities. Rear Admiral Fukudome, head of the First Division of the Naval General Staff, Captain Tomioko, head of the First Section, and Commander Miyo, Air Staff officer, were among the most vocal. One of the prime reasons for their opposition was the belief that the plan constituted simply too much of a gamble. What guarantee was there that the American Fleet would even be in Pearl Harbor at the time of the attack? they asked.

Those favoring the plan clung to Yamamoto's main argument, that if war was indeed unavoidable, the only possible method of attack would be to destroy the enemy's predominance at the outset, thereby placing him at a disadvantage. Foremost among the champions of the plan was Commander Genda, head of the air units aboard the carriers.

Meanwhile, as the debate between the naval commanders continued, the Japanese Army cast fate to the wind and took advantage of the situation in Europe by announcing in July that it had negotiated an agreement with the Vichy French Government to form a joint protectorate of Indo-China. This proved to be the straw that broke the camel's back as far as the United States was concerned. They countered the move by freezing all Japanese assets in the United States and halting all shipments of oil. Great Britain and Holland soon followed suit. The oil embargo was critical, since Japan was entirely dependent on imports of this vital resource. It was an ultimatum. Japan's oil reserve

---

*Taranto harbor was forty-two feet deep, Pearl Harbor forty-five. It was considered too shallow for the use of torpedo bombs. Admiral Cunningham's Mediterranean Fleet proved otherwise.

was good for at least eighteen months, but after that, there would be nothing. Japan had therefore to agree to humiliate itself by kowtowing to the United States, or it had to fight.

The navy was taken back by the army's action in Indo-China, since not once did the two branches of the service consult regarding the potential consequences of the move. In August, the navy began to prepare itself for the inevitable. War games were conducted, consisting of dry runs of the proposed Hawaiian operation. The air unit from the carrier *Akagi* traveled to Kagoshima Bay for training exercises. The interesting point about this harbor was its close resemblance to Pearl Harbor. A fiery young aviator, Lieutenant Commander Mitsuo Fuchida, was posted to the carrier as its flight commander at the time. It was Fuchida whom Yamamoto had selected to lead the attack force against the American naval base.

Various problems had to be overcome before the operation could in fact be performed. Foremost among them was the monumental opposition to the plan. This negativism had to be surmounted. Of a more technical nature was the problem of the depth of Pearl Harbor. Could torpedoes be used similiar to the ones utilized by the British at Taranto—torpedoes that could not sink beyond the forty-five foot depth of Pearl Harbor? Yamamoto discovered that fitting them with wooden fins would keep the torpedoes from sinking too deep. That, he knew, would become one of the keys to success. The other would be whether or not the operation could be conducted in secrecy. Would it be a surprise? Again Yamamoto was sure it would be, and, despite all opposition, he stuck to his guns.

Two strong voices against the Pearl Harbor strike were Admirals Kusaka and Onishi, Chiefs of Staff of the First and Eleventh Air Fleets respectively. During fleet war games that simulated a mock attack on the United States, the Japanese Fleet suffered (on paper) a great deal of damage. Kusaka, who greatly respected Yamamoto, felt that the plan was too risky. Seeing the results of the war games, he concluded that the Hawaiian attack was like "putting one's head in the lion's mouth."[11] Another voice added to the opposition was that of Admiral Chiuchi Nagumo, commander of the Aircraft Carrier Fleet itself. The opposition decided to write to Yamamoto requesting that the entire concept be abandoned. After reading the document in silence, Yamamoto remarked that as long as he was commander-in-chief, the operation would proceed. Emphasizing that the action was vital, he resented having it called a gamble.

Through careful persuasion both Onishi's and Kusaka's resistance was broken. Yamamoto personally placed his hand on Kusaka's shoulder and explained that the Pearl Harbor raid had become an article of faith to him and that he would be most grateful if Kusaka would stop resisting. The latter finally came around, and along with Onishi, pledged to help prepare for the operation.

At an Imperial Conference on September 6, the decision to go to war with the United States was reached. Exactly a month later, five days of map maneuvers were held on board Yamamoto's flagship, the aim being to acquaint various levels of commanders with the Hawaiian operation. Yamamoto reiterated his absolute intent to carry it through if war became inevitable. He was so optimistic regarding the plan's success that even the Chief of the Naval General Staff, Admiral Nagano, dropped his opposition. After that, most of the others went along, following a dramatic scene during which Yamamoto threatened to resign if the plan were not adopted.

Outwardly Yamamoto gave the impression of a man chomping at the bit for action and intent on proving his plan feasible. Inwardly, however, he was deeply depressed over the whole turn in political affairs. More now than ever he did not want war. It was ironic that the man who, through the sheer power of his will, overcame all opposition to the Hawaiian plan was in fact the most reluctant of all.

Yamamoto was an enigma. He prepared for a war he did not want. He preached restraint while preparing one of the most infamous acts in history. He cautioned against underestimating his opponents, yet based his future plans on the premise that once beaten by a surprise attack, the enemy would simply turn over and give up. On September 18, during a speech in Tokyo to some old Nagoaka schoolmates, Yamamoto gave numerous reasons why Japan should avoid war with the United States.

> "It is a mistake to regard Americans as luxury loving and weak. I can tell you that they are full of spirit, adventure, fight, and justice. Their thinking is scientific and well advanced. Lindbergh's solo flight across the Atlantic was an act characteristic of Americans—adventuresome but scientifically based. Remember that American industry is much more developed than ours—and unlike us—they have the oil they want. Japan cannot vanquish the United States. Therefore we should not fight the United States."[12]

Prime Minister Konoye immediately branded Yamamoto as pro-American and pro-British upon hearing these words.

Yet Yamamoto continued to plan. A major question was what was the best route for the fleet to travel in order to insure the vital secrecy of the operation. There were three possible alternatives: a northern route, a central Pacific route, or a southern one. Yamamoto felt that the northern route held the greatest prospect for success because the warships could then travel the little-used waters of the Northern Pacific. There were problems with that route. The seas would be rougher, making refuelling next to impossible. But even with that problem the chance of success would be better since the prospect of the fleet's detection would be greatly lessened.

Meanwhile, information regarding the disposition of the American fleet was being received from spies. Yamamoto wanted every scrap of information regarding the enemy's habits. U.S. Intelligence units were able to monitor the transmissions of these secret agents but paid little attention to them because, as part of Yamamoto's cover plan, Japanese spies were relaying information from Portland, Oregon, San Francisco, Manila, Panama, and San Diego.

Pearl Harbor was but one of the many areas the Japanese were watching.

On October 17, the winds of war blew more stormily, as Japan once again underwent a change in government. Army General Hideki Tojo became the new prime minister.

During the first week in November the Hawaiian Operation finally became a fully accepted plan. Flight Commander Genda, who was supervising the flight training, could now inform his pilots that the target was Pearl Harbor. Genda unrolled a large map of Oahu containing a detail of Pearl Harbor. A cold chill was felt among the pilots as they heard the outline of the plan for the first time. On the 5th Yamamoto issued Operation Order No. 1, the Hawaiian operation. Eight days later he held a conference at Iwakuni Naval Air Base to which all commanders-in-chief, chiefs of staff, and senior staff officers were summoned for a detailed explanation and discussion of the operational order. There, Yamamoto informed the gathering that it had been formally decided that December 8 (December 7 Hawaiian time) would be the official date for the opening of hostilities. He then went on to describe the route to be taken by the attacking force and to explain that the fleet would assemble by November 22 at Tankan Bay (Hitokappu Bay) in the Kuriles. This fleet would contain six carriers and have 423 planes as its strike force. The force would sortie on November 26 and take the northern route to the vicinity of the Hawaiian Islands. A force of twenty-seven submarines were to be part of the force. This force would be largely composed of the large I-Class submarines but would include a number of midget submarines, as well. The latter were to slip into Pearl Harbor just before dawn and remain submerged while the aircraft attacked. They would then make a surprise attack after sunrise when the Americans thought they were safe. That portion of the plan was later modified to allow the midget submarines to attack at will.

The commander-in-chief then cautioned everyone that negotiations were still in progress, and if an agreement was reached, the fleet, upon receipt of appropriate orders, would return to base. At this, Admiral Nagumo, commander of the task force, responded that it would be demoralizing to turn back a force already in motion. Yamamoto retorted that if there was anyone present unable to obey an order when given, he should resign then and there. All remained silent.

Feverish days of activity now engulfed the fleet. All inflammables, personal possessions and unnecessary items were taken ashore to be replaced by weapons, ammunition and food supplies. The planes too were prepared. Rudders and flaps on aircraft were treated with a special antifreeze grease to protect them from the anticipated cold of the northern Pacific. Each vessel involved in the operation assembled in November at the rendezvous. Yamamoto took part in a ceremony with Nagumo on board the carrier *Akagi*, flagship of the task force. Eyewitnesses attest to the fact that Yamamoto's expression was somber, approaching gloomy. On the 22nd, the *Akagi* entered Tankan Bay. In all, thirty-one vessels assembled there for the historic voyage.

On the 25th, Yamamoto issued his sailing orders, giving the time the fleet would move out of the bay, which direction to take and what to do upon conclusion of the attack. Included in these orders was the statement:

> "Should negotiations with the United Staes prove successful, the task force shall hold itself in readiness forthwith to return and reassemble.[13]

The commander-in-chief continued to cling to the hope that war could be avoided.

Plowing eastward, the task force crossed the International Dateline on December 1. Meanwhile, in Washington, negotiations proceeded in earnest even while Tojo and his cabinet were putting the finishing touches on the war plans (*See Map 5*).

Among the many fears harbored by Yamamoto was that Japan's act of war would not follow the conduct of war. That is, he insisted that Washington should receive a

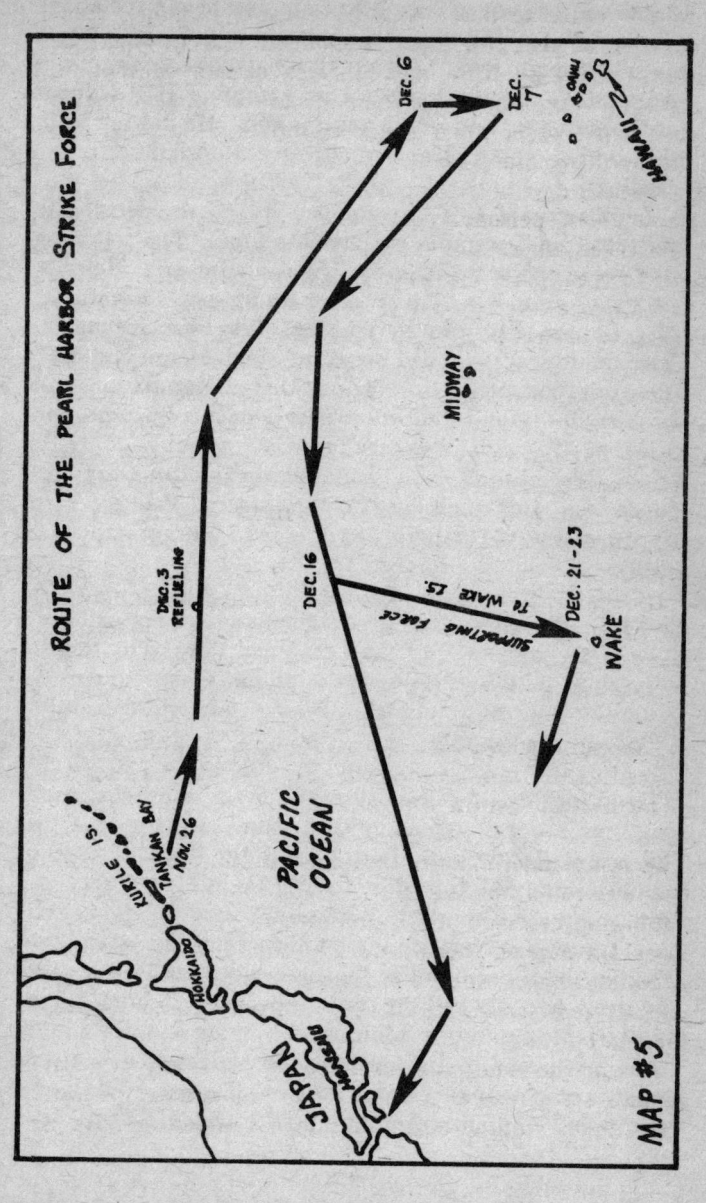

declaration of war at least a half an hour before the attack was scheduled to begin, should the negotiations break down. Though some believed this was unnecessary, since Admiral Togo had attacked Port Arthur in 1904 without announcement, Yamamoto was insistent. He did not want this attack to take place without such a declaration's preceeding it.

On December 1, Tojo's cabinet ratified the decision to start war on December 8 (Japanese time). The following day the emperor reluctantly signed an Imperial Rescript formally committing Japan to a path of war. That was it. Negotiations had proven fruitless. War was inevitable. Yamamoto sent the coded message "Climb Mount Niitaka." This brief statement told Nagumo that all negotiations had broken down and that hostilities would commence on schedule. Yamamoto was saddened.

On December 3, the commander-in-chief of the Combined Fleet was summoned to the Imperial Palace for an audience with the emperor, who received him cordially and issued the following injunction:

> "In commanding our forces into action we entrust to you the command of the Combined Fleet. The task facing the Combined Fleet is of the utmost importance, and the whole fate of our nation will depend on the outcome.[14]

Ironically, neither the emperor nor the admiral desired war, yet one was commanding the other to fight, and the other was pledging his life to fight to the finish.

Meanwhile, the United States' Pacific Fleet at Pearl Harbor under the command of Admiral Husband Kimmel sat unsuspecting as Nagumo's task force steamed its way across the Northern Pacific. The Japanese code had been broken by the Americans and the secret messages sent from Tokyo to the Japanese Ambassador in Washington had, for a long time, been read by U.S. code breakers. However, if asked where the anticipated war would begin, most would have said the Philippines, Malaya, or the Dutch East Indies.

Pearl Harbor was not suspect. It was simply too far from Japan to be endangered. The United States would pay dearly for this gross underestimation of the Japanese ability.

At Pearl Harbor sat eight battleships, two heavy cruisers, six light cruisers, twenty-nine destroyers, five submarines, and forty-four other types of ships. There were two aircraft carriers assigned to the Pacific command as well. These, of course, were the most desirable targets of all.

By December 5, the Japanese task force had left the chilly North Pacific behind for the calmer waters of the temperate zone. Throughout the journey Yamamoto worried. Would the fleet be discovered? How was the weather? Would the American fleet be in harbor at the time of the attack? Luckily, the Japanese fleet remained undetected. The decision to take the northern route was the correct one. As for the weather, once again Yamamoto's luck held. A Siberian high had brought an extraordinary spell of calm weather to the area, which was usually buffeted by severe winds during that time of the year.

The fear regarding the presence of the American fleet was perhaps Yamamoto's greatest. His only hope here was the American custom of bringing the fleet into harbor for the weekend. Since the date of the attack was a Sunday, hopefully all the ships would be present. On the 6th, Japanese spies related that the two American carriers were not present. Perhaps they would be there, however, by the time of the attack.

That same day, Yamamoto sent a message to the fleet. It was an obvious coincidence that this message was similiar in style and content to Admiral Togo's address just before the Battle of Tsushima during the Russo-Japanese War. Nagumo read it to the fleet.

"The rise or fall of the empire depends upon this battle. Everyone will do his duty to the utmost."[15]

At that point a huge battle flag was broken out on the masthead of the *Akagi*. It was the famous "Z" flag of Admiral Togo, which had been run up on his flagship, the

Mikasa, in the Straits of Tsushima. The shouting of *banzais* echoed across the fleet.

Admiral Chiuchi Nagumo, the man who led the Pearl Harbor attack, possessed little experience in aviation. This was unfortunate, since it was this man who was placed in command of the First Air Fleet and saddled with an awesome responsibility. In chapter three we will present a complete discusson of Nagumo. For the present it is essential to highlight one of his traits in order to comprehend what followed. He was a timid man, lacking in self-confidence and uncertain about the Pearl Harbor plan. It was most unfortunate for Yamamoto that Japanese command assignments were not given out on the basis of ability, but on seniority. There were so many other more aggressive and capable commanders who might have commanded what was supposed to have been Japan's decisive punch.

In the early morning darkness of December 7, 1941, amid the loud screams of *banzais,* the six Japanese carriers turned into the wind and began to launch the planes containing their deadly cargo. Fuchida commanded the first wave of 183 aircraft. The complete story of Pearl Harbor will be related in the chapter on Nagumo. The main trends of the attack, however, will be covered here, as they relate to Yamamoto.

The attack plan contained two options. If complete surprise was achieved the torpedo planes would lead the attack, followed by the level bombers. If American resistance was encountered, however, the fighters would first gain control of the air. Then, the dive bombers would lead the attack, while the level bombers attacked the enemy antiaircraft installations as they opened up. In the midst of this confusion the torpedo planes would descend upon the battleships.

During the approach to Pearl Harbor everything was strangely quiet. Fuchida tapped out the prearranged attack code indicating that complete surprise had been achieved: To-To-To. Nagumo, two hundred miles away aboard *Akagi,* and Yamamoto, aboard his flagship *Nagato* in the

Inland Sea, both heard the magical words. Surprise was complete. No American fighters appeared in the air. With this message, hostilities began all across the Pacific and Indian Oceans. Thus began a string of Japanese victories that would not be blunted for six months.

When the To message was received aboard *Nagato*, jubilation broke out. Only Yamamoto remained as still as a Buddha statue. Finally, he turned to his aide and said:

> "Check the time of the attack carefully. It is very important to know when the attack began. It seems to have come earlier that we expected."[16]

Indeed it had, thanks to carelessness and ineptitude on the part of the Japanese embassy. Yamamoto's fears were realized. The ultimatum was delivered thirty-five minutes after the attack. Japan entered the war without a formal declaration, the very thing Yamamoto wished to avoid at all costs. On top of this, word was received that no American aircraft carriers were present at Pearl Harbor.

When word of the attack was made known to the people of Japan the name of Yamamoto suddenly acquired a new importance in the minds of the public. The vast majority were jubilant. Such a great victory with such little loss of life!

In fact, Pearl Harbor was an incomplete victory. When Fuchida landed aboard the *Akagi* he reported to Nagumo that four battleships had been sunk, numerous other ships had been damaged, and most of the American planes had been destroyed on the ground. Unfortunately, he went on, no aircraft carriers were present. Nagumo seemed pleased with the results and was ready to set sail away from Hawaiian waters. Fuchida, however, pleaded for another attack wave aimed at facilities—the dry docks, repair shops, and fuel storage tanks. Nagumo, whose losses were a mere twenty-nine aircraft and fifty-five men, felt he had accomplished enough. Fuchida's protests were to no avail. Nagumo's sense of caution held sway.

At Yamamoto's headquarters a debate also ensued over

whether or not another attack should be launched. Yamamoto said:

> "No. Wait, it would be fine, of course, if it were successful. But even a burglar hesitates to go back for more. I'd rather leave it to the commander of the task force. . . . I imagine Nagumo doesn't want to."[17]

Thus the second attack never took place and Japan lost an ideal opportunity to cripple the United States even more.

Was Yamamoto wrong in not demanding that Nagumo launch another attack? His operations officer, Admiral Kuroshima, told the commander-in-chief that Nagumo was responsible for the partial failure of Pearl Harbor. He should have been more aggressive. Kuroshima went so far as to recommend that Nagumo be relieved from duty. Yamamoto, however, could not do this, for he knew the kind of person that Nagumo was. If he were relieved, Yamamoto felt that Nagumo would probably commit *hari-kiri*. John Dean Potter, in his study of Yamamoto, wondered:

> "Was the village schoolmaster's son a little in social awe of the ineffectual but aristocratic admiral who served under him? For by keeping Nagumo, Yamamoto went a long was towards dooming himself and his navy."[18]

Was Pearl Harbor necessary? The historical verdict has answered this negatively. Samuel Eliot Morrison, America's eminent naval historian, said this of the attack:

> ". . . thus, the surprise attack on Pearl Harbor, far from being a 'strategic necessity,' as the Japanese claimed even after the war, was a strategic imbecility. One can search military history in vain for an operation more fatal to the aggressor. On the tactical level, the Pearl Harbor attack was wrongly concentrated on

ships rather than permanent installations and oil tanks. On the strategic level it was disastrous."[19]

American's prewar plan, Rainbow Five, called for an American counterattack if Japan attacked the Philippines. This counterattack would be against Japanese positions in the Marshalls and Carolines before moving to relieve the Philippines or other areas. Prewar estimates said that it would take approximately six to nine months for this to be accomplished. Had the Japanese not attacked Pearl Harbor, they would have had at least half a year to consolidate their gains without running the risk of uniting the populace of the United States in anger. The American people would not have been so unified in a common cause if it were only the Philippines that were attacked. The infamous attack on Hawaii, however, was soundly condemned, with a unanimous desire for revenge. Ironically, America's Rainbow Five plan coincided almost exactly with Japan's orthodox view of waiting for the enemy to come to them rather than carrying the attack to the opponent.

The Pearl Harbor attack thrust Yamamoto onto the world stage and portrayed him as a criminal. To every American he was the embodiment of the back-stabbing, aggressive, treacherous enemy. One sentence, taken out of the context of a letter written by Yamamoto a year earlier as a means of raising morale in Japan, made Americans determined that when the war was over, that murdering warmonger Yamamoto would be put on trial as a war criminal. This sentence read:

> "If there should be a war between Japan and America, then our aim, of course, ought not to be Guam or the Philippines, nor Hawaii or Hong Kong, but a capitulation at the White House, in Washington itself.[20]

These words appeared to be sheer bravado and convinced Americans that Yamamoto was a fanatical warmonger. In fact, the letter was not intended to be that at all. If the entire letter had been published the readers would have seen that the next sentence went on to say:

> "I wonder whether the politicians of the day really have the willingness to make sacrifices."[21]

Yamamoto meant the letter as a warning to the then Prime Minister Konoye and the Navy Minister Oikawa, that if war came, it would not be a limited one but a conflict of great magnitude. A limited war with the United States was impossible. That was the feeling that Yamamoto wished to express.

We must again return to the initial question. Was Pearl Harbor necessary? Yamamoto certainly felt so. Granted, it branded him as a criminal. He still felt it necessary to destroy the enemy fleet at the outset. Japan could ill afford to wait for the United States Fleet to come to them. Time would work against Japan. If he could have survived the war, Yamamoto would have had a heated debate with Morrison.

After Pearl Harbor, victory followed victory. A few days after the Hawaiian attack another victory occurred that gave Yamamoto an acute sense of satisfaction, for it vindicated his belief that air power could cripple battleships—not just battleships lying at anchor as at Pearl Harbor, but battleships on the high seas. This victory, of course, was the sinking of the British battleship *Prince of Wales* and the battlecruiser *Repulse*. Where he had been sullen at the news of Pearl Harbor, Yamamoto was elated over the latest success.

These twin victories of air power over capital ships should have served to convince the Naval Ministry that the age of the battleship was past and the age of airpower had dawned. Yet, at noon on December 21, the gigantic battleship *Yamato*, whose construction Yamamoto had vehemently opposed for five years, made its first appearance at Hashirajima anchorage. The *Yamato* was the world's largest battleship, displacing seventy-eight thousand tons and mounting 18-inch guns. Two months later this mammoth became Yamamoto's flagship.

The Japanese Navy continued to string together an unprecedented series of victories. Thanks to the destruction of the *Repulse* and the *Prince of Wales* the army was able to conquer Malaya and Singapore by mid-February. On the 27th of the same month, the Japanese won a convincing victory over an Allied fleet in the Java Sea.

As the successes continued to mount, Yamamoto remained troubled. Japan had the Dutch East Indies with all its oil. However, what was Japan's next step to be? The lightning conquests left his planners agog. Without any long-range strategic goals, a difference of opinion now divided the naval leaders. Should Japan remain on the offensive or should she hold fast and consolidate her swift conquests? If she did go on the offensive, where would she go? India? Australia? Hawaii?

Yamamoto realized that the fleet had to prepare for future operations. His chief of staff had suggested consideration of any of the aforementioned objectives with special emphasis on Hawaii. Again the same reasons for the initial attack on these islands surfaced. The natural resources of the United States were so numerous that if Japan did not engage the American fleet in a decisive fleet battle near Hawaii once and for all, the enemy would recover quickly and counterattack the Imperial Navy.

Other officers, however, were studying the possibility of an assault against the British aimed at achieving supremacy in the Indian Ocean with the possibility of an eventual linkup with the advancing German Army in the Middle East. While Yamamoto's staff debated over India or Hawaii, the Naval General Staff planners in Tokyo were thinking along the lines of an operation toward Australia. They rightly observed that Australia would probably be used as the springboard for any future Allied counteroffensive. Australia, they felt, must either be conquered or cut off and neutralized. The army, however, vetoed any invasion of Australia since there were not enough troops available, thanks to the demands of the war in China. Actually, the army preferred an attack on Russia, which at that time was embroiled in a life-and-death struggle with Nazi Germany. The Japanese anticipated a German victory and were eager to participate in it by stabbing their ancient foe in the back.

Yamamoto's primary concern, though, was the bringing of the war to a successful conclusion as swiftly as possible. He knew that the amazing string of victories could not continue for more than a year. Which then, of the three areas under consideration, would have the best chance of insuring peace?

While the debate continued, Yamamoto decided to send Nagumo's carriers into the Indian Ocean to deal a decisive blow to the Royal Navy. Though this action proved to be another victorious campaign for the Imperial Navy, it was, like Pearl Harbor, a hit-and-run operation. There was no follow-up attack. In fact, this was the last time the Japanese Navy ranged west of Singapore.

Finally, after two months of debate, Yamamoto made his decision. He resolved to seize Midway Island, believing that not only could it be used as an advance base for air and submarine patrols, more importantly, it would, he felt, draw out the American fleet for a decisive naval battle. The admiral was convinced that this operation would accomplish what Pearl Harbor had left undone. With a conclusive victory, the American will to fight would be undermined, and they would be forced to sue for a negotiated peace on Japanese terms.

On April 2, Yamamoto's planning officer, Commander Watanable, traveled to Tokyo to present Plan AF, a joint Midway and Aleutian operation, to the Naval General Staff. The plan was overwhelmingly rejected as too risky. The General Staff's negative view was that Midway was much too far away and would prove difficult to keep supplied. As an alternative, they proposed an attack on New Caledonia, Fiji, and Samoa in order to isolate Australia from the United States. That, they claimed, would serve to draw out the American fleet even more so than a Midway operation.

Watanable telephoned Yamamoto to inform him of the Naval General Staff's opinion. Yamamoto replied that

Watanable should tell them that it would be Midway or nothing. The Naval General Staff quickly gave their consent, basing their decision on the fact that Yamamoto was considered the greatest admiral since the great Togo. Therefore, if he felt that strongly about Midway, the plan should proceed.

The commander-in-chief wanted the assault to take place during the first week of June when the moon was full. The Naval General Staff, however, requested more time to prepare and suggested instead that the operation take place at the end of the same month. Yamamoto would not hear of this delay, reasoning that the longer the attack was postponed, the more the chance of success was reduced. Though they gave in, the Naval General Staff did not have complete confidence in the plan. During the debate, neither of the two key admirals slated to command the operation, Nagumo and Kondo, was asked his opinion. The primary reason for this was that they were busy elsewhere with other operations. Unfortunately, this was a great mistake, since both of these commanders could have added their own insights, particularly about the readiness of the fleet. After all, the fleet had seen nonstop action since late November and it was exhausted and in urgent need of a rest. When this was presented to Yamamoto as a reason for delaying the Midway operation, again he would not hear of it. The commander-in-chief seemed obsessed by the fear that the United States would soon counterattack.

Even more than Yamamoto's anxiety over an American counterthrust was his fear that Tokyo, or even worse, the Imperial Palace, would be bombed. So obsessed was he that he daily asked for the weather forecast for the Tokyo area and would be happy for the rest of the day when he heard that it was cloudy near the capital. Then he could rest secure that no bombing raids would take place on that particular day. To many, this was an ungrounded fear. Where could American bombers come from? Any enemy carrier would have to come within two hundred miles of Japan and by that time they could easily be destroyed by the air force.

Then the impossible happened. On April 18, two American carriers were detected 720 miles from Tokyo. When he received the warning, Yamamoto did not demonstrate undue alarm. The carriers would not be in position to launch their aircraft until the following morning. That would give the Japanese defenders ample time to deal with them. Kondo's Second Fleet was immediately dispatched to intercept and deal with the enemy.

Suddenly, as the defensive dispositions were being made, Yamamoto's worst fears became a reality. Tokyo was bombed. How could this be? Reports quickly followed that American B-25 bombers were also attacking Nagoya, Yokohama, and Kobe. Where had these army planes come from? Midway?

Actually, the B-25s were led by Lieutenant Colonel James Doolittle, who flew the planes (after many weeks of practice) from the decks of the aircraft carrier *Hornet*, part of Admiral William Halsey's task force. These planes were capable of flying much further than the conventional carrier aircraft; thus the attack was launched from a position approximately six hundred miles from Japan. Since these large planes could not land aboard the carriers, they were ordered to fly into China and land behind friendly lines. Therefore, as soon as the launch was complete, the American task force reversed course and hightailed it for home, completely eluding the pursuing Japanese.

Only sixteen planes were used in the American attack, and in reality, they did little damage. The Japanese punned on the commander's name and called it the "do-little" raid. As far as Yamamoto was concerned, however, the raid was a disgrace and served to confirm his conviction that the United States' fleet had to be brought to battle and destroyed. Meanwhile, in late April, Nagumo's fleet arrived back in Japan with worn-out crews. Upon its arrival, the fleet commanders were apprised of the Midway operation for the first time and were so overconfident that they were certain that victory would finally be theirs.

While the preparations for the Midway attack proceeded, Yamamoto also initiated an operation aimed at advancing the Japanese position in the South Pacific via the seizure of the New Guinea port of Port Moresby. Three Japanese carriers, the small *Shoho* and the big fleet carriers *Zuikaku* and *Shokaku*, were dispatched to the Coral Sea as protection for the Port Moresby invasion fleet.

Thanks to their ability to read the Japanese code, the Americans took immediate countermeasures. A task force under Admiral Frank Fletcher, containing the carriers *Lexington* and *Yorktown*, was hastily dispatched to the Coral Sea.

Speed was of the essence for the Japanese, since the Midway operation was only a month away. Admiral Inouye, commanding the Japanese forces, planned to seize Tulagi in the Solomon Islands on May 3, a week before launching the Port Moresby attack. Inouye commanded a fleet of seventy ships and Japanese confidence ran high. When Yamamoto received word that American aircraft carriers were in the area he was delighted and immediately ordered Rear-Admiral Hara, commanding the carriers, to swing around the Solomons in the hope of finding and destroying the American carriers. (*See Map 6*).

The two fleets searched for each other for a number of days. Then, on May 7, the *Shoho* was located and attacked by U.S. carrier planes. Meanwhile, Japanese planes spotted what they thought to be a carrier but was in fact the oil tanker *Neosho* and the destroyer *Sims*. The latter was quickly sunk and the *Neosho* was left burning. By nightfall both sides were aware of the proximity of the other and looked forward to the morning when each hoped for a decision in its favor.

In the early morning mist, carriers from both fleets turned into the wind and launched their scout planes. At 8:24 AM a Japanese scout plane sent the electrifying message: "Two American carriers 235 miles away." Almost simultaneously came reports from American scout planes who had located the Japanese fleet. Both sides scrambled to launch their attack planes. The great battle was about to commence. The Japanese attacked the *Yorktown* first, then

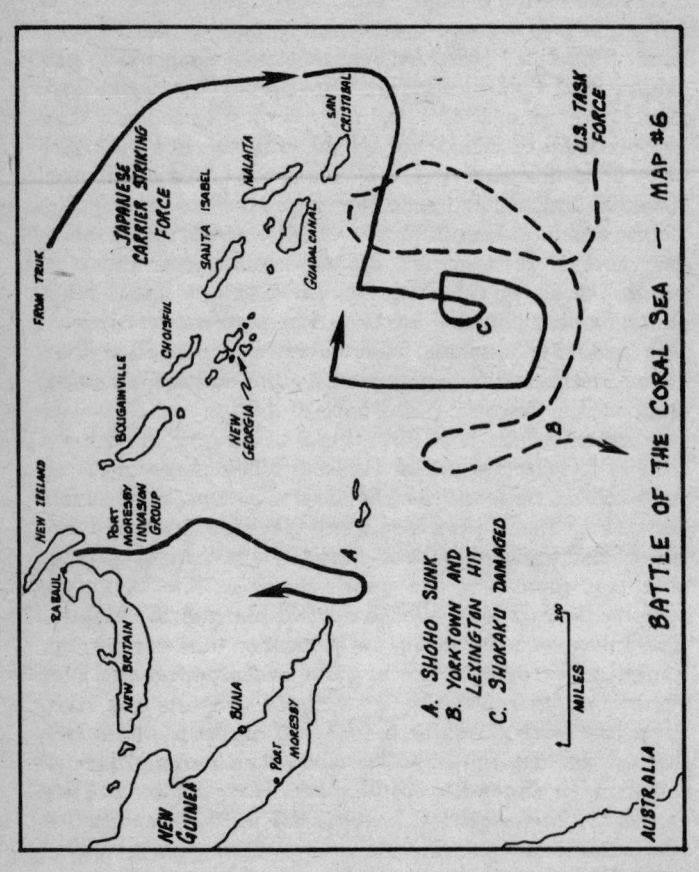

concentrated on the *Lexington*. The placid, idyllic Coral Sea was turned into a churning inferno. Both American carriers were soon hit, but at the same time their planes were attacking the Japanese carriers. The *Shokaku* was quickly hit, but the *Zuikaku* managed to evade the attackers by hiding under a nearby rain squall.

By midday, the first naval battle in which the ships of both sides never came into contact with each other was over, and the planes were en route home. The *Shoho* had been sunk on May 7, the *Shokaku* was burning so badly that her planes were forced to detour to the *Zuikaku*. Unfortunately, there was not enough room to land all the planes, so many of the pilots had to ditch at sea.

On board the American carriers, fires blazed, but damage control parties felt they had a handle on them. It seemed as if the Japanese had come off second-best, since the *Shoho* was gone and the *Shokaku* was burning furiously. The returning Japanese aviators, however, reported that both American carriers had been sunk, and they jubilantly celebrated a victory.

Meanwhile, the fires aboard the *Lexington*, originally thought to be under control, were reaching vital sections of the ship, resulting in a series of severe explosions, which doomed it. The *Yorktown* was ordered back to Pearl Harbor, where it was estimated that the ship would require months of repair.

Three hours before the *Lexington* plunged to the bottom, Inouye ordered the Japanese invasion fleet to return to Rabaul and cancelled the invasion of Port Moresby. Obviously, he did not believe the optimistic reports that both American carriers had been sunk. He did know, however, that one of his carriers was lost and that a second lacked sufficient air strength to protect the invasion force if even one of the enemy carriers was still intact. Thus ended the attempted invasion of Port Moresby and the Battle of the Coral Sea.

What had the Americans lost? The Japanese were convinced that both American carriers had been sunk, but they could only confirm the loss of the *Lexington*. What of the

Yorktown? Many were convinced that it had followed the *Lexington* to the bottom of the Coral Sea. Unfortunately, Japanese optimism was ill founded.

Yamamoto was ecstatic when he received reports that both American carriers were destroyed and was angry at Inouye for ordering his ships away from the battle scene. He countermanded the order, but it was too late.

The Battle of the Coral Sea had a great bearing on the subsequent battle at Midway. In addition, it represented the first time since Pearl Harbor that the Japanese had to call off an operation. More important, however, was Inouye's failure to pursue the retreating American ships. By failing to do this he had allowed the *Yorktown* to escape, and her presence at Midway was to be decisive. Finally, the damage to the *Shokaku* and the heavy loss of aircraft from the *Zuikaku* meant that both of those ships could not be part of the Midway carrier force. Without these two carriers, Nagumo was deprived of one-third of his air power.

Yet, Yamamoto remained optimistic. After all, Nagumo still had four carriers, and if Japanese intelligence was correct, the American fleet was reduced to two carriers, the *Hornet* and the *Enterprise*.

During the month of May Yamamoto prepared the fleet for the Midway operation. Pilot training was the highest priority. It seemed that the new generation of pilots did not equal the caliber of those who had participated in the Pearl Harbor attack. Yamamoto's greatest fear was that there would not be enough veterans to staff the fleet. Midway, he felt, would be the decisive battle he had sought for so many months. The final outcome of the Pacific war hinged on this battle.

The Japanese armada assembled. Its size was so enormous that no one could doubt its invincibility. All together Yamamoto had two hundred ships. Among them were eleven battleships, two of which were the largest in the world, the *Yamato* and *Musashi*, four fleet carriers, and four light ones, twenty-two cruisers, and sixty-five destroyers. There was a total of seven hundred planes.

The plan, however, suffered from a number of defects. The Nagumo chapter will cover these in detail, but a few were vital enough to warrant mention here.

Lack of concentration was perhaps the greatest defect. Although Yamamoto commanded the largest fleet ever assembled for any operation, the various elements were scattered—some to the Aleutians and the main fleet of battleships three hundred miles behind the carrier fleet. Even the enthusiastic Admiral Yamaguchi of the *Hiryu* felt that the battleships and destroyers should act as a screening force for the carriers. Yamamoto, however, disagreed. He felt that the carriers would do all right on their own. In this he was supported by the normally conservative Nagumo.

Another defect was the lack of accurate military intelligence. Where the United States had their code-cracking teams who could accurately relate the Japanese intentions, the Japanese proceeded blindly. They had no idea where the American fleet was. Yamamoto hoped it was at Pearl Harbor but had no way of knowing this for sure. He ordered a screen of submarines to concentrate in the Hawaii-Midway corridor, but by the time these arrived, the American fleet had already passed, en route to Midway. Yamamoto also ordered a reconnaissance of Pearl Harbor to be made by seaplane (Operation K). This plan had to be scrubbed because the area where the seaplane was to be refueled by a submarine was being patrolled by an American destroyer. Instead of moving to another area to refuel, the Naval Staff cancelled the operation entirely. This careless overconfidence on their part was crucial, for had that reconnaissance been made, the Japanese would have known that the fleet was not where it was thought to be.

Finally, the presence of Yamamoto himself on board the *Yamato* would prove costly. Thanks to his own order to maintain radio silence, he was condemned to become a spectator rather than a participant in the battle.

On May 27, 1942, the main body of Nagumo's fleet sailed from Hiroshima Bay, one day prior to Admiral Kakuda's Aleutian force. The Midway invasion force left Saipan on May 28, protected by the Second Destroyer

Squadron under Rear Admiral Raizo Tanaka. That same day, Rear Admiral Takeo Kurita's Seventh Cruiser Division left Guam. Finally came the main fleet, with battleships, cruisers, and destroyers following in the wake of Kondo's invasion force. In this last group, Yamamoto, aboard the *Yamato*, assumed direct control of the armada.

In total, the Japanese flotilla represented virtually the entire strength of the Combined Fleet. It far exceeded the size of the force that had attacked Pearl Harbor and was much superior to anything the United States could muster. Unfortunately for Yamamoto, as his fleet left its anchorage in Japan, the United States' fleet sailed from Pearl Harbor, with the carriers *Hornet* and *Enterprise*, under Rear Admiral Raymond Spruance. Yamamoto had no idea what he was heading for. Two days after Spruance sailed, the *Yorktown*, supposedly sunk, having had three months' worth of repair work miraculously complete in two days, also set out for Midway and passed through the area where the Japanese submarines were to establish a screen twenty-four hours later.

Admiral Nimitz, commander-in-chief of the U.S. Pacific Fleet, had cast his lot to fate. However meager his forces, he threw everything he had into the fray. It was truly a David-and-Goliath situation, but in this case, the American David came equipped with code-breaking intelligence instead of a slingshot.

Nagumo, meanwhile, was left in the dark about the American strength. Because of the restriction on breaking radio silence, whatever information was received by Yamamoto was not passed on to Nagumo. The commander-in-chief reasoned that Nagumo would have probably picked up the same radio transmissions anyway. Unfortunately, that was not the case, for the radio receivers on the *Akagi* were in no way as powerful as those aboard the *Yamato*. (*See Map 7*).

The primary aim of the entire operation was the occupation of Midway itself. The second was to lure out the United States' fleet, believed to be at Pearl Harbor, for a decisive battle on the open seas. The second objective was by far the

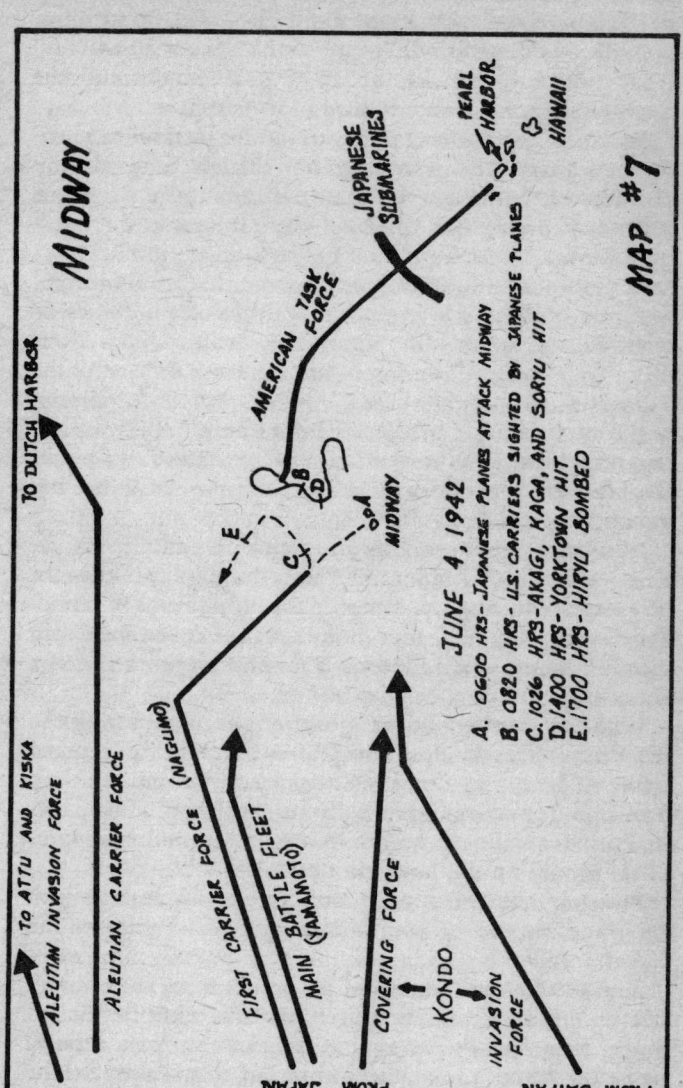

most important, but in order of precedence, the occupation of Midway came first. It was not clearly stated, however, which objective should have priority if things failed to go according to plan.

In the early morning hours of June 4, planes from Nagumo's carriers sped towards the islands of Midway. After the first attack Nagumo received the message to ready another wave. The planes on the carriers were already armed with torpedoes in case the American fleet was spotted. Believing that this fleet was nowhere in the vicinity, and having just been attacked by land-based high-level bombers from Midway, Nagumo agreed that another strike against the island was necessary. He therefore ordered the torpedoes replaced with bombs. Unfortunately, a scout plane from one of his cruisers, having been delayed on its reconnaissance flight because of technical problems, radioed back that it had located ten enemy vessels. By the time this report was received, the second attack wave had already been rearmed with ordinary bombs. Nagumo felt uneasy, but the scout plane did not report any American carriers. Then came another message that a carrier was indeed with the American fleet. Impossible, thought Nagaumo! He quickly ordered the armaments changed once again. The unloaded bombs were carelessly stacked together loosely on the decks, since the overworked crews had no time to store them safely below.

While all this activity was going on, each carrier was in the process of relanding the planes from the first attack wave. At 10:20, the order went out for the second attack to take off. The carriers promptly turned into the wind. At that crucial moment, American dive bombers dropped out of the clouds on the Japanese fleet.

Five hundred miles westward, Yamamoto had no idea what was happening with Nagumo's fleet. There was no way he could be aware of the time-wasting armament changes. When he first heard the report from the cruiser's scout plane about the sighting of the U.S. fleet he felt optimistic, since was not Nagumo's second attack wave ready to strike? Thus, Yamamoto was forced to stake everything on the quick judgment of Nagumo. This was a costly mistake.

For two hours Yamamoto sat in the dark waiting for word. Then, at 10:50, he was handed a radio message.

"Fires raging aboard *Kaga*, *Soryu*, and *Akagi*, resulting from attacks by enemy carrier and land-based planes."[22]

Yamamoto groaned aloud. Unfortunately, there was little he could do since Nagumo's forces were over five hundred miles away. He immediately ordered his battleships to full speed and made for Midway to support the beleaguered Nagumo. Yamamoto would assume personal command of the battle. Just as he set off, however, a thick fog shrouded his own fleet and reduced its speed. Zigzagging to avoid American submarines, proceeding through heavy fog, Yamamoto cast caution aside and risked the threat of collisions in his efforts to reach the carriers. The carriers that had accompanied the Aleutian force were ordered to reverse course and head toward Midway. Yamamoto was determined that the long-sought fleet engagement would not elude him.

Only the *Hiryu*, flagship of the aggressive Rear Admiral Yamaguchi, remained capable of launching planes. Yamamoto heard reports that one American carrier was burning. This, of course, was the *Yorktown*. The appearance of the *Yorktown* shocked Yamamoto. Reports of the heavy damage incurred by the carrier at the Coral Sea were obviously unfounded. Then came additional reports that still another American carrier was on fire. The Japanese could not know that, thanks to excellent fire control, what was thought to be another carrier burning was in fact the same *Yorktown*.

Yamamoto was still hopeful. If only one American carrier remained, victory was still a possibility. The best course, he decided, was a night action. The fate of his fleet had to be gambled in order to destroy the Americans. The hastily recalled Aleutians force, Kondo's screening force, and the main fleet all made for a rendezvous with destiny, the great admiral at the helm of the entire force.

The final agony came later in the day when Yamamoto received word that the *Hiryu* was also on fire. This report filled him with remorse. Still, he was anxious to proceed with the operation. The light carriers *Hosho* and *Zuiho* accompanying the main fleet remained intact, and the Aleutians force contained two additional carrriers that would arrive in less than two days. The Americans had, he thought, only one carrier remaining.

Yamamoto's opponent, Admiral Spruance, was a very cagey individual. Instead of heading west toward the Japanese fleet, he wisely reversed course, and the American fleet proceeded eastward, away from Yamamoto's main fleet. It appeared as if the sought-after night action was not to be.

Meanwhile, in Tokyo, the Naval General Staff, which had been monitoring the battle closely, knew that the operation had failed. Still, they refused to interfere. It was Yamamoto's fight. They were, however, concerned that if Yamamoto continued to press for the decisive engagement, more of the fleet might be destroyed.

Near midnight, two Japanese heavy cruisers, *Mogami* and *Mikuma*, were on their way toward the Midway atoll in order to relieve the submarine I-168, which had been shelling the island for a number of hours. Spruance thought that this was the prelude of the invasion, so he moved his fleet closer to Midway.

Yamamoto was now faced with a decision. The chance of a night action was now gone. If he continued on toward Midway the fleet would not arrive there until daybreak. This would make the ships sitting ducks for American planes. He also knew that he could not afford any additional losses. Debates raged aboard the flagship. Some pressed for continuing on toward Midway, while others claimed it would be suicide to do so and advocated retreat. But retreat would mean to lose face. One officer then asked the vital question, "How can we apologize to His Majesty?"[23] Yamamoto's reply was, "Leave that to me. I am the only one who must apologize to His Majesty."²⁴.

With that, the staff knew that Yamamoto had accepted the reality of the situation. A general withdrawal was ordered, and at 2:55 AM it was issued with the public admission that the Imperial Navy had suffered a defeat. Yamamato was left with one final, agonizing decision. What should be done with the burning *Akagi*, the only one of Nagumo's carriers still remaining afloat? Never in Japanese naval history had one of its own ships been scuttled by another. But it would be even more humiliating if the ship fell into enemy hands. At 3:50 AM, Yamamoto made the painful decision and ordered the *Akagi* torpedoed.

Meanwhile, the cruisers *Mogami* and *Mikuma*, which were approaching Midway, also reversed course, but were followed by the American submarine *Tambor*. When the sub's periscope was sighted the two cruisers collided in the panic of trying to avoid the torpedo wakes. The bow of *Mogami* was severely damaged, while one of *Mikuma's* fuel tanks was badly ruptured, causing oil to leak out and leaving an easy trail to follow. Within a few hours the *Mikuma* was battered by bombs from stalking American planes, and it plunged to the bottom. The *Mogami* was seriously damaged but managed to make good its escape, limping to the naval base at Truk.

Spruance pursued the retiring Japanese fleet. Yamamoto held out one final hope for revenge, but even this was denied him. Spruance was too wise and refused to push his luck any further. He called off the pursuit. Had he not changed course, he would have fallen into a trap. Unhappily for Yamamoto, another chance passed.

The fleet that had everything going for it limped back to Japan in defeat. Yamamoto retired to his room aboard the flagship and closeted himself for several days. To him, this defeat shattered any hope he had of giving Japan a second chance for an early peace settlement. The only part of the entire operation that had been successful was the attack on the two Aleutian islands of Attu and Kiska. Without victory at Midway, however, these two islands proved more a liability than an asset.

When the fleet arrived in Japan heavy press censorship denied the public the truth about what had happened. Yamamoto always despised false news reporting and must have been highly upset by the lies spread by the mass media. The surviving officers and men were dispersed to various bases and confined there. Many were hastily sent to the South Pacific without any opportunity to converse with their families. Thus the big lie was spread that the operation was a huge success. The truth would have to wait for the day when Japan lay in defeat.

Before we leave our discussion of the Midway Operation a review of what was wrong with the plan is in order.

First of all, the battle planning was faulty. None of Yamamoto's senior admirals was briefed fully on the plan. Kondo and Nagumo only heard of it after it had already been drawn up and had no opportunity to add to it.

Second, the fleet was used piecemeal. The Aleutian operation was totally useless. What superior power there would have been had the two carriers from this force along with those assigned to the main fleet been combined with Nagumo's four to form one huge strike force!

Third, faulty intelligence doomed the operation from the outset. The cancellation of the seaplane reconnaissance of Pearl Harbor was fateful. If that had only been accomplished, the Japanese would have known that the American fleet was at sea. The fact that their code was broken was beyond Yamamoto's control, but its effects were deadly. Morrison calls Midway "A victory of intelligence, bravely and wisely applied."[25]

Next was the lax security. Where before Pearl Harbor secrecy was stringently practiced, for Midway the destination of the fleet was common knowledge. Masanori Ito has said:

> "Blame for the defeat at Midway . . . must be placed directly on Japan's relaxed security measures. This relaxation of security was attributable directly to the

fantastic victories Japan had enjoyed early in the war."[26]

Fifth was the faulty disposition of the submarines. Not only did they arrive at their destination too late, but they were placed in static positions. Had they been allowed to range freely, chances are they would have stumbled on the American fleet.

Finally, the critical decisions were left to Nagumo's discretion. Admiral Nimitz, commander-in-chief of the United States' Pacific Fleet remained ashore in Hawaii and from there was able to assess the battle with the entire picture before him. In contrast, Yamamoto was on board the *Yamato*, hundreds of miles away from where the battle was raging. Because of the threat of discovery, he was forced to maintain radio silence. He was unable to communicate with Nagumo when it was imperative that he do so.

When one takes all these facts into consideration only one conclusion can be reached. The Japanese threw away their golden opportunity. Yamamoto was forced to accept defeat. It was Japan's first major defeat at sea in over three hundred years. Yamamoto now knew that with the loss of his four carriers he would have to adopt a defensive strategy. His worst fear, a long, drawn-out war, was about to become a reality. This, he knew, could only result in Japan's ultimate defeat, for, with America's industrial might, the opponent would continue to grow, while Japan's strength, spread out, would continue to decline. Japan simply could not equal the industrial potential of the United States.

With the Midway operation a failure, Yamamoto turned his attention to the South Pacific. Forced onto the defensive, he was still determined to do his utmost for his emperor and country.

A month prior to Midway, during the Battle of the Coral Sea, Lieutenant Commander Okamura, at the head of a small force, landed on the unknown island of Guadalcanal in the Solomons. There, in the island's thick malarial jungles, the Japanese began construction of an airfield for use as a potential springboard for a future movement to New Caladonia, Fiji, and Samoa. With the destruction of his carrier force, Yamamoto had more than ever to protect against an Allied counteroffensive originating from Australia. Now that General MacArthur was in that country, this area truly appeared to be the headquarters for such a counteroffensive. This could not be allowed to happen. Australia had to be isolated. Thus Yamamoto began to regard this little-known island of Guadalcanal as the forefront of a limited offensive aimed at isolating Australia.

When the Americans discovered that the Japanese were constructing an airfield on the island, they knew that they had to react quickly and capture Guadalcanal. On August 7, 1942, the 1st Marine Division crashed ashore on Guadalcanal and a regiment of the 2nd Marine Division assaulted Tulagi, just north of Guadalcanal. There was little opposition on the former, where the marines moved quickly inland and captured the airfield, which they promptly renamed Henderson Field in honor of a marine pilot who had perished at Midway. On Tulagi, the story was a bit different. The staunch Japanese defenders put up a bitter but uneven fight. This twin attack initiated a six-month-long campaign on land, in the air, and on the sea.

Yamamoto viewed the coming struggle in the Solomons as an opportunity to gain revenge on the American fleet for the humiliation at Midway. (*See Map 8*). His first chance for this revenge came within a day of the landings on Guadalcanal. Yamamoto ordered Admiral Gonichi Mikawa to steam from Rabaul towards the island and engage the enemy fleet in a night action. The American aircraft carriers supporting the marine landings had, however, already left the vicinity, but six Allied cruisers and numerous transports remained behind. In the ensuing naval battle, known as the Battle of Savo Island, the Japanese won an astounding victory, sinking four cruisers, damaging another, and mauling two destroyers. The only thing that saved the transports from destruction was Mikawa's overcautiousness. Fearing enemy air attacks if he lingered in the area until daylight, he withdrew. Had he stayed, he would surely have

The Naval Battles for Guadalcanal

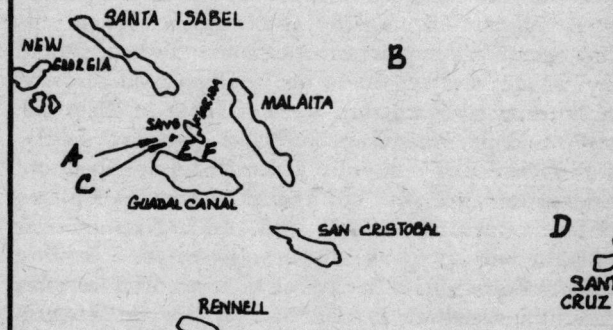

A. BATTLE OF SAVO ISLAND   AUG. 9, 1942
B. BATTLE OF THE EASTERN SOLOMONS AUG 23-25
C. BATTLE OF CAPE ESPERANCE OCT. 11-12, 1942
D. BATTLE OF THE SANTA CRUZ ISLANDS OCT. 26
E. NAVAL BATTLE OF GUADALCANAL - NOV. 13-15, 1942
F. BATTLE OF TASSAFARONGA - NOV. 30, 1942

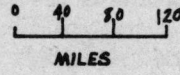
MILES

MAP #8

disrupted the entire American operation, since most of the supplies needed to supply the marines were aboard those helpless transports.

> "If he had done this, he would effectively have halted American operations in the South Pacific. He would have left the 1st Marine Division in a serious plight, low on food and ammunition and an easy prey to an Ichiki* counterattack."[27]

The Guadalcanal story would have been one of Japanese supplying and reinforcing by night, while the Americans held sway in the air and at sea during daylight hours. The full Guadalcanal story is covered in the chapter on Admiral Tanaka, but the major outlines of the various battles and how they relate to Yamamoto warrant discussion here.

On August 17, Yamamoto set sail on the *Yamato* for the South Pacific, never again to see his homeland. On the 26th, the mighty battleship steamed into the fleet anchorage at Truk. Meanwhile, the land and naval battles continued on and around Guadalcanal. Yamamoto adopted a strategy of attrition. Though aware that this type of warfare favored the nation with the larger industrial capacity, he felt there was no other alternative.

By late September the Japanese navy had severely damaged the American carrier *Enterprise*, while Japanese submarines did the same to the *Saratoga* and scored a coup by sinking the *Wasp*. This meant that the United States had only one healthy carrier in the South Pacific, the *Hornet*.

In mid-October Yamamoto made a concentrated effort to destroy Henderson Field and the American defensive perimeter. This resulted in a simultaneous effort by both sides to reinforce Guadalcanal. The result was the Battle of Cape Esperance. Once more it was a night action, but this time the Japanese were taken by surprise and came out with the heavier losses. Nevertheless, two days later the Tokyo

---

*Commander of a Japanese Regiment on Guadalcanal.

Express* made its nightly delivery to Guadalcanal and Yamamoto retained the hope of destroying Henderson Field.

The Americans knew that Yamamoto meant business and recognized the need for an aggressive leader of their own to counter the Japanese commander. That leader was appointed in mid-October: Admiral William (Bull) Halsey. He was just the type to oppose Yamamoto.

Halsey did not pause to rest. On October 26 a fleet carrier engagement near Santa Cruz island took place. Like the Coral Sea and the Eastern Solomons (which witnessed the loss of the *Wasp* and damage to the *Saratoga* and the *Enterprise*), it was a battle of aircraft versus ships. The *Hornet* was hit, but so too were the Japanese carriers *Junyo*, *Zuiho* and *Shokaku*, the last of which was severely damaged. A second strike was sent by both sides. The *Enterprise*, recently returned to the South Pacific after having the damage incurred in August hastily repaired, launched its planes. They struck the already damaged *Shokaku*. The *Hornet*, already in tow, was hit again in turn by the Japanese. This was the fatal blow to the famed ship, which sank into a watery grave soon after. Yamamoto was disappointed that the *Hornet* had sunk, since he wanted it captured intact so that he could bring the ship that had launched Doolittle's raid back to Japan in triumph. That raid still visibly affected him.

After the battle off Santa Cruz, Yamamoto sent the remaining carriers back to Truk for repairs, then home to the Inland Sea. This was the last carrier engagement until 1944. Yamamoto could not afford to risk them anymore in the face of the increased air power of the enemy in the South Pacific.

November would be the month of decision around Guadalcanal. A huge naval battle took place in the middle of the month, lasting three days and costing the Americans the lives of Rear Admirals Scott and Callaghan. This battle

---

*Japanese means of sending reinforcements from Rabaul to Guadalcanal.

determined once and for all who would control the waters around Guadalcanal. It was a murderous action fought at extremely close range, battleship versus battleship, cruiser versus cruiser, destroyer versus destroyer. The action truly resembled the old-style naval battles. When it was all over, Yamamoto's forces had suffered the loss of two battleships, a heavy cruiser, and seven destroyers, as against the American toll of three cruisers and seven destroyers. The battle was decisive. It proved to be the final attempt by the Japanese to capture Henderson Field. After that, there were so many American ships around Guadalcanal that Yamamoto had to resort to using his submarine force to bring in the needed supplies to the Japanese soldiers on the island, an island soon to be known as Starvation Island.

The use of the submarine force in this role rather than as an attack force has since been hotly debated. Granted, the men on Guadalcanal needed supplies desperately, but it must be remembered that only one submarine had accounted for the destruction of the *Wasp*. If used offensively, the submarines might have proved a devastating weapon. Instead they ran supplies to the beleaguered Japanese troops, and in the interim, lost over twenty of their number.

One last battle was fought near the island, this time at Tassafaronga on November 30. Though the Japanese forces accounted for another American heavy cruiser, this battle foretold the climax of five months of bitter naval battles.

On the first anniversary of Pearl Harbor, Yamamoto was still at Truk observing the mounting losses at Guadalcanal. New Year's Day found him aboard the *Yamato*. Though outwardly giving an appearance of his old energetic self, inwardly he was tired. It had become apparent to him that Guadalcanal could not be held. This proved a bitter pill to swallow after six long months of attempting to drive the Americans off, the heavy losses incurred, and the death of so many men. What had been accomplished? Abandonment.

However, the fact that thirteen thousand Japanese were evacuated from Guadalcanal was a great tactical success, though it was accomplished in the face of defeat. Deception was used to convince the Americans that the Japanese were still sending in reinforcements, when in reality they were doing just the opposite. While the Yano battalion, a specially trained force of rear-guard troops, threw the Americans off guard by attacking, the evacuation was conducted in secrecy. By the first week of February, the last Japanese troops were gone.

Why were the Japanese defeated at Guadalacanal? On the whole, they had outmaneuvered the Americans in almost every battle. Yamamoto wanted to destroy American ships, and that is precisely what he did. The Americans lost two carriers, five heavy cruisers, two light cruisers, fourteen destroyers, and suffered varying degrees of damage, ranging from light to severe, and to the loss of many other warships. In this sense, Yamamoto had not failed in his objective. Then why did he lose? The difference was that the Americans quickly made good their losses. Just as Yamamoto had always predicted, America's huge industrial capacity had ultimately to triumph. The Japanese Navy had shot its bolt in little over a year. Yamamoto wrote to a friend,

> "Guadalcanal was a very fierce battle. I do not know what to do next. Nor am I happy about facing my officers and men who had fought so hard without fear of death."[28]

He knew he was beaten.

On February 11, 1943, the admiral moved his headquarters from the *Yamato* to its sister ship, the mammoth *Musashi*, also anchored at Truk. In early April it was decided that Yamamoto should visit the stronghold of Rabaul as a morale booster. On the third of that month he left the *Musashi* and traveled to Natsushima seaplane base where he boarded one of the planes, which carried him and his party to Rabaul. The following day he celebrated his birthday. Three days later he viewed the takeoff of a combined fighter and bomber assault destined for Guadalcanal and personally waved his cap to each passing plane. After a week in Rabaul, with his scheduled visit coming to a close, Yamamoto decided to wind up his stay with a one-day tour of bases in the northern Solomons in the Shortland area. This, he felt, would raise the morale of the men stationed there. In the late afternoon of the 13th, his itinerary was broadcast, listing the places he would visit and the estimated times. He personally wanted to visit and inspect Ballale, Shortland, and Buin. The latter was on the large jungle island of Bougainville, while Ballale and Shortland were just east and west of Bougainville, respectively.

Admiral Ozawa, commander-in-chief of the Third Fleet in Rabaul, objected to the tour, feeling that it was too dangerous. Others also tried to dissuade their chief, but to no avail. He was determined to go. Rear Admiral Jushima, commander-in-chief of the Eleventh Air Flotilla on Shortland, read the lengthy radio message of April 13th and stated that it was foolish to send such a lengthy and detailed wire. On the 17th, one day before the tour was to begin, Jushima flew to Rabaul in an attempt to dissuade Yamamoto personally. Again, his objections fell on deaf ears. Yamamoto refused to listen.

Joshima was right. It was foolish to have sent the long itinerary over the air. American code breakers read the message and forwarded the information to Nimitz. Here was an ideal chance to lay a trap. Nimitz, however, was hesitant to act, so he forwarded the information on to the secretary of the navy, Frank Knox. Unaware of the ramifications of the message, Knox glanced at it and left it on his desk while he went to lunch. While eating, he overheard a remark that in the old days wars were settled by a duel between the opposing commanders. Wasn't Yamamoto the most hated of all Japanese leaders? What better way, he thought, of revenging Pearl Harbor than to kill the very man responsible for that infamous act.

Upon returning to his office, Knox sent for the chief of the army air forces, General Henry "Hap" Arnold and informed him of the decoded message. Arnold was enthusiastic about the possibility of laying a trap for

Yamamoto. Looking at a map and comparing it with the itinerary, the two figured that the best place to intercept Yamamoto would be over Bougainville as he came in for a landing at Kahili airstrip. Since the distance from Henderson Field on Guadalcanal to Bougainville was five hundred miles, he realized that the distance was beyond the range of the new P-38 fighters stationed there.

Arnold then sent for the famed Atlantic soloist, Charles Lindbergh, who was acting in the capacity of advisor to the army air forces. Lindbergh and another expert both agreed that the plan was feasible, but the P-38s would have to be fitted with long-range tanks. After reviewing all the details, Operation Vengeance, as the plan was called, was on. Knox sent two messages, one to General Kenney, commander of the South-West Pacific Air Forces, the other to Guadalcanal. Kenney was directed to send a large number of 165- and 310-gallon fuel tanks to Guadalcanal. When Major John W. Mitchell, the commander of 339 Squadron on the island, received the message it electrified him. When he briefed his pilots, they were unanimously enthusiastic.

The fateful tour began on April 18. Two planes contained the dignitaries and six Zero fighters served as escorts. As Yamamoto's plane flew over Bougainville, more than a dozen P-38 fighters pounced on the unsuspecting Japanese. The plane carrying Yamamoto was hit and crashed into the dense jungle.

Around noon, Watanable and Kuroshima, two of Yamamoto's staff officers who had remained at Rabaul, heard of the crash. Watanable wanted to go to Bougainville immediately but bad weather delayed him until the following day. The search for the victims lasted two days. The jungle was so thick that the only way to penetrate to the crash site was by following Bougainville's meandering streams. Finally, an army search party located the wreck on the evening of the 19th. There they found Yamamoto's body still strapped to his seat but thrown clear of the plane. The army unit moved the bodies to a separate location and left the scene because of the approach of nightfall. While leaving the area, they came upon the naval search unit, which had been looking all day. They asked the army unit to guide them to the crash site in the morning, which they did.

Meanwhile, the Americans were congratulating themselves for a job well done. Admiral Halsey sent a message to Henderson Field.

"Congratulations Major Mitchell and His Hunters, sounds as though one of the Ducks in their bag was a Peacock."[29]

The news was jubilantly received by the American leadership. The actual story of how it was achieved was, of course, suppressed for years, in order to cover up the fact that American code breakers were reading the Japanese code. But Americans were elated that the warmongering, fanatic Yamamoto was dead. A measure of revenge for Pearl Harbor had been gained.

Around nooon on April 20th, Watanable received the remains of his beloved commander-in-chief. A post-mortem was immediately performed to determine the cause of death. The medical team found that a bullet from one of the American planes had pierced Yamamoto's lower jaw and emerged at his temple. This, they felt, had probably killed the admiral even before the plane crashed.

The bodies (eleven in all) were placed in coffins and taken to a tent where a wake was held in the burning heat of Bougainville. The next day, the bodies were cremated. Watanable collected the admiral's ashes, which he placed in a wooden box lined with fresh papaya leaves. On the following day, though suffering from a high fever, Watanable flew back to Rabaul with the remains. Admirals Kusaka, Ozawa, and others then accompanied the remains to Truk for the sad reunion of the ashes with the admiral's flagship, the *Musashi*. In this ship, Yamamoto's ashes were to be returned home to Japan.

The emotion among those who accompanied the ashes was enormous. Yamamoto was more to them than their commander-in-chief, he was a symbol, and one might even say, a friend.

Following the ambush, no one except high political and military leaders knew of Yamamoto's death. From May 7, when the *Musashi* sailed for Japan, until its arrival on May 21, not once did the press mention anything at all about the commander-in-chief of the Combined Fleet. Even his wife and children were not informed until the 18th. Finally, on May 21, the nation was informed that their brave leader had met death at the front lines. He was posthumously promoted to the rank of fleet admiral on the same day, while a nation grieved.

A state funeral was held in Hibiya Park in Tokyo on June 5, 1943. At 8:50 that morning, crew members of the *Musashi* carried the white-draped coffin from the room in the Navy Club where it had lain in state, to a black gun carriage that carried the ashes in procession to the somber sounds of Chopin's *Funeral March*. Watanable carried the sword depicting the rank of full admiral. After the elaborate ceremony, Yamamoto's ashes were divided, half brought to the Tama Cemetery and placed next to the legendary Admiral Togo of Tushima fame, the other half to Yamamoto's home in Nagoaka. His grave stands today on the grounds of a Zen temple. A simple stone marks the spot and on the stone are carved his name and the words "Killed in Action in the South Pacific, April 1943."

Every Japanese felt Yamamoto's death. The war had truly touched home. The admiral's demise was a sure sign that no matter what the media said, things were not going well for Japan. Over two more bloody years would pass before the conflict's cataclysmic end in a nuclear nightmare. How often Yamamoto's prophetic words about avoiding war must have haunted Japan's leaders. How ironic that this man, who more than anyone wanted to avoid war, became himself the target of an ambush purposely designed to snuff out the life of the bandit of Pearl Harbor.

Little was really known about the man in America at the time. Americans didn't know that more than once Yamamoto's life had been in jeopardy because of his opposition to the warmongers and rightists. All they knew was that it was this man who had perpetuated the crime of the century.

Though objecting to war, Yamamoto was forced to fight it the only way he knew how—totally. He made mistakes, but he was only building on the biggest mistake of all, that of precipitating a war with a country that Japan could not defeat. True, Japan felt no other choice was open to them but war. The United States' oil embargo saw to that. With war imminent, however, Yamamoto was left with no choice but to prepare. He knew that a quick decision was the only hope, a decisive destruction of the American fleet was Japan's only chance. This elusive quest led him to Pearl Harbor and Midway. Unhappily, the decision went against him and Japan faced a war of attrition. Before his death, Yamamoto knew that Japan was finished, and himself as well. In one of his final letters he wrote,

"Wait but a while, young men! One last battle, fought gallantly to the death, and I will be joining you."[30]

Yamamoto died as he had lived, in the line of duty to his country and his emperor.

Chapter 3

The great Admiral Isoruku Yamamoto forged the fiery sword that was the Imperial Japanese Navy at the outbreak of World War II. After devising plans for the use of this magnificent weapon, Yamamoto placed it in the hands of Admiral Chiuchi Nagumo. This great samurai then wielded the sword mightily and rewarded Japan with an incredible string of victories during the first six months of the war. Indeed, no other admiral in Japanese history even approached the exploits of Nagumo, whose amazing series of triumphs throughout the Pacific left the heart of the mighty American fleet at the bottom of Pearl Harbor and drove the proud British navy from the Indian Ocean.

But despite his success, Nagumo was an enigma. His prior naval career as a recognized torpedo expert hardly qualified him to command Japan's potent carrier fleet. However, command assignments in the Japanese Navy went strictly by seniority. Thus, the outbreak of World War II found Nagumo commanding Japan's mightiest weapon. He was a man of contrasting personalities, on one hand jovial and friendly when all went well; on the other hand, when he lacked confidence in an operation he tended to sulk and was subject to moods of severe depression. Above all, he was a cautious man, unwilling to gamble. So much so that in the heat of battle more often than not he was indecisive. It was this latter trait that eventually led him to disgrace and nullified his early victories at a heavy cost to the Imperial Navy.

Chiuchi Nagumo was born in the northern Honshu Prefecture of Yamagato on March 25, 1887. The Nagumo family had a long record of service as samurai warriors to a succession of emperors. Although by the time of Chiuchi's birth the days of the proud warrior caste were, for the most part, but glorious memories, the family's tradition of service had resulted in their being considered minor aristocracy. From as early as he could remember, Nagumo was fascinated by the lure of the sea. Since he was an excellent student, it came as no surprise to his family when, upon graduation, he passed the entrance exams for the Naval Academy at Eta Jima. Despite the harsh discipline at the academy the fledgling officer managed to do quite well and ranked in the top ten of his class at graduation.

There followed the usual routine duty of junior officers with service on board destroyers, cruisers, and battleships. Nagumo zealously attacked each new assignment. He knew that his life would forevermore be devoted to the navy and was eager to absorb as much knowledge as possible about his chosen profession.

Early on, his superiors had marked Nagumo as a doer. His ability to learn quickly and his desire to excel earned him a succession of glowing fitness reports from various commanders. As a result, in 1926 he was selected to make a tour of Europe and America to learn firsthand what the other great powers of the world were accomplishing with their modernization programs. The tour of the United States left Nagumo with a lasting respect for the industrial capacity of that nation.

Upon his return from abroad, Nagumo was appointed torpedo instructor at the In Service School at Yokasuka. Although considered something of an expert in the field, he was not content to rest on his laurels. He quickly plunged himself wholeheartedly into his field and increased his proficiency by absorbing all there was to know about the technical aspects of the torpedo. By the time his tour of duty was up, Nagumo was considered one of the navy's leading overall authorities on the subject.

In addition to his knowledgeable grasp of his course of study, Nagumo's kindly manner and pleasing personality earned for him the admiration of his students. These were the young officers who would eventually command the ships of the fleet. As a result, in later years, Nagumo would be remembered with fondness and respect by his former students and became one of the most popular commanders in the Japanese Navy.

In 1930 Nagumo left the school to assume command of the 2nd Destroyer Flotilla. His expertise in the use of torpedoes, coupled with his earlier service in this type of ship, made him the logical choice to fill the vacancy with this squadron. One of the officers serving in the 2nd Flotilla at the time was Lieutenant (later Captain) Tameicha Hara, who was assigned to the destroyer *Fubuki* as torpedo officer. Hara later went on to become one of Japan's most brilliant destroyer captains. His comments about Nagumo give insight into the latter's character.

> "During my one year tour of duty aboard this ship (*Fubuki*), I developed a friendship with another of the unforgettable people in my life. He was our squadron commander, Captain Chiuchi Nagumo. He was one of the most brilliant destroyer experts in the Imperial Navy. It was certainly enlightening to live with him for a year. Nagumo encouraged me to study hard by loaning me various books he had obtained in the United States. Nagumo liked me and insisted that I should enroll in the Staff College. Later, Nagumo was subjected to all kinds of criticism. In my memory, however, he remains a brilliant naval officer, and a most kindhearted man."[1]

There followed tours of duty with the Naval Staff College, the captaincy of the cruiser *Naka*, and the command of a destroyer division. In July of 1937 Nagumo was given command of the 8th Cruiser Division. This formation was sent to Shanghai to participate in the Sino-Japanese War then raging in China. Since the Chinese Navy was virtually nonexistent, the cruiser division's primary responsibility was blockade duty and shore bombardment in support of the army.

In November, 1939, Nagumo attained flag rank when he was promoted to vice admiral and given command of the 3rd Battleship Division, the pride of the Japanese fleet. A year later, he went ashore once more to assume the presidency of the Naval Staff College. By now he was one of the more senior officers of the fleet. Since appointments in the Imperial Navy went stricktly by seniority, when the First Air Fleet was created in 1941, Nagumo was selected to command this new formation consisting of the bulk of Japan's carriers in April of that year. Unfortunately, at the time he knew little about naval aviation and had never served aboard carriers. Thus his appointment was met with much trepidation and resistance in the corridors of the naval hierarchy.

At the time of Nagumo's appointment, the war in Europe had been raging for over a year and a half. Japan's alliance with Germany, coupled with her aggressive overtures in Southeast Asia and the war with China, caused relations with the United States and England to decrease rapidly. Accordingly, the commander-in-chief of the Combined Fleet, Admiral Isoruku Yamamoto, had developed a plan aimed at dealing a lethal blow to the American Pacific Fleet. This, of course was the proposed attack against Pearl Harbor.

Having spent his entire career on smaller warships, with the exception of his year in command of the 3rd Battleship Division, Nagumo was an adherent of the orthodox plan calling for an attack on the Philippines in the event of war with the United States. This attack, it was hoped, would succeed in drawing out the United States Fleet where it could be destroyed in a decisive battle. He did not like the Pearl Harbor plan at all.

To overcome Nagumo's obvious deficiencies in the knowledge of naval aviation, the Naval General Staff reserved the right to appoint his chief of staff. The man selected to fill this vital position was Rear Admiral Ryunosuke Kusaka.

At the time, Kusaka appeared the ideal choice. He had been involved in naval aviation for almost a decade, having commanded the light carrier *Hosho* and later the big fleet carrier, *Akagi*. Thanks to Nagumo's outgoing and friendly personality, the two admirals quickly developed a cordial and harmonious working relationship that served the navy well in the succeeding months.

The second key appointment to the First Air Fleet was that of air officer. Selected for this vital assignment was Commander Minoru Genda, Japan's leading expert in the field of naval aviation. Genda's reputation was so high that, although he was a relatively junior officer, the Naval General Staff had chosen to show him Yamamoto's daring plan almost as soon as the ink was dry. Genda's subsequent recommendations for modification of the original plan were adopted in short order.

The First Air Fleet comprised the 1st and 2nd Carrier Divisions. In addition to responsibility for the First Air Fleet, Nagumo and his staff were saddled with the additional burden of direct command of the 1st Carrier Division. The heart of this formation were the carriers *Kaga* and *Akagi*.

Kaga was one of the navy's older carriers, having been launched in 1931. However, at that time she was also Japan's largest carrier, weighing thirty-eight-thousand tons and capable of handling ninety aircraft. *Akagi*, Nagumo's choice for flagship, was launched four years later, and although slightly smaller than her sister, was also capable of handling ninety planes.

The 2nd Carrier Division was commanded by Rear Admiral Tamon Yamaguchi. Although he too was deficient in aviation experience, he overcame this handicap with an energetic and aggressive character and the ability to quickly grasp the essentials of this revolutionary type of warfare. The core of Yamaguchi's division were the sister carriers *Hiryu* and *Soryu*. Both ships had been completed in the late 1930s and were capable of handling seventy-three aircraft, despite the fact that their tonnage was half that of the *Kaga*.

While the job of creating a cohesive fighting force from the foundations of the First Air Fleet began in earnest, Kusaka was summoned to Naval Headquarters where Admiral Fukodome showed him the final draft of Yamamoto's plan for an attack on Pearl Harbor. Kusaka was somewhat taken aback by the audacity of the plan, but nevertheless felt it was feasible. That, of course, was what Fukodome had been fishing for: approval. Kusaka was ordered to take the proposal and develop an operational plan to carry it out.

It is significant that the Naval General Staff saw fit to confide in the chief of staff of the First Air Fleet rather than its commander. Obviously they felt that Kusaka would be more amenable to the plan and less likely to raise strong objections. Nagumo's attitude toward the plan was no secret. In addition, Fukodome felt that Kusaka could sway Nagumo.

The Naval General Staff's reservations regarding Nagumo's attitude were well founded, for when Kusaka returned to the *Akagi* and briefed his chief on the concept, the latter called the plan mad. Nagumo set forth a host of reasons why the proposed attack could not work and wasted little time in hurling these objections at the astounded Kusaka.

Perhaps Nagumo might have been more discreet regarding his opposition to Yamamoto's grand plan, but he wasn't. Word of his reservations reached the staff of Admiral Yamamoto and the members of his staff. Admiral Ugaki, angered at Nagumo's reaction, called for his resignation.

> "If Nagumo and his chief of staff strongly oppose this operation, and feel they cannot carry it out, they should resign their posts."[2]

There would of course, be no resignation. Neither was there anything Ugaki or anyone else was able to do about Nagumo's appointment, since the seniority system was too deeply rooted in the Japanese philosophy.

Nevertheless, orders were orders. So Nagumo set about implementing them. Genda was set to work training air crews. Coordination of air attacks utilizing high level and dive bombers in conjunction with torpedo planes was practiced. Destruction of enemy warships was rehearsed again and again and heavy emphasis was placed on large-scale air battles where the fighter plane would predominate.

The rest of Nagumo's staff concentrated on training the various fleet elements. The ships were put through their paces, maneuvering to avoid enemy attacks and polishing their antiaircraft gunnery and antisubmarine tactics. The pace was demanding and hectic, as Nagumo had set the end of August as the date when the fleet should reach the peak of efficiency. Shortly before that deadline, Nagumo's staff was bolstered by the addition of still another key figure. Commander Mitsuo Fuchida, Genda's personal choice to lead the Pearl Harbor attack, arrived aboard the *Akagi* amidst the hearty cheers of the ship's air crews.

Fuchida was the final link in the chain for the Pearl Harbor attack. A pilot with more than a decade of experience, he was an ex-classmate of Genda's and was considered one of Japan's most brilliant aviation tacticians. It would be his assignment to personally lead the attack against the American fleet.

Despite the success of the training exercises, Nagumo continued to harbor grave reservations about the feasibility of the entire concept. In contrast to his willingness to accept technical progress, he was not ready to concede the ability of aircraft alone to strike a decisive blow. As an advocate of the "big gun" theory, he was simply unable to comprehend the potential of this revolutionary concept of naval warfare. When his mind was set, Nagumo could be a stubborn and dangerous man indeed. As an example, despite his well-known generosity and kindly disposition, when Admiral Inoue had proposed some radical administrative changes in the navy, during a party, Nagumo, a staunch supporter of the traditionalist Fleet Faction, threatened Inoue.

> "You're a fool. It would be the easiest thing in the world to get rid of you. One thrust with a dagger under the ribs, and that would be it."[3]

Yamamoto set about to convince his stubborn subordinate that the attack could indeed succeed. It would be compromised, however, if the man responsible for carrying it out did not have faith in the plan. Therefore, unless Nagumo gave his wholehearted support to the operation, the prospect of success was seriously reduced.

By the end of the summer, the prospect of war with the United States loomed larger and larger with each passing day. Although negotiations between that country and Japan continued, no significant progress was made, nor did it appear that any would be. Yamamato knew that the fleet had to be ready.

On September 16, the commander-in-chief held a conference of all key commanders of the Pearl Harbor striking force. The key items on the agenda were which route to take toward the target area and the ramifications of refueling at sea. Among those present at the meeting were Nagumo, Yamaguchi, and Genda.

The argument over which approach to use was paramount. All prior suggestions had boiled down to two alternatives, a northern route from the Kuriles or a southern approach from the Gilberts. Basing his argument on the problems of logistics, *i.e.*, refueling at sea, Nagumo favored the southern approach.

Genda and Yamaguchi, on the other hand, favored the northern approach, since this route would take the fleet through an area whose skies were usually overcast and whose sea lanes were infrequently used, thus reducing the risk of detection. Their arguments carried the day. The fleet would use the northern route.

Despite the agreement of most key figures that the attack would be successful, Nagumo continued to have his doubts. What if the fleet were detected? What if he were ambushed en route? Could he be absolutely certain that the U.S. fleet would even be in Pearl Harbor on the date fixed for the attack? Since he was a chronic worrier to begin with, all of these possibilities and more weighed heavily on his broad shoulders.

The ever optimistic Fushida harbored doubts about Nagumo's ability to carry off the operation, despite the admiral's popularity with the fleet.

Late in September, the First Air Fleet was bolstered by

the addition of two additional carriers forming the 5th Carrier Division. Commanded by Admiral Hara, the brand-new sister ships *Shokaku* and *Zuikaku*, weighing twenty-five thousand seven hundred tons apiece and capable of handling eighty-four aircraft, proudly dropped anchor alongside their older sisters. Nagumo was delighted with this apparent increase in his striking capacity. Unfortunately, his happiness was short-lived.

Meanwhile, preparations for the attack proceeded in earnest. Nagumo felt overwhelmed during actual aviation exercises, but when it came time to maneuver the fleet, his gloom changed, since he was then in his element.

On October 2, Nagumo summoned all senior First Air Fleet commanders to a conference aboard *Akagi*. Besides his own staff and Admirals Yamaguchi and Hara, present were the captains of the six carriers along with their air officers. Although rumors about a possible strike against the American fleet were rife in the Japanese Navy, this conference marked the first time the assembled officers were officially informed of the Pearl Harbor attack. To a man they were enthused. Genda then proceeded to outline the plan of attack.

Fuchida and Genda had decided on a two-wave attack, because it was impossible to launch all their planes in a short period of time. Consequently, the air squadrons that had reached the highest peak of proficiency were selected to carry the torpedoes. The remaining squadrons would be split between high-level and dive-bombing duties. Since Nagumo still considered himself a novice in the field, he was content to sit back and allow his two air officers to make all the plans and decisions regarding air operations. If anything, Nagumo remained too remote from the aerial planning.

A few days after the aforementioned meeting, just when he found himself beginning to warm up to the operation, Nagumo was dealt a stunning blow. Admiral Yamaguchi stormed into the former's cabin and informed Nagumo that he had received orders that the 2nd Carrier Division was being scratched from the Pearl Harbor expedition. Instead,

Yamaguchi went on, the *Hiryu* and the *Soryu* were being reassigned to support Admiral Kondo's simultaneous operations in the Philippines. Nagumo merely shrugged his shoulders and said that since the orders had come from a higher authority, there was little he could do. Yamaguchi was enraged.

Despite not being willing to admit it to Yamaguchi, Nagumo was in fact upset at having his strength reduced by one-third. Just when he was beginning to accept the concept, the last thing he needed was something of this nature.

On October 12, a planning session for the entire fleet was held aboard the *Nagato*, Yamamoto's flagship. During the course of this session Nagumo insisted on assurances from Kondo that he would not initiate any hostile action in the Philippines until word was received that the Pearl Harbor attack had succeeded. Kondo readily agreed to this stipulation and one more of Nagumo's fears, that of compromising secrecy, was laid to rest.

Following the session aboard *Nagato*, Yamaguchi once more demanded that Nagumo intercede on behalf of the 2nd Carrier Division. Again Nagumo refused. In response, Yamaguchi shouted, "If you are wrong, I will kill you".[4] The unhappy Yamaguchi then pleaded his case to Kusaka and Genda. Were the many weeks of intensive training to be thrown away? The two officers agreed to try to get Nagumo to change his mind.

Knowing full well that Nagumo was still not fully convinced of the feasibility of the entire project, Kusaka played on these fears and convinced his chief that any reduction in his striking ability might prove disastrous. After all, Nagumo could conceivably lose the entire war in a few hours if his fleet was sunk. Wasn't it better therefore to have as much strength as possible to guard against this eventuality? Finally, Nagumo endorsed his chief of staff's recommendations and sent him off to convince the Naval General Staff that perhaps Yamaguchi was right, after all.

When the General Staff refused to alter their stance, Kusaka wisely took his case to Yamamoto. The commander of the Combined Fleet threatened the General Staff with his resignation unless Nagumo was allowed all available strength with which to carry out his attack. The Naval General Staff caved in under the weight of this argument. Yamaguchi and his carriers would accompany Nagumo to Pearl Harbor.

The next few weeks were filled with feverish activity. For the rest of October and far into November dress rehearsals for the forthcoming grand attack went ahead full tilt. A series of war games were held during which the feasibility of the attack was confirmed. However, there still remained the problem of torpedoes.

At the time that the Pearl Harbor attack was drawn up, it was possible for low-flying planes to drop torpedoes that would dive to a depth of sixty feet before achieving their desired level. Since the average depth of Pearl Harbor was approximately forty feet, this was totally unacceptable, because the torpedoes would simply stick in the mud. Genda was directed to see what he could do to correct this deficiency.

Fortunately, Genda's commanding officer had been one of Japan's foremost torpedo experts in his younger days. Consequently, when Genda and Nagumo pooled their knowledge, a torpedo was developed that would sink to a level of around thirty-five feet with the use of wooden fins. This obstacle overcome, the fleet prepared to go to war.

On November 17, Admiral Yamamoto sailed into Ariake Bay aboard the *Nagato*. As soon as the anchor was dropped, the commander-in-chief headed for the *Akagi*, where he wished Nagumo well and addressed the assembled officers and crew.

"Although we hope to achieve surprise, everyone should be prepared for terrific American resistance in this operation. Japan has faced many worthy opponents in her glorious history—Mongols, Chinese, Russians,—but in this operation we will meet the strongest and most resourceful opponent of all.

"You may have to fight your way in to the target.

> "It is the custom of Bushido to select an equal or stronger opponent. On this score you have nothing to complain about—the American Navy is a good match for the Japanese Navy."[5]

After the traditional meal, the parties toasted the success of the mission and parted company.

On November 27, the last ship in the fleet dropped anchor at the rendezvous point. Besides the carriers, Nagumo's fleet was supported by the battleships *Hiei* and *Kirishima*, the heavy cruisers *Tone* and *Chikuma*, the light cruiser *Abukuma*, and nine of the navy's newest and most modern destroyers. A force of submarines would precede the fleet to Hawaii and take station there to act as watchdogs and report any unusual American activity. Some of these submarines carried midget submarines affixed to their decks. These two-man units would be launched prior to Nagumo's attack and make their way to Pearl Harbor, where it was hoped their presence during the air raid would add to the confusion.

When all the ships were assembled at the rendezvous point, Nagumo called a meeting of his entire staff to review the latest intelligence reports and discuss the operation. The Japanese were relying on the fact that the American fleet routinely returned to Pearl Harbor to spend the weekend. Over a period of months, Japanese spies in Hawaii had been monitoring the American anchorage and reporting this fact. Since the date fixed for the attack, December 7, was a Sunday, the Japanese should catch the Americans napping.

However, the American carriers held to no such routine and tracking them was more difficult. Since one of the primary objectives of the entire plan was the destruction of the American carriers, most of the discussion at the staff meeting centered around these ships.

In November of 1941 the Americans had a total of six fleet carriers available. Commitments to the protection of the Atlantic seaways demanded the attention of the *Wasp*, the *Hornet* and the *Yorktown*. Consequently, the Pacific fleet was left with the *Enterprise,* the *Saratoga* and the *Lexington.* These three ships were the prize the Japanese sought. Unbeknownst to them, however, even as they made their final preparations, the *Saratoga* was on the West Coast of the United States undergoing a refit. Therefore, the Pacific fleet was reduced to just the *Enterprise* and the *Lexington.*

The lack of hard intelligence regarding the whereabouts of these two ships caused Nagumo a great deal of concern. It was entirely possible that the Japanese strike force could run into one or both of the Americans en route to Hawaii. In addition, what if the American carriers were not present at Pearl Harbor at the time of the attack? Should Nagumo proceed anyway? Genda and Fuchida argued that yes, the attack should go ahead just as planned. Nagumo agreed. Had he had any way of knowing it, he might have been consoled by the fact that the American intelligence community had lost track of all six Japanese carriers.

The following day, November 23, the captains of all the ships involved were summoned to a meeting aboard the *Akagi.* Heretofore, only the captains of the carriers were privy to the objective of the last few months of frantic training. When the other captains were informed of their operational plan, their reactions ranged from enthusiasm to outright glee.

Nagumo then announced that as soon as each wave returned to the carriers, it would be rearmed for another attack. This was the desire of Genda and Fuchida. In addition, he ordered each captain to institute tight security measures. There was to be no shore leave, and no garbage was to be thrown overboard from that moment on. Finally, the operational plan itself was revealed.

The attack would go forth in two waves. The first, consisting of fifty horizontal bombers, forty torpedo bombers, fifty-four dive bombers, and forty-five fighters, would be launched one half hour before the second. After the fighters secured the air lanes over Hawaii and strafed the airfields, the dive bombers would concentrate on the airfields at Hickham, Wheeler, Kaneohe, and Ford Island, leaving the high-level and torpedo bombers free to deal with the American fleet. Thirty minutes later, the second wave, minus torpedo bombers since these should have achieved their goal during the first wave, would send its fifty-four horizontal bombers and thirty-six fighters against the airfields, while eighty-one dive bombers concentrated on finishing off what was left of the American fleet. The heavy emphasis on the airfields indicates that the Japanese feared American retaliation and were taking no chances.

On November 26, in the middle of a driving snowstorm, the First Air Fleet weighed anchor and sailed off on its historic voyage. Meanwhile, at Pearl Harbor, all was serene. The military forces had received word that war might come at any time and to prepare accordingly. However, this merely constituted a war warning, not a war alert, since negotiations in Washington were still under way. Furthermore, the United States had concluded that any potential Japanese attack would be aimed at the Philippines. Few thought the Japanese Navy capable off carrying out a full-scale attack on Pearl Harbor.

In one sense, the Americans were correct. Even as Nagumo sailed toward Hawaii, another strong Japanese fleet was moving steadily toward the Philippines, intent on launching its own attack in that area immediately upon receipt of word that the Pearl Harbor attack was a success.

Nagumo's fears sailed with him. The night before sailing was a sleepless one as he attempted to come to grips with the awesome magnitude of his undertaking. Then there were the ever present dangers. Would the American fleet, including the carriers, be present at the time of attack? Or could it be lying in ambush, waiting for Nagumo to sail into a trap? One of his ships might be torpedoed by a lurking submarine. Then, of course, there was the ever present danger of discovery. It had already been decided to sink any ship they might run across, but what if that ship managed to get off a radio warning before it could be sunk? Based on the earlier war games, the Japanese Navy expected to lose half of Nagumo's fleet. Which of the ships was now on its final voyage? Nagumo's fears would not abate until he was en route home.

Fortunately for the Japanese, the weather was with them. Overcast skies reduced the possibility of discovery to a minimum while the selected route itself, normally buffeted by storms during that time of the year, remained relatively calm. A good omen. The selection of the northern route had been the proper one.

On December 2, Yamamoto sent the signal "Climb Mt. Niitaka." The brief wording of this message told Nagumo that any hope of reaching a negotiated settlement with the United States was past. The attack could proceed on schedule. Two days later, the First Air Fleet left the cold water of the North Pacific and began the final run in towards Pearl Harbor.

On the morning of December 7, 1941, Admiral Kimmel's United States Pacific Fleet swung peacefully at anchor under a warm, sunny sky. Present that morning at Pearl Harbor were eight battleships, the pride of the fleet. Seven of them were moored on the east side of Ford Island rocking lazily at anchor. Two heavy cruisers, six light cruisers, twenty-nine destroyers, five submarines and a host of other shipping cluttered the harbor. The *Lexington* and the *Enterprise*, the two aircraft carriers, were absent from their berths. The former was off ferrying a squadron of planes for Midway, while the *Enterprise* performed a similar service for the marine detachment on Wake Island.

If Kimmel was not anticipating trouble, neither was his army counterpart, General Short. The general's primary concern was, since the time of the war warning, sabotage. To guard against this the planes at Hickham and Wheeler Fields had been bunched together, making it easier for sentries to protect them. There they sat, like ducks on a pond.

That Sunday morning, Honolulu went about its business just as if nothing was amiss. Ship's crews prepared to embark for liberty, sailors and citizens alike prepared to attend church services, and the radio stations played many of the popular tunes of the day. On board Nagumo's ships these radio transmissions were monitored, so the Japanese knew that the Americans suspected nothing.

Fuchida and Nagumo had risen early. At 5:00 AM the flight commander reported to the admiral's cabin. Nagumo wished him well and went on to say that he was confident of the mission's success. The two then proceeded to the briefing room where the *Akagi*'s pilots eagerly awaited the final briefing. Nagumo addressed them briefly and wished them all well.

At 5:30, the cruisers *Chikuma* and *Tone* launched their scout planes. It had been decided that these planes would fly over the target area to determine if the American fleet was actually present. Naturally this increased the risk of compromising secrecy, but Nagumo was prepared to accept the risk.

Then the "Z" flag flown by Admiral Togo at Tsushima broke out at the *Akagi*'s masthead to the shouts of *Banzai!"* from those members of the fleet within viewing range.

Twenty minutes later at a point approximately 220 miles north of Oahu, the six mighty carriers turned into the wind and prepared to launch their planes. Rough seas delayed the launching for almost half an hour, but shortly thereafter, the entire strike was airborne. Then the fleet turned south once more, to hover 180 miles north of the target area.

Meanwhile, thanks to their ability to read the Japanese code, American code breakers in Washington had intercepted a diplomatic message whose wording could only mean that war was imminent. General Marshall, the American chief of staff, immediately sent off a telegram to Honolulu suggesting that a Japanese attack against American installations could be expected at any time. Unfortunately, the message went out over regular Western Union channels instead of the military one. The telegram was received in Hawaii at approximately 7:30 that morning, but since it was not marked urgent, the Western Union operator simply pigeonholed it for routine delivery.

Fifteen minutes later, Fuchida, flying with the high-level bombers, entered the air space above Oahu and gave the message "To-To-To" over his transmitter. This was the signal for attack. As the Japanese squadrons dove on their respective targets, Fuchida could see that total surprise had been achieved. He grabbed his microphone and shouted the words "Tora-Tora-Tora," the signal indicating that the enemy had been surprised.

Aboard *Akagi*, Nagumo waited nervously on the bridge with his staff in total silence. The die had been cast. There was no turning back. All sorts of fears coursed through his brain and the staff could see that their commander was deeply troubled. Then came the signal from Fuchida. Surprise was complete. The American fleet was present. Nagumo and Kusaka turned toward each other, smiled, and wordlessly shook hands.

At Pearl Harbor itself the arrival of the Japanese air armada attracted little notice initially. American radar had discovered the flight, but since a flight of American B-17s from the mainland was due to arrive that very same morning, the radar reports were ignored. Others thought that the planes were simply army planes out for maneuvers. Once the bombs began to fall and the rising sun insignia on the wings was noted, reality struck home. The call went out: "Air Raid—Pearl Harbor—This is no drill!"

Over the airfields the Zeros peeled off and began their strafing runs. At Wheeler and Hickham the Japanese pilots could hardly believe their eyes as the American planes sat idly in bunches waiting to be destroyed. The Japanese fighter pilots had a field day with the sitting ducks. American aircraft were quickly destroyed where they sat and not one rose in opposition. Dive bombers followed the Zeros in and quickly destroyed hangars, runways, and installations. The American Air Forces were wiped out in the space of a few minutes.

Over the harbor the Japanese encountered little initial opposition. Thanks to a misinterpretation of Fuchida's attack signal, the torpedo planes and high-level bombers attacked simultaneously. Many of the ship's crews were already ashore enjoying their weekend. Others lolled in their bunks. Some of the ships were undergoing repairs. Only a handful were ready to raise steam at short notice. The Japanese attack had indeed taken everyone by surprise.

Those few antiaircraft batteries that were quickly manned found no shortage of targets as the enemy planes attacked from all angles. Unfortunately, because of the total lack of readiness of the fleet the initial response to the attack was feeble at best.

By the time the first wave's attack began to subside, Battleship Row was a shambles. The *Oklahoma* had taken five torpedo hits and had capsized. The *Arizona* took two torpedo hits and had blown up when a bomb found her magazines. The *West Virginia* and the *California* were beginning to settle into the mud at the bottom of the harbor. The *Maryland*, the *Tennessee* and the *Nevada* had received heavy bomb damage.

Elsewhere in the harbor the old target ship *Utah*, mistaken by the Japanese pilots for a capital ship, had overturned. The cruisers *Helena* and *Raleigh* were struggling to remain afloat. Then the next wave arrived.

The flagship of the American fleet, the battleship *Pennsylvania*, was in drydock and unhappily found herself the object of attention. Bombs fell aboard the flagship. Those that missed found the destroyers *Cassin, Downes,* and *Shaw* berthed nearby. The *Shaw* erupted in a spectacular explosion visible for miles. The cruiser *Honolulu* was also hit. Other planes concentrated on those ships that had managed to raise steam and were beginning to make for the open seas. Foremost among this group was the *Nevada*. Swarms of Japanese planes concentrated on the battleship. Eventually, the *Nevada*'s skipper ran the ship aground rather than run the risk of having it sunk at the entrance to the harbor and blocking the escape of any further ships.

When the last Japanese flight headed out to sea it left behind a shattered and broken American fleet. Ninety-eight planes had been destroyed and another hundred and six damaged, including some of the aforementioned B-17s who blundered into the middle of the Japanese attack. American casualties were twenty-four hundred dead and almost a thousand wounded. Although the second Japanese wave encountered heavier antiaircraft fire, the cost of the entire operation was incredibly low: five torpedo bombers fifteen dive bombers, and nine fighters failed to return to their mother ships, most of these from the second wave.

Even as the first wave began to arrive back aboard the carriers, the reports of widespread destruction were received with elation. However, Nagumo had not put the American carriers out of his mind. Where were they? Surely by that time they must know of the attack. Were they ready to retaliate? It was a threat that could not be ignored.

Nevertheless, Fuchida and Genda urged another attack. They were sure that Pearl Harbor's defenses were shattered. Even though the U.S. fleet was battered, the installations at Pearl Harbor remained relatively unharmed. Genda and Fuchida insisted that a second attack be directed against the oil storage tanks, repair facilities and other vital installations. The American fleet was certainly in no position to resist, they argued. The two aviators were, of course, entirely correct.

Nagumo was torn between the prospect of inflicting more damage or withdrawing with his fleet intact. Surely he had achieved his goal. The American fleet was critically wounded. Why risk the fleet?

Back in Japan aboard the *Nagato*, Yamamoto was hearing those very same arguments. As the reports filtered in from the Pearl Harbor strike force he listened in silence. In his heart he knew that Nagumo would elect to withdraw and admitted as much to his staff. However, he refused to interfere, preferring instead to leave the decision to the man on the spot.

Nagumo has been severely criticized for not sanctioning a follow-up attack. Had the port facilities at Pearl Harbor been destroyed the American fleet would have had to retreat all the way to the West Coast of America. However, it must be remembered too that Nagumo felt out of his realm in regard to aviation. Until the enormity of what he had accomplished sank in, he remained uncomfortable. Consequently, he was vulnerable to outside influence. His chief of staff, Kusaka, whose opinion Nagumo valued, turned a deaf ear to Fuchida's and Genda's pleas. After listening to their arguments he suggested that the fleet set a course for home. Relieved that someone else had eased the burden for him. Nagumo simply said, "Please do."

The two aviators continued to protest vehemently, but Nagumo's mind was made up and Kusaka was unconvinced. Although technically it was Kusaka's decision to withdraw, Nagumo held the power of veto over that decision but refused to exercise his option. The First Air Fleet set a course for the Marshalls as Nagumo issued a message to the fleet.

> "Brilliant success was achieved for our country through the splendid efforts of you men. But we still have a great way to go. After this victory we must tighten the straps of our helmets and go onward, determined to continue our fight until the final goal has been won."[6]

Upon reaching the refueling point at Truk, the First Air Fleet was ordered to detach the *Hiryu* and the *Soryu* to aid the Japanese attack against Wake Island. The rest of the fleet reached Hiroshima late in the afternoon of December 22. The following day, Nagumo reported to Yamamoto.

Despite having commanded the greatest victory in Japan's history, Nagumo found himself taking a back seat to Fuchida. Even during an audience with the emperor himself four days later it was the pilot who was the center of attention. Fortunately, jealousy was not part of Nagumo's character, so he accepted his plight magnanimously.

After the fall of the Philippines appeared imminent, the Japanese turned their attention to the Dutch East Indies. Nagumo took his carriers into the South Pacific and supported the various landings on Borneo, Java, Bali, and the rest of those fabled islands. The East Indies campaign was primarily fought by the surface warships and Nagumo's contribution was essentially one of scouting, bombing enemy positions ashore and attacking enemy merchant shipping. With one enemy, the United States, licking its wounds, Japanese attention turned to the other Western enemy, Great Britain.

As forecast by Yamamoto Japan began to run wild. The British battleship *Prince of Wales* and the battlecruiser *Repulse* were sunk in the Gulf of Siam by land-based aircraft from Indo-China on December 10. The small American Asiatic fleet was driven from Philippine waters shortly after the first of the year. General Yamashita drove down the Malay Peninsula and captured the great British base at Singapore. General Homma's army in the Philippines pushed the defenders of that country into the confines of the Bataan Peninsula.

The British Eastern fleet was based on Ceylon at the bases of Trincomalee and Colombo. In March of 1942 this force was comprised of five old battleships, two modern carriers, one older carrier, eight cruisers, and a handful of submarines and destroyers. (*See May 9*).

On April 4 Nagumo's carriers were sighted by a patrolling British plane. The Japanese force was south of Ceylon. Although the spotter was quickly shot down it managed to get off a sighting report. The next morning Nagumo, believing that the British fleet was at Colombo, approached to within two hundred miles of Ceylon and sent a two-hundred-plane raid winging toward the British base. Unfortunately, the British commander, Admiral Sir James Somerville, had split his force and ordered it to sea. Consequently, when the Japanese planes arrived over the harbor no British ships were present. Nonetheless, the port facilities were all but destroyed by the attackers. Shortly afterward one of the cruiser *Tone*'s scout planes sighted two British cruisers steaming to join the main British fleet.

Nagumo quickly ordered another attack. The British ships were overwhelmed. The heavy cruisers *Cornwall* and *Dorsetshire*, the latter being the ship that had administered the coup de grace to the German battleship *Bismark*, were sent to the bottom of the Indian Ocean.

To minimize the risk of detection and retaliation by land-based bombers, Nagumo drew off. In addition, he had no idea of the whereabouts of the British carriers. Three days later, however, he was back. This time it was the turn of the fabled base at Trincomalee. A heavy attack was dispatched

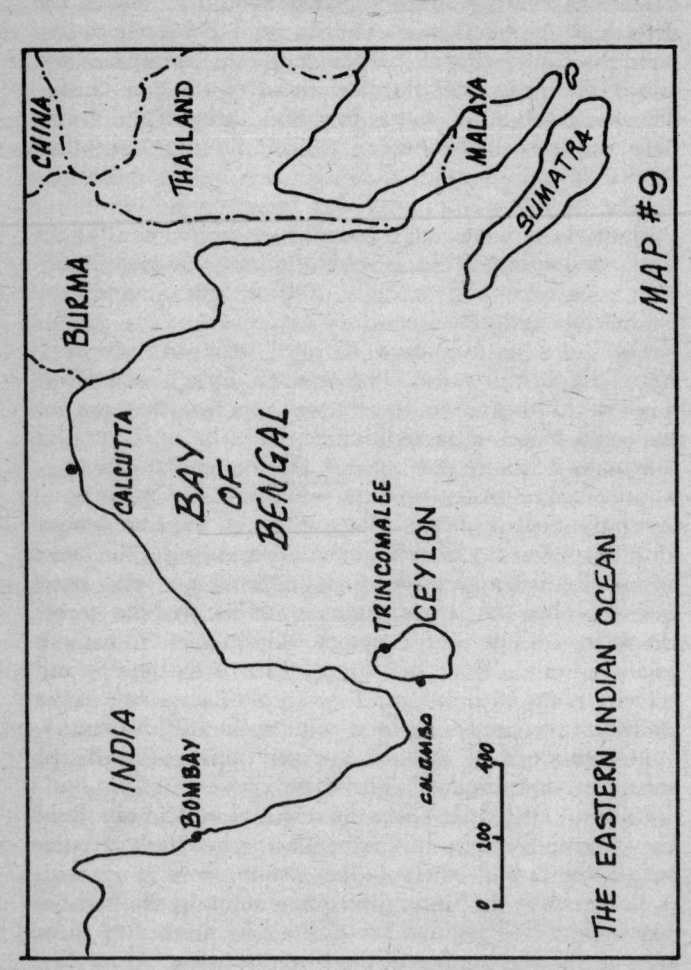

toward that base in a repeat of the Colombo raid. The old British carrier *Hermes* was caught returning to base escorted by the destroyer *Vampire*. *Hermes* was virtually defenseless, having left her planes behind to aid in the defense of the naval base. The carrier and her escort suffered the same fate as the *Cornwall* and the *Dorsetshire* and joined the cruisers at the bottom of the Indian Ocean. Somerville concluded that he had had enough. The British fleet withdrew to the Persian Gulf. Thus, the last Allied fleet in the central and South Pacific exited the stage. Nagumo turned his forces toward Japan.

Meanwhile, Admiral Yamamoto had been looking about for other horizons to conquer. Finally, after much deliberation, he settled on the island of Midway. This strategically located island would make a good advance base for air patrols and submarine operations against the Allied forces. Additionally, Yamamoto felt that an attack against Midway might serve to draw the rest of the American fleet out for the coveted decisive naval battle.

Yamamoto set his staff to work developing plans for Midway. It was to be an elaborate operation with a simultaneous attack against the Aleutian Islands. Almost all of the Combined Fleet would take part, with ships from all points in the Pacific rendezvousing at sea. Nagumo's carriers would soften up the island for the invasion force, which would sail independently. Meanwhile, Yamamoto would be at sea with a powerful fleet of battleships and cruisers ready to oppose the American fleet if the latter chose to intervene. Between his force and Nagumo's, Yamamoto felt confident that the Japanese possessed enough strength to deal with any threat.

Unfortunately, while the planning for Midway went ahead full tilt, the two key admirals charged with carrying out the operation, Nagumo and Kondo, were at sea with their respective fleets conducting operations in the East Indies and the Indian Ocean. Therefore, neither of them knew of the plan until after their return home. At no time during the formative stages of the plan were Kondo and Nagumo consulted, nor were their ideas solicited.

On April 22, the First Air Fleet reached home minus the carriers *Zuikaku* and *Shokaku*. These two ships were left behind to support the Japanese operations against Port Moresby in New Guinea. Kondo's Second Fleet had reached home a week earlier, only to be hastily sent back to sea to search for the American task force that had carried Dolittle's raiders on their bombing mission against Japan. This attack was the final straw as far as Yamamoto was concerned. Midway had to be captured.

Both Nagumo and Kondo pleaded for a delay of the Midway operation. Their crews were worn out and their ships badly in need of overhaul. Both fleets had been in constant action since early January, Kondo in the East Indies and the Philippines, Nagumo conducting raids in the Solomons, Darwin, and the East Indies. Both fleets had then joined hands to drive the British from the Indian Ocean.

But Doolittle's raid made Yamamoto determined that such an event would never occur again. He took it as a personal insult. Although Nagumo too felt that the conquest of Midway was necessary, surely, he said, it could wait until the fleet had rested and the ships were in shape to go to sea again. Kondo opposed the operation completely. Yamamoto would not be swayed. The Midway operation would proceed on schedule. Nagumo and Kondo were ordered to have their respective fleets ready for sea by the end of May. The Japanese fully expected to have the entire fleet available for the Midway operation. As we have already seen, however, the *Zuikaku* and the *Shokaku* had been detached to support the attack against Port Moresby.

On May 7, these two ships along with the light carrier *Shoho* joined battle with an American task force east of New Guinea. The American force consisted of the carriers *Lexington* and *Yorktown*.* When the battle was over the *Lexington* lay at the bottom of the Coral Sea, and the

---

*Shortly after the debacle at Pearl Harbor, the Americans had rushed the carriers *Hornet* and *Yorktown* to the Pacific.

Yorktown was limping back to Pearl Harbor, seriously damaged.

On the Japanese side, the *Shoho* was lost, bombed into destruction by American carrier planes. Even more important, however, was the fate of the two fleet carriers. The *Shokaku*'s flight deck was holed in several places by American bombs. Although the *Zuikaku* escaped physical damage, her air crews had suffered heavy losses. Consequently, before either ship could take part in further battles, new air crews would have to be trained and the *Shokaku*'s damage repaired. Neither of them would be ready to take part in the Midway operation. The setback in the Coral Sea failed to deter Yamamoto. He still had the four large carriers of the 1st and 2nd Air Divisions. In addition, there was no assurance that the Americans would even oppose the Midway operation.

Unlike the Pearl Harbor attack, where security had been relatively tight, a looser veil of secrecy cloaked the plans for Midway. On the other hand, even if Nimitz did oppose the Japanese moves he could do so with only two carriers, since it was assumed that the damage to the *Yorktown* would lay that ship up for many months.

Since the Americans had broken the Japanese naval code it was no trouble for them to determine that the enemy was planning another major move. Every wireless transmission between the various Japanese headquarters and fleets was quickly read and carefully scrutinized by American code breakers. Only the eventual target remained a mystery, since the Japanese did not refer to Midway by name. However, the code name AF kept popping up in Japanese messages.

Commander Joseph Rochefort, one of Nimitz's code breakers, suspected that the Japanese were planning to attack Midway. Unfortunately, there was little concrete evidence to support his conclusion. On May 10th he approached his commanding officer and asked that Midway be ordered to send a message in the clear indicating that its fresh-water distilling plant was out of operation and that the base was short of fresh water. Two days later the

Americans intercepted a Japanese message stating that AF was short of fresh water. The secret was out. The Japanese were planning to attack Midway.

Yamamoto's plan was an elaborate one calling for the various fleets involved to set out from dispersed locations. Nagumo's carrier force was to bombard Midway prior to the invasion. Behind him would come Yamamoto with the main body of the fleet: seven battleships, a light carrier, two seaplane carriers, two light cruisers, twenty destroyers and four oilers. Once at sea, a portion of this fleet would separate from the main body and take up station halfway between Midway and the Aleutians, where it could be ready to support either operation.

The task of Admiral Kondo's Second Fleet was even more complicated. His main body of two battleships, seven heavy cruisers, one light carrier, one light cruiser, ten destroyers, and six auxillaries was to leave Japan and link up with the occupation force sailing from Guam and Saipan. Escorted by Admiral Tanaka's ten destroyers, one seaplane tender, and one light cruiser, the occupation force was made up of twelve transports carrying five thousand troops for the invasion of Midway. As the entire group approached the target, Kondo was to detach Admiral Kurita from his main body with four heavy cruisers and two destroyers to provide close-in support for the invasion.

In addition to the elaborate plans for the capture of Midway, the Japanese planned a simultaneous invasion of the Aleutian islands of Kiska and Attu. A force of three heavy cruisers, three light cruisers, two light carriers, thirteen destroyers, six submarines, three transports, and three minesweepers under Admiral Hosogaya was designated to carry out this operation.

On May 27 the action began as Nagumo, Kondo, Hosogaya, and the occupation forces put to sea. Yamamoto would personally lead his force to sea early the next day and maintain station approximately six hundred miles to the rear of Nagumo's four carriers, two heavy cruisers, two battleships, one light cruiser, twelve destroyers and five oilers.

From that point forward all the various elements would

be out of touch with each other, since Yamamoto demanded that absolute radio silence be maintained at all times. Just as at Pearl Harbor, Nagumo would exercise tactical command of the 1st Carrier Division of *Kaga* and *Akagi* as well as overall command of the entire First Air Fleet. Admiral Yamaguchi with the *Hiryu* and the *Soryu* comprised the 2nd Carrier Division. Nagumo's flag flew from the masthead of the *Akagi*, Yamaguchi's from the *Hiryu*.

On the days following Nagumo's departure, Admiral Nimitz ordered Admiral Raymond Spruance to sea with the carriers *Hornet* and *Enterprise*, the cruisers *Pensacola*, *Northampton*, *New Orleans*, *Minneapolis*, *Vincennes*, and *Atlanta*, eleven destroyers and two tankers. Nineteen submarines were positioned around Midway to warn of the Japanese approach. As for the *Yorktown*, after her return to Pearl Harbor from the Coral Sea on the 27th, it was estimated that it would take three months to repair her battle damage. Nimitz emphasized the importance of having the ship available for immediate duty, so repair crews began to work on the mighty ship around the clock.

In order to alert himself to the movements of the American fleet, Yamamoto had designed two plans. One called for a seaplane to lie at French Frigate Shoals and conduct daily reconnaissance flights over Pearl Harbor. The second called for two submarine picket lines to be established, one near the area that the seaplane was operating from and the other between Midway and Hawaii, directly astride the route any American fleet would have to travel en route to Midway. Thus assured of accurate intelligence, with his flag flying from the monstrous battleship *Yamato*, the commander-in-chief of the Combined Fleet took his force to sea.

As the old saying goes, "The best-laid plans of mice and men often go astray." In the Japanese case it proved prophetic. When their submarine scouting unit arrived at French Frigate Shoals it found the area patrolled by an American seaplane tender. After watching the area for a few days in the vain hope the American ship would leave, the commander of the submarines radioed Kwajelein and told them not to dispatch the seaplanes. Operation K, as the plan was known, would have to be scrapped.

Meanwhile, on the 30th, thanks to a mammoth effort on the part of dockyard workers, the *Yorktown* sailed from Pearl Harbor in company with two cruisers and six destroyers. Admiral Fletcher's small fleet's course would take it directly over the anticipated position of the second Japanese submarine picket line. But the picket line failed to materialize. The sailing of the submarines had been delayed. Consequently, by the time they arrived in position on June 2, Fletcher and the *Yorktown* had long since passed through the position.

The next day, however, radio operators aboard the *Yamato* began to intercept numerous American transmissions. Although they were unable to decipher the messages, Yamamoto was notified of the activity. His staff accurately concluded that the American fleet was at sea. Yamamoto concurred with his staff's conclusion but refused to break radio silence and notify Nagumo. The commander-in-chief incorrectly assumed that Nagumo's force had monitored the same enemy transmissions and could draw their own conclusions. Unfortunately, the receivers on the *Akagi* were nowhere as strong as those on the *Yamato*, so the First Air Fleet was unable to intercept the American transmissions. Prior to sailing, Nagumo's chief of staff had urged that Yamamoto forward all messages, but the latter was so intent on maintaining radio silence that he flatly refused. Yamamoto seemed obsessed with the need for secrecy.

Thus the two fleets groped for each other, each unaware of the other's presence. Nagumo seemed in high spirits as the fleet sailed serenely toward the target. Seemingly he had little to fear. No messages had been received from the patrol planes at French Frigate Shoals or the submarine pickets. The American fleet was probably still in Hawaii.

Late in the afternoon of June 2, the First Air Fleet ran into heavy overcast weather. All through the night the fleet steamed through dense fog. It was Nagumo's intention to hover out of range of land-based planes until the night preceding the actual attack. Under cover of darkness he would then run in toward the target. Since the fleet was approaching Midway, this necessitated a temporary change of course.

When dawn arrived on June 3, Nagumo's ships found themselves still shrouded in dense fog. Consequently, the order to change course could not be given by signal lamp or flags. Nagumo therefore ordered a low frequency message sent to all ships informing them of the intention to change course. He was lucky. Although Yamamoto's flagship picked up the *Akagi*'s weak signal, the American fleet, even closer than Yamamoto, did not.

Later that same day Fletcher and Spruance linked up northeast of Midway. Unlike his opponent, Fletcher knew that the enemy fleet was at sea. Admiral Fletcher was the senior of the two American commanders and was thus in overall command. However, since Spruance was totally familiar with the operation of his own Task Force 16, Fletcher decided that although he would retain overall responsibility, during the battle his own Task Force 17 and Spruance's would operate independently. He then moved both groups to a position approximately two hundred miles north of Midway. Fletcher suspected that the Japanese carriers would approach Midway either from the west or the northwest. Thus the American carriers were ideally positioned to intercept the Japanese fleet.

Meanwhile, Tanaka's force of transports from Saipan was discovered by an American Catalina aircraft during the morning of June 3. Tanaka immediately notified Yamamoto. Later in the day the troop convoy came under attack by B-17 bombers from Midway. The attack failed to do any damage, but Tanaka dutifully reported the attack to Yamamoto, who now knew that the Americans had discovered the Japanese forces. Nagumo, unfortunately, had not intercepted Tanaka's transmissions and was unaware of the American attack. Neither did Yamamoto rescind his radio silence order to inform Nagumo of the attack on Tanaka. Unsuspectingly, the First Air Fleet sailed on toward Midway.

At 4:00 AM on June 4, Nagumo's four carriers burst into activity. Pilots were awakened and given breakfast before being briefed for their assignments. Half an hour later seven search planes were launched from the escorting battleships and cruisers. There should have been eight, but the cruiser *Tone* encountered problems with one of its catapults. The search planes were to fan out and search for any enemy ships that might be lurking in the vicinity of Midway.

At 4:45 Nagumo's carriers, having turned into the wind, launched their first strike against Midway. Yamaguchi's two carriers launched thirty-six level bombers, Nagumo's launched thirty-six dive bombers, and each of the four carriers added nine Zero fighters as escort, for a total of a hundred and eight planes. As soon as the launching was complete. The ships' crews began to arm another equally strong strike with bombs and torpedoes. Thus, in the event enemy ships were located, the Japanese would be ready to strike at a moment's notice. In addition to those already airborne and the ones waiting on the carrier decks, a formation of fighters hovered over the fleet as a combat air patrol.

Standing on the bridge observing the launch, Nagumo exuded confidence. Thanks to the lack of intelligence reports there was no reason for him to feel otherwise. No enemy fleet had been reported in the region. This meant that there would be no fleet action until at least after the invasion. At that point he would be ready to meet any threat. In the meantime he stood confidently watching the activity. The Japanese strike winged its way toward Midway. It would be an hour or more before they arrived over the target.

At 5:00 the *Tone* finally ironed outs its catapult problems and launched its remaining scout plane. That half-hour delay proved fatal, since the American fleet was positioned precisely in the area that the *Tone*'s second plane was to search.

As they approached Midway, the Japanese planes were discovered by a patrolling American aircraft, which immediately sounded the warning. Almost immediately all

American planes on the island began to scramble and were airborne before the enemy arrived over the target. A few minutes before 6:30, American fighters located the flight of Japanese bombers and maneuvered to intercept. The Zeros managed to beat back the American attack without loss to the bombers, which arrived over Midway exactly on schedule.

The Japanese planes peeled off and began to hit the American installations. To their misfortune all the American planes had managed to get airborne, but hangars, runways and installations took a severe pounding.

In thirty minutes, the attack was over. Midway was a shambles. However, the Japanese flight commander was disappointed with the results of the raid. It was fine to destroy installations, but the striking arm of the island's defenses, the aircraft, remained intact. Accordingly at 7:00 AM he radioed the fleet suggesting that another strike was needed. Since losses were relatively light, three level bombers and one dive bomber to antiaircraft fire, and two Zeros to the enemy fighters, the flight commander was sure that one more strike would finish the job.

Nagumo hesitated. Was another strike warranted? As he stood contemplating his next move, bombers from Midway arrived over the fleet and began to drop their lethal loads. Thanks to skillful maneuvering on the part of the ship's captains, none of the bombs found their target, but the attack convinced Nagumo that another strike was called for. He therefore ordered that the planes carrying torpedoes be rearmed with bombs. Those planes being held in reserve to attack any American naval forces would be used to deliver a second strike against Midway. Of course, it would take time to rearm these planes.

At 7:30, while the rearming proceeded, *Tone*'s plane made contact with the American fleet but reported that no carriers were present. Based on *Tone*'s sighting report, Nagumo began to second-guess himself. If *Tone*'s plane had only been launched on time he would not now be faced with this dilemma. Nagumo's primary objective was, of course, the American fleet, so once again he changed his mind. The order went out to cancel the rearming of the planes for another attack on Midway, to replace the bombs with torpedoes. Aboard the *Hiryu*, Yamaguchi raged. Why not attack with those aircraft that were already waiting. However, Nagumo knew that his fighters, both those en route back from Midway and those flying combat air patrol, were low on fuel. He refused to consider sending off an attack without the proper escort and decided instead to refuel the Zeros while the rearming proceeded.

While the activity proceeded furiously another American attack by planes from Midway took place. Again no hits were achieved on the Japanese fleet, but half an hour later, just as the Midway flight was returning to the carriers, a force of B-17s flew high over the fleet and dropped their loads. Once more violent evasive maneuvers succeeded in throwing off the aim of the American bombardiers and no hits were made, but the furious maneuvering caused additional delays. In the midst of all this confusion, another message was received from *Tone*'s scout plane repeating that no carriers were with the American fleet.

Now Nagumo had another choice to make. Should he recover the planes returning from Midway or should he launch the strike first? Since the first strike was dangerously low on fuel, he chose to recover it. As the carriers made preparations to receive the returning planes, *Tone*'s scout sent another message at 8:20 reporting the presence of one carrier with the American fleet. The *Yorktown* and her group had been discovered. Spruance's two carriers remained undetected. The American fleet had not sat idly by while the Japanese formation was in a flurry of activity. At 7:45 Spruance launched fifteen torpedo planes from both the *Hornet* and the *Enterprise*. Unfortunately, the Americans were unsure of the exact location of Nagumo's formation. Consequently, both torpedo squadrons flew slightly divergent courses, which gradually drew them apart. An hour later, Fletcher launched a full strike from the decks of the *Yorktown* consisting of torpedo and dive bombers with a handful of fighters for escort.

Around 8:30 the recovery of the Japanese planes returning from Midway commenced. Below decks the rearming of the next strike continued for the second time. Because of the urgency of the situation and the succeeding conflicting orders, there had not been enough time to properly stow the removed armaments. Torpedoes and bombs were stacked loosely around the decks and in hangars as the furious pace of the crews took priority.

By 9:15 the recovery was complete. If no further problems were encountered, Nagumo felt that the entire complement of planes could be refueled, rearmed, and ready to launch in a little over an hour.

While the sailors aboard the Japanese carriers continued their frantic pace, the *Hornet*'s Torpedo Squadron 8 located the Japanese fleet and dove to sea-top level to attack. The slow, lumbering torpedo planes were easy targets for the circling Zeros. The next few minutes witnessed a slaughter. All fifteen of Lieutenant Waldron's planes were destroyed by the tenacious Japanese pilots before they could even draw into range. Out of forty-five pilots and crewmen only one man survived.

Right behind Torpedo 8 came the *Enterprise*'s Torpedo 6. Selecting as their targets the *Kaga* and the *Akagi*, Torpedo 6 suffered almost the same fate as had the planes from the *Hornet*. Nine of the fourteen attackers fell victim to the experienced Zero pilots. For the terrible price they paid, the American torpedo squadrons had nothing to show. No hits were obtained on the Japanese ships.

By now Nagumo was deeply concerned. His staff and the carrier captains exhorted their crews to a greater effort in completing the task of readying the planes. At 10:00 the third American torpedo squadron, Torpedo 3 from the *Yorktown*, arrived on the scene. Again the American squadron paid a heavy price. The swarming Japanese fighters made short work of the vulnerable torpedo planes, and their attack on the *Soryu* went for naught. The Japanese carrier emerged unscathed. But this time the sacrifice of the American pilots was not in vain. Unlike the torpedo squadrons from the *Hornet* and *Enterprise*, the squadron from the *Yorktown* was accompanied by a full strike of fighters and dive bombers. Arriving over the Japanese fleet, the torpedo planes skimmed the waves and launched their attack first.

Meanwhile, Nagumo's spirits were lifting. It was obvious that this latest American attack was doomed to suffer the same fate as its predecessors. In addition, his original estimate that his own planes would not be ready until 10:30 had proved erroneous. Fifteen minutes ahead of schedule all planes were ready for launching. At 10:20 Nagumo ordered all carriers to turn into the wind and begin launching planes. In the midst of this maneuver all hell broke loose. Screaming out of the sky came Lieutenant Wade McClusky's thirty-seven Dauntless dive bombers from the *Enterprise*. McClusky's formation had been searching without success for the Japanese fleet, and low on fuel, were returning to their ship when they stumbled across Nagumo's formation by accident. Splitting his formation, McClusky gave the order to nose over and attack the *Kaga* and *Akagi*.

At the same time, the *Yorktown*'s eighteen dive bombers, which had accompanied the torpedo planes, focused their sights on the *Soryu*. Their leader, Lieutenant Commander Max Leslie, soon had his squadron in a steep dive with their fingers poised on their bomb releases.

The unsuccessful torpedo attacks had drawn the Japanese fighters down to sea level to meet the threat. After having successfully turned back the torpedo bombers the Zeros were flying at wave-top level searching for any American planes that might have eluded them. In that position, they never saw the American dive bombers.

The Zeros did not have the capability of climbing quickly enough to intercept the American dive bombers. Consequently, except for the feeble antiaircraft fire from the carriers, the Devastators found the field clear. Within minutes, three Japanese carriers lay blazing. The *Kaga* took four hits immediately. Fires and explosions erupted as the frantic crew attempted to clear the deck of the fuel lines still lying about. Almost immediately, the carrier's captain knew that his ship was doomed. As the crew of the *Soryu* looked on in awed amazement at the fate of the ships of the 1st Carrier Division, their awe turned to terror as three hits, ideally placed along the length of the ship, turned the *Soryu* into a blazing inferno. From stem to stern the flight deck was one huge mass of flame.

Aboard the *Akagi*, Nagumo's flagship, the story was the same. One bomb hit forward, another landed on the stern and destroyed the ship's rudder. The fatal blow, however, was the second hit that plunged through the central elevator to explode among the torpedoes on the hanger deck. As we have already seen, the Japanese sailors, in their haste to obey the order to rearm the planes, had left them strewn about the deck. Fuchida recalls,

> "I was horrified at the destruction that had been wrought in a matter of seconds. There was a huge hole in the flight deck just behind the midship elevator. The elevator itself, twisted like molten glass, was drooping into the hangar. Deck plates reeled in grotesque configurations. Planes stood tail up belching livid flames and jet-black smoke. Reluctant tears streamed down my cheeks as I watched the fires spread."[7]

In the very brief span of a few minutes the once proud First Air Fleet was a wreck as crews struggled to contain the fires. Only the *Hiryu* managed to escape. When the American attack came in she was conveniently shielded by a nearby rain squall.

Aboard the flagship, Nagumo's chief of staff, Kusaka, urged the admiral to leave the ship and transfer to another. Nagumo refused. His depression was so deep by that time that he seemed intent on sharing the fate of his fleet. The *Akagi*'s skipper, Captain Aoki, attempted to convince Nagumo that he was perfectly capable of handling the activity aboard ship without the admiral's assistance. Once again, Nagumo refused to listen. Finally Kusaka used the argument that the surviving portion of the fleet required direction and that it was Nagumo's duty to provide guidance. There was no disputing this argument. Nagumo gave in. The destroyer *Nowaki* came alongside and sent its launch to fetch Nagumo and other members of the staff. At 10:45, the admiral boarded the launch for the trip to the cruiser *Nagara*, whose facilities were more suited to that of a flagship than that of the destroyer. Forty-five minutes later, Nagumo climbed the *Nagara*'s ladder, still shaken.

At the very moment Nagumo was leaving the *Akagi*, the entire crew was abandoning the *Soryu*. The fires aboard the ship could not be contained. It was a losing battle. Captain Yanagimoto therefore gave the order to abandon ship. There was no question but that the ship was doomed.

Yamamoto was not the only one to realize that the Japanese still had teeth that had not been yanked by the Americans. Admiral Yamaguchi, in his flagship, the *Hiryu*, came to the same conclusion. At 10:55 he launched his long-delayed attack. An hour later this force located the *Yorktown*.

Although most of the planes were either destroyed by American fighters or diverted from their target by heavy antiaircraft fire, three pilots pressed home their attacks and dealt a crippling blow to the hastily repaired veteran of the Coral Sea.

Even as the attackers were winging their way home, Yamaguchi was preparing another strike with orders to find any undamaged American carrier, since by then it was obvious that the *Yorktown* was not alone. By 1:30 that afternoon this second strike of torpedo planes was streaking for the American fleet.

Precisely one hour later, the second strike located the already crippled *Yorktown*. Admiral Fletcher had transferred to the cruiser *Astoria*, but *Yorktown*'s commander, Captain Buckmaster, remained aboard and maneuvered to avoid the enemy torpedoes. Unfortunately, his efforts proved futile as the great ship's reduced speed made maneuvering difficult. Two torpedoes slammed home and the *Yorktown* stopped dead in the water. She would take no further part in the battle. Then minutes after the first torpedo hit, Captain Buckmaster ordered the ship abandoned.

Admiral Yamaguchi glimpsed a ray of hope on the horizon. The returning torpedo pilots reported that they had not attacked the same ship as the dive bombers had. Based on their reports, Yamaguchi concluded that the odds were now even, one Japanese carrier against one American. He erred, of course, since the *Hornet* and the *Enterprise* were both in full fighting trim. At 4:00 Spruance ordered both his carriers to launch a strike and destroy the remaining Japanese carrier.

While Spruance's planes were revving their engines on the carrier decks in preparation for takeoff, Yamaguchi was passing the order for yet another attack. Thanks to the heavy losses incurred during the two attacks on the *Yorktown*, few Japanese planes answered the call. However, Yamaguchi was perfectly willing to sacrifice them to achieve victory. Refueling and rearming began. That remaining American carrier had to be found and put out of action.

Precious little time was available since, as we have already seen, the two fleets were by now only an hour's flying time apart. Before the *Hiryu*'s planes were ready, the American planes arrived. The result was the same as in the morning. Four bombs struck the *Hiryu* in rapid succession. In minutes the ship was wrapped in a pall of smoke and flame. Its forward elevator was blown up against the bridge and leaned at an odd angle. The *Hiryu* was doomed, and with it, Yamaguchi's hope for victory.

It was obvious that there would be no salvaging of the *Hiryu*. When the order went out to abandon ship the valiant Yamaguchi decided to remain aboard and go down with his ship. He addressed those members of the crew still remaining:

"As commanding officer of this Carrier Division, I am fully and solely responsible for the loss of the *Hiryu* and the *Soryu*. I shall remain on board to the end. I command all of you to leave the ship and continue your loyal service to His Majesty, the Emperor."[8]

Even with the news of the *Hiryu*'s loss Yamamoto continued to press on in the vain hope of bringing the American fleet to battle. Eventually though, he realized that it was hopeless, so around 3:00 the following morning, he ordered the entire operation scrapped and all ships to retire.

Two postscripts remained to the battle. Yamamoto had earlier ordered Vice Admiral Kurita of the Close Support Group to take his Cruiser Division 7 to carry out a night bombardment of Midway. Shortly after midnight these orders were cancelled and Kurita was directed to withdraw. Just as the ships were reversing direction a report was received that one of the lookouts had sighted a submarine. In the resulting confusion the cruiser *Mogami* collided with the *Mikuma*, causing extensive damage to both ships. Kurita left two destroyers behind to escort the damaged cruisers home at a reduced speed and made off at high speed with his remaining ships. On the afternoon of June 5, American planes located the small flotilla and attacked. The *Mikuma* was sunk and the *Mogami*'s upper decks shattered. Nevertheless, she managed to limp safely home.

The second postscript involves the *Yorktown*. Although heavily damaged, the ship remained afloat. Admiral Fletcher decided to attempt repairs in hopes of towing the carrier back to Pearl Harbor. Around 1:30 PM on June 6, the Japanese submarine I-168 spotted the carrier and fired a spread of torpedoes. The fish struck home. One of them also broke the back of the destroyer *Hammann*, which was tied up alongside giving aid to the stricken carrier. The *Hammann* sank immediately. A short while later, the *Yorktown* herself rolled over on its side and plunged beneath the waves.

As Nagumo leaned out over the bridge of the retreating *Nagara* he watched in silence as his once mighty carrier fleet burned before taking its final plunge. He was acutely aware of the ramifications. The back of the Japanese Navy was broken. Not only had four valuable ships been lost, many skilled pilots had lost their lives. These were irreplaceable.

The experts have called Midway the turning point in the entire Pacific War, and rightly so. No more would the awesome Japanese carrier fleet roam the Pacific leaving death and destruction in its wake. The Japanese Navy did not have the ability to recover from the blow.

Who was at fault for the debacle at Midway? Certainly Nagumo must shoulder a great deal of the burden. His indecisiveness at the crucial time was a major factor in the subsequent events of June 4, 1942. However, there were extenuating circumstances.

Nagumo approached Midway blind. No intelligence reports had been received by his fleet, so there was no way he could know of the American presence. In fact, the lack of intelligence indicated to Nagumo that just the opposite was true. Yamamoto's assumption that the American fleet was at sea was not forwarded to Nagumo. Neither were the reports of American attacks on Tanaka's convoy. Therefore, there was no way Nagumo could know that the secrecy of the entire operation was compromised. Instead, he steamed serenely on toward the fate that awaited him.

Another major factor contributing to the outcome of the battle was the splitting of the Japanese fleet. Of course, Nagumo had nothing to do with this. Yamamoto, with a powerful battle fleet, was six hundred miles to the rear of the carriers. One light carrier was with this force, another with Kondo's invasion force, and two others with the Aleutians strike force. Had these four ships been assigned to Nagumo and combined in one powerful striking force, perhaps the scales of victory would have tipped the other way. Then, too, there was the absence of the *Shokaku* and the *Zuikaku*. The damage incurred by these two ships in the Coral Sea served to keep them out of the battle completely. Thus the Battle of the Coral Sea had a direct influence on the outcome of the Battle of Midway. The presence of the *Shokaku* and the *Zuikaku* would have given Nagumo a two-to-one superiority.

The Imperial Navy now found itself faced with the task of rebuilding its carrier fleet, but it would never again be the same. It would be months before another viable force could be put together. When it was, the man selected to lead it was Chiuchi Nagumo.

Yamamoto accepted full responsibility for the defeat at Midway. He refused to blame anyone else. Despite the urgings of his staff, he would not hear of replacing Nagumo. Yamamoto knew that Nagumo was an immensely proud man. Being replaced would be tantamount to loss of face and might result in Nagumo's committing suicide. Thus Nagumo received a respite.

While the battle of the Coral Sea was taking place, Japanese forces seized the island of Tulagi in the Solomons and constructed a seaplane base there. As soon as their position was secure they jumped to the neighboring island of Guadalcanal and began to construct an airstrip. When the Americans learned of this latest Japanese move they scrapped their plans for operations elsewhere. Guadalcanal, Nimitz concluded, had to be seized. The U.S. Navy could not afford to have an enemy airfield so close to their lines of communication in the South Pacific. On August 7, 1942, therefore, General Alexander Vandergrift led a force of U.S. Marines ashore on Guadalcanal and Tulagi. The latter fell quickly, while on Guadalcanal the marines encountered little initial opposition and quickly moved inland, took the incomplete airfield, and renamed it Henderson Field.

Yamamoto was determined to hold on to Guadalcanal. After having restructured the fleet after the horrendous defeat at Midway, he had taken the Combined Fleet south to the naval base at Truk in the Carolines. Other units of the fleet were based at Rabaul on New Britain and at bases in the northern Solomons. Nagumo commanded the carriers of the fleet, but overall responsibility for operations at sea was vested in the hands of Admiral Nobutake Kondo.

Two days after the American invasion of Guadalcanal a Japanese cruiser force under Admiral Gunichi Mikawa destroyed an Allied cruiser force guarding the beachhead. Thanks to a Japanese air raid the previous day Admiral Fletcher had withdrawn his covering carriers to a position of safety and was powerless to intervene in the Battle of Savo Island.

Meanwhile, Yamamoto was planning another more ambitious operation. Reinforcements were hastily assembled, loaded aboard transports, and dispatched to Guadalcanal, intent on driving the Americans back into the sea. Kondo's fleet, supported by Nagumo's carriers, was put to sea to provide cover for the convoy.

Meanwhile American code breakers had concluded that the Japanese were preparing a major operation and the fleet was ready to move south. Nimitz ordered Fletcher to move his force, containing the carriers *Enterprise, Saratoga* and *Wasp* to the east of the Solomons and intercept the Japanese fleet moving south from Truk.

On August 23, the Japanese forces approached the Solomons. Admiral Tanaka, with his flagship *Jintsu* and three destroyers, provided the escort for the seven-ship troop convoy. Kondo's main force included six cruisers, ten destroyers, one battleship, and the seaplane carrier *Chitose*. A second force consisting of the light carrier *Ryujo*, the cruiser *Tone* and destroyers, sailed ahead of the main body. It was hoped that the *Ryujo*, by launching attack against Guadalcanal, could draw the American fleet into battle.

Nagumo's fleet was made up of the *Shokaku*, the *Zuikaku*, four battleships, four cruisers, and ten destroyers. A powerful force indeed.

Throughout the day of the 23rd the two enemy fleets probed for each other. Reconnaissance planes from Guadalcanal located the Japanese fleet, but the two opposing admirals were unable to get an accurate fix on each other. Consequently, around 6:00 that evening, Fletcher sent the *Wasp*, already low on fuel, south to refuel. The American force was thus reduced to two carriers.

Twelve hours later Kondo, who had reversed course after being sighted the previous day, turned south once more. The *Ryujo*, along with its escort, was detached to carry out her mission of attacking the American positions on Guadalcanal.

A little after 9:00 an American Catalina aircraft sighted the *Ryojo*'s group and reported that the Japanese carrier was at that moment located less than three hundred miles from the American force. Fletcher ordered a strike off.

An hour and a half later, Nagumo launched a two-carrier strike against the Americans, but thirty minutes prior to this, his own fleet had been discovered by one of the *Enterprise*'s scout planes. Upon receipt of the report that Nagumo's force had been located, Fletcher made an unsuccessful attempt to contact the strike en route toward *Ryujo* and divert it toward Nagumo. Unfortunately, *Saratoga*'s aircraft never received the message. Around 4:00 this formation pounced on the hapless *Ryujo* and quickly turned it into a blazing wreck. The Japanese carrier sank about six hours later.

Meanwhile, Nagumo's strike was winging its way towards Fletcher's force. At 4:30 the Japanese planes made contact. The *Enterprise* was hit by three bombs, which did heavy damage. Fortunately, skillful damage-control parties brought the ship's fires under control and shortly afterward the "Big E" was ready to receive planes. Heavy antiaircraft fire from Fletcher's escorting warships and the skill of his combat air patrol prevented further damage. As soon as all planes were back aboard, Fletcher reversed course and made off to the south. Kondo continued to pursue him, but shortly after midnight called off the chase and headed for Truk.

The next morning land-based planes from Guadalcanal attacked Tanaka. One transport and a destroyer were sunk and the *Jintsu* damaged. The reinforcement operation was called off.

The Battle of the Eastern Solomons was a tactical victory for the Americans. The reinforcements for Guadalcanal were turned back. In addition, the Japanese light carrier *Ryujo* was sunk. Nagumo, however, had conducted his phase of the battle with confidence and skill. On this occasion he had waited until the right moment before launching his strike. Only after he was absolutely sure of Fletcher's position did he commit himself. Although no American ships were lost, Fletcher was forced to withdraw after the damage to the *Enterprise*. The American commander's timidity and poor handling of his force resulted in his being shunted off to a shore command. It was small consolation, though, for the disaster at Midway.

Two months later Nagumo was handed another opportunity to avenge himself. Yamamoto was determined to destroy the American naval units guarding the approaches to Guadalcanal. Only after destruction could the island be reinforced with ease. Once naval superiority was achieved, the Japanese could drive the Americans from their foothold in the Solomons.

On October 22, the Combined Fleet was ordered to sea again, once more under Kondo's command. His force of heavy ships would form the van of the fleet that included two battleships, five cruisers, fourteen destroyers and the light carriers *Junyo* and *Hiyo*. It was hoped that the American forces would attack the vanguard, thereby exposing their position. Once this occurred, Nagumo, with the main force, could attack and destroy the American fleet. Nagumo's force was by far the most powerful. In addition to the veteran *Shokaku* and *Zuikaku*, he had the light carrier *Zuiho*, five cruisers, two battleships and sixteen destroyers.

Meanwhile, his old antagonist Fletcher had been replaced by Admiral Halsey. Admiral Nimitz had decided that Fletcher was not aggressive enough and that a change of leadership was called for. Halsey was probably America's most aggressive naval commander. He formed his two carrier groups into two task groups under Admirals Kinkaid and Murray. The heart of these two formations were the carriers *Enterprise* and *Hornet*, veterans of the Doolittle raid and Midway. The *Enterprise* had rejoined the fleet on October 24th, after having the damages suffered at the Eastern Solomons speedily repaired.

October 25 found the two fleets steaming directly toward each other. Around noon that day an American reconnaissance plane from Guadalcanal sighted Nagumo's force approximately 350 miles north of the American fleet. The *Enterprise* launched search planes to verify the location at around 1:30, and followed it up with a full strike an hour later.

Nagumo, however, was taking no chances. His force had spotted the American reconnaissance plane, so just around the time the Americans were launching their strike, Nagumo reversed course. As a result the American planes failed to locate the Japanese fleet. After dark, Nagumo turned south once more. Shortly after midnight his position was again reported by an American reconnaissance plane. An abortive one-plane attack lasting a few hours failed to damage the *Zuikaku* or to deter Nagumo from his goal.

At approximately 4:15 that morning Nagumo's battleships and cruisers launched their scout planes with orders to find the enemy fleet. Nagumo had bitter memories of what the lack of sufficient intelligence had meant to the Midway operation. Therefore, half an hour later, thirteen additional scout planes were launched from the carriers. He was taking no chances.

Meanwhile, the *Enterprise* launched a formation of scouting planes, each one armed with a five-hundred-pound bomb. If any of these managed to locate the Japanese fleet they were to attack only after reporting the enemy's position.

At 6:30 Nagumo was handed a radio dispatch informing him that the American fleet had been sighted by one of the scout planes. Unfortunately the message made no mention of the size of the enemy fleet. Half an hour later though, one of the *Shokaku*'s scouts reported the presence of a large enemy fleet including a carrier. This was the message Nagumo was waiting for.

In anticipation of locating the U.S. carriers early, Nagumo had directed the carriers to have their planes armed, fueled and waiting on the flight decks. Fifteen minutes after receipt of the sighting report, a force of forty bombers escorted by twenty-seven fighters was winding its way south. Nagumo had struck first. Kinkaid's strike from the *Hornet* was not launched until a quarter of an hour later.

Each of the two fleets was a beehive of activity. Second strikes were being readied by both sides when, at 7:40, two of the *Enterprise*'s scout planes dove out of the clouds and unloaded their bombs on the *Zuiho,* tearing a fifty-foot hole in her flight deck. Although her speed was unimpaired, the *Zuiho* found herself unable to launch or recover planes. Nagumo ordered her back to Truk. Once more the Americans had managed to land the first blow. Nevertheless, Nagumo, although visibly upset, pressed on. Precisely on schedule, at 8:00, the *Shokaku* and the *Zuikaku* launched their second waves.

During the next few hours events occurred rapidly. Shortly after the Japanese launched their second strike, the *Hornet* and the *Enterprise* launched theirs. In fact, the *Enterprise*'s outbound strike passed within sight of the Japanese planes heading in the opposite direction. Around 9:00, the Japanese planes hit pay dirt.

When the American carriers located the incoming Japanese attack the *Enterprise* hurriedly sought the refuge of a nearby rain squall. This left the entire Japanese flight free to concentrate on the *Hornet*. That ship was not as fortunate at her sister. Every Japanese plane in the formation swarmed around the vulnerable American flat top. The *Hornet*'s combat air patrol and the antiaircraft fire of her escorts managed to bring down twenty-five of the attackers, but there were just too many of them. Four of the Japanese planes scored direct hits with their bombs and two torpedo planes struck through to successfully unload their lethal cargoes against the side of the helpless ship. These smashed into the *Hornet*'s engine room. Ten minutes after the attack had begun, the *Hornet* was dead in the water, burning furiously and listing heavily. It took over an hour to get the fires under control. When this was accomplished, the cruiser *Northampton* moved in to effect a tow. Despite superb damage control though, it was painfully obvious that the ship that had launched Doolittle's raiders was in dire straits.

While the *Hornet*'s crew were struggling to save their ship, her pilots were exacting retribution. At 9:30 they found the *Shokaku* and dove for the attack. Once more Nagumo found himself gaping in helpless awe as bombs rained down on his flagship. Four direct hits tore open the flight deck and started numerous fires. Fortunately, most of the ship's planes were aloft and escaped the fate of the planes at Midway.

Then it was Nagumo's turn again. His second strike located the *Enterprise* half an hour after the attack on the *Shokaku*. The Japanese pilots managed to score two hits, one on the forward part of the ship and one on the forward elevator. Another attacker dove his burning plane into the destroyer *Smith*, killing eight men and wounding twenty-three. Prior to the attack the submarine I-21 had torpedoed the destroyer *Porter*, another member of the *Enterprise*'s screen. That ship had to be abandoned and sunk by gunfire by its own colleagues.

The ordeal was not over for the Americans. An hour later a strike from the *Junyo* arrived over the *Enterprise* group. The carrier itself managed to avoid further damage, but the battleship *South Dakota* and the cruiser *San Juan* took bomb hits. Fortunately, damage to the two ships was minimal.

Nagumo was not satisfied. Thirsting for revenge, he launched another strike in midafternoon as soon as his planes were refueled and rearmed. Two hours out from their mother ships, this flight pounced on the hapless *Hornet* again.

The Americans were unsuccessfully attempting to tow the stricken carrier. Thanks to the efforts of her crews, however, steam was raised and the great ship managed to get under way at a greatly reduced rate of speed. Then Nagumo's third strike arrived. Another bomb hit and a further torpedo in her side and the *Hornet* was finished. Her captain gave the order to abandon ship. A few hours later, Admiral Kinkaid ordered her sunk by escorting destroyers.

Meanwhile, the Japanese were aware of the *Hornet*'s plight. Kondo sent a squadron of destroyers racing to the scene. What a coup it would be if the *Hornet* could be towed triumphantly into Tokyo Bay and displayed for all to view! Early that evening the Japanese destroyers arrived on the scene and drove off two American destroyers who, try as they might with torpedoes, had simply been unable to sink the *Hornet*. The ship was ablaze from stem to stern and all efforts by the Japanese to affect a tow proved unfeasible. With some reluctance, the Japanese destroyers launched their torpedoes and finally sent the *Hornet* to her watery grave.

The American fleet was hard pressed. Faced with the loss of one carrier and with the other heavily damaged, Kinkaid withdrew. Kondo knew that the Japanese had won a significant victory and was not anxious to press his luck. Late that night, after a halfhearted pursuit, he gave the order to withdraw.

The Battle of Santa Cruz was without a decisive Japanese victory. Thanks to Nagumo's aggressiveness the Americans were kept constantly off balance and had been dealt a crippling blow. As a result, the Japanese Army units on Guadalcanal were able to continue the struggle for three more bloody months. Nagumo had learned the lessons of Midway well. He made sure that enough search planes were used; then, as soon as the sighting reports were received, the first strike was launched immediately. Unlike Midway, where he waited for the results of the initial strike and held half of the total complement of aircraft in readiness for use elsewhere, at Santa Cruz the second strike was launched as soon as it was ready. There was no hesitation or indecisiveness. Every plane except those required for the protection of the fleet was directed against the enemy. Finally, when he knew that the Americans were suffering, Nagumo did not hesitate to launch additional strikes in an attempt to deliver the knockout blow. The onset of darkness was the only deterrent to perhaps an even more decisive victory. Unfortunately, the triumph was short-lived.

Despite the heroic efforts of the Japanese forces in the waters around Guadalcanal, the island was eventually abandoned early in 1943. Immediately after the Battle of Santa Cruz the Japanese carriers returned to Japan for urgently required repairs. Thanks to the losses at Midway there was no carrier reserve available to carry on the struggle. Admiral Nagumo never went to sea again with the carrier fleet.

Nagumo was a tired man. At Santa Cruz he seemed to have caught his second wind, but there was no denying the fact that his energy was spent. Those who had known him before the war were shocked at his appearance. His face was lined, he walked with a stooping gait, and he seemed perpetually weary. The old spirit was gone.

Upon reaching Japan with his fleet, Nagumo was handed new orders. Yamamoto, never completely satisfied with Nagumo's performance, finally gave in to the demands of the latter's detractors, and using poor health as an excuse, transferred Nagumo to a shore command. He was appointed commander of the Sasebo Naval District. Seven months later Nagumo was reassigned to command of the Kure Naval District and pronounced himself fit and ready to go to sea once more. Claiming that his health was restored, Nagumo requested another seagoing command. Unfortunately, by that time Admiral Yamamoto himself was dead. His successor, Admiral Koga, was not convinced that Nagumo had completely recovered. His supicions were confirmed by the observations of Nagumo's old friend, Captain Hara. The latter had dinner with the admiral near the end of November, 1943.

> "His health was restored. He looked much better than the sorry man I had seen at Truk a year earlier. But his conversation lacked spirit. In fact, all through our long dinner he urged me to speak of my experiences. I did not know it at the time but despite his return to health, this wrinkled old officer was forlorn."[9]

The veteran carrier commander did receive his seagoing command, but it was not what he had hoped for. Nagumo was appointed commander of the First Fleet, a training command. He held this appointment from November 1943 until March of the following year when he was sent to Saipan in the Marianas as commander-in-chief, Central Pacific and the 14th Air Fleet. By this time, however, Japan's fortunes were unquestionably on the wane. Vast armadas of American carriers roamed the Pacific uncontested, leaving death and destruction in their wake.

On Saipan Nagumo had little with which to counter any American advance. Although the title was impressive, in reality his command consisted of a handful of small patrol craft, an infrequent destroyer, and a few auxiliaries.

Eventually, the Americans got around to the Marianas. On June 15, 1944, U.S. Marines fought ashore at Saipan. Nagumo stood helplessly by as Ozawa led the Japanese carriers in their last major offensive during the Battle of the Philippine Sea. Since the defense of the island itself was primarily an army show, Nagumo took no part in the action (*See Map 10*).

Despite a fanatical defense, the Japanese defenders of Saipan were steadily pushed back. By the end of the month only a small perimeter on the northern portion of the island remained in Japanese hands. Nagumo knew that the battle was lost. Surrender, however, was out of the question for a samurai. On July 1, after bidding his staff farewell and wishing them the best, the proud admiral put a loaded pistol to his head and pulled the trigger. Thus perished one of the most gallant Japanese officers.

How does Nagumo stack up as a commander? There have been many critics of his failure to follow up the attack at Pearl Harbor, so as to destroy the American installations. Had he done so, the American fleet would have been required to retreat all the way to the West Coast of the United States. But this alone would not have altered the final outcome of the war. It may have delayed the inevitable for six months, but certainly not much more. One must remember, too, that this was Nagumo's first experience with handling carriers in combat. In fact, it was a first for the entire Japanese fleet. Taking this into consideration, all in all the Pearl Harbor attack was an unqualified success.

At Midway Nagumo was handicapped by the total lack of intelligence. True, his indecisiveness was one of the major causes of defeat. However, what if *Tone*'s scout plane had been launched on time and had found the American fleet? Would he then have reacted differently? There is enough evidence to support the claim that he would have.

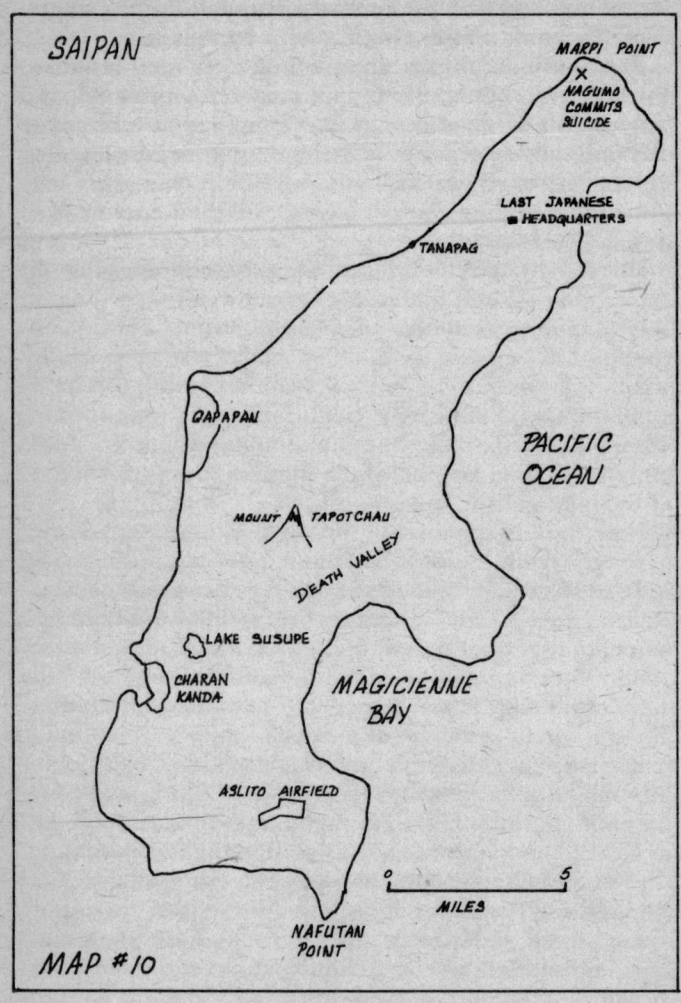

At the Eastern Solomons and at Santa Cruz Nagumo's performance clearly demonstrated that he could profit from his mistakes and experience. He was confident and aggressive, and handled his forces in an intelligent manner. Unfortunately, he was also worn out by that time.

It was the Americans who profited most from Nagumo. At Midway their performance was uncoordinated and spotty. At that time they were still novices at conducting fleet engagements requiring the use of carriers. By learning from Nagumo's dispositions and his mistakes, the Americans were eventually able to gain the upper hand.

All in all, there can be little doubt that Admiral Chiuchi Nagumo was indeed one of the great commanders of World War II, despite his ignominious end.

Chapter Four

Until the eve of World War II the world's navies operated primarily on the "big gun" or surface ship theory. The aircraft carrier did not begin to receive serious attention until the 1930s. Even then, a mere handful of enthusiasts boarded the carrier bandwagon. Even fewer of these envisioned the great carrier battles of the 1940s where huge fleets would duel each other while the opposing ships never came in sight of each other. Thus, the between-war period was the era of the specialist, *i.e.*, submarines, battleships, destroyers, and only later, aircraft carriers.

One such specialist was Admiral Raizo Tanaka of the Imperial Japanese Navy. Until he was abruptly placed on the shelf, Tanaka was one of the foremost destroyer tacticians of the war. During the first year of the conflict wherever Japanese operations called for destroyers to play a vital role, Tanaka was at the fore. His brilliance was acknowledged by friend and foe alike. In fact, many prominent naval historians, to this date, insist that Tanaka had few peers.

Raizo Tanaka was approaching his fiftieth birthday by the time the Japanese went to war with the United States. At the time, unaware of what lay ahead, he was contemplating his retirement. Perhaps after the China conflict was resolved. Once that war was over, the navy could afford to part with his services.

Tanaka could look back on his career with a sense of pride—the series of naval schools, the many months at sea, and the assortment of appointments in all types of ships before attaining enough seniority to find a permanent home in destroyers. For almost twenty years those small ships were his home.

During those years Tanaka contributed mightily to the creation of what was by the 1930s, a formidable force. He had conducted extensive experiments with the new Japanese torpedo during its initial stages. These 24-inch oxygen-fueled missiles of destruction far exceeded anything in the arsenals of any potential enemy. Leaving little wakes to be spotted by enemy warships thanks to their oxygen fuel, they packed a wallop almost two times that of those used by the Americans and the British. Even more important was the fact that the Japanese "long lances" had a range almost four times that of the torpedoes used by the Western nations.

Not only had Tanaka aided in the development of this weapon, he drilled his crews long and hard until they became proficient in its use. The torpedo was the backbone of any destroyer's weaponry. Even the threat of their use could cause captains of much larger ships such as cruisers and battleships to pay close attention to the activity of enemy destroyers.

Not only were the conventional tactics developed to a high state of efficiency, the handling of destroyers in night actions became a speciality, indeed a trademark, of Tanaka. In fact, the entire Japanese fleet became masters of night action. With their superior optical equipment, range finders, binoculars, etc., the Japanese navy in night actions was more formidable than one could reasonably expect. In short, during World War II, the Japanese sailor was equal to or superior to almost every opponent at night. This superiority was only offset by technological advances such as radar. Sometimes, though, even radar was not enough to offset the advantage. Tanaka had been part of this development.

During the first week in October, 1941, Tanaka, by now a rear admiral, sailed his 2nd Destroyer Squadron into Hiroshima Bay where virtually all of the Combined Fleet lay at anchor. On the 9th, the commanders of all ships were summoned to a conference aboard the *Nagato*, flagship of the fleet. There, they were addressed by the commander-in-chief of the Combined Fleet, Admiral Yamamoto. The assembled captains sat in awed silence as Yamamoto summarized the world situation.

> "The current situation suggests Japan may be forced to take up arms against America, Britain, Australia, and the Netherlands rather than succumb to strangulation through their blockade."[1]

For many of those present this was the first hint that war was imminent. Still others considered it the culmination of their wildest dreams. A handful of the more senior officers, of course, had been privy to the secret for some months.

Admiral Nagumo's mighty carrier fleet was selected to make the first strike against the American fleet at Pearl Harbor. Success there would achieve a primary goal: destruction of the enemy fleet. After that America's bases in the Philippines would have to be eliminated before moving on to one of the primary objectives, indeed perhaps one of the main reasons for going to war. If the enemy were unable to use the Philippines to harass Japanese shipping, the latter could take advantage of the vital natural resources of Malaya and the Dutch East Indies. In fact, conquest of these regions was one of Japan's foremost reasons for going to war in the first place. An American embargo of fuel oil, iron, and other essential natural resources was threatening to slowly strangle Japan. If she could not obtain these critical items via free trade, she would have to seize her own sources. The Dutch East Indies were among the richest areas in the world of those items Japan considered essential.

Not all ships could accompany Nagumo to Hawaii. Since secrecy was paramount the fleet would have to be as small as possible to insure against detection. However, since this operation was such a momentous one, many captains and squadron commanders vied for inclusion in this attack force. Most were disappointed. Tanaka was one of the latter, although, being the type of person he was, he did not attempt to push his prospects. Instead, secure in the knowledge that the entire Combined Fleet would eventually see its share of action, Tanaka was prepared to carry out whatever assignment he was given to the best of his ability. Of course, since war was expected shortly, any thoughts of retirement were shunted aside.

Tanaka's 2nd Destroyer Flotilla was assigned to the Philippine operation. The flotilla was comprised of the 15th Destroyer Division with the destroyers *Kuroshio*, *Oyashio*, *Hayashio*, and *Natsushio* along with the 16th Destroyer Division made up of the destroyers *Hatsukaze*, *Amatsukaze*, *Yukikaze*, and *Tokitsukaze*. The ships were all of the new Kagero class, capable of 35½ knots speed and mounting six 5-inch guns to complement their eight 24-inch torpedo tubes. As was the custom in the Japanese navy, the Flotilla Commander flew his flag in a light cruiser. In Tanaka's case it was the *Jintsu*, an eighteen-year-old veteran. Tanaka took his force to the Kuriles in mid-November, where it made final preparations for action. On the 26th, the flotilla sailed for Palau, the Japanese staging area. On the 1st of December, the graceful line of Tanaka's squadron entered the harbor at Palau and dropped anchor.

The following day Tanaka called a meeting of all his captains aboard the *Jintsu*. He was a precise and demanding leader and had not risen to the rank of rear admiral by being careless. Thus, he wanted to be sure that all the captains understood every letter of their orders. Tanaka reiterated that no offensive action was to be initiated until after Nagumo's strike against the American fleet. That operation had to be cloaked in secrecy and was not to be compromised. This brought up the inevitable question of what to do in case an enemy submarine was sighted, since the Philippine invasion force would be at sea prior to Nagumo's strike. On that point there was no option. Tanaka bluntly told his captains to sink any prowling submarines regardless of country of origin.

The next few days were ones of frantic activity, with final maneuvers and preparations rating a high priority. Finally, on the 6th, Tanaka led his fleet out to sea to patrol off Mindanao. The entire South Philippine Force to which Tanaka was attached was under the overall command of Admiral Takagi. Tanaka's destroyers would provide close escort for the troop convoys while Takagi himself, with the heavy cruisers *Haguro*, *Myoko*, *Nachi*, and the light carrier

Ryujo, provided covering support.

By the 8th of the month, the force was off its destination. Tanaka sent the 15th Division into Davao harbor to search for American shipping. The destroyers found none. Meanwhile, an assault force of one cruiser, four destroyers, one seaplane carrier and seven transports left Palau.

The next few days were busy ones. On the 10th Tanaka's flotilla rendezvoused with the assault force for the final run in. That night he detached the *Oyashio* and the *Kuroshio* to cover a mine-laying operation in San Bernadino Strait while his own *Jintsu* led the rest of the 15th Division to cover a similar operation in Surigao Strait. The following morning Tanaka took up station offshore as the 16th Infantry Division embarked from their transports at Legaspi on southern Luzon. After patrolling offshore for a few days while the army consolidated its beachhead, the entire forced hurried back to Palau where it picked up a second invasion convoy destined for Mindanao.

Meanwhile, a second strong Japanese fleet hovered closely near landing beaches in Malaya while still other formations covered landings on Northern Luzon. All this while Nagumo was returning from the successful raid on Pearl Harbor. Thus the Japanese navy was spread over the width of the Pacific, but the Allies were too weak to resist, since they had been taken totally by surprise.

On the 19th, Tanaka was back off the Philippines as his destroyers covered landings at Davao on Mindanao. The next day, the Japanese secured the area and began immediate construction of a seaplane base.

Then it was back to Palau to escort the 56th Brigade's nine transports to the island of Jolo. This time Tanaka's force was bolstered by the light carrier *Ryujo* and the seaplane carrier *Chitose*. On Christmas Eve, the troops were put ashore and quickly overran the island. As at Davao, the Japanese planned to use Jolo for a seaplane base.

Finally, after over three weeks at sea, Tanaka took his flotilla back to Palau for a hard-earned but brief respite. After the fall of the Philippines, the great prize of the

Dutch East Indies was next. Back at the Palau anchorage, Tanaka summoned his captains to the *Jintsu*. During an informal discussion of the just-concluded operation, he praised their efforts, particularly the teamwork of both destroyer divisions. Close cooperation between the elements of the squadron was a subject dear to Tanaka's heart. Coordination of effort was a tactic repeatedly practiced and stressed by the entire formation. Tanaka was a firm believer in the fact that close teamwork could overcome superior force and result in the Japanese having a distinct advantage when the odds were equal.

January 9th, 1942, found the Japanese forces at sea again. Once more the plan was an elaborate one calling for a wide dispersal of forces to conduct simultaneous operations at key points in the Dutch East Indies. Borneo, Bali, Sumatra, Timor, Celebes, and other key points were to be captured before combining to concentrate on Java. Tanaka's flotilla was assigned to escort six transports, crammed with troops of the Sasebo Landing Force, to Menado on northern Celebes. The overall operation was commanded by Admiral Kubo who, in addition to Tanaka's force, commanded the cruiser *Nagara*.

The landings were a complete success. Aided by a parachute drop earlier in the day, the troops waded ashore and quickly overcame the sporadic resistance encountered.

Using Menado as a staging area, the Japanese tentacles reached out for additional territory. Tanaka's squadron covered the landings at Kendai on January 24th and Ambon Island on the 31st. Landings on the latter were bitterly contested by a combined Dutch and Australian force. During the height of the battle, Tanaka risked his ships by ordering them to move in close to shore to evacuate the wounded. This humanitarian act earned him the respect and admiration of the Japanese army.

In February, Sumatra and Timor fell to the advancing Japanese forces. Finally, near the end of the month, a large force began assembling at Balikpappan on Eastern Borneo. The invasion of Java was next. On the 25th, this force set sail for Eastern Java. Meanwhile, the ABDA* fleet was poised waiting to strike at the Japanese convoys. From its base at Surabaya, Admiral Doorman led his fleet to sea on the 27th after reports of a Japanese convoy approaching the northern coast of Java.

The Dutch Admiral Karel Doorman was operating at a distinct disadvantage from the beginning. His fleet consisted of ships from the Netherlands, England, the United States, and Australia. Not only was language a barrier, but the ships were not used to operating with each other. In addition, both of his heavy cruisers, *Exeter* (G.B.) and *Houston* (U.S.), were minus the use of one turret, the result of bomb damage earlier in the week. Despite these handicaps, the ABDA fleet was determined to turn back the Japanese invasion.

Escorting the forty-one troop-laden transports to northern Java was an impressive array of warships. Admiral Takagi with the heavy cruisers *Nachi* and *Haguro* was in overall command. Besides Tanaka's 2nd Destroyer Flotilla the force included Admiral Nishimura's 4th Destroyer Flotilla of six destroyers and the light cruiser *Naka*.

The passage to northern Java was an eventful one. On the 26th a Dutch hospital ship hove into sight. Tanaka sent two of his destroyers racing to intercept her. When the Dutch ship's identity was established, he ordered it taken to the rear, out of harm's way. The next day, an American B-17 bomber discovered the Japanese force. As it maneuvered for the attack, the *Jintsu* put up a furious barrage of fire that drove the American plane off.

On the 27th, the Japanese convoy approached the Java coast precisely on schedule. Landings would begin the next morning. Just before noon, two more American bombers made a futile attack on the formation. No hits were recorded.

Later that same afternoon, Takagi received reports from Japanese reconnaissance planes the Doorman's fleet was

*The designation given the American, British, Dutch, Australian force.

speeding north to intercept. Takagi was mildly surprised since his intelligence had led him to believe that earlier bombing attacks had left the Allied fleet incapable of interfering. Now, here it was steaming to intercept him.

Takagi ordered the transports off to the north escorted by two destroyers. Unencumbered by the slow-moving transports, he prepared to do battle. If Doorman was looking for a fight, Takagi would be happy to oblige.

The Japanese warships were deployed in a horseshoe-shaped formation. Tanaka in the *Jintsu* led the eastern leg of the shoe while Nishimura's *Naka* was the point ship of the other leg. At the base was Takagi with his two heavy cruisers.

Around 4:00 lookouts on *Jintsu* sighted the Allied fleet, barely visible on the eastern horizon. Fifteen minutes later, the British destroyer *Electra*, steaming with two others in line abreast, sighted the Japanese force. The Allied destroyer, however, only spotted Tanaka's column. Takagi's and Nishimura's formations were still out of sight. A few minutes later, after Doorman's force had made contact, the *Nachi* and the *Haguro* opened fire.

The fight quickly became a landscape of milling ships as each side maneuvered to gain the most advantageous position. Tanaka boldly led his column forward in a daring attack, only to be thwarted when Doorman ordered a change of course and increased the range. Although many near misses were sighted near the *Electra*, Tanaka's attack failed to do any real damage.

Eventually, additional course changes found the two fleets steaming parallel with each other, Doorman's force inboard between Takagi and the Java coast. The Japanese commander ordered Nishimura's ships and his own cruisers to launch a torpedo attack. Once again the Japanese attack was unsuccessful as Doorman changed course once more in an attempt to close the range so that the guns of his light cruisers could be brought to bear.

Thus far the battle had consumed the greater part of an hour. Shortly after 5:00, Tanaka again raced in to launch a torpedo attack against the Allied line. At the same time, the 8-inch guns of the *Haguro* rang out. One of these hit the *Exeter* and forced it out of line. Thinking that the leading ship, the *DeRuyter,* Doorman's flagship, had ordered another change in course, the rest of the Allied line, sailing in line ahead, followed the *Exeter*'s example. The British cruiser, however, her speed drastically reduced, was out of the fight.

Meanwhile, in the confusion, one of Tanaka's torpedoes found a target. The Dutch destroyer *Kortenaer* took one squarely amidships and broke in half. Doorman ordered a retirement.

Tanaka now ordered his ships to close on the damaged *Exeter*. The destroyer *Electra* moved to intervene. Soon the British destroyer and the *Jintsu* were locked in a fierce but uneven gun duel. The *Jintsu* was hit once and was damaged slightly but in such an uneven duel the outcome was a foregone conclusion. A few minutes after the fight began, *Jintsu*'s shells began to rain down on the hapless *Electra* and within five minutes the gallant British ship was on fire and had begun to sink. However, her sacrifice was not in vain. The *Exeter* took advantage of the uneven fight and made good her escape to Surabaya.

Doorman began to pull off. Takagi, recognizing his adversaries' intention, took his two cruisers in pursuit. Tanaka's column also closed the enemy and launched a spread of torpedoes that all ran wide of their target. In the interim, the Japanese transports returned to the battle zone.

Takagi, concerned lest the distance between his ships and the transports became too great, broke off the chase and retired on the convoy. He was not about to be lured away from his primary responsibility, protection of the convoy.

Tanaka was fuming. After all the months of intense practice with the mightiest and most accurate torpedo in the world, his entire spread had failed to find a target. Obviously, more work needed to be done.

Shortly after withdrawing, Doorman again reversed course and began probing for the Japanese convoy. For the next few hours what remained of the ABDA force searched the darkness for the vulnerable transports. Tanaka had wisely positioned his formation between the convoy and the enemy fleet. Should the Allies manage to find the formation, Tanaka was ideally positioned to intervene.

Around 9:30, Doorman's formation received another severe jolt. The British destroyer *Jupiter* blew up and sank when it struck a mine. Half an hour earlier, the four old American destroyers of Doorman's force had left the formation for the return trip to Surabaya due to a shortage of fuel.

Even these events failed to deter the brave Dutch admiral. He continued to grope in the darkness for the enemy convoy until around 11:00 PM, when ships were sighted. Unfortunately, the ships were not the troop transports, but instead were the *Nachi* and the *Haguro*. Tanaka was miles away escorting the convoy safely through the Java Sea towards its final destination. A brief gun duel followed during which neither side scored a hit. But Takagi was stalking his prey.

Half an hour after the initial contact the two Japanese cruisers launched a spread of torpedoes. Fifteen minutes later the *DeRuyter* erupted in a ball of flame and went dead in the water. A few minutes later the *Java* suffered the same fate. Both ships quickly sank with heavy loss of life as the remaining ABDA ships beat a hasty retreat.

The next day the *Houston* and the *Perth* were caught by the Japanese cruisers the *Mogami* and the *Myoko* as they attempted to escape to Australia via the Sunda Strait. Both ships were reduced to burning wrecks and plunged beneath the waves. *Exeter* later suffered a like fate. Thus ended the Battle of the Java Sea.

Tanaka was unhappy with the performance of his squadron during the battle. He berated his captains for so many torpedo misses. Of all the torpedoes launched, only one had found a target in the bowels of the *Kortenaer*. The *Electra* had succumbed to the gunfire of the *Jintsu*. Nevertheless, the formation's aggressive behavior was the cause of Doorman's frequent alterations of course and added to the confusion in the Allied fleet. Whenever

Doorman attempted to close with the Japanese formation, Tanaka's destroyers seemed to appear as if by magic and drove him off. Thanks to the Battle of the Java Sea, the Allies had no ships worthy of mention with which to oppose the Japanese in Southeast Asia. The fall of the Dutch East Indies was therefore a foregone conclusion. Java fell on March 9, 1942.

The 2nd Destroyer Flotilla remained in the Southeast until April 17, when Tanaka received orders to bring his ships home to Japan. Yamamoto, meanwhile, was putting the finishing touches on yet another one of his grandiose schemes.

While the destroyer flotilla lay at anchor in Kure, rumors began to circulate of an ambitious operation aimed at the capture of Midway. Tanaka harbored reservations regarding the feasibility of such an ambitious adventure. After six months of war Japan had achieved every one of her projected goals. Just as Yamamoto had predicted, she had run wild. To bite off more than one could chew was to court disaster.

Tanaka expressed his reservations during a conference with his captains. When Captain Hara of the *Amatsukaze* asked Tanaka if the Midway plan was a fact, the admiral replied, "As a matter of fact, I am not sure of it. I hope it's untrue."[2]

The plan was a fact. On May 21, *Jintsu* led six destroyers out of harbor for the four-day voyage to Saipan. Tanaka had been chosen to command the escort for the troop convoy from Saipan to Midway.

Like the earlier Japanese operations, the Midway plan called for precise coordination and timing, as various elements of the fleet were scattered. Sailing from different points, these elements would be mutually supportive and were eventually to link up for the final invasion of Midway once that island was neutralized and any American naval forces in the vicinity disposed of. The makeup of the Japanese fleet for the Midway operation is covered in the chapter on Nagumo and need not be repeated here. So too is the actual Battle of Midway. Therefore, only Tanaka's role will be covered here.

On the morning of May 27, an armada of ships left the anchorage at Saipan. Twelve transports carried five thousand troops destined for the anticipated attack against Midway. In addition to the troop transports, eight other ships vital to the operation, such as oilers and minesweepers, were part of the formation. The seaplane carrier *Chitose* and her escort, the destroyer *Hayashio*, were part of the escort. Tanaka was in overall command of the escorting force with his two veteran destroyer divisions from the South Pacific, the 15th and 16th Destroyer Divisions. The escort was strengthened by the addition of the 18th Destroyer Division, comprised of the destroyers *Arare*, *Kagero*, *Shiranui*, and *Kasumi*.

At the same time a covering force of heavier ships, commanded by Admiral Kurita, left Guam. This force consisted of the 7th Cruiser Squadron with four heavy cruisers and two destroyers. Kurita's force was to rendezvous with Tanaka's at a point west of Midway for the final assault.

The slow-moving formation plodded eastward toward its destination without incident until June 3rd. Around 6:00 that morning a patrolling American float plane discovered Tanaka's force about six hundred miles south of Midway. Tanaka immediately radioed Yamamoto, who was aboard the battleship *Yamato* with the main body of the fleet. Tanaka informed his commander that the cat was out of the bag—he had been sighted. Unfortunately, Yamamoto never informed Nagumo's carriers that the invasion convoy had been detected. The commander-in-chief assumed that Nagumo could monitor Tanaka's transmissions. Of course this was not true, and Nagumo sailed blindly into the Battle of Midway.

Now that the occupation force was discovered, Tanaka knew that it was only a matter of time before the Americans made him the object of their attention. He was right. Late in the afternoon a formation of B-17s flew over the convoy. As soon as the enemy planes were sighted Tanaka ordered the fleet to begin a predetermined series of evasive maneuvers aimed at throwing off the aim of the American bombardiers. The skillful evasive tactics proved successful and the Americans' bombs fell harmlessly into the sea. Conversely, despite a heavy barrage of antiaircraft fire, no hits were obtained on the bombers.

Tanaka now sensed that the Americans would do everything in their power to contest the invasion. He never did have complete confidence in the venture and during the lull of the preceding weeks he was able to think of even more reasons why the plan might fail. With his presence discovered, his reservations deepened even further. Consequently, he spent a restless night aboard the *Jintsu*.

The next morning Tanaka listened incredulously to the radio reports of the systematic destruction of Nagumo's carrier force. Nevertheless, a message was received ordering him to proceed with the attack. An hour later, however, this order was cancelled and the transports were ordered to return to base. But Tanaka was directed to proceed with his destroyers and carry out a bombardment of Midway.

The admiral was furious. If the Americans possessed enough power to annihilate Nagumo's powerful force, what could his puny destroyers hope to accomplish?

Fortunately, just before midnight, Tanaka received contrasting orders telling him to join up with the main fleet. The entire Midway operation was cancelled and the Japanese fleet limped home to lick its wounds.

On the 14th of July, Yamamoto announced a sweeping reorganization of the fleet. As commander-in-chief of the Combined Fleet he would retain personal command of the First Fleet. Tanaka was assigned to Admiral Kondo's Second Fleet. Nagumo remained in command of the carriers now redesignated the Third Fleet. Admiral Mikawa was elevated to command of the newly created Eighth Fleet.

Three weeks later, on August 7th, the Americans launched Operation Watchtower, the invasion of Guadalcanal. In May of that year the Japanese had captured Tulagi in the lower Solomon Islands. A few weeks later they sent a construction force to the neighboring island of Guadalcanal and began to build an airstrip. This

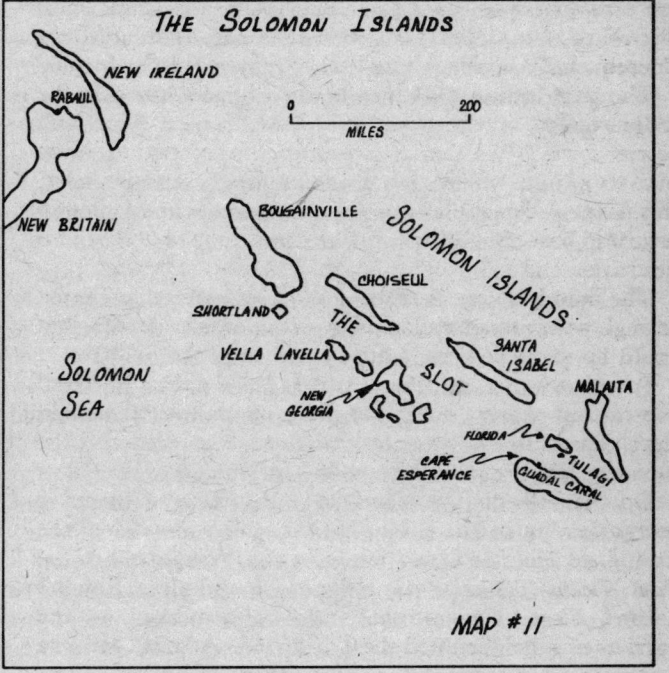

forced the commander-in-chief of the U.S. Pacific Fleet, Admiral Nimitz, to reconsider his plans for a counteroffensive, in order to eliminate the threat to the flank of his supply route.

In the interim, Mikawa's fleet was ordered to Rabaul, the Japanese base on New Britain in the Bismarck Archipelago. Consequently, when the Americans launched their invasion, Japan had a strong formation ideally poised to strike back (*See Map 11*).

The Solomons are a twin chain of tropical islands northeast of New Guinea. For the most part the entire chain consists of steaming, jungle-clad islands featuring marshy swamps. Situated just below the equator, the climate is atrocious.

"The heat, humidity, and torrential rains are never ending, and malaria-bearing mosquitoes and a host of tropical diseases thrive in the lush jungles."[3]

Running from northwest to southeast, the chain of islands is bisected by a sea passage known as "the Slot." The southern exit is dominated by the large islands of Guadalcanal to the south and Malaita to the north. San Cristobal Island sits a little further south directly astride the exit.

The strait between Malaita and Guadalcanal is dotted with the smaller islands of Florida, Savo, Sealark, and Tulagi. Between Florida and Guadalcanal is a broad expanse of water heretofore known as "Ironbottom Sound," so called because of the large number of ships soon to be resting on the ocean floor there. Thus began one of the longest and bloodiest conflicts of the war: the six-month-long battle for Guadalcanal (*See Map 12*).

The American invasion force was protected by a force of carriers commanded by Admiral Fletcher, veteran of the battles of Midway and the Coral Sea. Although the U.S. Marines met little initial resistance and quickly captured the incomplete Japanese airstrip, Fletcher was fearful of exposing his carriers to nighttime Japanese aerial raids from

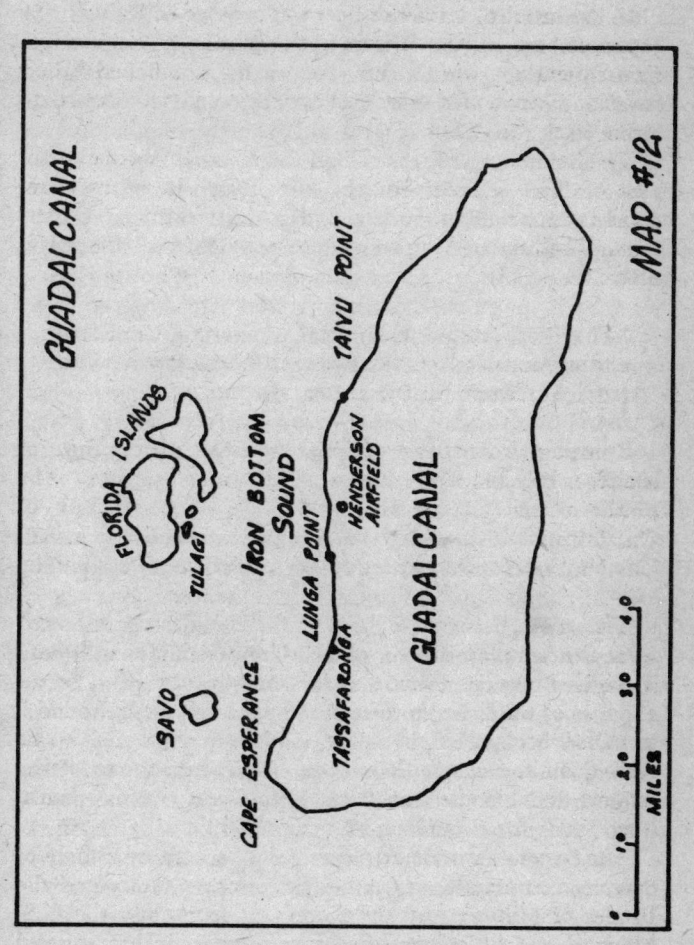

the north. Consequently, at night he drew his valuable carriers out of range of Japanese aircraft and left the American transports unprotected except for a force of cruisers and destroyers patrolling the waters between Tulagi and Guadalcanal.

With his target, the vulnerable American transports, at their unloading positions off the beach, Admiral Mikawa brought elements of his Eighth Fleet into Ironbottom Sound on the night of August 8th. Shortly after midnight he made contact with the Allied force patrolling between Savo and Tulagi. With the element of surprise on his side Mikawa's force of cruisers and destroyers inflicted heavy damage on the USS *Chicago* and left HMAS. *Canberra* ablaze and sinking. Mikawa then maneuvered around Savo and caught the three American cruisers guarding the area between that island and Guadalcanal napping. Once again, taking the Americans totally by surprise, the Japanese force blasted the American cruisers *Astoria*, *Quincy*, and *Vincennes* into scrap metal. With their covering force destroyed, the American transports were sitting ducks, unprotected and vulnerable.

Then Mikawa did an incredible thing. With nothing left to stop him, satisfied that he had just won a great naval battle, Mikawa reversed course and headed back up the Slot, any opportunity for an even greater victory lost forever.

Yamamoto was visibly upset by Mikawa's failure. A great victory had been achieved, but the American invasion fleet, the primary objective of the entire operation, remained intact.

Meanwhile, the commander-in-chief brought the First and Third Fleets south to Truk. Kondo's Second Fleet was already operating in that area. Yamamoto was determined to dislodge the American forces on Guadalcanal, but he knew that the Japanese forces already on the island were insufficient for the task.

Availability of troops was no problem at that point. Those units originally scheduled for the occupation of Midway were sitting idle at Guam and Palau. Transporting them safely to Guadalcanal, however, was another matter. The presence of the American carriers and Marine planes on Henderson Field precluded a large scale invasion. The only alternative, therefore, was to ferry the reinforcements to Guadalcanal piecemeal.

The Japanese had failed to consider one thing, the fighting ability of the United States Marines. The Marine Corps was America's shock troops, their toughest fighters. In addition, Yamamoto had no way of knowing just how many Americans were actually on the island. In a sense, he was proceeding blindly.

Faced with the problem of how to reinforce Guadalcanal, Yamamoto created the Guadalcanal Reinforcement Group. The question of a commander for this force was an easy problem to overcome. Since the primary role would be borne by destroyers, a top-notch destroyer commander was called for. In Yamamoto's eyes, Admiral Tanaka was one of the finest destroyer commanders in the entire navy. His exploits to date attested to this fact and he had already proven his ability for escorting convoys. Furthermore, not only was Tanaka's brilliance recognized throughout the fleet, he was extremely popular. It thus surprised no one except Tanaka himself when he was summoned to Yamamoto's headquarters and entrusted with the heavy burden of reinforcing Guadalcanal.

When confronted with the facts of this latest venture, Tanaka expressed his displeasure. Piecemeal reinforcement of Guadalcanal was not the answer. "Bamboo Spear Tactics" he called the effort, and made no secret of his disagreement with the methods. Tanaka argued that the entire concept would serve no other purpose but to keep feeding men and material into a meat grinder. In addition, unlike his superiors, Tanaka was a bit more respectful of his opponents. After the war he stated,

> "We were flushed with victories and we never imagined we could lose. We had victory disease, a blind arrogance, supreme confidence and utter contempt for the enemy. My superiors were certain

that single battalions and a few guns would easily dislodge the enemy from Guadalcanal. In the end, this tactic of piecemeal reinforcements led to tragic consequences."[4]

Nevertheless, Tanaka loaded almost one thousand troops of the Ichiki detachment* aboard his destroyers and set off for Guadalcanal and his new assignment with the Eighth Fleet. Thus began a series of exploits that would earn for Tanaka the grudging respect and admiration of his opponents and the nickname "Tenacious Tanaka."

Covered by the darkness of night, Tanaka's destroyers crept up to the coast of Guadalcanal on the evening of August 18th and landed the troops without incident. It all seemed so easy that Tanaka decided to press his luck even further and took his ships farther down the coast to carry out a bombardment of the American positions near Henderson Field and on Tulagi. But he lingered too long at the well.

The only thing the bombardment accomplished was a precious waste of darkness. Consequently, Tanaka found himself steaming back up the Slot in broad daylight. Since the operation had gone off without a hitch, the pace was unhurried. Suddenly, U.S. Army B-17s arrived over the formation and dropped their loads of bombs. One hit was made on the destroyer *Hagikaze*, but Tanaka ordered full speed ahead and drew out of range, the damaged destroyer limping along.

Precisely as Tanaka had cautioned, the effort was in vain. Armed with faulty intelligence reports vastly underestimating the American strength on Guadalcanal, Colonel Ichiki launched an attack on August 24th. At the Battle of the Tenaru River his force was annihilated. Those who survived were fair game for the American fighter planes that strafed their positions. The proud Colonel Ichiki wrapped himself in his colors and committed *hari-kiri*.

---

*After the commander of the formation, Colonel Ichiki.

Another effort to reinforce Guadalcanal was hastily prepared. The second part of Ichiki's command was to be delivered to the island. This time, Tanaka's force would have the support of not one, but two heavy forces. Kondo's and Nagumo's fleets sailed with him albeit at a distance and on a slightly different course. If the two latter fleets succeeded in bringing the American fleet to battle, it would allow Tanaka to land his precious cargo while the enemy was preoccupied elsewhere.

A few hundred miles north of Guadalcanal, Tanaka's force of destroyers and transports were discovered by an American PBY around 10:00 AM on the morning of August 23rd. Knowning that the Americans were aware of his presence, Tanaka ordered his force to reverse course. Thus, when planes from the U.S.S *Yorktown* arrived at the position where they estimated the Japanese convoy would be, they found nothing but empty sea. A few hours later, Tanaka doubled back again and continued on toward his destination.

Tanaka's decision to reverse course had a dramatic influence on the subsequent Battle of the Eastern Solomons. When *Yorktown*'s planes failed to locate Tanaka's formation, Admiral Fletcher concluded that the Japanese force was returning to base. Therefore, he felt that it was safe to dispatch the carrier *Wasp* for refueling. Consequently, when the battle erupted the following day, the two sides were more evenly matched. Were it not for Tanaka's decision to reverse course, Fletcher might have been able to achieve a decisive victory. As it turned out, minus the *Wasp*, the best the Americans could do was sink the light carrier *Ryujo* in exchange for damage to the *Enterprise*. Tanaka might have taken credit for making a positive contribution to the battle, but this was not his style. He freely admitted that his change of course was simply dictated by the desire to move out of range of the American carriers.

In one respect the Japanese plan worked. At the height of the battle Tanaka steamed unmolested towards Guadalcanal, while the two main forces fought each other. That night, four of his destroyers, which were not a part of the main body, raced down the Slot and spent the night bombarding American positions. Shortly before daybreak they broke off the action and headed to join up with the rest of Tanaka's force.

Tanaka was scheduled to land his troops on Guadalcanal after darkness. Unfortunately, early in the morning, his force was again sighted by a patrolling American aircraft. Around 8:30 on the morning of the 24th, planes from Henderson Field arrived overhead and formed up for the attack. Tanaka was in trouble.

The first group of American planes to come swooping down decided to concentrate their efforts against the largest target. This naturally was the *Jintsu*, Tanaka's flagship. Almost immediately a bomb hit the deck between the two forward turrets, destroying radio communications, starting a large fire, and throwing Tanaka to the deck. Stunned, he was briefly unable to conduct the defense of the formation even if he had been able to communicate with the rest of the ships. Skillful damage control by the *Jintsu's* captain prevented the fires from reaching the ship's magazines, and the danger passed, but the ship was heavily damaged, and she turned for Truk.

A few minutes after the hit on *Jintsu*, an American bomb struck the transport *Kinryu Maru*. The ship began to burn furiously and stopped dead. Seeing the transport's plight, the captain of the destroyer *Mutsuki* ordered his ship alongside the stricken transport. The *Maru* was crammed with over one thousand troops and they hastily began to board the rescuing destroyer.

Unfortunately, the ordeal was not over. While the *Mutsuki* was engaged in her rescue mission, B-17s arrived. In short order the destroyer was hit by three bombs and found itself in desperate straits.

By now Tanaka had recovered his senses. Seeing the plight of the *Mutsuki* and the transport, he ordered the remaining transports to proceed to Truk at full speed. It was imperative that they get out of range of any further American attacks. Two destroyers were ordered to provide escort.

Then he turned his attention to his two stricken ships. The *Yayoi* was ordered to aid in rescuing survivors from the two helpless ships. When the flotilla had completed as much as possible, Tanaka ordered a submarine that had arrived on the scene to sink the *Mutiuki*. He certainly did not want the destroyer to fall into American hands. Then he set sail for Truk, his mission unaccomplished.

Back at Truk, Tanaka ranted about the futility of further attempts to supply Guadalcanal in this fashion. His mood was not enhanced by the fact that he was forced to order the *Jintsu* back to Japan for extensive repairs. The ship that had served for so long as his flagship and had become like a second home would be sorely missed. Reluctantly, he lowered his flag and transferred it to the destroyer *Suzukaze*.

While Tanaka was busy reorganizing his command, Yamamoto sent another force down the Slot. This time it was the 20th Flotilla commanded by Captain Arita. American planes caught this force steaming south in broad daylight and heavily damaged three Japanese destroyers, killed Arita, and forced the rest of the convoy to turn back. Once more Tanaka pointed out the folly of continuing these tactics. A few short weeks before he had been seen as the brilliant destroyer expert. Now, however, his outspoken criticism was beginning to irritate his superiors, although they still conceded his ability. Were it not for this ability, Tanaka might have found himself without a command.

Yamamoto still refused to alter his stance. He was determined to hang onto Guadalcanal at all cost. Therefore, on the 28th, Tanaka dispatched seven destroyers crammed with one thousand soldiers to Guadalcanal with orders to unload the troops, bombard American shipping and positions, and retire at high speed. This time he remained behind in the Shortlands.

Unfortunately, the officer in charge of the operation did not possess Tanaka's mettle. After hurriedly unloading the troops he beat it back up the Slot without firing a shot against the American positions. Tanaka was incensed. The hapless destroyer commander was relieved of command a few minutes after stepping ashore.

Meanwhile, plans were proceeding for another full-scale reinforcement run. The commander of the troops designated for the next trip, General Kawaguchi, suggested that the troops be transported by barge. He pointed out that this was a tried-and-true system used in New Guinea. Tanaka stared at the general in amazement. Even his fast destroyers were unable to avoid attacks by American planes. How could slow-moving barges hope to get through? Tanaka shouted that not only was the entire idea stupid, so was anyone who might even consider such a possibility. After venting his wrath, he turned on his heel and stormed from the room.

Nevertheless, Tanaka still faced the problem of transporting Kawaguchi's men to Guadalcanal safely. Rather then risk large formations that required many hours to unload, Tanaka decided to ferry the troops down the Slot a few ships at a time. By taking advantage of the speed of the destroyers, he concluded that the ships could remain out of range of American aircraft until darkness, dash in, unload their passengers, and be well up the Slot before daylight.

For the next few weeks, daily sorties left the Shortlands. The tactic worked. Kawaguchi's troops were delivered safely to Guadalcanal. These nightly runs were observed by Allied coastwatchers on other islands in the Solomons. The coastwatchers dubbed the nightly forays the "Tokyo Express," a name that was shortly on the lips of every American on Guadalcanal. During the first two weeks in September alone, the Tokyo Express transported over six thousand troops to Guadalcanal.

During the second week in September Kawaguchi launched an all-out offensive aimed at the recapture of Henderson Field. In a three-day battle he failed to make a significant dent in the American defense. A good part of Kawaguchi's force perished attempting to infiltrate the American positions. The greater portion of those who gave their lives for the emperor did so in a frontal assault or *banzai* charge against the well-dug-in marine positions along "Bloody Ridge." Although the defenders paid a high cost, they continued to hang grimly on.

Faced with the failure of all previous efforts, Yamamoto finally turned a sympathetic ear to the pleas of Admiral Tanaka. The latter's squadron could not maintain the pace. The crews had been pushed to their limits. Recognizing this, Mikawa enhanced the strength of the Tokyo Express with the addition of the 20th Destroyer Flotilla, but even this was not enough. The nightly runs were taking their toll of men and ships.

Almost from the beginning, Tanaka had urged that an all-out effort be made instead of the wasteful piecemeal efforts. Yamamoto was so anxious to recapture Guadalcanal that the relatively small Japanese formations attacked the American positions almost as soon as they arrived. Now he began to realize that the Americans outnumbered his own forces, and until both sides could fight on more even terms, offensive action would have to be limited. Therefore, it was decided to halt all but absolutely necessary action until a significant buildup could occur.

Throughout the first week in October the Tokyo Express continued its nightly run, ferrying over twenty thousand troops of Hyukatake's 2nd Army Division to Guadalcanal. Japanese aircraft from the 11th Air Fleet on Rabaul made daily attacks and kept the Americans pinned down.

The Japanese plan for the final recapture of the island called for a combined operation featuring the navy, the air forces, and the army. Heavy air attacks would pin down the American forces; then a strong attack by the 2nd Division would be supported by heavy shelling of American positions by Japanese naval forces.

In the interim, the American naval forces around Guadalcanal had recovered from the debacle of Savo. They too were pouring reinforcements into Guadalcanal with close-in support provided by a force of cruisers and destroyers, while another force of carriers furnished long-range support.

Before launching the attack the Japanese needed a few more runs by the Tokyo Express to deliver the remainder of the 2nd Division, the unit's heavy equipment, and its supplies. To escort one of these final deliveries, Admiral Mikawa ordered a force of cruisers and destroyers with Admiral Goto in command to sail with the convoy. While the unloading proceeded, Goto would sail into Ironbottom Sound and bombard the American defensive perimeter around Henderson Field.

On the night of October 11/12, Goto unsuspectingly led his force into the waters off Guadalcanal. There he was ambushed by a force of American cruisers and destroyers under Admiral Norman Scott. In the ensuing battle of Cape Esperance, the Japanese lost the cruiser *Furutaka*, the destroyer *Fubuki*, and suffered damage to the cruiser *Aoba*, Goto's flagship. Goto himself was mortally wounded during the battle. The following day planes from both sides took a hand and two additional Japanese destroyers were sent to the bottom. On the American side, the cruisers *Salt Lake City*, and *Boise* were damaged, and the destroyer *Duncan* was lost. Tactically, the battle was a victory for Scott, but the Americans were unable to prevent the Japanese transports from delivering their precious cargo.

As a result of the losses incurred at Cape Esperance, Yamamoto delayed the beginning of the all-out offensive. Nevertheless, the Tokyo Express continued to run. Japanese efforts were intensified. Admiral Kurita took the battleships *Kongo* and *Haruna* into Ironbottom Sound on the night of October 13th. Escorted by Tanaka's 2nd Destroyer Flotilla, the Japanese heavies lobbed over nine hundred shells into the Henderson Field area. Tanaka's small ships sailed back and forth along the shore hurling smaller-caliber shells into the American positions. After exhausting his ammunition, Kurita returned from whence he had come. In his wake he left fifty aircraft destroyed.

Because of Kurita's feat and the continual bombing raids from Rabaul and the Shortlands, the Japanese felt that aerial supremacy over Guadalcanal had finally been achieved. Another supply run was sent down the Slot even as Kurita was steaming north. Six transports anchored at Tassafronga the following night and began to land over four thousand troops.

While the transports were discharging their passengers, Admiral Mikawa attempted a repeat of Kurita's effort. The cruisers *Chokai* and *Kinugasa* paraded up and down offshore heaving 8-inch shells into the marine positions on the night of the 14th. A few hours after midnight, Mikawa broke off the action and returned up the Slot, leaving Tanaka and his destroyers to cover the unloading of six transports.

Since they were confident that Henderson Field was out of commission once and for all, the Japanese thought that it was safe to unload the transports in broad daylight with relative impunity. Unfortunately, they were unaware of the existence of an auxiliary airstrip behind the American lines.

Kurita and Mikawa's bombardment caused heavy damage not only to the American planes but also to the stocks of aviation fuel as well. Nonetheless, the Americans set to work salvaging whatever they could. Early in the morning after Mikawa's raid one plane managed to take off from the auxiliary airstrip. The pilot soon sighted the Japanese transports near Tassafronga and managed to hit one of them with a bomb. Tanaka felt that the attack of one lone plane was no cause for alarm. If this was all the enemy had to strike back with, there was nothing to fear.

The Americans were far from beaten, however. A remarkable effort on the part of their ground crews succeeded in securing some aviation fuel. Others worked furiously to patch together some of the damaged planes. Around noon, a strike was ready to take off.

An hour later the small flight of planes roared over the Japanese transports. Within minutes, three of the ships were on fire and in a sinking condition. A shocked Tanaka ordered the remaining ships to haul off at high speed until nightfall. There was no way he could have known that the American attack represented a maximum effort on their part.

Two nights later the Tokyo Express was back. While the transports unloaded under cover of darkness, Tanaka's destroyers, accompanied by the cruisers *Myoko* and *Maya*, bombarded the American positions once more. This time the auxiliary airstrip came in for its share of attention.

Admiral Nimitz was fed up. The Americans simply had to do something about the nightly sorties of the Tokyo Express and the relative impunity with which Japanese warships shelled the American positions. Admiral Ghormley, the Southwest Pacific commander, was replaced by a fighter. Admiral William "Bull" Halsey became the new theater commander.

After several days of postponement the Japanese finally launched their offensive on the night of October 24th. Whether it was army or navy, the Japanese seemed to have a fondness for elaborate operations requiring precise timing and perfect coordination between dispersed units. And so it was on Guadalcanal. Unfortunately for them, the timing was far from precise. Consequently the Americans were able to defeat each wing of the offensive in turn. After four bloody nights the attackers called off the assault and began to retreat on the 29th. The cost was over four thousand casualties.

At the height of the battle, Admiral Nagumo, in support of the army's effort, inflicted a costly defeat on the American carrier forces at the Battle of Santa Cruz. The *Hornet* was sunk and the *Enterprise* damaged. Added to the loss of the *Wasp* a few weeks earlier to the torpedoes of a submarine, and the temporary loss of the *Saratoga* undergoing repairs for similar damage, the defeat left the Americans with only one carrier in the Southwest Pacific. This was, of course, the *Enterprise*, and she was unable to operate at full strength. Fortunately, they still retained their stationary "aircraft carrier"—Guadalcanal.

Two days after the Japanese offensive on Guadalcanal ground to a halt, the Americans themselves swung over to the offensive. During the preceding weeks the Tokyo Express was not the only unit ferrying in supplies. The Americans, too, were steadily pouring in supplies, fresh troops, and, even more important, a new supply of planes for Henderson Field's Cactus Air Force. The fresh troops were immediately sent into the line to relieve the battle-weary marines. Both sides suffered from tropical diseases:

dysentery, malaria, and assorted other ailments.

Commanded by Admiral Hiroki Abe, this strong force was comprised of the battleships *Hiei* and *Kirishima*, the cruiser *Nagara* and fourteen destroyers. Abe's proposed bombardment of Guadalcanal was to be followed up the next night by another commanded by Admiral Nishimura. The latter was intended to cover Tanaka's delivery of eleven transports. Admirals Kondo and Mikawa, with the balance of their respective fleets including the carriers *Hiyo* and *Junyo*, would stand off to the north and provide distant cover.

After delivering their convoys to Guadalcanal, Admirals Scott and Daniel Callaghan stood by to protect the unloading. Eventually, reports began to filter in of a large Japanese force moving south. Admiral Turner, in charge of the transports, ordered his ships to retire out of harm's way while Scott and Callaghan combined their forces and took up station in Ironbottom Sound. As senior admiral, Callaghan in the cruiser *Salt Lake City* assumed overall command. The balance of his force consisted of the cruisers *Atlanta (Scott's flagship), Portland, Helena, Juneau,* and eight destroyers.

Shortly after midnight on November 13th, the two opposing forces met head-on southeast of Savo Island. A wild melee broke out with neither side quite sure of just what was happening. Destroyer took on battleship, cruiser versus cruiser, every ship firing wildly at any target in sight. Early in the battle, both Admirals Scott and Callaghan were killed, leaving what little control of the battle there was in the hands of relatively junior officers, since communications on the ships carrying more senior officers were out of commission. In one respect, the battle, at least on the American side, deteriorated into a series of minor battles with every ship for itself.

The remarkable Japanese talent for night fighting swayed the battle. The U.S. destroyers *Cushing, Monsenn,* and the cruiser *Atlanta* were reduced to blazing wrecks. All three ships eventually sank. Torpedoes and concentrated Japanese gunfire damaged every other American warship with the exception of the destroyer *Fletcher*, some more heavily than others. The *Juneau*, with the five Sullivan brothers aboard, was sunk the next day by a Japanese submarine while making her way to port at a greatly reduced speed. The five Sullivans perished with their ship.

On the other side of the coin, the destroyer *Akatsuke* was sunk and the *Yudachi* reduced to a burnt-out hulk. The battleship *Hiei* was the focus of attention of the American destroyers, and although their small guns were unable to dent the goliath's armor, over fifty small-caliber hits set fires and caused cracks in the aging ship's hull. Out of control, the *Hiei* floundered north of Savo, her steering wrecked. The next morning she was fair game for marauding American planes from Guadalcanal and the hastily patched-up *Enterprise*. Abandoned by the rest of her comrades, the *Hiei* was attacked repeatedly and reduced to a blazing pile of scrap iron. Unable to save her, Abe ordered the battleship scuttled. It was the first Japanese battleship to be lost in the war.

The other major loss was of Abe's nerve. With the American cruisers fighting for their lives and the 14-inch guns of the *Kirishima* available, Abe overreacted to the tenacity of the American destroyers and the damage to the *Hiei*. Over the vehement objections of his captains, the Japanese commander turned his fleet around and headed north. Yamamoto relieved Abe of his command on the spot and the unfortunate admiral was retired from the navy.

The following night, Mikawa sent Admiral Nishimura with three cruisers and four destroyers racing into Ironbottom Sound. For half an hour the Japanese force pounded Henderson Field. The action was abruptly broken off when Nishimura received word of heavy American reinforcements approaching.

Meanwhile, Tanaka brought his convoy south. Originally scheduled to land on the 13th, Tanaka was ordered to reverse course and mark time when Abe's forced joined battle with the Americans. The landings were postponed for one day.

Around 7:00 on the morning of the 14th, Tanaka's

lookouts spotted a flight of American planes heading north. The escorts went to action stations and prepared to initiate defensive procedures. But the American planes ignored the convoy and continued on course. A bewildered Tanaka could not understand why his force went unmolested.

The answer was that the Americans felt that Tanaka's formation could wait. They were after bigger game. An hour after passing Tanaka, planes from Henderson Field hit Mikawa's force retiring up the Slot. The cruiser *Kinugasa* was torpedoed and the *Isuza* hit with bombs. Two hours later the *Enterprise* planes arrived. The *Kinugasa* was finished off and the *Isuza* damaged further. The *Maya*, the *Chokai* and the destroyer *Michishio* were also damaged to a lesser degree. Then the Americans turned their attention to Tanaka, who had elected to press on.

Just before noon thirty-seven enemy planes dove out of the sky over the vulnerable convoy. Tanaka immediately ordered evasive maneuvers and the destroyers were directed to lay smoke over the convoy. All the Japanese efforts were in vain. The transports *Nagara Maru* and *Canberra Maru* were hit by torpedoes and began to sink immediately. Bombs landed on the crowded decks of the *Sado Maru*, causing heavy casualties among the troops and disabling the ship to the extent that Tanaka ordered it back to the Shortlands escorted by two of his destroyers. Although the day was still young and Tanaka knew that he could expect more attacks, his mind was on the suffering of the Japanese troops on Guadalcanal. Delivery of the convoy was vital. Therefore, he decided to continue on despite the contrary advice of his staff.

While Tanaka was determined to reach Guadalcanal, Halsey was just as determined to prevent him from doing so. The American commander ordered that the attacks be repeated over and over.

The next attack sank the *Arizona Maru*, the *Shinangowa Maru*, and the *Brisbane Maru*. Tanaka sent destroyers alongside the blazing transports to rescue as many of the troops and crew members as possible. The Americans continued to apply the pressure. The succeeding attack hit the *Naka Maru*, which began to settle almost at once with heavy loss of life. In addition to the transports the *Enterprise*'s planes gave some of their attention to the destroyers *Takanami* and *Hayashio*, Tanaka's flagship. Both ships were slightly damaged by near misses but were able to continue on. Then friendly planes from the carrier *Junyo* arrived overhead and drove off the attackers. The *Junyo*'s planes remained on the scene until darkness closed down over the grateful convoy. The battle had cost the Japanese over three thousand troops killed.

Serious as his prediciment was, Tanaka knew that the plight of the troops on Guadalcanal was even more critical. There could be no question as to whether to continue on or not. The easy thing would be to use the darkness to cover his retreat up the slot, but Tanaka was sympathetic to the needs of the Army. The delivery of even one ship would be of immeasurable value to the beleaguered garrison.

Callaghan and Scott's defeat left the American beachhead temporarily defenseless. That situation was alleviated twenty-fours hours later when Admiral Willis "Ching" Lee, with his task force, comprised of the new battleships *Washington, South Dakota* and four destroyers, arrived off Guadalcanal. Meanwhile, Admiral Kondo was leading a strong Japanese force south with the intention of delivering the final knockout blow to Henderson Field.

Around 11:00 on the night of the 14th, Lee's forces sighted the leading elements of Kondo's force entering Ironbottom Sound east of Savo Island. Fifteen minutes later the American battleships opened fire. The Japanese ships immediately made smoke and retired. Ten minutes later, two more Japanese formations were sighted rounding Savo. The American destroyers opened fire at once. Again the superior ability for night fighting came to the fore. The Japanese destroyers lashed out with their "long lance" torpedoes, and moments later, three of Lee's destroyers, the *Walke*, the *Benham*, and the *Preston* staggered to a halt with enemy fish in their bowels. The American battleships, however, nailed the Japanese destroyer *Aganami* with their heavy-caliber shells. The latter retired from the action mortally wounded.

Lee then altered course to pass between Savo and the nearest point of Guadalcanal, Cape Esperance. West of Savo, Kondo, with the battleship *Kirishima*, was hurrying to the fray. Kondo got in the first blow as the *South Dakota*, suffering from technical difficulties, took a few hits from the enemy battleship. Then the *Washington* added the weight of her broadsides to the battle. *Kirishima* was battered unmercifully as salvo after salvo of 16-inch shells rained death and destruction on the hapless Japanese battleship.

With his flagship ablaze and two of his cruisers hit, Kondo gave the signal to retire. As he did, two destroyers came racing by and let loose a salvo of torpedoes at the *Washington*. Fortunately for Lee, all the torpedoes ran wide.

Fearful of becoming caught up in the battle, Tanaka had reduced speed. Since the night provided a protective blanket of darkness and the American forces were occupied elsewhere, Tanaka concluded that he could spare a few of his escorts. He sent three of his destroyers to the scene of the battle to see if they could aid the harassed Kondo. Two of these destroyers carried out the unsuccessful attack on the *Washington*. This was exactly the type of aggressive behavior that had brought Tanaka his well-earned reputation.

However, by now Tanaka knew that he could not reach Guadalcanal and expect to unload before daylight. Accordingly, he ordered the four remaining transports beached on the island while he turned his surviving destroyers for home, their decks crowded with survivors.

The following morning, at first light, American planes and long-range artillery decimated the beached transports, slaughtering over half of those attempting to come ashore, and destroyed not only the cargo aboard those ships, but those that had already been unloaded and were stacked on the shore. The two naval battles for Guadalcanal had proven a dismal failure for the Japanese. The reinforcement run was a total flop; two battleships lay at the bottom of the sea along with three destroyers, a heavy cruiser and all but one of the transports. Furthermore, Henderson Field remained operable, and from the time Kondo sailed back up the Slot, increased in strength daily. The twin battles marked the last time heavy Japanese units would sail into Ironbottom Sound to confidently shell the American positions. The tide had finally turned in favor of the Americans. But they hadn't heard the last of Tenacious Tanaka.

Yamamoto was now forced to reassess the entire Japanese effort. His resolve to hold on Guadalcanal at all cost was severely shaken. No more would large troop-laden convoys attempt to fight their way through to the island supported by the heavy ships of the Combined Fleet. The Japanese simply could not afford to pay the price. Tanaka's prophetic words rang loud in the commander-in-chief's ears. Attempting to supply Guadalcanal was an exercise in futility. Nevertheless, those troops remaining on the island simply could not be written off and allowed to starve. Another method of supplying them had to be found.

Two methods of achieving this were finally adopted. First, submarines would be used to run supplies in. These boats could sail to Guadalcanal undetected underwater, surface off the beach at night, and return beneath the waves before daylight, thus avoiding detection. Unfortunately, because of the relatively small size of these boats, the number of supplies they could deliver was restricted.

Tanaka came up with an alternative to the submarine plan. He sent his crews scavenging for old steel drums. Once a sufficient number of these were collected, he directed the men to scrub the interiors until they were spotless. The drums were then filled with rice, other foodstuffs, medical supplies, and ammunition, lashed together, and placed on the decks of high-speed destroyers. Tanaka then took the ships south under cover of darkness and dropped the drums overboard. The tide would then carry them near the beach, where troops would wade out into the water and haul them ashore. Tanaka's Tokyo Express rode again.

Thus began a series of nightly runs down the Slot.

Taking care to remain out of range of American planes during daylight hours, Tanaka's laden ships dashed in towards Guadalcanal under the cover of darkness. Near the island, ship's crews shoved the drums overboard without the necessity of having the ships reduce speed. The destroyers then hightailed it back up the Slot and were usually out of range of Henderson Field's aircraft by daylight. Even if they were detected, the ships could take high speed evasive maneuvers unencumbered by the responsibility of protecting lumbering transports.

Regrettably, this latter method was far from foolproof. Many of the drums floated harmlessly out to sea or found their way to American beaches. During daylight hours, unretrieved drums and those soldiers attempting to retrieve them were easy targets for marauding American planes.

This was the pitiful state to which the Japanese navy found itself reduced in November of 1942. On the 27th of that month, Tanaka, with his flag in the destroyer *Naganami*, left Rabaul accompanied by seven other destroyers, their decks piled with drums, over one hundred apiece. Six of the squadron were forced to leave their spare torpedoes behind to make room for additional drums. After pausing at the Shortlands, Tanaka led his flotilla to sea in the darkness on November 28th.

Meanwhile, the Americans had become wise to the Japanese technique. Admiral Halsey was hell-bent on halting the pesky Tokyo Express once and for all. A task force under Carleton Wright was directed to intercept the next run.

When compared to Tanaka's formation, Wright's force was formidable indeed. The American Admiral flew his flag in the heavy cruiser *Minneapolis*. Other heavy cruisers in the task force were the *New Orleans*, the *Pensacola*, the *Northampton* and the light cruiser *Honolulu*, bristling with fifteen 6-inch guns. Wright's formation was rounded out by the presence of six destroyers.

On the 28th, American intelligence reported that Tanaka's destroyers would make a run into Guadalcanal during the night of the 30th. Admiral Wright took his task force north to intercept them.

Meanwhile, Tanaka himself had received reports of enemy naval forces near Guadalcanal. Radio reports from fleet headquarters warned him of the possibility of encountering American forces. Nonetheless, moved by the plight of the troops on the island, he was determined to carry out his mission.

> "Almost daily came radio messages reporting the critical situation on the island and requesting immediate supplies. It was indicated that by the end of November, the entire food supply would be gone, and by the latter part of the month we learned that all staple supplies had been consumed. The men were now down to eating wild plants and animals. Everyone was on the verge of starvation, sick lists increased, and even the healthy were exhausted."[5]

Before leaving the Shortlands Tanaka cautioned each destroyer captain that the delivery of supplies was the primary mission, but that all ships should be prepared to do battle in case the Americans attempted to intervene. When informed of the presence of American warships, the Admiral ordered the following signal sent to each of his destroyers:

> "It is probable that we will encounter an enemy force tonight. Although our primary mission is to land supplies, everyone is to be ready for combat. If an engagement occurs, take the initiative and destroy the enemy."[6]

Shortly after 11:00 PM, Tanaka's force rounded Savo Island and began the final run in to the beach. With the exception of the destroyer *Takanami* off to port, the Japanese destroyers moved in a single file, led by Tanaka's own *Naganami*. The flagship and *Takanami* were the only two ships carrying a full load of torpedoes. Behind *Naganami* trailed the *Makinami*, the *Oyashio*, the *Kuroshio*, the

Kagero, the *Kawakaze*, and the *Suzukaze*.

Wright's ships were also steaming in single file. The destroyers *Fletcher*, *Perkins*, *Maury*, and *Drayton* led the line of cruisers, the *Minneapolis*, the *New Orleans*, the *Pensacola*, the *Honolulu*, and the *Northampton* in that order. The two remaining destroyers, the *Lamson*, and the *Lardner*, brought up the rear.

At approximately 11:15, Tanaka approached Tassafronga Point and reduced speed to allow the drums to be pushed overboard. Suddenly, the night erupted.

The *Fletcher*'s radar had picked up the *Takanami* gaurding Tanaka's flank. A few minutes later, numerous blips appeared on the radar screen of the *Minneapolis*. These were Tanaka's remaining destroyers readying their drops. Incredibly, Wright would not give the order to open fire until he was absolutely sure of the situation. Since none of the American ships was authorized to fire independently, Wright's few moments of hesitation gave Tanaka all the opportunity he needed.

As Wright attempted to decipher the situation, the keen eyes of the lookouts on the *Nakanami* sighted the American formation. Not one to waste an opportunity when he saw one, Tanaka ordered the supply drop temporarily suspended, straightened his battle line, and sailed into the attack.

The *Takanami*, meanwhile, had fired a spread of torpedoes at the American line and reversed course. Being the closest Japanese ship to Wright's task force, she now became the target of concentrated American gunfire. The little destroyer was hit repeatedly and fires began to spread through out her length. But her sacrifice was not in vain.

By drawing attention to herself, the *Takanami* allowed the rest of Tanaka's squadron to sail down the port side of the American battle line. The *Minneapolis* soon swung her guns around the began to fire at the Japanese flagship. Too late! Tanaka's destroyers had already launched their deadly "long lances."

Five minutes after firing, the Japanese fish began to strike home. The *Minneapolis* was the first victim. A torpedo decimated her fire room. A second exploded forward of the bridge. Officers on the bridge stared down incredulously at the peculiar angle of over sixty feet of the American flagship's bow. *New Orleans*, next in line, swerved out of line to avoid ramming the *Minneapolis*, and a torpedo plowed into her forward magazine, blowing the entire bow completely off clear back to the second turret.

Seeing the two ships in front suddenly stop dead, the *Pensacola* was attempting to avoid them when a "long lance" blew a huge hole in the cruiser's side, amidships.

The *Honolulu* was more fortunate than her sisters. Her captain wisely took his ship down the disengaged side of the confused American formation. Protected by the three blazing cruisers, the *Honolulu* continued to blaze away with all her guns. In all the confusion, however, her firing was innacurate.

Next in line, the *Northampton* was the most unfortunate of all. Two torpedoes smashed into her side and set the ship's fuel tanks on fire. Burning like an inferno, the *Northampton* went dead in the water and took on an immediate list to port.

Tanaka assembled his destroyers and headed north at top speed. When he noticed that the *Takanami* was not present he ordered the *Kuroshio* and the *Oyashio* to return to the scene of battle and search for their comrade. They found the *Takanami* burning from stem to stern and sinking. The *Kuroshio* and the *Oyashio* stood by rescuing survivors until the approach of American destroyers forced them to break off and rejoin the rest of Tanaka's formation for the race up the Slot. The actual battle had lasted for a little over twenty minutes.

No drums of supplies reached the Japanese troops on Guadalcanal that night. That was not to say that the Japanese force had been defeated. Tanaka had truly lived up to his nickname. Three badly damaged American cruisers were left in his wake and would require months of extensive repair. As for the stricken *Northampton*, she rolled over and sank a few hours after the battle. The Battle of Tassafronga was a smashing Japanese victory.

Outgunned, outnumbered, and ambushed, Tanaka had turned the tables and inflicted a crushing defeat on his enemy. With the exception of the loss of the *Takanami*, he took on a highly superior force and emerged without a scratch.

It was typical of Tanaka's generosity that he wished to share the credit. After the war he said,

> "I have heard that U.S. naval experts praised my command in that action. I am not deserving of such honors. It was the superb proficiency and devotion of the men who served me that produced the tactical victory for us.
>
> "We were able to defeat Admiral Wright's ships in this action only because of the *Takanami*. She absorbed all the punishment of the enemy in the opening moments of battle, and she shielded the rest of us. Yet we left the scene without doing anything for her valiant crew."[7]

But he had attempted to do something for *Takanami*'s crew. Hadn't he dispatched two of his precious destroyers to the scene in a rescue attempt? To risk them unnecessarily, however, when the American forces approached, would have been foolish.

But if Tanaka was reluctant to take credit, others were willing to heap praise on him. One of the greatest of all naval historians, Samuel Elliot Morrison, had this to say:

> "It is always some consolation to reflect that the enemy who defeats you is really good, and Rear Admiral Tanaka was better than that—he was superb. In many actions of the war mistakes on the American side were cancelled by those of the enemy; but despite the brief confusion of his destroyers, Tanaka made no mistakes at Tassafronga."[8]

Incredibly, when Tanaka arrived back at base it was not

to the acclaim of his superiors. Instead, he was criticized for not delivering the supplies.

Tanaka was undeterred. On December 3, again on the 7th, and once more on the 11th, the Tokyo Express sailed down the Slot and unloaded the drums into the waters off the island. But the Japanese had overused their tactic. More and more drums failed to reach the shore. During the sortie on the 11th of December, Tanaka's formation was attacked by American PT Boats. His flagship, the destroyer *Teruzuki*, was torpedoed and sunk by the small enemy torpedo boats. Tanaka was wounded during the action but managed to transfer his flag before the *Teruzuki* sank. Returning to Rabaul, the gallant little admiral was hospitalized for treatment of his wounds.

Yamamoto finally began to realize that the Guadalcanal effort would have to be written off. The very last thing that a commander who is forced to admit defeat wants to hear is "I told you so." This is precisely what Yamamoto thought of every time he heard the name Tanaka glorified and praised. Throughout the entire operation the latter had repeatedly spoken out against the folly of it all. With defeat at Guadalcanal imminent, Yamamoto decided that he could dispense with the services of this insubordinate destroyer commander. Tanaka's days were numbered.

Yamamato was not foolish enough to get rid of Tanaka though, while there was still work to be done. The troops remaining on Guadalcanal needed to be evacuated. Without informing the men in the field of his decision, Yamamoto began to evacuate Guadalcanal. The Japanese troops were being pushed back all along the line by superior American forces under General Alexander Patch,* and Yamamoto felt that if the defenders knew that they were shortly to be evacuated, all defenses would break down. Consequently, almost right up until the end, the Japanese troops remained uninformed of the plan to evacuate them.

Small packets of troops were evacuated during nightly trips by destroyers and submarines to Guadalcanal. The

---

*See Volume III in this series, *The Americans*.

formation charged with this operation was the famed Tokyo Express, commanded by Admiral Raizo Tanaka, now fully recovered from his wounds.

During January and February the Express made numerous runs to Guadalcanal, loading ships to overflowing with troops, and speedily retiring up the Slot under cover of darkness to avoid being overwhelmed by American aircraft. During the last week in January and the first week in February, the Tokyo Express managed to evacuate over twelve thousand Japanese troops. The commander-in-chief of the American Pacific Fleet, Admiral Nimitz, praised Tanaka's efforts.

> "Only Admiral Tanaka's skill in keeping his plans disguised, and his bold celerity in carrying them out, enabled the Japanese to withdraw the remnants of their Guadalcanal garrison."[9]

It was unfortunate that Yamamoto failed to share his opposite number's opinion. With Guadalcanal marked down as a failure, the commander of the Combined Fleet cast about for a scapegoat. Who better to fill this role than his most vocal critic, Tanaka? The latter was held responsible for the failure of the relief efforts. He was relieved of command. For the balance of the war, Tanaka languished in disfavor and never again held a seagoing command. Japan could ill afford to squander such talent. A few months later, Yamamoto himself was dead, victim of Tanaka's old antagonists, American aircraft from Guadalcanal.

When one reflects on Tanaka's deeds, one must, if objective, heap the same praise on the man that his enemies have. Despite the intense hatred for anything Japanese, the Americans did not hesitate to respect and (sometimes) to stand in awe of Tanaka's achievements. When his star was at its zenith, at Tassafronga, he was truly incredible and demonstrated the mark of a great commander.

Yamashita

Chapter 5

Last spring, one of the authors interviewed a Filipino who as a young boy lived in the Japanese-held Philippine Islands. One of his earliest memories was of the ill treatment his mother received at the hands of Japanese soldiers. He was in Manila in February 1945 and witnessed the orgy of rape and pillage inflicted on the city's population by Japanese troops gone amok. Throughout the interview, he repeatedly channeled his hatred toward one man. This man, who took upon himself the collective hate of the Filipino people, was General Tomoyuki Yamashita.

From our studies of the personalities of World War II, we have found some to have been mediocre, some good, and still others who were outstanding. We have always felt that Yamashita belonged in the latter category. The aforementioned interview, therefore, posed a dilemma. Was Yamashita a mass murderer who deserved what he got—death by hanging—or was he the "Tiger of Malaya," one of Japan's most capable and, dare we say, one of her most honorable soldiers?

Tomoyuki Yamashita was born on November 8, 1885, in Osugi Mura, a remote village on Japan's smallest of her four main islands, Shokaku. Nestled in the quiet isolation of this mountainous district, cut off from the stress and strain of modern civilization, young Tomoyuki grew up to be "healthy, clean cut, peace-loving, open, responsible, industrious, and straightforward."[1] At Yamashita's war crimes trial, a former chief of staff of his said this about the general:

> "As a boy, Tomoyuki Yamashita was carefree, healthy, and mentally as well as physically alert. He was fond of spending his time out in the open, roaming the hills and fields he loved best, which

caused some concern to his parents and teachers, especially the latter."²

His parents and teachers often scolded him for his truancy.

Yamashita's father was a poor country doctor. Traditionally, one of the sons in a Japanese family follows in the footsteps of his father. Tomoyuki's elder brother showed an interest in medicine, but not the future general. Tomoyuki had a stubborn streak in him, which caused his father endless headaches, concerns that only a parent could appreciate. In order to break down that stubbornness, he was packed off at the age of twelve by his father to an uncle at Kochi to attend the strict Kainan State School. The headmaster of the school was a noted disciplinarian, descended from a line of ancient samurais. He ran the school as if he were the shogun* of all Japan. After two years in this atmosphere, young Tomoyuki changed his academic perfomance and began to give serious consideration to his future goals. During summer vacation in 1899, he informed his mother that he wanted to become a soldier.

The turn of the century was an auspicious time for a young man to embrace a military career. Japan had only recently embarked on the road to fulfilling what it considered its divine destiny. Having only recently industrialized, Japan vitally needed the raw materials and markets of China. In 1895 Japan fought a war with China, only to find its rightful fruits snatched away by the European powers. Not to be undone, Japan simply aspired to more expansion as part of its divine destiny.

The military was the forger of the empire, and as such was held in high esteem by the Japanese people. At the age of fifteen, young Tomoyuki applied to one of the recently opened military academies. Years later, when asked why he, the son of a doctor, chose a military career, he answered,

*Military Leader.

"It was perhaps my destiny. I did not choose the career. My father suggested the idea, perhaps because

I was big and healthy, and my mother did not seriously object because she believed . . . that I would never pass the highly competitive entrance examination."[3]

He did pass, and in the summer of 1900 he entered the academy at Hiroshima. From there he was admitted to the prestigious Central Military Academy in Tokyo, graduating fifth in his class of 1908 and being subsequently assigned to the infantry.

While at the academy, he had seen Japanese military might express itself successfully, this time against the mighty Russian Bear. For his first posting in 1908, Yamashita was appointed to the 11th Regiment that had recently fought against the Russians. He found routine garrison life boring, as peacetime duty usually appears to any young, energetic officer eager for action. However, he used his time to the best advantage and sought admission to the War College. Though he failed the entrance examination a number of times, his persistence finally paid off and he was admitted. The work was difficult, but he was determined to do his utmost. In 1916, while a student at the War College, he married Hisako, the daughter of a retired general. This marriage proved a true love relationship and would last until his execution in 1946.

Upon completion of the course of study at the War College, having finished sixth in his class, Yamashita found himself posted to the General Staff in Tokyo, where he worked on mobilization and financial estimates. In 1919, he was sent to Switzerland to serve as assistant military attaché. There he formed a close relationship with another aspiring young Japanese soldier, Hideki Tojo. Both were around the same age and both had attended the Military Academy and the War and Staff College. The two were destined for greatness. A deep animosity eventually developed between them; by the time they both reached high rank, their antipathy toward each other was obvious to all. Yamashita had once recorded, however, that he had "nothing against Tojo, altough Tojo has something against me."[4]

But in 1919 the two furure generals toured Austria and Germany together. The fact that both had studied German at the Military Academy made it much easier for them to gain firsthand knowledge of German's postwar plight.

In 1922, Yamashita returned to Japan and again was assigned to a staff appointment at Imperial Headquarters in Tokyo. Three years later, in 1925, he was appointed an instructor at the Staff College, but in 1927, before completing the usual three-year tour of duty, he was given the prestigous appointment of military attaché at the Japanese Embassy in Vienna. He thoroughly enjoyed the three years he spend in Austria, studying and learning all he could about European life and politics. In 1930 he returned to Japan, was promoted to the rank of colonel, and for the first time given command of a regiment, the 3rd Infantry Regiment. Soon afterward, he found himself reassigned to the war affairs section, which had to do with mobilization and budget. Unhappily, during his term of office, Yamashita had to draw up a drastic program of disarmament.

The twenties were an optimisitic decade. Japan, along with most other civilized nations, attempted to establish peace by limiting the size of the military. This resulted in the development of a latent hostility among the younger officers who felt that Japan was being ruined by corrupt politicians and businessmen. Because of Yamashita's role in the disarmament program, lasting hostility toward him was felt by a number of officers, Tojo being one of them.

Within the Japanese Army there were three main political groups or factions. All three held many common viewpoints. They resented the political and economic domination of Japan by the politicians and businessmen. They all espoused a sense of nationalism and were hostile to the civilian government, which attempted to reduce the size of the army and navy. The factions felt that this was tantamount to cutting off Japan's chance to fulfill its destiny. All three factions also viewed expansion into Asia to be part of Japan's manifest destiny.

One of these factions was the "Cherry Society," This group drew its membership from the majors and colonels of the Kwangtung Army, the military force based at Port Arthur for the purpose of protecting Japan's interests in Manchuria. The basic aim of the Cherry Society was to purify Japan's national life by securing more power for the army via elimination of the corrupt system of political parties financed by power-hungry businessmen. The Cherry Society held definite ideas on Japan's divine destiny and felt it should expand into Manchuria.

Another faction, which competed with the Cherry Society was the "Imperial Way" group. The goal of this group was to establish military rule under the emperor. Russia was viewed by this faction as the main enemy, and they felt that Japanese expansion should be at the expense of the Soviet Union.

Finally, there was the "Control Group." They too desired power and considered any method that brought about that power to be legitimate. The Control Group felt that Japan had to expand into China no matter what, even if this move escalated into a war with America and Great Britain.

The story of Japan in the 1930s was a story of these three factions vying with each other and against a government that they deeply resented. This led to much violence and many political assassinations. One foreign correspondent described Japan's government at that time as "government by assassination."

Meanwhile, in 1931, the Kwangtung Army unilaterally precipitated an incident which led to the invasion and eventual conquest of Manchuria by Japan. If any politician in Japan disagreed or complained about the army's action, he found his life in great peril. This wave of fear gradually led to the military's gaining more and more control of the government. The country's parliamentary days were numbered. The militarists, being ardent nationalists, spread xenophobia. The Russians, Americans, British, and Chinese were all out to strangle Japan and deprive her of her rightful place. Gradually, through propaganda, it led the people to see the rightness of their cause. The racist Americans and imperialistic British must stop their enslavement of Asia. The militarists were able to present their cause cloaked in idealistic phrases such as the "freeing of all Asian people" for the establishment of the Greater East Asia Co-Prosperity Sphere.

In November, 1934, the Control Faction was discredited when a plot of theirs was uncovered and reported to the emperor. The discoverer was none other than Yamashita, who had been ordered by one of the emperor's aides to keep an eagle's eye on the political activities in the Military Academy. Yamashita received the gratitude of Emperor Hirohito but the emnity of a man who was temporarily disgraced by the incident: Tojo.

By 1935, Yamashita had been promoted to the rank of major general and was appointed head of the Investigations Board at Imperial Headquarters. Politically, he was an advocate of the Imperial Way faction, but he was not a front-line activist of that group. Some of his closest friends, however, were extremely active, and the general knew that they would soon make a move against the government.

Two protégés of the general were Captains Nonaka and Ando. Both officers had served in Yamashita's old regiment and were actively involved with the Imperial Way faction. In December, 1935, they discussed the political situation at length with Yamashita and confided what they desired to do to set it right.

Nonaka and Ando felt that the current prime minister, Keisuke Okada, was detrimental to Japan and was hindering the nation's military aggrandizement, while the war minister, a member of the Control Faction, was hostile to the young officers of the Imperial Way. The only option, they felt, was to overthrow the government.

Why had the two junior officers approached Yamashita, a general officer? They looked upon him as a father figure and respected his opinions. Surprisingly, he did not disagree with their proposed action, though it must also be said that he did not commit himself either. One source said that Yamashita was very proud of the patriotic fervor of the two captains and thus did not caution them, nor did he advise them to drop their proposed plan.

The result was the February 26th attempted coup d'état by nineteen junior officers and nearly fifteen hundred soldiers of the 1st Division. The bloodletting was horrible, as assassination squads led by Captains Nonaka and Ando went to the residences of the prime minister and others whom they considered corrupt. There, they either shot or hacked their victims to death. The prime minister, fortunately, was saved by the quick actions of his staff.

Yamashita heard the news while having breakfast. He exclaimed, "They've done it."[5] He quickly hurried to the War Ministry in a state of exultation, but upon arriving his joy was soured as he found that the Emperor had not approved of the action of the insurgents. Soldiers of the Control Faction wanted to come down heavy on the rebels. Those of the Imperial Way, however, approved the righteousness of their cause.

A high-level meeting was quickly convened. Present at the meeting were the war minister, the army chief of staff, General Sugiyama, Generals Terauchi, Mazaki, and Araki, all prominent men in the Japanese Army. Also present was Major General Yamashita.

Since members of both the Control Faction and Imperial Way were also present, sharp discussions naturally ensued. Sympathizers urged that the rebels be treated leniently by simply allowing them to disband without any reprisals. Sugiyama and Terauchi, however, wanted the assassins dealt with by force.

Meanwhile, the insurgents consolidated their position, bringing life in Tokyo to a grinding halt. The emperor decided to take a firm hand in the situation and summoned each individual attending the meeting into his presence. Speaking to each, he impressed upon them the army's responsibility for suppressing "these violent rioters."[6]

In the meantime the rebels presented their demands, which included the request that the Emperor assume full power and that various corrupt politicians be arrested, along with the dismissal of several senior officers.

Ironically, the job of presenting the emperor's response fell to Yamashita. He went out among the rebels and said:

> "The emperor has been told of your intentions, the war minister recognizes the sincerity of your motives, the War Council has met and decided to uphold the national prestige."[7]

This vague answer puzzled Nonaka and Ando who, after Yamashita finished, questioned his statement's phraseology. It was obvious from the tone that the emperor viewed their act with disdain. The only answer Yamashita could give was to repeat the emperor's vague answer. He remained with the rebels until 5:00 PM and then returned to the palace. At 9:00 PM, a meeting took place between representatives of the rebels and Generals Araki, Mazaki, and Yamashita. At that meeting Nonaka demanded that a new government of direct military control be formed. Mazaki's answer was that the rebels must disband before any consideration could be given to their demands. Nonaka replied that they would not disband.

Another meeting was held on the 27th. Again no move was made by the rebels. The emperor, meanwhile, was fast losing patience. On the 28th he ordered that a direct order be issued to the rebels demanding that they return to their barracks. If they agreed to do so, they would be pardoned, but if they failed to accede, they would be regarded as traitors. Yamashita had to pass this bitter message on to the insurgents.

Upon hearing the message, Nonaka asked Yamashita's advice. In a manner that was both ice cold and brutally blunt, the general said that Nonaka and his fellow officers should commit suicide. This, it was felt, would dramatically portray the seriousness of the cause. Drawing aside, Nonaka discussed the issue with the other insurgent leaders. Returning to Yamashita, he stated that the rebels would take his advice. At this, Yamashita's icy demeanor broke down and he burst into tears.

On the following day February 29th, the army forcefully put down the rebellion. Ando and Nonaka, along with many other rebels, committed ritual suicide. Those insurgents who did not choose this route were subsequently court-martialed and either executed or cashiered out of the army.

The emperor then demanded that the army purge those who had backed these young officers. He knew that those rebel leaders were simply stooges of the Imperial Way. The responsibility for carrying out the purge fell to the new war minister, General Terauchi. More than two thousand of the eight thousand commissioned officers in the army were either dismissed, forced to retire, or exiled far from Japan. Inevitably, Yamashita fell victim to the purge and was posted to command a brigade in Korea. He had reached the nadir in his professional life and gave vent to the thought of leaving his chosen field and seeking employment in civilian life. Then came December 1936. During that month he received a personal note of encouragement and appreciation from the "Son of Heaven," the emperor himself. This note did wonders for his morale and revived his drooping spirit.

From Korea Yamashita was assigned as chief of staff to the North China Army in Manchukuo and was later given command of the 4th Division. While he was in the latter capacity, the famed "China incident" at the Marco Polo Bridge near Peking precipitated the long Sino-Japanese War. Yamashita's reputation as a war leader soon began to soar and in November 1938, he was promoted to lieutenant general.

In July of the following year Yamashita returned to Tokyo to assume the position of inspector general of the air force, succeeding Hideki Tojo. Within a few months, however, Tojo became war minister. Yamashita was sent to Europe as head of a military mission whose job it was to study the German and Italian methods of waging war. It was rumored that Tojo had sent Yamashita because he desired to remove the latter from Tokyo for fear of his popularity and the possibility of his becoming a rival. This rumor was possibly true, for Tojo was one who carried grudges and, as we have already seen, his dislike for Yamashita went back a long way.

The trip to Berlin brought Yamashita and thirty-nine other observers across the frozen wastes of Siberia. At a ceremonial meeting typical of the pomp revered by the Nazis, he met Hitler. The German dictator promised the Japanese delegation that he would withhold no secrets from his friends and allies. But after six months of touring training camps and depots in both Germany and Italy, Yamashita realized that Hitler's promises were meaningless. He recorded:

"There were several pieces of equipment the Germans did not want us to see. Whenever I tried to persuade the German General Staff to show us things like radar—about which we had a rudimentary knowledge—the conversation always turned to something else."[8]

Nevertheless, Yamashita was highly impressed by the industrial and military strength of Germany.

After months of observation, which included a trip to the French coast to witness the German Luftwaffe's efforts against Great Britain, Yamashita realized that the Japanese Army lagged far behind the European armies. He particularly noted Japan's deficiency in medium tanks and long-range bombers. Upon returning home, he wrote a lengthy report noting these deficiencies and expressly suggested that war plans be halted until Japan could modernize its armed forces.

Tojo was not pleased with the report nor with the advice and sought to remove Yamashita's presence from Japan once more. He promptly assigned Yamashita to command of the Kwangtung Army in China, where he remained until November, 1941, when he was recalled to Tokyo and informed that he would assume command of the Twenty-Fifty Army. This unit was already in training for the invasion of Malaya should Japan decide to go to war. If war came, then, Yamashita would be responsible for conquering the "Pearl of the Orient," the British naval base at Singapore.

Even before Yamashita was named commander of the Twenty-Fifth Army, both army and navy staffs debated strategies to be used in the invasion of Malaya and Singapore. The Navy wanted the landings to be preceded by a prolonged bombardment of the beach defenses coupled with an intensive attack on the British airfields. The navy felt that in order to insure the safety of the troop transports, the RAF had to be eliminated.

In contrast, the army staff felt that this strategy would eliminate the element of surprise, an element they felt was vital to insure the success of the operation. They reasoned that the British would not make any aggressive moves, even if they detected the approaching Japanese armada, and by the time the enemy realized they were at war, the Japanese air force would have already gained air supremacy by having surprise on their side. After much debate, the commander of the Japanese Fleet for the invasion of Malaya, Vice Admiral Jisaburo Ozawa, accepted the army's proposal. This ended the debate, and Ozawa stated, "I say that the navy should accept the army's proposal even at the risk of annihilation."[9]

The actual site of the invasion was also decided before Yamashita assumed command. The narrow neck of land known as the Kra Isthmus, which joins Thailand to Malaya, was the area slated to be attacked. The three points on the isthmus were Singora and Patani in Thailand and Kota Bharu at the mouth of the Kelantan River in northern Malaya. Each of these three ports had excellent anchorages and nearby airfields. The main landing was to take place at Singora, for it possessed the best beach for exploitation.

Did Yamashita feel that Japan had a just cause for war preparation? In his own words he bluntly stated the rightness of its cause:

"The cause of this war is fundamentally economic. Fifty years ago Japan was more or less self-sufficient — the people could live off the land. Since then the population had almost doubled, so that Japan had to rely on outside sources of food supply and other economic requirements. In order to buy or import her commodities she had to pay ultimately in commodities. This effort on her part was prevented for one reason or another by other countries. Japan made attempts to solve the misunderstandings through peaceful methods, but when all her efforts were thwarted or negated she felt it necessary to engage in open warfare."[10]

He wrote these words shortly after the attack on Pearl Harbor. Along with most other Japanese, he did not consider war an infamous act, but rather a sacred duty.

For the proposed invasion, the Twenty-Fifth Army was allotted five divisions. When Yamashita arrived at his new headquarters on Hainan Island, he reviewed the situation and made a startling suggestion. During an interview with Army Chief of Staff Sugiyama, he stated that three divisions would be more than enough for the operation, instead of the allotted five.

This was most surprising, since most commanders usually requested more forces, not less. Yamashita, however, was astute enough to realize that the terrain of Malaya would mitigate against the use of large numbers of troops. Fewer troops of superior quality, he felt, could move more rapidly.

A total of sixty thousand men were thus allotted to Yamashita for this operation. They consisted of the 5th and 18th Divisions, two of the best-trained and most experienced divisions in the Imperial Army; and the third division was the Imperial Guards. These forces would be supported by two regiments of heavy artillery and a tank brigade. The army forces were to be protected by 450 land-based planes and 150 naval aircraft, along with the combined firepower of a battlecruiser and 10 destroyers.

Two of Yamashita's divisional commanders were also extremely experienced and well liked by their men. The 5th Division, veterans of China, were commanded by Lieutenant General Takuro Matsui. His counterpart with the 18th Division was Lieutenant General Renya Mutaguchi. Yamashita liked both men but felt a much closer bond with Mutaguchi, who had served as his chief of staff in 1937 when Yamashita was with the Kwangtung Army. The other division, the Imperial Guards, was commanded by Lieutenant General Takuma Nishimura, a man who disliked Yamashita and attempted to be as uncooperative as possible. Besides being uncooperative, Nishimura was close friends with the commander of the Southern Area Army, Yamashita's immediate superior, General Terauchi. He was also close to the army chief of staff, General Sugiyama. This friendship was to cause Yamashita many problems during the coming battle.

In addition to the problem of Nishimura, another individual who caused difficulties for Yamashita was his own chief of operations, Colonel Masanubu Tsuyi, an austere and sinister-looking person. Tsuyi was more a government spy and dutifully reported all his impressions of the army commander to the prime minister. As we have already seen, Tojo was no friend to Yamashita either.

Thus Yamashita was faced with enemies above him, under him, and on his staff. Hardly an ideal situation for a man about to embark on the difficult venture of conquering the "bastion of Singapore."

The invasion plan called for the assaulting forces to land at three beaches in the north, two in Thailand and one in Malaya. It was a daring plan calling for an assault on Singapore from the north, something the British considered unlikely. The defenses of the naval base were designed to protect from the obvious direction of a possible assault, the sea. The idea of driving a force down the spiny, jungle-covered back of Malaya was considered possible but improbable. Yet that was precisely the route the Japanese planned to take.

The Malayan Peninsula is roughly four hundred miles long and varies in width from two hundred to sixty miles. It is joined to Thailand by the narrow Kra Isthmus. Malaya has a spiny backbone, a ridge of jungle-covered hills rising to about seven thousand feet in the north and to around three thousand feet in the south. On both sides of the mountains lie the coastal plains. These contain hundreds of rivers and streams, which meander their way from the mountains to the sea, cutting their way through endless areas of thick jungle and swamp. The great growth of jungle is so thick that in places visibility is reduced to yards. Cultivated areas feature miles of rice paddies or fields where six-foot-high elephant grass, so sharp it can cut a man like a thousand knives, grows wild. This then is Malaya, a land totally unsuited for military maneuver. Or is it?

For the invasion, portions of the 5th and 18th Divisions were to land at the two ports in Thailand between Singora and Patani, and at the Malayan port of Kota Bharu. Once the two divisions had established their beachheads, it was planned to land Nishimura's less efficient Imperial Guards. A reserve division, the 56th, was to remain on board ship in case help was required. Once the beachheads were consolidated, it was planned to move south towards Singapore.

In early December, reconnaissance flights were sent over Thailand and Malaya. These flights confirmed the suspicion that enemy troops were deployed in defensive positions around Kota Bharu. Opposition could thus be expected at this point, but the Thai beaches were clear.

From his headquarters in Saigon, Count Terauchi sent a signal to Yamashita confirming the date for the commencement of hostilities, December 8 (December 7, Hawaiian time). He also informed Yamashita that should a negotiated settlement occur in the diplomatic talks then taking place in Washington, the operation would be cancelled.

Meanwhile, Yamashita's forces were loaded onto the ships and set sail for Malaya. They were split into five convoys to avoid arousing suspicion. Two convoys headed for Singora, two for Patani, and one for Kota Bharu. The landing of Mutaguchi's forces at Singora was to form the spearhead of the invasion (*See Map 13*).

December 8 was Japan's day of destiny. The men of the Twenty-Fifth Army were filled with nationalist fervor. Finally, an opportunity had come to oust the hated "barbarians" and liberate Asia for the Asians.

What of the opposing forces? As previously mentioned, the British plan for the defense of Singapore was totally geared to preventing a seaborne invasion. Although in the 1930s a forward-looking commander had predicted the possibility of a Japanese attack from the north, most experts came to accept the fact that the jungle and mountains provided an impenetrable barrier. Gradually, in the latter part of the decade, after observing the Japanese performance in China, the British came to the conclusion that the Malayan jungle might not be the impenetrable barrier they thought it to be. Slowly the view that the defense of Singapore might have to begin with the defense of Malaya became accepted.

In a military appreciation forwarded to London, the British chiefs in Malaya discussed the possibility of a Japanese thrust down from China through Thailand into Malaya. They asked London for more troops, and in particular, more planes.

In December 1940, Air Marshal Sir Robert Brooke-Popham was appointed commander-in-chief of Malaya and Singapore. After duly investigating the situation, he sent his appreciation to London. In it he too said that more airplanes and men were necessary if any Japanese attack was to be halted. London complied, but lowered the number of planes sent and only dispatched one Indian infantry division. Middle East priorities took first place. In February 1941, an Australian division arrived, followed the next month by still another Indian division. In April, Lieutenant General Arthur Percival arrived to take over as GOC (General Officer Commanding) in Malaya. One historian has called Percival

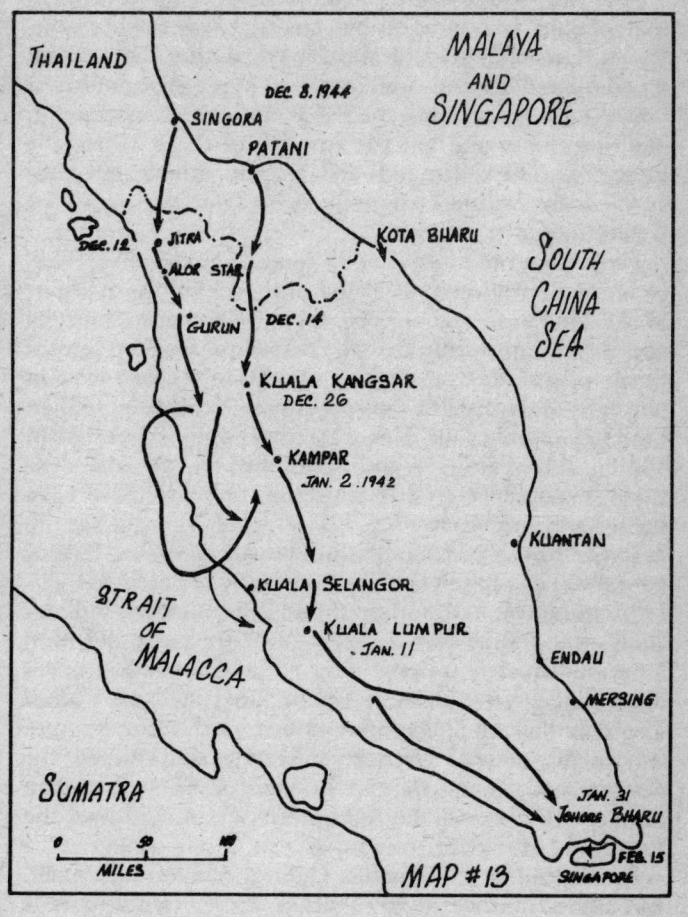

"a colorless character, more a staff officer than a commander and certainly not a natural leader."[11]

Nevertheless, at the time he was considered the ideal man for the job. Within a week Percival came to the conclusion that Malaya was indefensible unless it was further reinforced. He boldly told the British War Office that at least six additional divisions were required plus two regiments of tanks and more antitank and antiaircraft units. In addition, he urged that the strength of the RAF also be increased. These demands fell on sympathetic but deaf ears, since British commitments to North Africa and Greece took first priority.

Percival had to make do with what he already had. That included 88,000 men: 19,000 British, 15,200 Australians, 37,000 Indians, and 16,800 local volunteers. Since he accepted the principle that the defense of Singapore meant the defense of Malaya, forward airfields were constructed in northern Malaya. Unfortunately, these airfields lacked the necessary number of planes to defend the country. In addition, the airfields themselves had to be defended, which required Percival to scatter his forces to protect the fields from ground attacks.

So the British commander faced many obstacles. First of all, he did not have enough troops to do an adequate job. In addition, he had no tanks, and other modern military equipment was in short supply. What troops he did have were inadequately trained, most notably the Indian units. Thus Percival was short of troops, weapons, and planes. The only defense Singapore had besides these forces were two mighty capital ships recently sent to prop up the defense and the morale of the people of Singapore. The *Prince of Wales* and the *Repulse* arrived, but without the support of an aircraft carrier.

On December 4, Yamashita's convoy sailed from Hainan and arrived off the invasion beaches on the moonlit night of the 7th. Shortly after midnight, the British beach defenses at Kota Bharu were systematically shelled by the Japanese warships. Then the amphibious forces struck. The RAF did manage some bombing of the convoy and caused some initial confusion but the Indian troops defending Kota Bharu were soon overwhelmed by the superior Japanese forces. The Indian positions were situated only a hundred yards from the water, putting them in an excellent position to rake the invading forces. Quick action saved the day for the Japanese. By driving hard into the Indian fire, the invaders circled their positions and fired into the Indians from all sides. Panic spread among the defenders as rumor spread that the Japanese had broken through. In fact, at first the Japanese were having a difficult time. Percival's curse of having to rely on such poorly trained troops benefited the Japanese. As panic spread among the defenders, they evacuated their positions, including the airfields where they left the Japanese much booty. Besides the gift of an undestroyed airstrip, the defenders left behind bombs and fuel, all intact and ready for the invader's use. Kota Bharu was in Japanese hands within a matter of hours.

The landings at Singora and Patani were routine. There was some initial light resistance by patrols of the Thai Army and police but it failed to amount to anything significant. At 5:20 4AM, Yamashita came ashore at Singora and established his headquarters. It was there that he first received word of the attack on Pearl Harbor, the Philippines, and Hong Kong.

Within a few hours, a compromise was reached with the Thai government that gave the Japanese troops the right to pass through. Of course the Thai government did not have much of a choice. Either they complied or their country would be devastated.

The original British defensive plan was code-named Operation Matador. Basically, the plan called for British forces to advance to wherever the Japanese landed. With the invasion at Kota Bharu, the British decided that it would be useless to launch Matador, so the order went out for the British forces to fall back from the Thai border to a defensive position then under construction around Jitra. This position, in fact, was the key to the entire campaign. With only five hundred men and a mere ten tanks, General

Matsui reached the Jitra line with a burst of thunder. The fighting was heavy, but using the popular Japanese tactic of the hook—in which the troops infiltrated through the jungle and moved behind the enemy positions—the British position fell rapidly. The Jitra Line was breached and the Japanese were on their way toward their next immediate objective, Aloi Star. Arthur Swinson said of the action at the Jitra Line:

> "As for the action at Jitra itself, this had proved possibly the biggest disgrace to British/Indian armies since Chillianwala in the Second Sikh War of 1848."[12]

What was humiliating for the defenders was that the Japanese captured the line without even having to deploy the whole of the 5th Division. The task had been accomplished by only the advance guard. Japanese losses were a mere fifty men. Not only had they captured this important defensive position, but the panic-ridden Indians left food, ammunition, large quantities of guns and trucks behind. In their panic the Indians neglected to carry out the prescribed demolitions. Yamashita was heard to remark that if Indian troops made up the bulk of the British forces defending Malaya, the job would be easy.

In defense of the Indians, it must be said that they were handed a difficult job to do without benefit of the necessary training or heavy weapons. In fact, for many of the Indian troops, it was the first time they had even seen a tank.

Having breached the Jitra Line, the Japanese rolled south. Yamashita was optimistic. Speed was of the essence in the advance. The further south the Japanese advanced, the more confident they became. They quickly adapted themselves to fighting in the jungle. Their confidence bolstered by their recent victories, fattened on captured food, strengthened with captured fuel, truck, and ammunition they were convinced of their opponents' inferiority. The Japanese steamroller was unstoppable.

> "The   keynote   of   Yamashita's   campaign   in

Malaya—advance, breakthrough, pursuit, consolidation."[13]

The battle tactic used at the Jitra Line became the model for the balance of the campaign. Infiltrate the enemy line, hit them with tanks, always apply pressure. Constant pressure on the British line was deemed necessary. In doing so, they never allowed the defenders the time they needed to consolidate a new position. Japanese infantrymen even used bicycles to speed themselves along. They would peddle their way along roads and paths and carry the bikes across the rivers and streams, always maintaining the pressure on the retreating enemy.

In advocating the tactic of the hook, Yamashita had a disagreement with Tsuyi, his operations officer, who wanted to keep the pressure confined along the main roads of Malaya. Tsuyi considered Yamashita's tactic of wide encirclement along the jungle paths to be expensive in manpower. In a heated debate, Tsuyi was no match for the army commander, which caused the operations officer to lose face. He offered to resign but Yamashita refused to accept the resignation. However, from that time forth Tsuyi became an implacable enemy who began to talk against his commander. This vilification campaign was enthusiastically pursued in Tokyo by Prime Minister Tojo, who would manage, at the end of the campaign, to deny Yamashita the fruits of the great victory he would soon win.

Nevertheless, Yamashita continued to use the tactic of the hook. He even utilized seaborne flanking operations. That he never let up was the key to Yamashita's success.

For the British, one disaster followed another, even at sea, where within a few days of the Japanese landing the Imperial forces won a tremendous victory by sending the *Prince of Wales* and the *Repulse* to a watery grave. The days of the battleship were truly past. He who commanded the air dominated the sea.

With the fall of the Jitra Line, the defenders retreated southward. Within six weeks, the capture of Malaya was complete. The British routine during these weeks followed a pattern: retreat; halt and dig a defensive position; be attacked by the Japanese, which caused a further step backward. Over and over again, step by step, down the entire length of the peninsula, this routine was repeated. In the course of the British retreat, over twenty thousand Indian troops surrendered. Percival's only hope was the 8th Australian Division at Jahore in southern Malaya.

Thus far the Australians had done well against the Japanese. Though they too had been forced to retreat, they had given the Japanese a bloodletting, making the victory more costly. Unfortunately for the British, these better-trained troops were few in number, and when Yamashita's forces made an amphibious landing on the west coast of Jahore and launched a frontal assault against the inexperienced 45th Indian Brigade, Percival was left with no choice but to fall back on Singapore, to the disappointment of the Australians, who felt they could have held the enemy. The remnants of the Indian troops were withdraw across the stone causeway connecting Malaya and Singapore Island. The Australians and British troops formed the rear guard. On January 31, 1942, the last of the rear guard crossed to Singapore. When the last troops crossed the causeway, it was blown sky high.

Meanwhile, the newspapers in Japan were making a hero out of Yamashita. Ironically, he knew that this fact could have an adverse effect on his career because of Tojo's animosity and jealousy.

Yamashita's forces now massed for the final drive of the campaign, the attack on Singapore Island. The island measured twenty-seven miles from east to west and fourteen from north to south. The actual city of Singapore was in the southernmost part of the island. Most of the island was comprised of jungle and swamps, interspersed with rubber and coconut plantations. The major defenses of the island were at the naval base. Unfortunately, as we have already seen, the naval base's massive guns faced seaward and would prove useless during the forthcoming battle.

The Straits of Johore separating Singapore from Malaya measure from six hundred to five thousand yards in width.

The defense of the island was in the hands of eighty-five thousand men, including six recently arrived British battalions. General Percival had numerical superiority, so in theory, therefore, he should have been able to thwart any Japanese assault. However, there were some deep problems.

The northern portion of Singapore was literally defenseless. General Wavell, Percival's theater commander, had recently inquired why no defenses were being constructed in northern Singapore. Percival replied to the astonished Wavell that the construction of defensive works would have a negative impact on morale. Whereupon Wavell angrily responded by stating that the impact on morale would be even greater when retreating troops began to cross the causeway from the mainland. Churchill, however, ordered that Singapore be turned into a citadel. On January 20, he signaled Wavell.

> "I want to make it absolutely clear that I expect every inch of ground to be defended, every scrap of material or defenses to be blown to pieces to prevent capture by the enemy, and no question of surrender to be entertained until after protracted fighting among the ruins of Singapore city."

For the assault, Yamashita had only sixty thousand men. His heavy artillery was severely reduced, his ammunition inadequate, and his line of communication long and tenuous. Only in the air did he have the advantage, thanks to the support of some two hundred aircraft in comparison to a single squadron of Hurricanes remaining to the British. Yamashita realized that he had to strike quickly before the British realized the dire straits they were actually in. If British morale revived and they put up a staunch defense, he knew that he did not possess the tools for a long, drawn-out campaign.

While Yamashita's forces prepared for the assault, Japanese planes flew over the city and subjected it to a horrible attack. Approximately two hundred people perished daily in the city from the effects of the bombing.

Yamashita was a troubled man. Besides the shortages of critical supplies, he was being barraged by an interfering commander, Count Terauchi, the commander of the Southern Area Army. From Saigon, the latter issued orders to the Twenty-Fifth Army on how to conduct the assault on Singapore. Yamashita deeply resented this Monday-morning quarterbacking. He was incensed when Terauchi sent his own chief of staff to Yamashita's headquarters with voluminous notes and instructions on how to organize the assault. Yamashita dealt with the notes by tearing them to shreds.

By February 4, the Japanese were ready to begin the attack. Yamashita assembled two hundred collapsible launches equipped with outboard motors and a hundred larger landing craft. He then moved his three divisions into position, along with three thousand vehicles. After practicing for a few days, on February 6th he summoned his divisional commanders together to give them their final orders for the assault. Nishimura's division was ordered to make a feint to the east on the evening of the 7th, in an effort to draw the British in that direction. Then, after dark on the 8th, the 5th and 18th Divisions would cross to the northwest corner of the island. Once established, the Imperial Guards would follow. Nishimura, who already felt that the army commander had slighted him, added this to his list of grievances against Yamashita.

Yamashita was counting on Percival's falling for the feint. To add to the deception, the Japanese commander had erected dummy camps on the mainland directly opposite the invasion area. Each day, trucks headed eastward under the watchful gaze of the British. What the British failed to see were the trucks doubling back at night. All this activity confirmed what Percival already thought, that the Japanese were going to invade the northeast sector. The British commander sent more ammunition to that sector.

From the glass-domed tower on the grounds of the Sultan of Johore's palace, Yamashita watched the commencement of the assault on February 8. It was preceded by a heavy artillery bombardment and massive air strikes. British machine-gun fire raked the Japanese ranks. Nevertheless, by the morning of the 9th, thousands of Japanese were on the island and moving southward. Yamashita moved his headquarters to a rubber plantation on Singapore Island.

Before noon that day, with the 5th and 18th Divisions already across, it was time for the Imperial Guards to cross. Nishimura deferred because he felt a loss of face. In reprisal for what he considered humiliation, the Guards' commander ordered the brutal beheading of two hundred wounded Australians and Indians who had been left behind in Johore. Nishimura used every method at his disposal short of outright insubordination to make things difficult for the Twenty-Fifth Army commander. He questioned orders and made excuses. Yamashita said of Nishimura's attitude,

> "I ordered the Imperial Guards to cross the strait. Then their commander asked for further orders from me. I received a message from him that his troops were hesitating to cross because of oil flames on the surface of the water. It looked to me as if he was still upset about not being able to lead the attack. I ordered him to do his duty."[15]

Yamashita could ill afford this internal opposition because he was under pressure from above. Terauchi had promised Tokyo that Singapore would be captured on February 11, Japan's National Foundation Day. This only served to increase the pressure on Yamashita.

The fighting was intense. In many places it was a hand-to-hand battle. Percival had decided to establish a perimeter defense line around the city, reasoning that it was essential to hold the vital reservoirs supplying the city's water. Wavell made one last visit to Singapore on the 10th. He ordered an immediate counterattack but knew realistically that it would have little chance of success. He then left for his headquarters in Java.

By the 12th the Japanese had captured the vital road junction leading to the city. Panic hit the town. But

Yamashita himself was beginning to feel apprehensive. His chief supply officer had warned him that he was critically short of fuel and artillery ammunition. If the capture of Singapore required a long siege, the Japanese would not have the tools necessary to carry it out.

That evening, Yamashita held a conference at Mutaguchi's headquarters. The army commander stated that unless further supplies reached them, the guns would fall silent within five or six days. Yamashita knew that he had to continue the struggle without letup, for if he so much as briefly allowed the British the opportunity to consider the situation, their morale might revive. It was important to continue as if the situation was well in hand and hope that the British would capitulate before the ammunition ran out. To nudge the British in that direction, Yamashita had a note dropped onto Percival's headquarters demanding surrender but promising leniency. The note also threatened reprisals should resistance continue. The message read:

> "Your Excellency:
> I, the High Command of the Nippon Army, based on the spirit of Japanese chivalry, have the honor of presenting this note to your Excellency advising you to surrender the whole force in Malaya.
> My sincere respect is due to your army, which true to the traditional spirit of Great Britain, is bravely defending Singapore, which now stands isolated and unaided. Many fierce and gallant fights have been fought by your men and officers, to the honor of British warriorship. But the development of the general war situation has already sealed the fate of Singapore, and the continuation of futile resistance would only serve to inflict direct harm and injuries to thousands of noncombatants living in the city, throwing them into further miseries and horrors of war, but also would not add anything to the honor of your army. . . . In closing this note, I pay again my

sincere respects to your Excellency."

(signed) Tomoyuki Yamashita

"1. The Parliamentaire should proceed to the Bukit Timah Road."

"2. The Parliamentaire should bear a large white flag and the Union Jack."[16]

Percival had no intention of complying. That same day, the Japanese pushed forward and captured a main British ammunition dump and a large military hospital. At the hospital, the British medical officers attempted to surrender but the Japanese troops entered the hospital and savagely bayoneted 230 patients and 93 of the staff to death. Survivors fled to the city and told of the Japanese atrocities. The rumor quickly spread that this treatment was what everyone could expect if Percival continued to refuse to surrender.

Morale in the city was declining rapidly already. This deterioration accelerated like wildfire as news of the atrocities at the hospital spread. It appeared as if Yamashita's bluff was going to succeed. In his own words:

"My attack on Singapore was a bluff, a bluff that worked. . . . I knew that if I had to fight long for Singapore I would be beaten. That is why surrender had to be at once."[17]

From Percival's point of view, surrender seemed the only alternative. Wavell finally authorized him to make the decision once Percival was completely satisfied in his own mind that continued resistance was no longer feasible. By the 14th, the only water reaching the city came from a pumping station only half a mile from the nearest Japanese position. In fact, some parts of the city were already without water and there was concern that disease would hit the city. Percival was informed that within forty-eight hours there would probably be no water available at all.

On Sunday the 15th, Percival called a conference of his subordinate commanders to solicit their opinion. After speaking with these officers, he became convinced that the situation was hopeless. At 10:00 that morning, a party of British soldiers carrying a large white flag approached leading troops of Mutaguchi's division. A few hours later Yamashita was informed that the British were ready to discuss truce terms. The bluff had paid off. On hearing the news Yamashita commented, "I prepared myself against being deceived, and ordered the British commander to come in person."[18]

The British delegation returned to their lines and reported to Percival that he would personally have to go to the designated meeting place. The British commander arrived late that afternoon carrying a white flag to the slope of Bukit Timah. The hapless Percival, wearing a light tropical shirt and shorts, and Yamashita, dressed in the tunic of a Kwangtung Army officer complete with leggings and boots, sat down at the table.

Yamashita asked Percival if he wished to surrender unconditionally. The British commander replied in the affirmative. The next question was did the British have any Japanese prisoners of war? Percival said no. Then Yamashita placed the document of surrender on the table. Percival read the document, then asked permission to wait until the next day before signing. Yamashita could not afford any further delay. Feeling that perhaps the British might find out about his shortages, he wanted an immediate capitulation. Therefore, he told Percival that he had either to sign right then, or the fighting would resume. The Japanese interpreter at the conference was not particularly adept, and Yamashita was rapidly losing patience. In a loud voice he shouted to the interpreter, "Is the British Army going to sign or not? Answer yes of no."[19] At this, the dejected and startled Percival said yes. The surrender document was signed at 6:10 PM.

With the surrender official, Yamashita had gained the greatest victory of any Japanese general. The heralded bastion of Singapore had fallen in only seventy-three days. The loss of Singapore sent shock waves throughout Asia and forcefully demonstrated that the stature of all white man in the east would never again be the same. In all, Yamashita had captured 130,000 British, Australian, Indian, and Malay troops at a cost of 9,823 Japanese casualties.

Without a doubt, Yamashita justly deserved the nickname "Tiger of Malaya." Without enough strength and lacking supplies, he conducted a superior campaign. His 'hook' tactic was highly successful and his ability to coordinate amphibious and ground operations was masterful. The bluff during the final days of the campaign saved Japan from a long, drawn-out, attritional campaign. Granted, he faced many inferior forces, but there were enough British forces who could have inflicted tremendous losses. It was primarily Yamashita's forcefulness that brought the campaign to its successful conclusion. He deserves all the accolades,and honors due to a victor. Unfortunately, these honors were not forthcoming.

With the conquest of Singapore, Yamashita now faced the difficult task of getting the city back into working order. It took engineers five days just to get fresh water flowing into the city again. Yamashita also had to deal with the vast numbrs of Allied prisoners. Many pages have been devoted to this aspect of the Japanese effort. It must be said, however, that under Yamashita, the POWs were accorded relatively humane treatment. Unfortunately, he did not retain command for very long after the campaign, with the issuance of Tojo's order regarding the treatment of prisoners, the situation deteriorated rapidly.

Like Admiral Yamamoto, Yamashita knew that the pressure on the Allies could not cease if Japan could hoped to win the war. He advocated an invasion of Burma and Australia. In July, while he was preparing the Twenty-Fifth Army for future operations, Yamashita was abruptly relieved of command and transferred to command of the First Army Group in Manchukuo. Why had the "Tiger of Malaya" been shuttled off to this obscure command? What was the reason one of Japan's most successful generals was being sent to a backwater of the war?

Yamashita considered the transfer a slight, since he was positive that he would get command of the army in Burma.

The answer to the puzzle lay with Tojo. The prime minister wanted Yamashita out of the limelight: Of course, Tojo argued that this appointment was to a vital sector, since there was always the danger of an attack by Russia. However, Russia was in no position to attack Japan in 1942, and Tojo knew it. Yamashita's transfer was the result of jealousy and vindictiveness on Tojo's part. He did not even allow Yamashita to travel to his new position by way of Japan, where, as a successful general, he had earned the right to the honor of a private audience with the emperor. Instead, Yamashita was ordered to proceed directly to Manchukuo. Tojo had deftly managed to get rid of his rival. The prime minister also refused to allow Japanese newspapers to print anything about Yamashita. A complete news blackout was ordered. He was determined not to allow Yamashita any publicity.

As compensation, Yamashita was promoted to full general, but it was small satisfaction, for from his obscure post, he saw Japan's fortunes turn sour. Primarily, his time was consumed with training and preparing for a war with Russia. Sadly, he saw the empire shrink, but the greatest shock came in July, 1944, with the fall of Saipan. Yamashita knew now that the homeland was in grave danger.

The resignation of Tojo following Saipan's loss was one positive occurrence, as far as Yamashita was concerned. The new prime minister, General Koiso, dedicated himself to the successful prosecution of the war. With the empire in jeopardy, Koiso ordered the "Tiger of Malaya" back home and into the heart of the war.

Japan's situation was ominous. The Americans were about to make their grand entrance into the Philippines. To avert this potential disaster, Japan was willing to commit everything it had left, knowing that if the United States recaptured the Philippines, Japan itself would be cut off from the southern region and all its vital natural resources. To forestall this inevitable invasion, the Japanese planned an all-out operation, known as the Victory Plan (Sho Plan).

Both the army and the navy prepared to do battle. In the Philippines the Japanese had amassed two hundred and fifty thousand troops, each one ready to fight to the death. What was urgently required was an inspired leader who could lead those men to victory. Who else could fill that role but the hero of the Malayan campaign, General Tomoyuki Yamashita?

Upon arriving in Tokyo on September 29, 1944, Yamashita was briefed on the situation and about the details of his new command. He was also granted the long overdue private audience with the emperor. During the audience, Hirohito himself invested Yamashita with command of the Fourteenth Area Army in the Philippines. He was informed that the very future of Japan's war effort depended on retaining command of the islands.

Yamashita arrived in Manila on October 5 and wasted no time in getting down to work. He called a conference of all senior members of his staff and the commanders of all fighting forces who were able to attend. Yamashita told the assembled officers:

"I have been told by our emperor that the crisis will develop on this battlefield. This gives us all a heavy responsibility."[20]

Yamashita established his headquarters on Luzon, where he made plans for the anticipated battle. His prime force was Lieutenant General Sosaku Suzuki's Thirty-Fifth Army, which was charged with defending the central and southern Philippines.

Another force in the Philippines was Lieutenant General Kyoji Tominaya's Fourth Air Army. Both Yamashita and Tominaya reported on an equal basis to Field Marshal Count Terauchi, the Southern Area Army commander. Yamashita was not happy with the thought of once more serving under Terauchi, but he had little choice in the matter. He was also dismayed with the fact that the air force was an independent command.

A third independent command in the Philippines was the

naval force. This divided-command situation represented one of the biggest problems faced by Yamashita. There was no joint overall headquarters responsible for coordinating strategy. Instead, three separate commands, army, navy and air force, each split by animosities and jealousy, attempted to meet the enemy.

Yamashita realized that his appointment had come a good six months too late. He hardly knew his command and was unhappy with what he had already seen, particularly the separate commands. He also felt that the Americans would invade soon. In addition, Yamashita felt that he lacked adequate troops and that the ones he did have were dreadfully untrained. Food, fuel, and equipment were in short supply. Compounding these problems was the activity of the Filipino guerrillas, who harassed the Japanese supply and communication lines. There was simply too much to do and too little time to do it in.

Nevertheless, as a soldier of Nippon, one who had lived by the Code of Bushido, Yamashita was determined to do his best. He took care to personally inspect as many units as possible. He encouraged, reprimanded when necessary, and did his utmost to prepare for the American attack.

The major question in his mind was where that attack would be. Before leaving Japan Yamashita had been told that the Americans might land in the central Philippines, but it was on the all-important island of Luzon where he was to prepare to fight an all-out decisive battle.

On October 17, 1944, the Americans landed on a couple of small islands in the Gulf of Leyte. Three days later the main invasion struck Leyte itself. The long awaited invasion of the Philippines had begun. By noon, Yamashita knew that the Americans had established a deep bridgehead. He heard the historic speech of General Douglas MacArthur who, when he landed again on Philippine soil, stated, "I have returned" (*See Map 14*).

By nightfall of the first day, the American Sixth Army held two large beachheads more than a mile deep on Leyte's eastern shore. The next morning, the attacking forces drove inland, and within a week the American grip

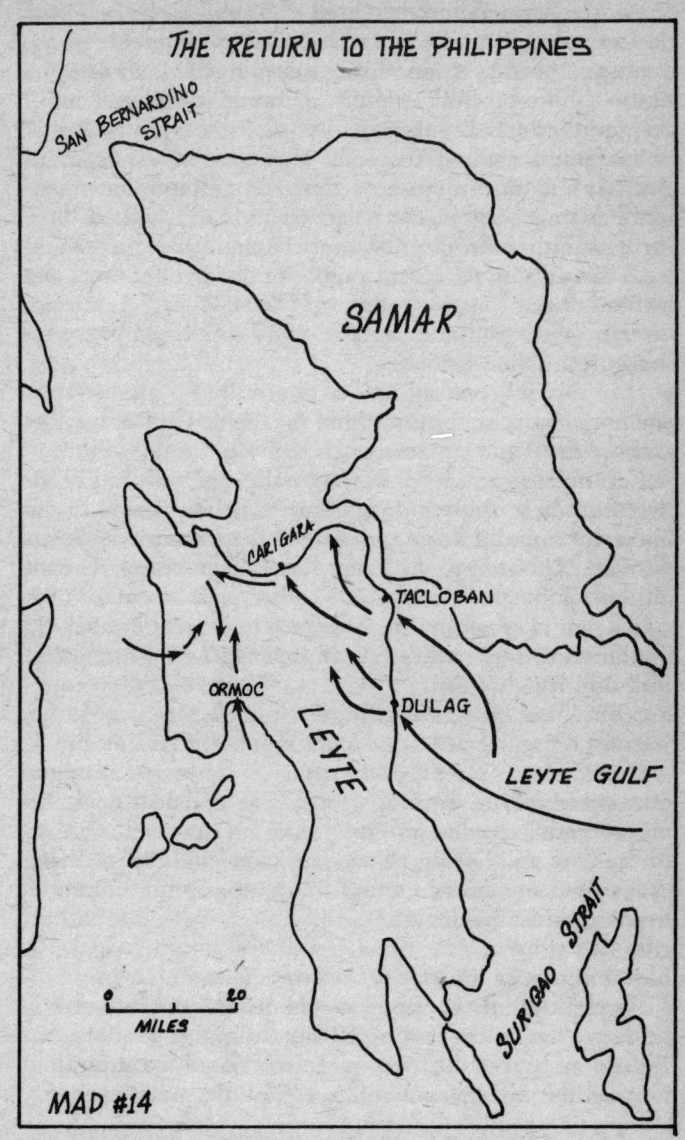

on the eastern shore was secure.

As MacArthur's forces blasted their way onto Leyte, the Japanese Navy, as part of the Sho Plan, prepared for an all-out naval confrontation. The ensuing battle, known as the Battle of Leyte Gulf, wound up being the largest naval battle in history. For the Japanese the result was the loss of some three hundred thousand tons of combat shipping. Included in that massive total were one large and three light aircraft carriers, three battleships, six heavy and three light cruisers, and ten destroyers. American losses totaled only forty thousand tons, comprising one light carrier, two escort carriers, two destroyers, and one PT boat. As a result of the catastrophe, the Japanese Navy ceased to exist as an effective fighting force.

The great naval victory secured MacArthur's communication and supply lines. By the end of October the Sixth Army had completely occupied the Leyte Valley and all of the airfields in the east-central portion of the island. Unfortunately, those airfields proved useless, thanks to the incessant rains on Leyte that turned the airstrips into rivers of mud. This proved the biggest American disappointment of the campaign. Not until December, near the end of the campaign, was an airfield constructed on solid ground. In the interim, aerial support was provided by the aircraft of Admiral Halsey's Third Fleet.

With the Americans firmly established on Leyte, Yamashita was faced with a dilemma. He had originally accepted the reasoning that the main battle for the Philippines would be fought on Luzon and had made his dispositions accordingly. The Americans, however, were on Leyte. At this point, Terauchi interfered by ordering Yamashita to send additional troops to Leyte. Yamashita's reply reflected his fury:

> "Without air superiority the movements of large-scale reinforcements to Leyte would be subject to grave risk. Also, there is not sufficient shipping available, and it is still difficult to determine with certainty whether the invasion of Leyte is the main enemy

effort, or whether it will be a limited operation, followed quickly by a major attack in Luzon."²¹

Yamashita was a cautious commander, and he knew that MacArthur had the ability to attack not only on Leyte, but in Luzon as well. Strategically and politically he viewed Luzon as the American objective and did not want to weaken his position there by sending troops to Leyte only to find out too late that MacArthur was planning to invade Luzon and was just waiting for him to make such a move. Terauchi, however, was his superior. The latter had long favored an all-out fight wherever the enemy landed. He thus ordered Yamashita to throw everything available into the defense of Leyte.

The latter was shocked by this order. He warned his superior that risking everything for Leyte would strip Luzon of its strength and leave it vulnerable to attack. His arguments fell on deaf ears and he had no choice but to comply with his orders. Therefore, he began shifting troops to support General Suzuki in Leyte. Yamashita said:

"The die was now cast for an all-out battle on Leyte, a grim struggle that would determine the fate of the Philippines."²²

Protected somewhat by the cover of incessant rain, the convoys from Manila ferried Japanese reinforcements to western Leyte near Ormoc. These reinforcements turned Leyte's central mountain range into a bastion. By November 1, over thirteen thousand men had been sent to bolster the Thirty-Fifth Army, and more were on the way. These reached Ormoc on the 9th and the 11th. U.S. planes attacked these convoys, killing and wounding thousands, but thousands more landed safely. Before the battle was over, forty-five thousand reinforcements were sent to Leyte.

Yamashita was astute enough to see that with American domination of the air and sea, the battle for Leyte was already lost, just as he had predicted. He therefore felt that the only logical move was to pull out. On November 7, he sent his chief of staff, Lieutenant General Akira Muto, to see Terauchi's chief of staff and express that very opinion, emphasizing the importance of not dispatching additional reinforcements to Leyte. Terauchi's chief of staff disagreed and a tremendous argument ensued, ending with Muto's angrily stamping out of the meeting. Imperial Headquarters and the Southern Army were both out of touch with the real situation, he shouted.

The following day, a stern Terauchi summoned Yamashita and reiterated the need to continue the struggle for Leyte. Yamashita attempted to convince his superior that this policy was simply draining the Fourteenth Army's strength, but the Southern Area commander remained adamant. Leyte, Terauchi said, was far from lost. Thus, Yamashita was directed to make every effort to bring the battle to a successful conclusion. He had little choice other than to yield, but deep down he lamented the fact that in the two campaigns of the war that he had commanded, Terauchi was his superior. In Malaya, Terauchi had taken exception to Yamashita's conduct of the campaign, and now, here in the Philippines, he interfered with the way Yamashita felt the campaign should be run.

During November, the ground battle was bitter and costly. The Japanese were relentlessly pushed further westward and southward. The American objective was Ormoc, which, if captured, would eliminate the main Japanese port of entry. Accordingly, the defenders contested the approaches to Ormoc with great vigor. The fighting in the jungle-clad hills north of the port was the most savage of the campaign. Up and down, through the steaming green hell, the fighting continued, at time deteriorating to small-arms action and hand-to-hand combat. Savagery was matched by more savagery. The sheer weight of the American juggernaut, however, cracked the Japanese defenses. By the end of the month, the Americans were ready to descent from the heights into the Ormoc Valley. In other parts of the island, the story was the same. The Japanese were inexorably pushed back. Low on food, ammunition, and heavy weapons, but high on casualties, the resistance petered out.

By early December, the Thirty-Fifth Army found itself squeezed between the northern Ormoc Valley and the ridges south of the city. Yamashita was justifiably concerned over the desperate situation. Meanwhile, Terauchi shifted his headquarters from Manila to Saigon. Before leaving, however, he ordered Yamashita to continue to vigorously prosecute the Leyte campaign. The Fourteenth Army commander realized that the only way to fulfill Terauchi's order was to recapture the airfields on the eastern portion of the island. If he could accomplish this, he felt, he might prevent the Americans from using them, while at the same time allowing the Japanese air forces the use of the fields to bomb the American positions.

General Tominaga, the Fourth Air commander, agreed to cooperate by combining an airborne attack with the army's attack toward the airfields. This attack was given the name "Wa Operation." Orders for this final all-out attempt on Leyte were given on November 23, the launching scheduled for the first week in December.

The attack was preceded by heavy Japanese air attacks including the dreaded Kamikaze planes. These Japanese attacks placed a tremendous strain on the American carriers, which, from the beginning of the campaign, had provided air cover for MacArthur's forces. Admiral Halsey notified MacArthur that his Third Fleet would soon have to be withdrawn from the area. Had it not been for the constant rain, which had turned the airfields into quagmires of mud, Halsey's forces might have left weeks earlier.

The paradrops went off on schedule, and though initially successful, were soon repulsed with heavy losses. The ground offensive that was to link up with the paratroops failed miserably because of the difficult terrain, resulting in the attacking forces' being totally exhausted. The Wa Operation went down to bitter defeat. Ironically, the airfields, on which the Japanese placed such heavy emphasis, were temporarily abandoned by the Americans in late November because of the horrendous soil conditions, incessant rain, and poor drainage.

Meanwhile, the final American offensive on Leyte began on December 5, with a drive into the northern Ormoc Valley by the U.S. X Corps and a simultaneous attack by the XXIV Corps into central and southwestern Leyte. Though physically exhausted, the Japanese fought tenaciously, but they faced overwhelming odds. To cap the American drive, on December 7, General Krueger, the Sixth Army commander, ordered the 77th Division to make an amphibious landing at Ormoc. This operation would close the primary Japanese port on western Leyte. The landing at Ormoc was uncontested, but the Japanese reacted quickly with a heavy air raid, featuring Kamikaze attacks against the supporting vessels.

With the American capture of Ormoc, the Japanese were denied their main supply port. The defenders were trapped in a vise between the American forces. The battle was all but over for the surrounded, starved Japanese. General Suzuki was forced to bring his forces into the tractless wilderness of northwestern Leyte, where the Thirty-Fifth Army made its last stand.

Faced with the crisis on Leyte and the reduction of his forces on Luzon, Yamashita was confronted by yet one more crisis. On December 13, MacArthur's forces struck at the island of Mindoro, just south of Luzon. Sensing that MacArthur would use this move as a stepping stone for an eventual invasion of Luzon, Yamashita attempted once more to convince Terauchi to reverse his stand. The latter's first reaction was to order Yamashita to counterattack on Mindoro, but Terauchi's chief of staff convinced him that the Mindoro operation should be abandoned and in its place, Yamashita be allowed to concentrate his efforts on the defense of Luzon. Two days later, Terauchi finally gave Yamashita complete freedom to conduct the campaign as he saw fit.

One of Yamashita's first acts after receiving the good news was to signal the commander of the forces on Leyte, General Suzuki, telling him not to expect any more supplies or reinforcements, and that he should be prepared to evacuate Leyte as soon as possible.

But Mindoro was proving a thorn in Yamashita's side. The island provided the Americans with what Leyte could not: decent land for the construction of airfields. From the hastily established fields, the American air forces flew repeated sorties against Luzon and caused the Japanese untold difficulties. The movement of troops became a precarious venture, always under the watchful gaze of U.S. fighters and bombers.

Nevertheless, Yamashita had obtained what he desired from the start, authority to conduct the campaign without interference from Southern Army headquarters or from Tokyo. In preparing for the decisive campaign on Luzon, he moved his headquarters out of Manila during the last week of the year and into the village of Ipo, about twenty miles north of the capital. He wanted to declare Manila an open city, but the naval commander, Vice Admiral Mikawa and General Tominaya, the air force chief, violently objected to the prospect. In the city were twenty-five thousand naval troops who had vowed to fight to the death in defense of their position.

In the interim, the fighting on Leyte ground down to its inevitable conclusion. The battle had proved a disaster of the first class for the Japanese. Its navy was destroyed, its air forces suffered huge irreplaceable losses, and a large chunk of the Japanese army was gone. At least fifty thousand men had died during the preceding two months of battle. For Yamashita, it meant that with a greatly weakened force, he now faced a superior American invasion force.

Chief among Yamashita's problems was lack of air power. He also faced shortages of virtually every other commodity necessary to sustain an effective defense: ammunition, engineering stores, food, and fuel. Thanks to the sustained U.S. submarine effort and the lack of a Japanese convoy system, not a single cargo vessel carrying food got through to Luzon during the month of December. This caused the Japanese commanders to cut their daily rations by one-third at the beginning of the year. The problem of moving troops was another nightmare. Filipino guerrillas were not helping matters as they blew up bridges, sabotaged convoys, and greatly hindered the dispersement of supplies to the men in the field. In the face of these problems, one of Yamashita's staff commented about his commander:

> "He appeared to be much more human, indeed to some he seemed to be drifting into a fatalistic mellow calm."[23]

Luzon is the northernmost and largest of the thousands of islands that comprise the Philippine archipelago. Much of the island is mountainous, but as the Japanese found out in December 1941, it contains excellent landing beaches around Lingayen Gulf on its west-central shore. This passageway provided excellent access to the island's central plain, which contained good roads for quick exploitation southward towards the capital city of Manila. The American invasion force approached Luzon in early January, spearheaded by the battle-tested Sixth Army of General Krueger. Its mission was to duplicate General Homma's drive of 1941.

To resist this force, Yamashita had almost two hundred fifty thousand men. Unfortunately, this large number included many undertrained and poorly led troops. The cream of the Japanese forces had already perished on Leyte. In addition, many of the units suffered troop shortages along with shortages of food, ammunition, fuel and transport.

In the knowledge that numbers alone would not be enough to defend all of Luzon, Yamashita deployed his troops into three main groups (*See Map 15*). Directly under his command were approximately a hundred fifty-two thousand men known as the Shobu Group, whose responsibility was the defense of northern Luzon. A second group, the Kembu Goup, containing thirty thousand men under Major General Tsukada, was given the task of defending the central zone, including Bataan and the area around Clark Field. A third formation, the Shimbu Group of eighty thousand men under Lieutenant General

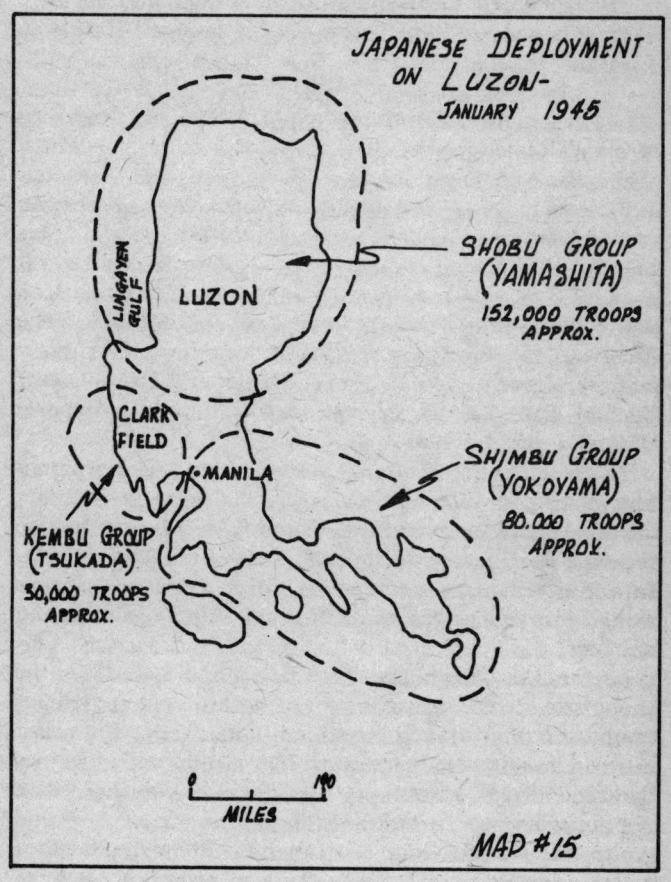

Yokoyama, was responsible for the area stretching from Manila down to the Bicol Peninsula. Yamashita retained overall control of all forces except for Admiral Iwabuchi's naval troops in Manila.

The U.S. invasion force was immense by Japanese standards. The Sixth Army contained four divisions, the 6th, 43rd, 37th, and 40th, all veterans of jungle fighting in either the Solomon Islands or New Guinea. Close support was provided by Admiral Kinkaid's Seventh Fleet, while strategic air cover was in the hands of General Kenney's Fifth and Thirteenth Air Forces.

The landings began on January 9, 1945. From the sea and air the beaches were pounded by massive firepower. At 9:00 AM, the American troops headed for the shore, and by nightfall, sixty-eight thousand men had landed on a beachhead seventeen miles wide and deep. Yamashita had planned to counterattack the beachhead, but his plans were foiled by the guerrilla attacks and American air strikes, which prevented the movement of troops and supplies to the key defensive sector. Without this, no prolonged resistance would be possible.

Crisis followed crisis as one position after another fell to the Americans. Whatever air power the Japanese had left was quickly dissipated in fruitless Kamikaze attacks. Despite murderous delaying tactics, the sheer weight of the American avalanche was overwhelming. American pincers headed in two directions—one toward the central plain at San Jose, the other toward Clark Field and Manila. The Kembu Group defending the Clark Field area incurred heavy losses. On the 29th, MacArthur's forces made another landing near San Antonio, about thirty-five miles north of the Bataan Peninsula. Its objective appeared to Yamashita to be an attempt to cut across the northern part of Bataan and a drive towards Manila.

Yamashita was like the little Dutch boy, plugging holes in a dam about to burst asunder. Some of his forces were cut off, others were bypassed as strong American forces drove past them in a relentless drive towards Manila.

At Manila, the Shimbu Group commander, General

Yokoyama, dug in. On the 31st, hoping to bring order to the situation in the capital, Yamashita invested the Shimbu Group's commander with complete control of all army and navy forces in the city. Yokoyama deployed the bulk of his army units east of Manila in the mountains, leaving the actual defense of the city in the hands of Rear Admiral Iwabuchi. The latter was a well-known fanatic who was aware of Yamashita's orders to make Manila an open city, but the admiral chose to follow the original plan calling for a fight to the death.

The Americans hit Yokoyama's forces by surprise on February 1. Two days later the Japanese withdrew, leaving the door wide open for the Americans to enter the northern suburbs of the capital. Yokoyama sent an order to Iwabuchi ordering him to withdraw from the city, but the admiral replied that his commitments would not allow him to pull out. Yokoyama repeated the order but Iwabuchi simply ignored it. Then, at this critical point in the campaign, both Yamashita and Yokoyama lost contact with Iwabuchi. Both generals had no knowledge of what Iwabuchi had planned for the city.

Iwabuchi ordered every street, building, and sewer to be manned by a fighting man. He ordered every inch of the city contested. A month of brutal fighting ensued. Iwabuchi himself held out in the old walled sector of the city known by its Spanish name, Intramuros. Taking reprisals against the native population, the Japanese forces ran amok.

> "In an intoxicated fury of revenge and despair, the wild-eyed sailors threw themselves into an orgy of burning, shooting, raping, and torture. Young girls and old women were raped and then beheaded; men's bodies were hung in the air and mutilated; babies' eyeballs were ripped out and smeared across walls, patients were tied down to their beds and then the hospital burned to the ground. The atrocities continued on seemingly without end, as the American troops fought to breach the naval forces' perimeters."[24]

By the time the horror was over, sixteen thousand Japanese were dead but a total of a hundred thousand Filipinos had fallen victim to the atrocities. All this was done without authority from Yamashita and without his knowledge.

Meanwhile, the army commander was facing his own problems as enormous American attacks hit the Japanese units holding out in Luzon's mountains. One area Yamashita was determined to hold on to was the Cagayan Valley, the island's breadbasket. It stretched from Aparri in the north almost one hundred miles south to the tributary of the Magat River. The valley's width was approximately forty miles. Yamashita considered it essential to hold this area and deny it to the enemy. Without the valuable rice crop, the Shobu Group could not hope to hold out much longer.

The areas surrounding the valley consisted of dense jungles and mountains dominated by high slopes and deep gorges. The jungle was so thick that some of its area had never been explored. Yamashita hoped to use the terrain to his favor.

At this time, a correspondent from the Domei News Agency interviewed the army commander. During the course of the interview, he spoke candidly about the campaign and the war in general. Yamashita said:

> "I think Japan has made a big mistake in the way she had administered foreign populations. . . . We really make no attempt to understand them. . . . Relatively speaking, Japan is a poor country. Scientifically, we simply cannot compete with the Western nations."[25]

He went on to express his regrets at the way the press had handled the surrender of Singapore. It was reported that he had yelled at Percival, when in reality, he said, he was simply upset with the interpreter, Hishikari, who was having difficulty making Percival understand the points. It was not Percival he was yelling at, he reiterated, it was the interpreter. "I wanted to treat the enemy most courteously," he said.

Meanwhile, MacArthur's forces smashed into the Shobu position in the mountainous jungles. From their caves and dugouts, the Japanese bitterly contested every inch. The casualty rate among the defenders was enormous but they continued to fight.

By April 15, the Americans had moved closer to Baguio, requiring Yamashita to move his headquarters further eastward.

The fighting continued for the next four months. Yamashita ordered a strong redoubt established around his new headquarters. Every foot of ground the Japanese gave up was paid for with blood. The natural elements were uncooperative. Rains pelted the troops, mosquitoes drove men to madness, leeches and flies fed upon the living and the dead. By mid-May, morale among Yamashita's own staff was sagging as one report after another confirmed more losses. Still, the general ordered the defense to continue.

By July, Yamashita knew he could not hold out much longer. At a staff conference he discussed the dismal war situation. After the staff officers were dismissed, he took General Muto, his chief of staff, aside, and said that they had three alternatives. They could continue to fight, they could attempt to break through the American positions to the west, or they could sacrifice themselves in a final grand *banzai* charge. Personally, he felt that the first alternative was the best. The third option was completely ruled out. Yamashita said that the only ones who would gain from a suicide charge would be the Americans. Consequently, the best alternative would be to hold out and attempt to link up with the scattered regiments. Then they could attempt to break out of the American ring and form guerrilla bands in the high mountains of northwestern Luzon.

On July 30, Yamashita sent the following message to Terauchi in Saigon:

> "We anticipate that it will be possible to mount a break-out operation by the beginning of September."[26]

By now, however, there were only about fifty thousand men remaining in the Shobu Group. Yet Yamashita retained strict control to the very end. Then, on August 14, he heard the news of Japan's surrender. One of his staff officers saw him the next day and remarked that the general seemed to have aged ten years overnight. His staff was anxious lest he commit *hari-kiri*, but he set them at ease by stating that his prime duty was to bring his soldiers home.

When confronted by another officer who felt that in order to save face the army commander should kill himself, Yamashita bluntly replied:

> "You're just a boy and you don't understand. I've been responsible for the deaths of many people here in the Philippines. . . . I expect to pay for them. . . . If I die now, who takes responsibility?"[27]

On August 24, Yamashita held a funeral service for those who had perished during the campaign. On the 31st, an American plane dropped a message from Major General Gill, the commander of the 32nd Division. The message gave instructions about what to do if Yamashita wished to surrender. He sent one of his officers with a reply. On September 2, Yamashita left his mountain retreat and surrendered himself. As he said farewell to his men, it was noted that tears flowed from his eyes. The general then turned and walked down the mountain path and into the eager arms of American MPs. For Yamashita, the war was over, but his trial was about to begin.

Yamashita's war crimes trial was scheduled for Manila during the latter part of 1945. The charges against him were entirely related to the Philippine campaign. Unknowingly, Yamashita was about to play a most important role in MacArthur's pacification plan. The Filipinos had suffered enormously during the war and someone would have to pay for all the suffering. A scapegoat was necessary; a sacrificial lamb is probably a more appropriate term. Yamashita fit the bill ideally. This would be MacArthur's means of satisfying the Filipino thirst for vengeance, while in Tokyo he dealt with the Japanese in a benevolent fashion.

The judicial proceedings opened on October 29 in a carnivallike atmosphere. Cameras, bright lights, and vocal broadcasters were everywhere. Outside the courthouse vendors hawked ice cream and other treats to excited crowds who waited with baited breath to wreak their revenge on this solitary figure.

When the charges were read to him, Yamashita showed no emotion. Most of the charges dealt with the horrible mutilation of the people of Manila by the half-crazed naval troops defending the city, an act, as we have already seen, not ordered by the defendant. However, that did not matter. Yamashita was the commander-in-chief and as such was responsible for the behavior of the troops under him.

The trial proceedings lasted nearly six weeks. All the while Yamashita's marked dignity earned the hostility of one of the prosecutors, who came to resent him immensely. Drearily, one after another, the Filipino survivors told their own personal atrocity tales. Women described the horrible rapings, young girls showed their bayonet wounds, distraught mothers told of their child's death. As each witness related his story, hostility toward the defendent increased.

Yamashita's defense was based on his humane treatment of POWs and his many attempts at mitigating the harsh directives emerging from Tokyo. As far as the crimes in Manila were concerned, they had been perpetrated by Admiral Iwabuchi and his naval forces. Yamashita was miles away at the time and had no means of communicating with the admiral.

Ironically, it was Yamashita who was brought to trial, while others who were actually guilty were not. The reason for this was perhaps that Yamashita was the most prominent officer in the Philippines. One crime after another was ascribed to him. In his own defense, the general stated that as a soldier he had done what he thought was best, and never once had he condoned any massacres.

Despite evidence to the contrary, the tribunal charged him for having failed to provide effective control over his troops. It concluded:

> "General Yamashita. The commission concludes (1) that a series of atrocities and other high crimes have been committed by members of the Japanese armed forces under your command against the people of the United States, their allies, and dependencies throughout the Philippine Islands, that they were sporadic in nature but in many cases were methodically supervised by Japanese officers and noncommissioned officers; (2) that during the period in question you failed to provide effective control of your troops as was required by the circumstances."[28]

His conviction then, was for his failure to do something, not for something he had actually done, a crime unknown in the annals of jurisprudence. This crime that he was reputed to have committed was an indictment of every military commander, for in effect, it said that a commander is responsible for every action committed by every soldier in his command, regardless of whether the commander had any control over the actions of his men. Realistically, how can any commander be sure that every soldier under him will obey every order?

One of Yamashita's defense attorneys, A. Frank Reel, said this of the trial:

> "General Yamashita was condemned unjustly, first because the evidence against him was obtained and accepted in violation of the laws that Anglo-Saxon jurisprudence had developed over centuries in order to protect such persons against the prejudices of judges and the demand of the mob for vengeance. He did not have a fair trial."[29]

On the fourth anniversary of Pearl Harbor, December 7, 1945, Yamashita was sentenced to death by hanging. He was condemned to death for a crime no one had ever before been charged with. It violated the Fifth Amendment by accepting hearsay evidence. Because of the unconstitutionality of the evidence, his defense lawyers applied to the Supreme Court of the United States in hopes of gaining a stay of execution.

Meanwhile, MacArthur refused to postpone the execution date. Yamashita's defense attorney, Reel, flew to Washington to appeal the case in person. After a month of deliberation, the Supreme Court upheld the verdict of the Manila Tribunal. Two justices, however, dissented and wrote a lengthy report stating their views. Unfortunately, these two opinions were not enough to overturn the conviction. The basic reason for the judges' dissenting view was their fear that a precedent would be set regarding the issue of due process of law.

When MacArthur received the dissenting justices' report, he countermanded them with a report of his own. He remained unmoved. Yamashita was to die.

Reel made one final attempt to save the general's life. He went right to the White House to appeal to the President. Truman stated that he would not meddle in MacArthur's business.

Yamashita accepted his fate calmly. On February 22, 1946, he was given his last meal, then brought to the condemned man's cell in the new Bilbid Prison on the outskirts of Manila, where he was billeted for the night. He awoke a little after 5:00 AM the following morning, dressed, and was allowed to talk briefly with a Buddhist priest. At 6:01 he was blindfolded and led away in handcuffs. With deepest respect, Yamashita turned toward Tokyo and bowed reverently toward the palace of the emperor. He then climbed the scaffold. Seconds later, the trap door opened, ending the career and the life of the "Tiger of Malaya."

After completing the interview referred to at the beginning of this chapter, an attempt was made to explain

Yamashita's position to the Filipino. It was like talking to a stone wall, for as far as he was concerned, Yamashita was a demon guilty of crimes against humanity.

In reality, however, Yamashita was a dedicated soldier who served his emperor with all his ability. He far surpassed most of his contemporaries in ability and was both a talented tactician and an innovative strategist, as evidenced by his Malayan campaign. In the Philippines, Yamashita never had the luxury of enough time to prepare adequately. He arrived only two weeks prior to the American invasion, and when the attack came, he was forced to follow a policy he totally disagreed with. When he finally did obtain total control of the battle, it was already too late, so that all he could fight was a defensive battle against superior odds.

When the war was over, he had to pay the supreme penalty. He was hanged not because he had commanded troops who committed atrocities, but because he was in command of troops who committed these crimes on the losing side. His sentence was a gross miscarriage of justice, one that American jurisprudence could not be proud of. Granted, atrocities were carried out, atrocities the Japanese were not proud of either, but why blame the one man whose entire career attested to the fact that he never once condoned any such action?

Kurita and Ozawa

Chapter 6

This chapter marks a deviation from earlier formats in this series in that, instead of focusing on one particular individual, the wartime exploits of two commanders will be traced simultaneously. Indeed, the careers of Admirals Takeo Kurita and Jisaburo Ozawa were, for the most part, so tightly entwined that it would be a difficult task to separate them. Malaya, The Dutch East Indies, Guadalcanal and the Solomons, the Philippine Sea, and finally Leyte Gulf saw both admirals fight with skill and determination.

Jisaburo Ozawa was born in 1886 and entered the Naval Academy when he was nineteen. Four years later, near the top of his class, he graduated. As a student he impressed his instructors as a clear thinker with the ability to analyze problems quickly and find the appropriate solution to them. Ozawa was a physical fitness buff and excelled in sports during his school days. Even in later years he prided himself on being in as good a physical condition as many men half his age. This devotion to conditioning served him well.

Takeo Kurita was four years younger than his colleague. Born to a family of scholars, he encountered few problems with learning, but the lure of the sea was stronger than the thirst for knowledge or the attraction of the academic community. Accordingly, as soon as he was eligible, Kurita too entered the Naval Academy. Unlike the analytical approach of Ozawa, Kurita's scholarly heritage influenced his solving of problems. He had a tendency to overanalyze puzzles, with the result that he frequently found many objections to his own solutions. Consequently, before settling on a final solution to a problem, he would consider all the ramifications and adopt the more conservative course. Nevertheless, he attacked all aspects of academy life with a zeal, be it athletics or books.

When Ozawa graduated from the Naval Academy, surface ships were the rulers of the seas. At that time submarines were still in their infancy and aircraft carriers in the distant future. The battleship was queen of the fleet. As was the case with most junior officers, Ozawa began at the bottom. This meant the dirtiest jobs on the smallest ships in the fleet, the destroyers.

From the beginning Ozawa was marked as a "comer." His eagerness to perform both menial or difficult tasks with equal aplomb caused his superiors to notice the young officer. Throughout his formative years Ozawa constantly received outstanding fitness ratings from a succession of commanding officers. As a result, Ozawa rose quickly through the ranks. By the 1930s he could look back with satisfaction on a varied and brilliant career in destroyers, cruisers, battleships and staff positions. His wide knowledge of tactics and his broad experience made him uniquely qualified for any command. In 1935, this well-rounded officer returned to the Naval Academy as professor of naval tactics.

Ozawa thoroughly enjoyed his brief term at the Naval Academy. He was justly proud of his extensive experience and enjoyed sharing his knowledge with the young cadets. He knew that the future of the Imperial Navy was in the hands of these young men, and since the navy was his life, he was eager to fill their youthful minds with as much knowledge as they could grasp.

Ozawa's term at the Naval Academy was all too brief for his own taste, but he was not one to question orders. Besides, even with his vast experience, Ozawa thought that there was still much he could learn, particularly with the great technological advances made after World War I. Accordingly, in 1935, he was promoted to captain and given command of the modern cruiser, *Maya*. Throughout World War II, his affection for this particular ship never wavered.

Towards the end of the following year Ozawa was promoted once more, this time to rear admiral. Flag rank demanded a more responsible command than a heavy cruiser so he raised his admiral's pennant in the battleship *Haruna*. A World War I vintage veteran, the *Haruna* was modernized for a second time and was ready for sea again in September of 1934. She was capable of attaining the astonishing (for a battleship) speed of just over 30 knots. The battleships of the other naval powers rarely exceeded 24 knots until later in the decade. Mounting eight 14-inch guns, the *Haruna* was a warship capable of engaging any potential enemy ship then afloat. However, by 1936, the aircraft carrier had joined the fleet. Many officers were, even then, proclaiming the carrier the ship of the future. Ozawa was skeptical about this drastic deviation from the orthodox, but vowed to keep an open mind until he could find out for himself.

Events began to move rapidly. The seniority system was deeply imbedded in the Japanese Navy. In the turmoil of frequently changing governments, unrest in the navy, and general confusion, the attrition rate of senior officers was high. As a result of this movement at the top, Ozawa found himself appointed chief of staff of the Combined Fleet in 1937. After a year in this post he was transferred once more, this time to command of the 7th Cruiser Division.

Back at sea Ozawa was content. The heavy cruisers of the fleet figured prominently in all war plans. Their versatility made them highly prized commands. Japan's modern heavy cruisers were a match for those of any of the world's navies and far outclassed most of them.

Unhappily, after a year with the cruisers, Ozawa found himself ashore once more. This time he was appointed head of the torpedo school. The use of torpedoes, particularly by cruisers and destroyers, was one tactic that the Japanese developed to a fine art. In addition, their oxygen-fueled torpedo far outclassed any other then in use worldwide and was a jealously guarded secret. The torpedo school's curriculum was designed to make cruiser and destroyer officers proficient in this craft. Later, results would prove just how proficient the Japanese captains really were.

Once more the assignment lasted for only a year.

Obviously, with the prospect of war looming larger as each week passed, the Naval General Staff desired that Ozawa become as versatile as possible. Therefore, with another promotion, now to vice admiral, he took command of the First Air Squadron in 1940. Finally, the opportunity to find out for himself about the much heralded aircraft carrier had arrived. The First Air Squadron was comprised of the carriers *Kaga* and *Akagi*, the pride of the fleet.

It was not long before Ozawa understood why other officers were predicting great things for the new method of naval warfare. He conducted a broad series of exercises that convinced him of the unlimited potential of using carriers. Now his keen mind began to contemplate even more radical proposals for the use of carriers. What if an entire fleet of these ships were combined to form a powerful striking force? Nothing could stop them. The power of such a striking force could be awesome.

Armed with such a proposal Ozawa approached his old friend, Admiral Isoruku Yamamoto. The latter, commander-in-chief of the Combined Fleet, thought Ozawa's idea unrealistic and refused to consider such a thought. Unhappy with the rebuff, in April, 1940, Ozawa forwarded his proposal to both the Naval General Staff and the Naval Ministry. After a few months of review, the staff officers concluded that Ozawa's proposals possessed merit. Shortly thereafter, Yamamoto himself warmed to the idea and began to develop the potential.

Eventually, the First Air Fleet was established, comprising the 1st and 2nd Air Squadrons of 4 large carriers. Later, another squadron with the large carriers *Zuikau* and *Shokaku* was added just prior to the launching of the Pearl Harbor attack.

Unfortunately, when the First Air Fleet was formed, Ozawa's lack of adequate seniority precluded his commanding this force. Instead, Admiral Chiuchi Nagumo was selected to command the powerful striking force. In addition to commanding the First Air Fleet, Nagumo elected to exercise direct command of the 1st Air Squadron. Consequently, there was no room for Ozawa. Yamamoto would have to find other employment for his old friend.

Another command for Ozawa was a problem. Although he preferred to have his friend command the carrier force, Yamamoto knew that even he could not buck the seniority system. The commander-in-chief was already making plans for the eventuality of war with the United States and Great Britain. He had already decided upon the strike at Pearl Harbor, but both he and the Naval General Staff knew that this blow alone was not enough. The Dutch East Indies and Malaya were designated targets along with the Philippines. Since Nagumo was to command the Pearl Harbor attack, other senior admirals were needed to command the fleet elements in these areas, particularly since for the most part, the demands of the southern campaign would require that the fleet operate in individual groups necessitating each commander to exercise independent command, In October, 1941, therefore, Ozawa was given one of these commands in Admiral Kondo's Second Fleet.

Meanwhile, Takeo Kurita had made a name for himself as well. Unlike Ozawa, who preferred a broad scope of experience in a variety of different types of ships, Kurita's first love was destroyers. Like his brother officers he was required to round out his experience with duty aboard cruisers and battleships, but he never lost his affinity for the small greyhounds of the fleet.

When he achieved enough seniority to allow him a voice in his choice of appointments, he elected to remain with destroyers. Kurita never ceased to admire the versatility of these small craft and was content to practice his craft with them. With the development of the "long lance" torpedo, Kurita felt that Japan's destroyer fleet was second to none. By the late-thirties he had become recognized as one of the Imperial Navy's leading authorities on destroyer tactics. He was, however, realistic enough to recognize that eventually the seniority system would catch up with him and he would have to assume more responsible commands if he wished to further his career.

As was the case with any senior officer, Kurita's career was interspersed with staff assignments and brief periods at the various naval schools both as student and instructor. He always considered these shore assignments to be tedious duty and by the expiration date of each commission found himself impatient to return to sea. It was therefore with a sense of reluctance that he left his destroyer flotilla in the fall of 1940 to assume command of the 7th Cruiser Division. The transfer from destroyers to cruisers was made easier with his promotion to rear admiral in September of that year.

A few weeks later, Kurita's cruiser squadron was added to Kondo's fleet. From that point onward, Kurita's and Ozawa's paths paralleled each other for the balance of the war.

Even while Nagumo was making his spectacular raid on Pearl Harbor, a large Japanese convoy approached Malaya. Ozawa and Kurita commanded the covering forces and were responsible for the safety of the convoys. At the same time, Japanese units elsewhere were launching their campaign against the Philippines.

On December 8, 1941, the invasion of Malaya formally began. Kondo had divided his Second Fleet, enabling the various elements to cover the widely dispersed beachheads. Then came word that the British battleship, *Prince of Wales,* and the battlecruiser *Repulse* had left their base at Singapore and were heading for the Japanese landing areas. Kondo immediately recalled the forces of Ozawa and Kurita and set out to intercept the two British ships. Before he could locate them, however, Japanese aircraft sent the *Prince of Wales* and the *Repulse* to the bottom of the Gulf of Siam.

The following week saw the Second Fleet covering the landings on Borneo. Later it was the turn of Java, Sumatra and the other islands of the Dutch East Indies. After that it was off to cover landings in Burma. Once the conquest of these valuable prizes was complete, Ozawa was directed to take a strong force into the Indian Ocean to attack shipping there (*See Map 16*).

In conjunction with Admiral Nagumo's carrier raids on the British naval bases at Colombo and Trincomalee,

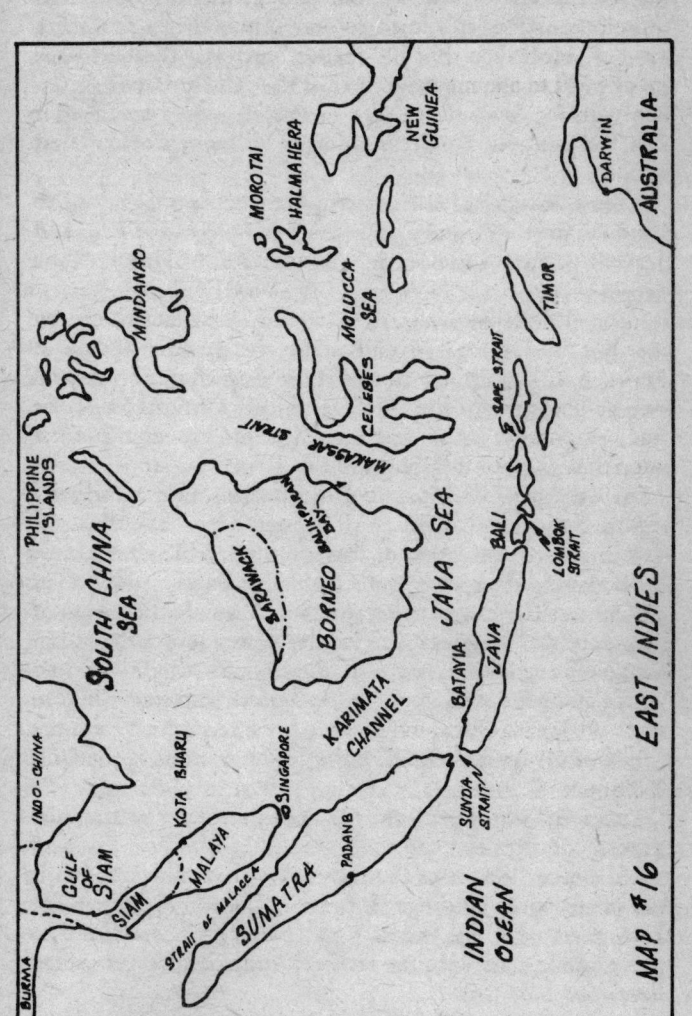

Ceylon, Ozawa took his force of five heavy cruisers, the light carrier *Ryujo*, and four destroyers into the Bay of Bengal on April 3. On the 5th, he divided his force into three separate sections, retaining command of the Central Force himself. For the next three days the three sections preyed on Allied shipping off the East Coast of India. The Southern Force of two cruisers and a destroyer managed to hunt down and sink three ships. Ozawa's own force accounted for four more.

The most spectacular success though, was achieved by Kurita's Northern Force, comprising the cruisers *Kumano*, and *Suzuya* and the destroyer *Shirokumo*. Taking his force deep into the Gulf of Siam, in a two-day period Kurita's ships sank nine merchantmen. Faced with the presence of the Japanese forces in the area, the British halted all shipping and confined all merchant ships to port. Lacking targets, Ozawa reunited his fleet and set a course for Japan. After four months at sea, his ships were in dire need of overhaul and the crews deserved a rest. In addition, the Battle of Midway loomed on the horizon and Yamamoto was anxious to use every ship available.

Yamamoto was greatly distressed when he met Ozawa upon the latter's return from the South Pacific. Ozawa was visibly tired. He had lost weight, was drawn, and seemed to have lost his old spark. As a result, Yamamoto ordered him to take a leave and regain his strength. It would serve the navy no useful purpose to have Ozawa collapse while on duty. Yamamoto wanted to retain his old friend's talents. Much to his consternation, therefore, Ozawa was ordered to the sidelines just before the great Battle of Midway. No amount of arguing or threats could change Yamamoto's mind.

Kurita, on the other hand, figured prominently in the plans for the invasion of Midway. He was to repeat his role at Malaya and the Dutch East Indies and command the group slated to provide close-in support for the actual invasion.

It would serve no purpose to rehash the Battle of Midway here since it is thoroughly examined in the earlier chapter on Nagumo. Kurita's force moved to center stage on the day following Nagumo's disastrous defeat. After learning of the loss of all four of Nagumo's carriers, Yamamoto refused to call a halt to the operation. Accordingly, Kurita was directed to take his force of four heavy cruisers and two destroyers toward Midway and proceed with the bombardment as scheduled. Shortly after midnight Yamamoto cancelled this order and instructed Kurita to rejoin the main body of the fleet. The 7th Cruiser Division was in the process of making its 180 degree turn when a lookout aboard the destroyer *Arashio* sighted what he thought to be the periscope of an American submarine. There was no submarine in the vicinity at the time, but Kurita could not afford to take chances so he ordered his ships to take evasive maneuvers. In the resulting confusion, the cruiser *Mogami* sliced into the side of the *Mikuma*. Both ships were heavily damaged and their speed drastically reduced.

Kurita pondered this latest dilemma. Should he risk exposing the entire formation to attack? Unwilling to accept this risk, he ordered the two damaged ships to proceed to port on their own escorted by the destroyers *Arashio* and *Asashio* while he set out for the rendezvous with the rest of the Combined Fleet with his two remaining ships, the flagships *Kumano* and *Suzuya*.

The next morning, American carrier planes were out hunting any cripples. Discovering the oil slick from where the *Mikuma*'s fuel tanks had been holed by the collision with *Mogami*, the American planes followed the trail and found the retreating cruisers just before 10:00 AM. The *Mogami* was the first to feel the wrath of the American aviators. Her rear turret was destroyed by bombs and many men were killed. Then attention shifted to the *Mikuma*, who was pounded unmercifully. Two and a half hours later another attack arrived over the hapless ships. Heavy fires blazed out of control on the *Mogami* while the *Mikuma* was pummeled into a blazing hulk. Her captain gave the order to abandon ship, but so intense was the heat that the *Arashio* could not approach to take off the crew. Consequently, they were required to jump over the side, where they were fished from the water by the escorting destroyers.

Two hours later, the final attack of the day set off *Mikuma's* torpedoes and the ship rolled over and sank. In this attack, *Mogami* lost an additional ninety men killed, making the total for the day over three hundred dead. Fortunately, after the third attack the Americans came no more. The *Mogami* managed to reach Truk on the 14th, but she was out of the war for thirteen months while her unrecognizable upper decks were replaced. The *Mikuma* was the first heavy cruiser lost during the war.

Neither admiral played a significant role during the long struggle for Guadalcanal. Ozawa remained in Japan until November, but Kurita did manage to carry out a hugely successful bombardment of Henderson Field during the night of October 13, following Goto's defeat at Cape Esperance. He boldly took the battleships *Kongo* and *Haruna* into Ironbottom Sound, where he stood offshore and lobbed shell after shell into the American positions until he had exhausted over nine hundred rounds of heavy ammunition. When he set sail up the Slot he left behind over forty-five American planes destroyed and another ninety heavily damaged. In addition, the airstrip itself was pockmarked with huge holes and rendered inoperable, and virtually the entire supply of aviation fuel was set on fire. All in all, a rather successful raid. However, Kurita was unaware of the existence of an auxiliary airstrip within the confines of the American positions. The following day, using this very airstrip, Guadalcanal's Cactus Air Force was back in operation, albeit at a greatly reduced strength.

Yamomoto's frustration with the inability to defeat the American forces caused him to cast about for scapegoats. Even his friends were not immune to his wrath. One of those who paid the price for the Japanese failure at Guadalcanal was Admiral Chiuchi Nagumo. Even though he had just achieved a victory over the Americans at the Battle of Santa Cruz, in November Yamamoto decided to dispense with the legendary Nagumo's services and ordered him to turn over command of the carriers, using health as his reason for relieving the veteran of Pearl Harbor.

Yamamoto's decision to get rid of Nagumo allowed him to bring Ozawa back to sea. The latter was formally named commander of the First Air Fleet containing the bulk of the Japanese carriers, or at least those that remained after Midway.

Many of those who had failed in the Solomons eventually lost their commands. Mikawa and Kondo did not escape. Both eventually lost their commands, with Kondo's Second Fleet going to Kurita. Both he and Ozawa were indeed fortunate that they had not been overly involved in the Guadalcanal campaign.

As 1942 drew to a close, Yamamoto decided to abandon Guadalcanal and withdraw to the central Solomons. No longer were the heavier units of the Combined Fleet capable of influencing the course of action. American air power in the Solomons was simply too great. From now on, Japanese aircraft from Rabaul and destroyers would bear the brunt of the fighting.

On January 29, 1943, a flight of Japanese planes located an American force of six cruisers and eight destroyers covering a reinforcement mission to Guadalcanal. The resulting two-day Battle of the Rennell Islands cost the United States the cruiser *Chicago*.

By the end of the month, only a handful of rear-guard troops remained alive on Guadalcanal. The bulk of the survivors had been skillfully evacuated by the "Tokyo Express." The rear guard was removed during the first week in February, via the same method.

The Americans began to build Guadalcanal into a staging area for use in the next phases of the Solomons campaign. Their overwhelming superiority in both men and equipment, not to mention aircraft and shipping, began to tell. Their plan called for them to bypass the Japanse garrisons on some of the smaller islands and to concentrate their efforts on key enemy strongpoints. Since the initiative was now with the Americans, they could afford to conquer one island, secure it, and pause to regroup before hitting the next objective.

Attrition on the Japanese side was costly, a price they

were ill prepared to pay. Once their resources were expended they could no longer be made good. Japanese air raids against the staging areas on Guadalcanal proved little more than a nuisance, with each attack costing the attacker dearly.

The next American objective was New Georgia. Their plan for the overall capture of the Solomons chain before jumping off to New Britain was designated Operation Cartwheel, and called for a series of amphibious landings in succession while climbing the Solomons chain. Operation Toenails was the next step in Cartwheel. The former was the code name for the invasion of New Georgia. On that island was located the Japanese air base at Munda. This airfield had to be neutralized before taking the next jump up the Slot.

The Japanese correctly guessed that New Georgia was the next American objective. U.S. planes conducted frequent bombing missions over the island, while American naval forces repeatedly bombarded key points on New Georgia. The Japanese fleet attempted to reinforce the garrison there and deliver supplies, but their efforts proved costly. On the night of March 7, Admiral Ainsworth's forces sank the destroyers *Murusame* and *Minegumo*, which were carrying reinforcements. Meanwhile, American planes continued to plaster the airfields at Munda and the smaller one at Vila.

April 18 was a black day for the Japanese. On that date, a squadron of American P-38 fighters shot down a Japanese plane over Bougainville. The plane was carrying the commander-in-chief of the Combined Fleet, Admiral Isoruku Yamamoto. Ozawa had urged that Yamamoto not attempt a tour of the Japanese island bases in the South Pacific. Yamamoto appreciated his old friend's concern but refused to pay heed to the advice. Ozawa then approached those members of Yamamoto's staff responsible for laying out the itinerary and implored them to at least provide a heavy fighter escort.

"If he insists on going, six fighters are nothing like enough. Tell the chief of staff that he can have as many of my planes as he likes".[1]

Again his pleas fell on deaf ears. Ozawa's proposal never reached Ugaki. Thus perished the guiding spirit behind the Imperial Navy. A search for his successor began immediately.

After the war, one former member of Yamamoto's staff offered the opinion that the eventual successor was ill chosen.

> "The only men who could have succeeded Yamamoto as commander-in-chief of the Combined Fleet were Yamaguchi and Ozawa, but Yamaguchi was killed at Midway, and the navy was too bound by the seniority system to appoint Ozawa."[2]

Thus, Admiral Mineichi Koga was named to command the Combined Fleet, but no one could fill Yamamoto's shoes.

During the second week in June, Koga ordered heavy air raids to be made on Guadalcanal. After the first two, during which the Japanese lost almost half of their planes, Koga called the operation off. Obviously he could not stop the Americans this way.

On June 21, American marines staged initial landings on the southern tip of New Georgia. This was followed nine days later by stronger landings elsewhere on the island and on the island of Rendova. To counter these landings, Koga rushed reinforcements to Vila on Kolombongara. One of these Tokyo Express runs ran into a force of American cruisers and destroyers on the night of July 5.

Although the Imperial Navy could never hope to keep pace with increasing American strength, this did not result in a deterioration of their basic skills. They were still masterful sailors. At the Battle of Kula Gulf, the Americans lost the cruiser *Helena*, a victim of the dreaded "long lances." In turn, the U.S. forces sank the destroyers *Nagatsuki* and *Niitsuki*.

A week later to the date, another Tokyo Express run clashed with the Americans at the Battle of Kolombongara.

This time it was no standoff. The Japanese lost the light cruiser *Jintsu*, Admiral Tanaka's former flagship. But the Americans paid heavily for their triumph. The Japanese destroyers executed a brilliant torpedo attack. Long lances smashed into the sides of the cruisers *Honolulu*, *St. Louis*, and the Australian cruiser *Leander*. The destroyer *Gwin* was broken in half by another torpedo.

However, the Japanese went to the well too often. By the end of the month their earlier efforts were offset by the loss of the destroyers *Hatsuyuki* on the 18th, *Yugure* and *Kiyonami* on the 21st, and the escort carrier *Nisshin* on the 22nd. Then, on August 6, Captain Frederick Moosebruger, with six destroyers, ambushed the destroyers *Hagikaze*, *Arashi*, *Kawakaze*, and *Shigure*, attempting to run reinforcements to New Georgia. During the Battle of Vella Gulf, only the latter escaped destruction at no cost to Moosebruger's force.

Meanwhile, the Americans had succeeded in their attempt to capture Munda Airfield on New Georgia. Electing to bypass Kolombongara, they staged landings on Vella Lavella. On the 24th of August, Koga decided that it was pointless to attempt to hold on to the central Solomons. He began to withdraw his forces to Bougainville and the Shortlands, at the top of the Slot. Throughout the campaign, these two areas served as staging points for supply runs down the Slot. The naval and air bases there were vital to the defense of the great base at Rabaul on New Britain.

During the Japanese attempts to evacuate Kolombongara, yet another naval battle in the long struggle for the Solomons occurred. On the night of October 6, the opposing forces ran into each other north of Vella Lavella. The battle was a standoff with each side losing a destroyer—the Americans the U.S.S. *Chevalier* and the Japanese the *Yugumo*.

In the interim, Koga began to contemplate sending heavy reinforcements to the area. Most of the Combined Fleet heavy units sat idly at Truk or in the Inland Sea of Japan. The loss of Bougainville would expose Rabaul, and Koga could ill afford to let this happen.

On November 1, American forces waded ashore at Empress Augusta Bay on Bougainville. Koga ordered Admiral Omori to attack the American landing beaches with his force of cruisers and destroyers. Rear Admiral "Tip" Merrill was lying offshore covering the landings with the cruisers *Denver*, *Cleveland*, and *Columbia*, and eight destroyers.

On the night of November 2, Omori led the heavy cruisers *Haguro* and *Myoko*, the light cruisers *Sendai* and *Agano*, and six destroyers into the waters of Empress Augusta Bay. Merrill was waiting for him. In a wild melee, three of Merrill's destroyers were damaged. It was, however, a small price to pay for the damage inflicted. The *Sendai* was blasted to the bottom, as was the destroyer *Hatsukaze*. The *Agano*, the *Myoko*, and the *Haguro* limped back to Rabaul heavily damaged and escorted by the remaining destroyers. The Battle of Empress Augusta Bay was the final surface battle in the struggle for the Solomons.

Following the debacle at Empress Augusta Bay, Koga ordered Kurita to take the fleet's heavy cruisers to Rabaul. Just as Yamamoto had been determined to hold on to Guadalcanal, so was Koga equally bent on saving New Britain and Bougainville. On November 2, Kurita left Truk with the heavy cruisers *Atago*, *Chokai*, *Maya*, *Takao*, *Mogami*, *Suzuya*, and *Chikuma*, the light cruiser *Noshiro* and four destroyers. Three days later, around 7:00 in the morning, Kurita's powerful force dropped anchor in Rabaul harbor alongside the light cruisers *Agano*, and *Yubari*, and seven destroyers.

Meanwhile, Admiral Halsey was planning to neutralize Rabaul with his carriers. When the Americans received word that Kurita's cruisers were approaching the naval base, the prospect became even more inviting. Halsey ordered Task Force 38 under Admiral Sherman, containing the carriers *Princeton* and *Saratoga*, to hit Rabaul.

On the morning of the 5th, even as Kurita's ships were dropping anchor, Task Force 38 approached Rabaul. Around 9:00 AM, when they were just over two hundred miles away, Sherman turned his ships into the wind and launched over a hundred planes. An hour later, the American planes arrived over the Japanese naval base. Incredibly, the Japanese never knew the Americans were coming.

Less than half an hour later, Kurita's fleet lay smoking. The *Atago*'s hull was stove in by three near misses. The *Maya* raised steam and made for the harbor entrance at the height of the attack. There she was pounced on by a flight of dive bombers that ripped out her innards. Unable to navigate, with seventy dead and sixty wounded littering her decks, the *Maya* went dead in the water. The *Mogami* was struck in the side by a torpedo that started heavy fires. The *Takeo*'s number two turret was destroyed by a bomb. The *Chikuma* was more fortunate than her sisters; damage from near misses was slight. Most of the destroyers, with the exception of the *Wakatsuki*, escaped heavy damage, since the American pilots preferred to concentrate on the larger targets. Not so the *Agano* and the *Noshiro*. Unlike their smaller comrades, the two light cruisers took their share of pounding.

Kurita stared in horror as the American dive bombers and torpedo bombers dove on his vulnerable fleet. Less than eight hours after his arrival, Kurita ordered the *Atago*, the *Chikuma*, the *Kumano*, the *Mogami* and the *Suzuya* back to Truk, escorted by six destroyers. The *Takeo* and the *Maya* were so badly damaged that they could not accompany the rest of the fleet. Koga's attempt to reinforce Rabaul was a total failure. Poor Kurita never had a chance.

Where were the Japanese carriers? Why hadn't Ozawa's ships taken part in the operation? The answer was that the decks of the Japanese carriers were barren. Koga had sent every available plane to Bougainville and New Britain including those assigned to carrier duty. The Japanese simply could not make good their losses quickly enough.

Six days after Kurita's ordeal, the *Princeton* and the *Yorktown* were back, this time in company with the *Essex*, the *Bunker Hill* and the *Independence*. The *Agano* and the *Naganami* were gutted and the destroyer *Suzunami* was sunk. American planes blasted shipping, airfields, and installations. Sixty-eight Japanese planes were destroyed on the ground. A hastily prepared counterstrike set out after the departing attackers, but the Japanese planes never reached their destination. The combat air patrol over the American carriers accounted for an additional forty enemy planes.

The following day, Koga reluctantly ordered the evacuation of all shipping and carrier planes from Rabaul. As a base, Rabaul was now worthless in the face of American strength.

With the eventual fall of the Solomons now a foregone conclusion, the Americans began to focus their attention on other Japanese bastions. Large fleets of carriers raided Japanese installations throughout the Pacific with impunity. On November 20, the Americans invaded Tarawa and Makin in the Gilberts. Three days later, after a bloody and costly battle, the Gilbert Islands were secured.

In December, Nimitz's fast carrier force raided Kwajalein and Wotje in the Marshalls. The day after Christmas, U.S. Marines landed on New Britain and in three days captured Cape Gloucester. Koga ordered the carrier planes to return to the island to aid in the defense. Four days after their arrival, Rabaul's airfield was the focal point of a heavy American air raid. Most of the Japanese planes there were destroyed before they had the chance to get into the air.

Hard-pressed as they were, the Japanese could not conclude where the next American effort would be. To what point should they dispatch reinforcements? The widely dispersed American raids kept the Japanese completely off balance.

On January 31, Kwajalein in the Marshalls was invaded. The battle was over in five days. Then the fast carrier force, Task Force 58, hit Truk, the great Japanese naval base. Fortunately, Koga had evacuated the Combined Fleet a few days prior to the February 17 raid. However, the Americans found the light cruiser *Naka* and a few transports at Truk. The cruiser was sunk along with most of the merchant ships. Attempting to flee, the light cruiser *Katori* and a destroyer were run down by American surface forces and sent to the bottom. Two hundred sixty-five Japanese planes were destroyed in the raid.

The next day the Americans returned, sunk the remaining ships and leveled the shore installations. Yamamoto's great bastion was a shambles.

A week later it was the turn of the Marianas. Saipan, Tinian, Rota and Guam were heavily punished by the marauding Task Force 58. More Japanese planes were destroyed. Then American attention turned to the Admiralties and Carolines. The former was invaded on January 29th, while the latter's islands of Yap, Palau, Ulithi, and Wotje were subjected to three days of round-the-clock raids. Over a hundred thousand tons of irreplaceable Japanese shipping was sunk.

At the end of April it was Truk's turn once more. The great naval base was not only strategically located, it represented a symbol. The earlier raids had all but eliminated Truk as a base and staging area. The raids of April 29th made certain of that fact. When Task Force 58 steamed away, only ten operable planes remained at Truk.

As the American forces ravaged Japanese bases throughout the Pacific, Koga began to lay down plans to bring the American fleet to battle once and for all. The bulk of the Combined Fleet Koga brought to the Philippines from Japan. He had reorganized the entire fleet in mid-1943, giving Kurita command of the Second Fleet with the rank of vice admiral. The First Mobile Fleet, including virtually all the remaining carriers and Kurita's Second Fleet, was placed in the hands of the most able Admiral Ozawa. Then, en route to the Philippines from Palau, Koga's plane crashed during a storm on March 31st. News of his death was withheld by the Japanese, so not until early May was a successor chosen. Command of the Combined Fleet passed to Admiral Soemu Toyoda.

Unlike his predecessor, Toyoda felt that the Americans would attempt to advance closer to the homeland instead of concentrating solely on the reconquest of the Philippines. The outer bastion of Japan's defensive perimeter was the Marianas. This, Toyoda concluded, was where the

Americans would strike next. With this in mind, he developed the A-Go plan, designed to defeat any American effort to capture the Marianas. Ozawa's Mobile Fleet would be responsible for the implementation of A-Go.

In fact, Admiral Nimitz had planned to capture the Marianas, but not exactly for the reason Toyoda thought. Rolling off the assembly lines at American aircraft plants was the B-29, a new heavy bomber with a range of four thousand miles. Rushed to the Pacific, the first few B-29 Superfortresses were sent to China, from where they could carry out a bomber offensive against the Japanese homeland. Unfortunately, there were too many drawbacks to the Chinese bases. Not only were they at the extreme range of the B-29s from Japanese targets, but also the route of the bomber formations took them through Japanese airspace every mile of the way. An advanced base in the Pacific was an urgent priority if the B-29s were to prove effective. The islands of Guam and Saipan in the Marianas were within fifteen hundred miles of Japan and large enough to facilitate the lengthy runways required by the Superfortresses. Thus, the Marianas suddenly rated high on Nimitz's shopping list. Mid-June was established as the target date for an invasion of Saipan.

In the interim, Task Force 58, built around the new powerful Essex class carriers, roamed throughout the Pacific. The Japanese never knew where the American carriers would strike next.

Toyoda ordered what remained of the Japanese fleet to assemble at Tawi Tawi, the Sulu Island base in the southern Philippines. Basing his A-Go plan on the assumption that the next major American offensive would occur in the vicinity of the Marianas, Toyoda's strategy was to strike at the American fleet first. If he could inflict a serious defeat, the Japanese ships could then destroy the American landing forces. To carry out the operation, not only were Ozawa's carriers available, but swarms of planes from Japan itself would be sent south via Okinawa to bases in the Marianas. Thus a twin-pronged force would be used to defeat the Americans (*See Map 17*).

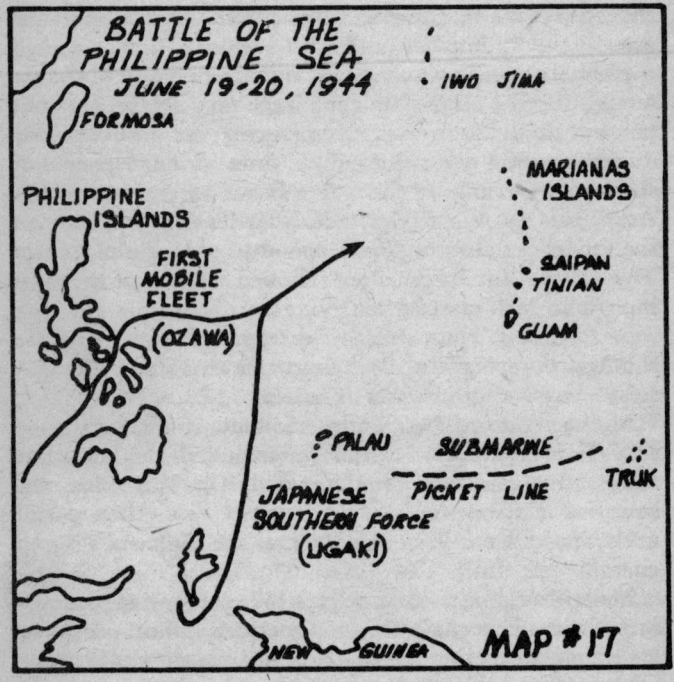

Even before the U.S. invasion of Saipan, Ozawa was ready to take his fleet to sea. The waters around Tawi Tawi were rapidly becoming too hot. American submarines roamed freely throughout the area and prevented the Japanese from conducting exercises safely. Between the 24th of May and June 4th, Ozawa's force was reduced by five destroyers and three tankers, all losses coming as the result of enemy submarine activity. After the *Tanikaze* was sunk on the 8th by the submarine *Harder*, Ozawa ordered the fleet to sea in an effort to escape the restricted waters around the Philippines.

Even though he was virtually certain that the Marianas represented the next American objective, Toyoda could not be absolutely certain. Adopting a tactic used unsuccessfully during the Midway operation, he ordered a picket line of submarines established between Palau and Truk. If the American fleet was indeed making for the Marianas, one of the Japanese submarines was bound to spot it and inform Toyoda's headquarters. What followed was one of the most incredible feats of the entire war.

American intelligence sources reported that Japanese submarine was making a supply run from Truk to Buin. A squadron of destroyer escorts* under commander Hamilton Hains was ordered out from the Solomons to intercept the sub. Hains's Escort Division 39 included the destroyer escorts *George*, *Raby*, and *England*. On May 19th, the squadron made contact with a Japanese sub. After several unsuccessful attacks by the *George*, the *England's* depth charges sank the I-16.

Meanwhile, the submarine RO-117, running on the surface, was discovered by an American plane. Admiral Halsey suspected that the Japanese had placed a picket line athwart the route to Saipan and ordered Hains to investigate. Early in the morning of May 22nd, Escort Division 39's radar located RO-106 running on the surface in

---

*A smaller, more lightly armed version of the destroyer. The destroyer escort's primary function was that of a submarine hunter.

the predawn darkness. As the three little ships raced in for the attack, the submarine dove beneath the surface. The *England* dropped depth charges where the sub had last been seen and was rewarded by the destruction of a second enemy submarine. But she was just beginning.

The next day, Hain's force located RO-104. The *George* failed in five attempts to sink the submarine. *England*'s second run was rewarded by a tremendous undersea explosion. Bits of wood, supplies, and human bodies bobbed to the surface, marking the end of RO-104. An hour later, the *England*'s asdic made contact with yet another submarine. By then her crew were becoming experts with depth charges. RO-116 joined her sister submarines at the bottom of the Pacific.

Hains was now certain that he had indeed stumbled across a Japanese picket line and continued the hunt. His diligence paid off. On the evening of the 26th, just before midnight, RO-108 surfaced to charge her batteries. The *England*'s radar located her immediately and the DE raced in for the kill. The Japanese submarine executed an emergency all-out dive, but to no avail. The *England*'s depth charges found her. Scratch RO-108.

Five days passed before another contact was made. By then the *England*'s crew were becoming rather cocky about the whole affair. Then, on the 31st, the *George* made contact with RO-105 running on the surface a little after midnight. Hains decided to allow his other two ships to share the glory. The *George* exhausted all her depth charges in a series of unproductive runs over the submarine, which had hastily submerged. Then the *Raby* attempted in vain to make the most of its opportunity. Finally, Hains told the *England* to go ahead. From that moment on, RO-105 was doomed. A short time later pieces of wreckage bobbed to the surface following an underwater eruption. Scratch RO-105. Scratch one Japanese picket line. The final submarine in the line was sunk by an American plane off Truk. There would be no warnings of an American fleet sailing north.

Task Force 58 arrived off Saipan on June 11th. That

same day, Ozawa was ordered to send the giant battleships *Musashi* and *Yamato* along with the cruisers *Aoba, Kinu, Haguro,* and *Noshiro,* and a force of destroyers to support the third of a series of Japanese landings on Buin (Operation Kon). Following that, the ships were to attack MacArthur's landings on New Guinea.

On the second day of the American carrier strikes at Saipan, ten cargo ships of various types were sunk. By now Toyoda was aware that the advance warning he was anticipating would not be forthcoming. Nevertheless, Task Force 58's activity confirmed his suspicions. The Marianas it was. Ozawa turned his fleet toward Saipan and ordered the Kon ships to abandon their task and rendezvous with the rest of the fleet at sea.

Ozawa's fleet contained nine carriers, split into three divisions of three ships apiece. It was his intention to split his force once they reached the vicinity of the Marianas by sending a third of his carriers toward the American fleet under heavy escort. This van force was under the command of Admiral Kurita and contained the battleships *Musashi, Yamato, Kongo,* and *Haruna*, eight heavy cruisers, eight destroyers, and the light carriers *Chitose, Chiyodo,* and *Zuiho* with ninety planes.

Meanwhile, since the Japanese planes had a greater range than the Americans', Ozawa would stand off, out of range, and attack the U.S. carriers with the longer-range planes from his two carrier divisions. Carrier Division One was commanded by Ozawa himself, flying his flag in the big new carrier, *Taiho*. The two remaining veterans of Nagumo's Pearl Harbor Task Force, the *Shokaku*, and the *Zuikaku*, represented the balance of the division.

Under Ozawa's overall command, Admiral Takaji Joshima's 2nd Carrier Division included the fleet carriers *Junyo, Hiyo,* and the light carrier *Ryuho*. Counting those aboard Kurita's carriers under the tactical command of Admiral Sueo Obayishi, the Japanese carriers carried a total of four hundred fifty planes. Kurita, however, controlled the bulk of the heavy escorting forces, and these would be one hundred miles forward during the battle. Ozawa's screen was reduced to three heavy cruisers, one battleship, and nineteen destroyers. There was some concern over the weakness of the destroyer screen, but with the losses of the previous few months, there was little Ozawa could do about the situation.

While the Japanese submarines were unable to provide reports regarding the activity of the enemy forces, just the opposite was true of the Americans. Their submarines were patrolling along the entire proposed route of the Japanese advance.

Near 9 AM on the morning of June 15th, Admiral Toyoda sent the following message to Ozawa.

> "The Combined Fleet will attack the enemy in the Marianas area and annihilate the invasion force. Activate A-Go Operation for a decisive battle."[3]

Ozawa was already en route. Ten minutes after receipt of Toyoda's directive, the 2nd and 4th U.S. Marine divisions swarmed ashore on Saipan following a softening-up bombardment by a force of American battleships.

From the very beginning, lack of communications between commanders doomed the Japanese effort to failure. Admiral Takagi never saw fit to report the loss of his submarines. Neither had Admiral Kakuta bothered to inform Ozawa that Task Force 58's three days of bombing had resulted in the loss of many Japanese planes and heavy damage to key airfields on Guam, Tinian, Rota, and Saipan. In addition, Takagi elected not to bring all his planes in from Yap and Peleliu. Ozawa was not only counting on these planes, he was plannning to use the air bases to refuel his planes so that they could be sent back into battle immediately, thus avoiding the time-consuming return flight to the carriers.

Unbeknownst to him, Ozawa's force was sighted by the submarine *Flying Fish* late in the afternoon of the 16th. The sub's report alerted Spruance's Fifth Fleet, of which Task Force 58 was a part, that the Japanese fleet was heading in their direction.

Task Force 58 was an awesome force in itself. Under the command of Admiral Marc Mitscher, the force was split into five sections, four of which were powerful carrier forces. The fifth section was Admiral Willis Lee's formation of modern fast battleships. At the Marianas, the composition of the fleet was as follows:

Task Group 58.1 — Rear Admiral Joseph J. (Jocko) Clark Fleet Carriers — *Hornet** and *Yorktown*, Light carriers — *Belleua Wood* and *Bataan*. Four cruisers. Fourteen destroyers. 267 planes.

Task Group 58.2 — Rear Admiral Alfred E. Montgomery Fleet Carriers — *Wasp* and *Cabot*, Light Carriers — *Bunker Hill** and *Monterey*. Four cruisers. Twelve destroyers. 244 planes.

Task Group 58.3 — Rear Admiral John W. Reeves Fleet Carriers — *Enterprise** and *Lexington*, Light carriers — *Princeton* and *San Jacinto*. Five cruisers. Thirteen destroyers. 288 planes.

Task Group 58.4 — Rear Admiral William K. Harrill Fleet Carrier — *Essex*, Light Carriers — *Langley* and *Cowpens*. Four cruisers. Fourteen destroyers. 163 planes.

Task Group 58.5 — Rear Admiral Willis Lee Battleships — *Washington, North Carolina, Iowa, New Jersey, Indiana, South Dakota, Alabama*. Four cruisers. Fourteen destroyers.

Mitscher was in the *Lexington* and Spruance's flag flew from the masthead of the cruiser *Indianapolis* in Task Group 58.3.

Ozawa knew Spruance by reputation. The Japanese commander guessed that his opponent would elect to fight a defensive battle. In fact, this was precisely what Spruance was planning. Unlike the Japanese, the Fifth Fleet Commander was less concerned with the destruction of the enemy fleet than he was with the protection of the American landing forces. With this in mind, and unaware that Ozawa's primary objective was the destruction of the American carriers first and the beachhead second, Spruance adopted a formation designed to provide the maximum defense and prevent an end run. In addition, Spruance initially labored under the impression that two Japanese forces were approaching Saipan. This misconception was brought about by reports from the submarine *Seahorse,* which had sighted the Kon force prior to its linking up with Ozawa's main body on the 16th.

The Japanese force sailed into the Philippine Sea on the 18th. All through that day Admiral Kakuta sent his planes roaring from bases on Guam, Saipan, Tinian, and Rota against the U.S. fleet. The inexperienced Japanese pilots were no match for Mitscher's highly trained veterans. Wave after wave of Japanese planes was intercepted far from their targets by Task Force 58's Combat Air patrols and beaten back with incredible losses to the attackers. By evening, Kakuta's powerful air force was but a skeleton of its former self. Those planes that had escaped destruction on the ground during the previous three days were easily outmaneuvered by the more experienced American pilots.

On the other hand, Kakuta never did have the quantity of planes that Ozawa was counting on. Instead of committing every plane in his fleet, Kakuta decided to hold back some planes for the defense of other areas such as the Palaus. Kakuta compounded this error by not informing Ozawa of the heavy losses or of the fact that many planes never did arrive in the Marianas. Confident that sheer weight of numbers would overwhelm the Americans, Ozawa continued on.

Around 6:00 on the morning of the 18th, Ozawa began to launch his search planes. Sixteen planes searched for the American fleet but failed to make contact. A few planes did, however, run across search planes from Task Force 58. Three of the search planes fell victim to the American guns.

Around noon, Ozawa launched another search of fifteen

planes. This flight fared a little better, as one of the pilots located the American fleet three hours later. The first sighting was followed three-quarters of an hour later by another. What the Japanese scouts had stumbled across, though, was not the entire American force but merely the northern Task Groups. Once the location and course of the enemy fleet was determined, Ozawa set his own course to keep his fleet approximately four hundred miles from his opponent. The Japanese commander was not about to throw away the advantage of the longer range of his aircraft. In addition, if necessary, he could shuttle his planes to bases on Saipan and Guam. Ozawa elected to wait until first light the next morning before launching his attack. After all, to the best of his knowledge, his fleet remained undetected.

A few of his subordinates did not agree with Ozawa's decision to wait. Admiral Obayashi of the 3rd Carrier Division, for one, prepared to launch his planes immediately following the receipt of the sighting reports. One flight of planes from the carrier *Chiyoda* was already airborne when Ozawa ordered them recalled, much to Obayishi's disgust. The aggressive carrier commander railed at the decision but to no avail. Ozawa steamed north, as did Kurita.

Over on the American side, Mitscher disposed his fleet in a manner best suited to meeting attacks. Twelve miles apart running from north to south he placed Task Groups 58.1, 58.3, and 58.2 respectively. Task Group 58.4 was positioned ten miles ahead of 58.1. Lee's battleships of Task Group 58.5 were ordered to take up station fifteen miles due west of 58.3. In turn, Lee sent two destroyers twenty miles further west to serve as an early-warning picket line. Any Japanese force attempting to reach the center of Mitscher's line would have to fly directly over Lee's circle of battleships, bristling with antiaircraft guns.

Up to that point, Ozawa had indeed remained undetected. At least for the last few days. Late that evening though, he made an incredible blunder. Wishing to insure a coordinated attack the next day, Ozawa ordered a radio transmission made to Kakuta, directing the latter to synchronize his attacks with those of the carriers. The Americans fixed on the Japanese transmission and reported their findings to Spruance. For the first time, the Fifth Fleet commander was reasonably certain of the location of the Japanese fleet.

Spruance pondered the question of whether to maneuver for attack or continue with his present defensive posture. There was always the possibility that the calculation of the radio interceptors were in error. The Japanese still had plenty of time to execute an end run in an attempt to get at the American landing areas. Protection of the latter was Spruance's prime objective. No. He would not close with the Japanese. The Fifth Fleet was to lie back and let the enemy come to them. Verification of Ozawa's location came two hours after midnight. The submarine *Finback* made contact with the enemy fleet and dutifully reported its findings immediately.

Ozawa's fateful transmission was a wasted effort. Kakuta had few planes left with which to attack the Americans. The heavy air raids of the three previous days had taken their toll of Japanese air bases and planes. On the 18th, the Japanese attackers had suffered unusually high losses. To compound the inaccuracy, not only did Kakuta fail to report his heavy losses, but he informed Ozawa that his attacks had been an unqualified success. Many American planes had been destroyed along with damage to several carriers, according to Kakuta. It remains unfathomable why Kakuta acted in this manner, unless it represented an attempt on his part to save face.

Half an hour after midnight, Ozawa made a move which typified the Japanese operations throughout the war. He divided his forces. Kurita took his van force and moved one hundred miles closer to the enemy. Not only was Kurita not a carrier expert, his force contained the bulk of the heavy ships. This move also necessitated diluting the already weak destroyer screen, since both formations required destroyers to screen them.

In the early morning hours of the 19th, Ozawa ordered his ships to take up battle stations. Unlike Nagumo at Midway, he was determined to avoid the pitfalls of using too few search planes. At Midway the lack of adequate search planes was decisive. Accordingly, at the Philippine Sea, in a two-hour period beginning around 4:15 AM, Ozawa's fleet launched over forty scout planes. An hour and a half later, Mitscher began to launch his.

Three and a half hours after the first search plane climbed into the sky, Ozawa was rewarded with a sighting report. Although his planes were armed and fueled on the decks of the carriers just waiting for the order to take off, Ozawa hesitated until reports of a second sighting could confirm the first.

One hundred miles ahead, the impulsive Admiral Obayishi refused to wait. Instead of biding his time to coordinate his attack with the main force from Ozawa's six carriers, an hour after the initial sighting, seventy of Obayishi's planes were winging their way east from the decks of *Chitose*, *Choyoda*, and *Zuiho*. Thirty minutes later, Ozawa, having exhausted his own patience, launched twenty-seven torpedo planes, fifty-three bombers, forty-eight fighters, and one plane carrying Window (strips of tinfoil which, when dropped, confused enemy radar). Meanwhile, while Ozawa was stalking Spruance, the submarine *Albacore* was stalking the Japanese admiral.

Just before 10:00, the U.S.S. *Alabama*'s radar in Lee's force picked up the first Japanese strike over one hundred miles out. In the meantime, Mitscher had ordered all his planes to return from their raids on Guam and Rota. In addition, he directed each Task Group to launch its torpedo planes and dive bombers to clear the decks for use by the fighters and reduce the possibility of having the attack planes destroyed on the decks. The torpedo and dive bombers were ordered to hover a distance from the fleet, out of harm's way. Then Mitscher ordered all carriers to launch their fighters. Five minutes before 10:30, the carriers began to comply. Fighters from the *Princeton*, *Essex*, *Hornet*, *Cowpens*, and *Monterey*, however, were already in the air returning from raids. These groups turned to intercept the enemy.

Even as Mitscher's remaining carriers were launching their fighters, *Essex* planes waded into the Japanese formation, which by that time had located Lee's formation. The American pilots had a field day with their inexperienced foes. Between the American planes and the heavy antiaircraft fire from Lee's battleships, the Japanese lost fifty-nine planes. The *South Dakota* was hit with a bomb that killed twenty-two men and wounded twenty-four, but it failed to reduce the ship's fighting ability. Two cruisers were damaged by near misses. That was the extent of the harm to Lee's force. Instead of waiting till they found the enemy carriers, the excited Japanese pilots had attacked the first group of ships they came across.

Ten minutes after the first Japanese wave headed back for their carriers, the next flight arrived over Lee's Task Group. Once more American fighter pilots pounced on the Japanese formation. One enemy plane smashed into the side of the *Indiana* but merely succeeded in scratching the battleship's paint. Half a dozen others made it through to attack Task Groups 58.2 and 58.3. The *Wasp* and the *Bunker Hill* suffered slight damage from near misses, but that was the extent of the damage inflicted by Ozawa's large strike. Only thirty-one Japanese planes returned from the attack.

Despite the lack of adequate destroyers, Ozawa elected to commit as many planes as possible to the attack instead of retaining a few to bolster his antisubmarine patrols. This was his most costly decision. Shortly after 9:00, six torpedoes from the *Albacore* streaked toward the Japanese flagship. One pilot who had just taken off from the *Taiho*'s deck dove his plane into one of the fish. Four others missed. One, however, smashed into the side of the huge ship, rupturing fuel lines and jamming the forward elevator. Competent damage-control parties secured the damage, and the carrier was able to maintain course and speed.

An hour later, the 2nd Carrier Division launched its first strike, the third for the Japanese that fateful day. Half of this flight was misdirected en route to the target and failed to find the American fleet. The other half was jumped by the *Hornet*'s combat air patrol and was driven off with heavy loss.

Impatiently marking time a short distance away from Task Force 58, the American torpedo and dive bombers requested permission to get involved in the battle by attacking the Japanese air bases. Mitscher quickly gave his consent, and for the second time that day, the airfields on Guam and Rota came under heavy attack.

The fourth Japanese strike fared even worse than its predecessors. Kurita's van force was busy recovering planes when Ozawa dispatched the next force. Consequently, the former's three carriers were unable to add their planes to the weight of the attack. This flight missed the Americans completely, and after a lengthy search, all but eighteen planes headed for the air bases on Guam and Rota, hoping to replenish their fuel tanks before setting off once more in an effort to find the American fleet. In the midst of landing, the Japanese aviators suddenly found the sky filled with American planes. All but a handful were destroyed either on the ground or in the air.

Shortly after launching his fourth strike, Ozawa stared in horror as the Pearl Harbor veteran, the *Shokaku*, seemed to erupt in a ball of flame. After eluding the weak destroyer screen, the American submarine *Cavella* had fired four torpedoes at the Japanese carrier. All four struck home. Within an hour, the carrier's bow was underwater, and her captain gave the order to abandon ship. Fierce fires blazed throughout the carrier and she took on a heavy list. She remained afloat, although it was obvious that the great ship was doomed.

Ozawa's shock over the fate of the *Shokaku* was nothing like his bewilderment over the fact that few planes seemed to be returning from the raids. Misled by Kakuta's glowing reports, Ozawa could only conclude that his planes were shuttling back and forth between the Japanese air bases and the American fleet. Never, in his wildest imagination, could he fathom the huge losses of aircraft. The Japanese had completely underestimated the enormous striking power of Task Force 58.

Three hours after being hit by the *Cavella*'s torpedos, the *Shokaku* was engulfed by a tremendous explosion and plunged beneath the waves. On the bridge of the *Taiho* Ozawa was still sorting out the day's events when the entire ship erupted beneath him. Fumes from the ruptured gasoline and oil lines damaged by the torpedo hit had seeped throughout the ship. One spark was all it took. This spark was provided by one officer's decision to activate the exhaust fans in an effort to rid the ship of the noxious fumes. The resulting explosion destroyed the flight deck completely, blew huge holes in the ship's bottom, and doomed the *Taiho*. Ablaze from stem to stern, the carrier slowed to a stop. Nothing could save her now.

Ozawa's staff pleaded with him to leave the burning ship. In his turn, Ozawa expressed his wish to follow the example of Admiral Yamaguchi at Midway and go down with his ship. Eventually, however, the staff's views prevailed. Ozawa ordered the emperor's picture removed from the ship and he slid down the *Taiho*'s side to the deck of the destroyer *Wakatatsuke*. From the deck of the destroyer, Ozawa watched in sadness as the mighty *Taiho* slipped beneath the waves, taking over sixteen hundred men and a dozen planes with her. Added to *Shokaku*'s twelve hundred casualties, the Japanese cost in lives was heavy.

Watatsuke's facilities were inadequate for Ozawa to conduct the battle. Around 5:00 PM, he again transferred ship, this time to the cruiser *Haguro*, whose facilities were only slightly better than the destroyer's. Since it was painfully obvious that the day's fighting was concluded, Ozawa ordered Kurita to join up and called a halt to activities.

Including the destruction of fifty more of Kakuta's planes and the twenty-two lost when the *Shokaku* and the *Taiho* went down, Japanese aircraft losses for the day totaled four hundred twelve. On the other hand, Mitscher's losses totaled thirty-one planes. The Americans dubbed the action "The Great Marianas Turkey Shoot," and rightly so.

The following morning, Spruance directed Mitscher to close the range. Ozawa's force was refueling when American search planes located it in midafternoon of the

20th. When the American scout plane was detected, Ozawa ordered the refueling operation suspended and the fleet to take up defensive battle stations. The Japanese commander knew that his turn had come.

Eighty planes were launched as a combat air patrol. It was a pitiful handful to throw at what was heading the Japanese's way. Mitscher threw the entire weight of his fleet against the enemy. By the time darkness began to settle in, forcing the American planes to return from whence they had come, the *Hiyo* had been hit by two torpedoes and sunk, the *Zuikaku* and the *Junyo* were battling raging fires, three tankers were gone forever, and two heavy cruisers were badly damaged. In addition, sixty-five of the eighty planes comprising the combat air patrol were splashed by American fighters. That night, Toyoda ordered the fleet to return to Okinawa. Ozawa left the Philippine Sea with thirty-five planes remaining on board his carriers.

As a postscript to the American attack of the 20th, many U.S. pilots remained over the target area too long. Some of these ran out of fuel before reaching their mother ships. Almost all of the pilots arrived over Task Force 58 in the darkness. Despite the threat of Japanese subs, Mitscher ordered all carriers to turn on their lights to guide the pilots in. Flashing different-colored lights to designate particular ships, Task Force 58 guided their planes in. For some, it was too late, but for most of the American pilots, the sight of that huge force glowing like a Christmas tree was the most welcome sight they had ever seen. Seventy-three planes ran out of fuel and never made it back. This, as opposed to only fifty-six lost to enemy action during the two-day battle.

En route home, Ozawa sat down at his desk and penned his letter of resignation. Manfully, he accepted full responsibility for the defeat. But was he really totally to blame?

Kakuta's actions contributed heavily to the American success. His inaccurate but glowing reports of many enemy planes shot down and carriers blazing misled Ozawa from the very beginning. Then, of course, there was his reluctance to report on the conditions of his airfields. Instead of waiting to coordinate the attack with Ozawa's to form one huge formation, Obayashi's impetuous premature launching of his strike certainly contributed to the debacle.

The inexperience of the Japanese pilots also weighed heavily. The veterans of Midway, Pearl Harbor, and Santa Cruz were long gone. The newer pilots were no match for their veteran American counterparts and their overzealousness and youthful enthusiasm caused the first two waves to hit Lee's battleships instead of their primary target, the American carriers. Furthermore, there was no way Ozawa could control the fact that half of the third strike and all of the fourth missed the American fleet completely. Blame for that rests with the flight leaders themselves.

Whatever the reasons for defeat, the Battle of the Philippine Sea marked the final time the Japanese carrier fleet was a viable force in battle. The once proud and mighty Mobile Fleet was a wreck. Any remaining hope lay in the hands of the surface forces, the bulk of which were commanded by Admiral Kurita.

Rebuilding the fleet would be, of course, an impossible task. The most pressing problem facing the Japanese was: Where would the Americans strike next? The Philippines, Formosa, Okinawa, or Japan itself? Whatever the next enemy move, it would most certainly be aimed at severing Japan's supply line from the East Indies. Without the natural resources and vast oil reserves of that area, Japan would be unable to wage war at all, since she had no resources of her own. Therefore, Admiral Toyoda directed his staff to prepare plans to meet any eventuality.

As far as General MacArthur was concerned, there was only one choice for the Americans. When he had evacuated Corregidor in 1942 the general left with a promise to the Philippine nation that he would return. And return he would, with a vengeance!

During the months following the Battle of the Philippine Sea the American Pacific Fleet starring Task Force 58 (renumbered 38 when Halsey was in command—58 was Spruance's number) kept the Japanese reeling with raids throughout the Pacific. The remaining islands of the Marianas chain were conquered, Palalu invaded, Iwo Jima and the Carolines bombarded, and the New Guinea campaign wound down to its inexorable conclusion. In September, the fleet conducted heavy raids against the Philippines.

By October, the Pacific Fleet had swelled to allow the Americans the luxury of conducting simultaneous raids against Japanese areas. Including the smaller escort carriers, Nimitz's forces numbered no less than eighty carriers—mind boggling when one considers that at the great Battle of Midway the carriers on both sides totaled seven.

On the 12th of October, Task Force 38 began a five-day raid against Formosa. The Japanese struck back, but Mitscher stood his ground. In the five-day battle Japanese losses in aircraft rivaled those of the Philippine Sea. So intent were the Japanese on the destruction of the American carriers that Toyoda ordered planes out from Japan itself as reinforcements for the hard-pressed defenders of Formosa. Many of these planes were in the process of training with what remained of Ozawa's Mobile Fleet—irreplaceable carrier pilots.

Then it was back to the Philippines. For four days the American fleet stood offshore and pounded key Japanese positions on the more important islands. Toyoda knew then where the next American invasion would be: the Philippines. He therefore ordered the implementation of the grandiose Sho-1 plan.

Despite previous disasters, the Japanese proclivity for complicated operations requiring precision timing by dispersed forces remained unabated. Sho-1 was the most elaborate of all these plans.

"People of the Philippines, I have returned." Thus spoke General Douglas MacArthur after he waded ashore at Leyte on October 20th. Early that morning, four American divisions swarmed ashore on the southern coast of that island. Toyoda ordered his fleet commanders to destroy the American transports (*See Map 18*).

The elaborate Japanese scheme called for a pincer move-

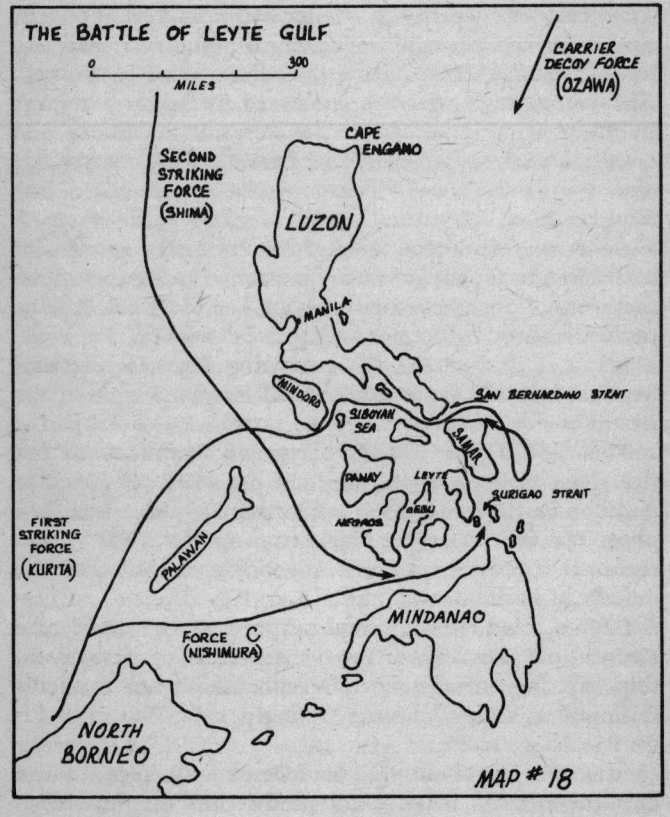

ment against the American beachhead by two powerful surface forces. Under the command of Admiral Kurita, the First Strike Force would leave its bases on Borneo in the East Indies, move through the Philippines, exiting through San Bernadino Strait, and move down the east coast of Samar and Leyte. Off Leyte Gulf, Kurita would rendezvous with a second striking force coming through Suragio Strait. This force was actually two different formations. The first was under the command of Admiral Nishimura, and like that of Kurita, based near the oil supplies of Borneo. Nishimura's force was to be bolstered by Admiral Shima's flotilla moving south from the Pescadores. Shima and Nishimura would link up at sea. Thus the elaborate timing. Shima links up with Nishimura — Nishimura and Shima rendezvous with Kurita.

After the war, Kurita confided to his interrogators that he fully expected to lose half of his ships during the operation. He did not approve of the plan, but there was little he could do about it short of asking to be relieved.

What of Ozawa and the remaining Japanese carriers? Surely these were not to be excluded from Sho-1. After the Battle of the Philippine Sea, the carriers remained in the Inland Sea. Ozawa retained command since Toyoda felt that no other Japanese admiral was experienced enough to lead the carriers in battle. Unfortunately, there were few pilots available to handle planes from carrier decks. Those that had trained for carrier operations were fed into the defense of Formosa and annihilated. Nevertheless, the carrier force could serve a useful purpose. Ozawa could take the heat off Kurita by luring the American carriers north, thus exposing the American beachheads. It was a suicide mission and Ozawa knew it. Willingly, he set out to do his duty to his country.

At 5:00 PM on the afternoon of October 20, 1944, Ozawa gave the order to weigh anchor and set sail for the Philippines. The following day, Shima left the Pescadores. Next it was Kurita's turn. With a powerful battle fleet, he left Brunei on the morning of the 22nd. In midafternoon of the same day, Nishimura followed from the same anchorage.

Kurita's route took him along the west coast of Palawan Island, through the narrow Palawan Passage, then across the Sibuyan Sea, and finally, through the San Bernadino Strait separating Luzon from Samar. Nishimura's force would steam directly through the Sulu Sea between the islands of Mindanao and Cebu. Shima's fleet was scheduled to join up when Nishimura reached a point south of the island of Negros.

Of all the Japanese forces involved, Kurita's was the most powerful by far. Five battleships, the *Kongo*, the *Haruna*, the *Nagato*, and the mammoth sisters *Yamato* and *Musashi* were the backbone of the formation. The finest of Japan's heavy cruisers, the *Haruna*, *Atago*, *Takao*, *Chokai*, *Maya*, *Myoko*, *Kumano*, *Suzuya*, *Chikuma*, and *Tone* were present. Fifteen destroyers were led by the light cruisers *Noshiro* and *Yahagi*.

Two additional battleships, the *Fuso* and the *Yamashiro* constituted the heart of Nishimura's fleet. They sailed in company with the heavy cruiser *Mogami* and four destroyers. Shima was to add the weight of the heavy cruisers *Nachi*, *Ashigara*, and *Abukuma*, and seven additional destroyers. Thus, seven battleships, fourteen heavy cruisers, two light cruisers, and twenty-six destroyers converged on the American landing beaches.

Task Force 38 stood off the Philippines providing an aerial umbrella for the invasion. Admiral Fukodome, commander of the Japanese air forces in the Philippines, was powerless. His meager force of two hundred planes was simply not powerful enough to influence the course of battle.

Task Force 38 had been at sea for months on end. Halsey felt that in view of the relative light opposition encountered to date, it was an opportunity to begin resting the ship's crews. On the 22nd, Admiral McCain was ordered to take his Task Group 38.1 to Ulithi for a brief period of rest. Admiral Davison, with Task Group 38.4, was scheduled to follow the next morning.

The *Darter* and the *Dace*, two U.S. submarines, were on patrol east of Palawan. In the early morning darkness of

October 23, the two boats were sailing side by side on the surface while their captains compared notes via megaphone. Suddenly, a contact was made and both submarines secured ship and dove beneath the waves. Steaming directly for their position was Kurita's battle fleet. It was a submariner's dream.

Aboard the *Atago*, Kurita paced the bridge impatiently, his mind filled with thoughts. He was in a foul mood that morning, since he was still not fully recovered from a bout with dengue fever. The admiral was no fool. Kurita knew that whatever the outcome of the coming battle, the Japanese Navy would have to pay a high price. Which of his ships would he leave behind at the bottom of the sea, even if the operation proved successful? His answer was not long in coming.

Just before 5:30, the *Darter* and the *Dace* attacked. The former launched a full spread of six torpedoes from her forward tubes at an inviting target before turning 180 degrees and firing all four of her stern tubes at another. Minutes later, two torpedoes slammed into the side of the *Atago*, knocked Kurita from his feet, and opened huge gashes in the cruiser's side. The ship began to settle immediately. Within moments, the order went out to abandon ship and Kurita found himself floating in the sea. The destroyers *Asashimo* and *Kishanami* moved alongside the dying *Atago* and picked up over five hundred survivors. Twenty minutes after the first torpedo hit, the *Atago*'s bow dipped beneath the sea for the last time, carrying over three hundred and sixty of her crew to a watery grave. While Kurita was temporarily incommunicado, control of the fleet passed to his second-in-command, Admiral Ugaki, Yamamoto's former chief of staff, then flying his flag in the *Yamato*.

The *Darter*'s second spread was rewarded with two hits on the *Takeo*, which caused serious flooding and started huge fires. Damage-control parties managed to save the cruiser but she was unquestionably unfit to participate in any battle. Ugaki ordered the destroyer *Naganami* to escort the stricken cruiser back to Brunei.

Meanwhile, on the other side of the formation, the *Dace*'s

attack was crowned by four direct hits on the cruiser *Maya*. A few minutes after 6:00, *Maya* exploded in a huge ball of flame and carried three hundred and forty of her crew to the bottom with her. Over seven hundred survivors were fished from the sea by escorting destroyers. In the brief span of three-quarters of an hour, Kurita found his force reduced by three heavy cruisers and a destroyer. Drying off on the deck of the *Yamato*, where the rescuing destroyer had transferred him, Kurita's mood was worsened by the ignominious events thus far. Nevertheless, he maintained course for Leyte and entered the Sibuyan Sea at around 6:30.

Upon receipt of the sighting reports from *Darter* and *Dace*, Halsey recalled Davison's Task Group, which was already on its way to Ulithi. From his flagship, the battleship *New Jersey*, the Third Fleet commander ordered his task groups to take up station off Luzon, San Bernadino Strait, and Samar.

At dawn the following morning Task Force 38's aircraft were airborne, seeking Japanese targets. Unfortunately, most of the searches were directed to the west, totally ignoring the northern flank. From that direction, Ozawa's fleet was approaching the Philippines. However, unlike Kurita and Nishimura, whose forces were located that morning, Ozawa was disturbed not over being sighted, but over not being detected. Unless he were discovered, Ozawa's force could not carry out its decoy role.

After confirmation of the sighting of Nishimura's and Kurita's formations, Halsey ordered strikes launched against both enemy fleets. Shortly after 9:00 AM, Nishimura's group came under attack but managed to escape with only one bomb hit on the battleship *Fuso*. Although some fires were started, the huge ship's fighting ability was not impaired and she was able to maintain course and speed. Shortly after the attack, the fires were extinguished. Nishimura was lucky. He had gotten off lightly, since the American effort was concentrated against the larger and potentially more dangerous threat, Kurita's fleet. Unfortunately, Nishimura never saw fit to notify

Kurita or Shima of the fact that his force had been discovered.

Meanwhile, the American carriers launched wave after wave of planes against Kurita. Admiral Fukodome took the opportunity to intervene with the handful of planes remaining in the Philippines. Soon after dawn he began readying counterstrikes against Task Group 38.3.

Fukodome's raid was intercepted by Admiral Sherman's combat air patrol and annihilated. One diligent Japanese pilot, however, did manage to sneak through and plant his bomb directly on the deck of the carrier *Princeton*. The bomb plunged into the ship's bowels, and after futile attempts to stem the resulting raging fires, the *Princeton* was scuttled later in the day. Her exploding magazines had caused heavy casualties not only to her own crew, but also to the crew of the cruiser *Birmingham* that lay alongside aiding in the fire-fighting efforts.

The Japanese air raid resulted in Fukodome's small air force being reduced even further in size. Kurita sent his scout planes to bolster the effort. Up north, Ozawa, chafing at having not been discovered, sent seventy-five of his one hundred planes winging toward the reported American positions. After failing to locate Halsey's force, these planes landed on Luzon and placed themselves at Fukodome's disposal. So too did Kurita's scout planes.

Kurita knew that Fukodome's decision to attack the American fleet meant that his own force was now on its own and could not rely on a combat air patrol from the Philippines for protection. The 24th saw swarm after swarm of American planes attack and reduce his fleet even further. From midmorning until late afternoon, no less than five major attacks were launched against Kurita's formation steaming through the Sibuyan Sea.

When the first American attack screamed down on Kurita's force hits were made on the cruiser *Myoko* and the battleship *Musashi*. Kurita ordered the cruiser to return to Brunei, but the *Musashi*'s fighting efficiency was hardly impaired. In anticipation of being short of air cover, before leaving Burnei Kurita had ordered all his ships fitted with additional heavy machine guns. These went a long way toward breaking up the American attacks and hindering the aim of the enemy pilots.

Nonetheless, the incessant American attacks continued without letup. The great *Musashi* and the *Yamato* seemed like magnets, attracting a great deal of attention, the former even more so after she was damaged in successive attacks. The *Yamato* was relatively fortunate in that she was hit by only two bombs, much to Kurita's consternation, since for the second time in two days, his flagship came under attack. Both leviathans, however, were capable of absorbing tremendous punishment. The *Yamato* and the *Musashi* were by far the largest and most powerful battleships ever launched, mounting an unheard of 18-inch main battery.

In contrast to the rest of the fleet, the *Musashi* received the bulk of the attention of the American planes. Even a ship as powerful as she was could not sustain the pounding she took. By late afternoon, the ship had been hit by fourteen torpedoes and numerous bombs. Her speed reduced and down by the bows, Kurita ordered the ship beached. Then the final American attack arrived before the order could be carried out. Three more torpedoes ploughed into her side and the mighty *Musashi* plunged to the ocean depths, carrying almost a thousand members of her crew with her.

As evening approached, Kurita ordered his fleet to reverse course. Anticipating even further attacks, the admiral considered it sheer folly to expose his formation further. Once night shrouded the fleet with the safety of its darkness, he could resume his original course.

Despite reports indicating the heavy damage to Kurita's force and Fukodome's air fleet, Toyoda ordered Kurita to stick to the original plan. But the latter had no intention of abandoning the operation completely, he simply desired to insure a measure of safety.

Kurita's reversal of course caused Admiral Halsey to play right into the Japanese hands. Around the same time that he received reports that Kurita had turned back, reports were also forthcoming telling of the Japanese carrier fleet moving south. Believing that Kurita was in full retreat as a result of the pounding he had taken, Halsey ordered his three task groups to rendezvous and set a course to intercept Ozawa. There was no way Halsey could have known that only twenty-five planes remained on board the Japanese carriers. While Task Force 38 sailed off to the north, Kurita did another about-face and resumed his original course. Contacting Nishimura, Kurita scheduled a rendezvous off Samar for 9:00 the next morning.

Nishimura never made it to the rendezvous. Unwilling to wait for Shima's forces, which were a little over an hour behind his own, the Southern Force commander steamed into Suragio Strait after informing Kurita that he was right on schedule. Admiral Kinkaid's heavy forces were waiting.

Kinkaid's Seventh Fleet was responsible for the close support and protection of the American landing areas. Three squadrons of small escort carriers were to the east providing aerial cover. These three groups, known as Taffy's, were therefore left behind when the Third Fleet sailed off in pursuit of Ozawa. In light of the activity of the previous two days, Halsey presumed that the Taffy's were more than capable of providing adequate protection. However, Halsey did move to cover all bets. He ordered Admiral McCain's Task Group 38.1 to refuel at sea and return to Leyte.

Kinkaid also had the services of heavier units. A force of cruisers and older battleships commanded by Admiral Jesse Oldendorf was charged with giving fire support to the landings. Their shore bombardment softened up the Japanese positions on Leyte. When informed of Nishimura's approach, Oldendorf positioned his force at the north end of Suragio Strait where it empties into Leyte Gulf.

At the head of the strait, Oldendorf placed the battleships *Mississippi*, *Maryland*, *Tennessee*, *West Virginia*, *California*, and *Pennsylvania*. With the exception of the first, all were veterans of Japan's attack on Pearl Harbor. Now, their wounds repaired, they sought revenge.

In front of the battleship line, at either end of the formation, steamed a squadron of cruisers. In Suragio Strait itself were three destroyer squadrons patrolling each side and the head of the strait. Finally, guarding the approaches and entrance to the strait, a swarm of PT Boats awaited the Japanese.

For almost four hours, beginning around 10:30 that evening, Nishimura's flotilla was harassed repeatedly by attacks from the American PT Boats. Finally, around 2:15 the next morning, the attacks ceased abruptly without having caused any damage. The small boat's luck changed an hour later when one of them planted a torpedo in the side of the light cruiser *Abukuma* of Shima's force.

An hour after the PT Boats drew off, Nishimura's formation began to register on the radar screens of the American destroyers. The little ships maneuvered themselves for the attack.

After entering the strait, Nishimura placed his force in line ahead with the four destroyers in the van, followed by the flagship *Yamashiro*, then the *Fuso* and the *Mogami*. The American destroyers raced into the attack. Around 3:00 the first group of destroyers launched their torpedoes. Eight minutes later two of these caved in the *Fuso*'s side. On fire and out of control, the battleship steamed in circles, mortally wounded. Half an hour later she blew up and broke in two, both halves sinking an hour later.

The second destroyer attack was even more devastating. *Yamashiro* took one torpedo hit that caused little damage and the flagship was able to proceed. The Japanese destroyers, however, did not fare as well. *Yamagumo* blew up and sank. *Asagumo*'s bow was blown off and the ship retired at a greatly reduced speed. *Michishio* was raised completely out of the water by the torpedo that struck her. When she came down, the destroyer was dead in the water and unable to maneuver. A second torpedo hit half an hour later finished her off.

Unaware of the carnage taking place around him, at 3:30 Nishimura radioed Kurita that he was under attack but intended to continue on. That was the last word Kurita received from his fellow admiral.

The final destroyer attack came in just before 4:00. Two

more torpedoes found *Yamashiro*'s hull and the battlesihp came to a halt. Moments later she was under way again, her speed cut in half, but by then Oldendorf's battleships and cruisers had her range.

Pummeled by the concentrated gunfire of the American battle line, the *Yamashiro* steamed in circles as 6-, 8-, and 14-inch shells rained down on her decks. No one knows at what point Nishimura perished, but his body was most certainly aboard when the *Yamashiro* plunged to the bottom around 4:20.

Meanwhile, the *Mogami* and the lone surviving destroyer, the *Shigure*, began to beat a hasty retreat. Pursued by heavy-caliber gunfire, the cruiser's upperworks were reduced to scrap iron. The lucky little destroyer escaped without a scratch. En route out of the strait, the two retreating ships came across Shima's force steaming on an opposite course. The *Mogami* collided with the cruiser *Nachi* and incurred even more damage. Her speed reduced, she was left to her fate by Shima, who, having seen enough, turned tail and headed for home without notifying Kurita of his intentions.

American cruisers pursued the retreating Japanese, sank the bowless *Asagumo*, and pumped shell after shell into the *Mogami*. Still the proud veteran refused to sink. Shortly after noon, she was scuttled by her own crew after the Americans had abandoned the effort.

The morning of October 25th dawned gray and overcast. Undetected, Kurita's force had moved through San Bernadino Strait during the night and was moving south along the east coast of Samar.

As already mentioned, three squadrons of American escort carriers were to the east coast of the Philippines, close into shore, providing cover for the American ground forces. Admiral Thomas Sprague's Taffy 1 was off Mindanao. Taffy 2 under Admiral Felix Stump was off Leyte Gulf. The northernmost task group, Admiral Clifton Sprague's Taffy 3, was off Samar. Kurita's force closed on the latter. Halsey was off to the north chasing Ozawa. The fox was in the henhouse amongst the chickens.

At first light the three Taffy's launched antisubmarine patrols and readied strikes against Japanese positions inland. On the bridge of the escort carrier *Fanshaw Bay*, Admiral Clifton Sprague was observing the activity when he was handed an urgent radio dispatch at 6:45.

> "Enemy surface force of four battleships, seven cruisers and eleven destroyers sighted twenty miles northwest of your task group and closing on you at thirty knots."[4]

Sprague remembers thinking.

> "Now there's some screwy young aviator reporting part of our own forces."[5]

Unaware that Halsey had slipped anchor and was off chasing Ozawa, Sprague ordered the scout plane to check the identification. Two minutes later he received the shock of his life.

> "Ships have pagoda masts."[6]

Lookouts aboard the Japanese ships sighted the Americans around the same time. Sprague had no choice. He was unable to turn his ships into the wind to launch his remaining planes, so he did the next best thing. Hoping that his planes would be able to take off in a cross wind, he set a course due east toward a rain squall. At the same time he ordered all ships in the formation, including the escort, to make smoke.

On board the *Yamato*, Kurita was straining out over the bows of the mighty ship hoping to get a glimpse of the enemy ships. At 7:00 he ordered his ships to open fire with their forward turrets as they came in range. One minute later, the huge 18-inch guns of the *Yamato* belched fire and smoke, sending her awesome projectiles toward Sprague's six helpless carriers. Then Kurita ordered the "General Chase" signal hoisted. This directive meant that each ship or squadron of ships was free to act independently. Thus, any advantage of a disciplined fleet action was thrown away.

Running at high speed toward the rain squall, Sprague watched in horror as multicolored shell splashes ringed his small fleet. The enemy shells were equipped with colored dye, thus allowing each ship to spot its own particular fall of shot. Furious orders issued forth from the flag bridge of *Fanshaw Bay*. Make smoke. Launch all available planes. The latter order was difficult to carry out since most of the Squadron's planes were already in the air over Leyte. Frantic calls for help went out to Kinkaid's headquarters.

South of Taffy 3, Admiral Stump, on Taffy 2's flagship, the *Natoma Bay*, heard Sprague's urgent call for help. Stump ordered those planes already airborne to abort their mission, and alter course for the Japanese force. That order was also received by Taffy 3's planes, who promptly complied.

Shortly after Kurita opened fire, the *White Plains* was badly hit by a heavy-caliber salvo. Then the Japanese ships found themselves under attack from the air. Taking violent evasive action, Kurita's ships managed to avoid damage.

Then occurred one of the most heroic acts of the war. Each Taffy was escorted by three destroyers and four destroyer escorts. The Japanese sailors stared in awe as, tearing through the smoke, came the destroyers *Johnston*, *Heerman*, and *Hoel*. Gnats attacking elephants. The destroyer attack threw the entire Japanese battle line into a state of confusion. Ships maneuvered frantically to avoid the destroyer attack. Fire was shifted from the carriers to the small destroyers. The *Kumano* was blasted by one of *Johnston*'s torpedoes. *Hoel* took on the battleship *Kongo* in an unequal contest.

From that point on the entire battle deteriorated into chaos. Planes from Taffy's 3 and 2 kept constant pressure on the Japanese fleet. The *Suzuya* took a bomb hit. Then one of the *Johnston*'s fish flew the bow off the *Kumano*, which had just found the range of the American carriers. The three brave destroyers were joined by the four even smaller destroyer escorts. Racing in for the attack, out and back again, the seven little ships totally distracted the Japanese gunners whose ships repeatedly altered course to avoid potential torpedo attacks and the fire of the escort's popguns that raked the bridges of the Japanese ships. But the little ships paid dearly for their heroism.

Only *Chikuma's* cruiser division was unaffected by the harassment. With her sister ships the *Tone* and the *Haguro*, the *Chikuma* closed the range on Sprague's formation, which by now had turned south. Sprague could not hope to outrun the enemy whose speed far exceeded that of his own ships. The *Gambier Bay* was hit repeatedly, abandoned, and shortly thereafter rolled over and sank. The *Kitkun Bay* and the *Fanshaw Bay* came under fire when incredibly, the Japanese broke off the action and reversed course.

From his vantage point on the *Yamato* at the rear of the battle line, Kurita was unable to keep abreast of the situation. Ships were steaming in all directions in an effort to avoid the American destroyer attacks. Enemy planes attacked repeatedly. Unable to use the decks of their own carriers, Sprague's planes used the airstrip at Tacloban to rearm, refuel, and take off for the next attack. Army ground crews serviced the planes as soon as they landed and got them airborne again in record time. Thus, what Kurita saw was a constant stream of attacks against his ships. Since he no longer had control of the battle, he ordered his fleet to reform.

Sprague could not believe his eyes. Just when the Japanese were within killing distance, they pulled off.

"At best I expected to be swimming by this time, saw the enemy ships disappear into the smoke haze to the north. I could not believe my eyes."[7]

For his part, Kurita was unaware that his force had been in action against a mere handful of escort carriers. As far as he knew, the battle was against the mighty Task Force 38. As a veteran of the Marianas Turkey Shoot, he was all too conscious of the awesome striking power of that formation.

The Japanese commander had no way of knowing that at that very moment Halsey was far to the north chasing Ozawa's decoy fleet. The latter made no radio transmissions to inform Kurita of what was transpiring. Furthermore, there was still no word of Nishimura's and Shima's fleets, forces that were supposed to rendezvous with his own fleet.

After sailing north for an hour and a half pursued every minute by the pesky American planes, Kurita altered course towards Leyte Gulf once more. A few minutes later, a strong air strike from Taffy 2 arrived. That settled the issue once and for all, as far as Kurita was concerned. Already four of his cruisers were cripples. Enough was enough. Ordering the cripples, the *Chokai*, the *Suzuya*, the *Chikuma*, and the *Kumano* to retire on their own, Kurita set course for San Bernadino Strait and made the following signal to Toyoda.

> "First Striking Force has abandoned penetration of Leyte anchorage and is proceeding north to search for enemy task force. Will engage decisively, then pass through San Bernadino Strait."[8]

Only the *Kumano* was in a position to follow. Japanese destroyers eventually scuttled the other three cruisers.

> "That he had his flagship sunk under him by underwater attack, had been without sleep for three days and had suffered a day and a half of almost incessant massed air attack, losing the splendid *Musashi* and two heavy cruisers in the process, must inevitably have clouded his judgment and played its part in bringing him to a decision to retire at 12:20 on October 25th."[9]

Later, Kurita confided to Captain Hara, "I made the retirement out of sheer physical exhaustion."[10]

Even though his mind was irrevocably made up, Kurita knew that his ordeal was far from over. He was absolutely certain that the American planes would allow him no respite. He couldn't have been more prophetic. Halsey had taken steps to cover his tracks.

Steaming full tilt to the Philippines was Admiral McCain's Task Group 38.1, hastily recalled from its scheduled rest at Ulithi. As soon as he was in range, McCain launched almost 150 planes from the decks of the *Wasp*, the *Hornet*, and the *Hancock*. Kurita's fleet was discovered in midafternoon. Fortunately, the only additional damage incurred was bomb damage to the *Tone*. The renewed American attacks, however, served to convince Kurita that he had indeed reached the correct conclusion. If he was harboring any thoughts of aiding Ozawa, these were quickly cast aside as he took his fleet full ahead for the San Bernadino Strait.

Three hundred miles to the north, Ozawa needed all the help he could get. Lingering two hundred miles off Cape Engano on the north coast of Luzon, Ozawa labored under the false impression that he was still undiscovered. How maddening. Hadn't he been obvious enough? Had he not, under the pretext of aiding Fukodome, sent seventy-five of his planes south in hopes that the Americans would be curious enough to investigate where those planes had come from? Frustrated, he had ordered Admiral Matsuda to move even farther south during the preceding night with the hybrid carriers *Ise* and *Hyuga** and a division of destroyers. It would not, however, be prudent to stray too close to the Philippines. The entire purpose of his mission would be compromised if the American carriers could strike out at his fleet with one hand and Kurita's with the other.

Ozawa's fears were unfounded. Halsey was indeed aware of his presence. The only uncertain thing was the exact location of the Japanese force. Around 2:30 AM, one of Mitscher's scout planes put the final piece of the puzzle in place. Ozawa's carriers were located.

The Japanese force was made up of the last remaining veterans of Pearl Harbor, the *Zuikaku*, the light carriers

---

*The *Ise* and the *Hyuga* were actually battleships whose rear turrets were removed, and flight decks capable of handling seaplanes were installed in their places.

Chitose, Chiyoda, Zuiho, and the aforementioned *Ise* and *Hyuga*. The light cruisers *Tama, Oyoda,* and *Isuzu* complemented the escort of eight destroyers.

Just before 9:00, Task Force 38 launched a 180-plane strike from all three Task Groups. This strike found the Japanese, blasted the *Chitose* to the bottom, put a torpedo into the destroyer *Akitsuki*, which blew apart in a spectacular explosion, and planted bombs on the *Zuicho*, the *Chiyoda*, and the *Zuikaku*.

Mitscher's second strike nailed the *Chiyoda* again along with the cruiser *Tama*. Meanwhile, with his flagship *Zuikaku* on fire, Ozawa transferred to the cruiser *Oyoda*.

All morning long, Halsey found himself besieged by urgent messages from Kinkaid telling of Sprague's plight. But the Third Fleet commander's attention was riveted on the destruction of the Japanese carriers. Kinkaid requested that Task Group 34, Admiral Lee's fast battleships with Halsey's fleet, be returned to Leyte posthaste.

Halsey's cardinal sin was that he had failed to notify anyone of his departure. Any commander worth his salt would have jumped at the opportunity to seek a decisive battle with the enemy carriers. Halsey had no way of knowing that Ozawa's force contained only twenty-five planes. Shortly after 11:00, Halsey was handed what he considered an insulting message: "Where is Task Force 34—the world wonders?" Reluctantly, Halsey ordered Lee's battleships to reverse course at 11:15, and make full speed for Leyte Gulf. Admiral Bogan with Task Group 38.2 was directed to follow.

Strike number three from Mitscher's two remaining groups planted several more bombs on the *Zuikaku* and finished the famous ship off with three torpedoes. *Zuiho* was hit again, as was the *Chiyoda*.

Even as the planes were warming up on the decks of the American carriers, Admiral Laurence DuBose took the cruisers *Santa Fe, Mobile, Wichita,* and *New Orleans* off to engage the Japanese fleet. Mitscher's carriers were drawing precariously close and it would not do to expose them to the heavy guns of the *Ise* and the *Hyuga*.

Zuiho took her final plunge before DuBose's cruisers could arrive on the scene, but the *Chiyoda*, although critically wounded, remained afloat. The American cruisers finished off the helpless carrier and managed to catch up with the damaged destroyer *Hatsusuki*. The hapless little ship was overwhelmed by the combined gunfire of the cruisers.

Ozawa's remaining few ships managed to slip from Halsey's grasp. However, as the Japanese force made their escape during the night, the submarine *Jallao* spotted the formation running north and put three torpedoes into the already damaged *Tama*. The light cruiser sank quickly with heavy loss of life, the last of Ozawa's force to be lost.

Kurita meanwhile, was making full speed for Brunei with the main body of his fleet. Strung out behind were the damaged *Kumano* and those destroyers that had been left behind to finish off the luckless *Chokai*, the *Suzuya*, and the *Chikuma*. Halsey detached his two fastest ships, the *Iowa*, and the *New Jersey*, with orders to guard the San Bernadino Strait. Around midnight, the two mighty battleships discovered the destroyer *Nowake* crammed with survivors of the *Chikuma* and easily overwhelmed it.

Near dawn, Clark's and Bogan's task groups rendezvoused off Luzon. At first light Kurita's ordeal began all over again. Repeated attacks by the American carrier planes succeeded in planting bombs on the *Yamato*, the *Tone*, and the *Nagato* without achieving much. The light cruiser *Noshiro* was stopped with a torpedo in her side during the first attack and was pummeled beneath the waves in succeding ones. In the afternoon, B-24 bombers from the *Moratai* kept up the pressure.

The *Kumano*, minus her bow, was hit again but managed to reach Manila. Admiral Koyanagi, Kurita's chief of staff, was critically wounded by a splinter from a near miss. Nevertheless, Kurita managed to reach Brunei the following day without additional loss.

Historians have been highly critical of Kurita's performance at Leyte, while at the same time scoffing at Ozawa's. To be objective, however, one must place oneself in the

Japanese admirals' place.

Kurita had gone without sleep for four days and was not completely recovered from a rather serious illness. For three of those days, his ships were attacked repeatedly. His flagship went down under him and he found himself swimming in the ocean. He saw other ships in his fleet pummeled to the bottom of the sea and was exposed to relentless and seemingly never-ending air attacks. Repeated efforts to contact the other units of the fleet (Nishimura and Shima) scheduled to rendezvous with his own force were in vain. Finally, he was under the impression that he was facing the entire might of Task Force 38 and could not have known otherwise in the face of the tenacious American air attacks. With this type of pressure, only a superhuman would have opted to continue.

As for Ozawa, he really never had much of a chance from the outset. No one can dispute that he made every conceivable effort to have his fleet discovered. Armed with the knowledge that discovery was tantamount to destruction, he nevertheless continued to play his decoy role to the best of his ability.

Leyte Gulf marked the last time the Japanese sought a fleet action against the Americans. In the following months, ship after ship was hunted down by American submarines or carrier planes and sent to their watery graves. At war's end, only a handful remained afloat.

Neither Ozawa nor Kurita ever went to sea again following the debacle at Leyte Gulf. Kurita was replaced as commander of the Second Fleet by Admiral Ito, the man who later took the *Yamato* on its suicide mission. In December, Kurita was named commander of the Naval Academy and served out the war in this capacity. After the war he went into retirement and died peacefully at his home in 1977.

Ozawa returned from Leyte Gulf to an appointment as vice chief of the Naval General Staff. After Toyoda's failure to prevent the seizure of Okinawa, Ozawa was tapped to command what remained of the Combined Fleet. At war's end, he was responsible for surrendering his few remaining ships to the Allies. Then he joined his colleagues in retirement and passed on at the age of eighty, in 1966.

Notes to Introduction

1. Saburo Ienaga, *The Pacific War*, p. 53
2. John Costello, *The Pacific War*, p. 232
3. Lawrence Taylor, *A Trial of Generals*, p. 43
4. *Ibid*, p. 45
5. *Ibid*, p. 66
6. Stanley L. Falk, *Bataan: The March of Death*, p. 129
7. *Ibid*, p. 187
8. *Ibid*, p. 188
9. *Ibid*, p. 199

Notes to Chapter 1

1. Alvin Coox, *Tojo*, p. 8
2. Courtney Browne, *Tojo: The Last Banzai, p. 21*
3. Coox, *op, cit*, p 19
4. *Ibid*, p. 28
5. Browne, *op. cit*, p. 64
6. *Ibid*, p. 67
7. Coox, *op. cit*, p. 49
8. David Bergamini, *Japan's Imperial Conspiracy*, p. 735
9. Coox, *op. cit*, p. 72
10. John Toland, *The Rising Sun*, p. 96
11. *Ibid*, p. 99
12. Bergamini, *op. cit*, p. 825
13. Coox, *op. cit*, p. 91
14. Browne, *op. cit*, p. 101
15. *Ibid*, p. 104
16. Toland, *op. cit*, p. 118
17. Coox, *op. cit*, p. 147

18. Toland, *op. cit*, p. 147
19. Browne, *op. cit*, p. 124
20. Toland, *op. cit*, p. 277
21. Browne, *op. cit*, pp. 139-40
22. *Ibid*, p. 141
23. Bergamini, *op. cit*, p. 1052
24. *Ibid*, p. 1063
25. Browne, *op. cit*, p. 182
26. *Ibid*, p. 209
27. *Ibid*, p. 210
28. *Ibid*, p. 236

Notes to Chapter 2

1. Sir Michael Carver, ed., *The War Lords, p. 134*
2. *Ibid*, p. 395
3. *Ibid*, p. 396
4. Hiroyuki Agawa, *The Reluctant Admiral*, p. 134
5. *Ibid*, p. 184
6. *Ibid*, p. 186
7. Carver, *op. cit*, p. 397
8. John Dean Potter, *Yamamoto*, p.43
9. Agawa, *op. cit*, p. 220
10. Potter, *op. cit*, p. 53
11. Agawa, *op. cit*, p. 229
12. Carver, *op. cit*, p. 397
13. Potter, *op. cit*, p. 79
14. Agawa, *op. cit*, p. 246
15. Potter, *op. cit*, p. 92
16. *Ibid*, p. 102
17. Agawa, *op. cit*, p. 265
18. Potter, *op. cit*, p. 123
19. Samuel Elliot Morrison, *The Rising Sun In The Pacific, Vol. III*, p. 132
20. Agawa, *op. cit*, p. 291

21. *Ibid*, p. 291
22. *Ibid*, pp. 244-45
23. Potter, *op. cit*, p. 253
24. *Ibid*, p. 253
25. Carver, *op. cit*, p. 400
26. Mansanori Ito, *The End Of The Imperial Japanese Navy*, p. 61
27. Potter, *op. cit*, p. 275
28. *Ibid*, p. 300
29. *Ibid*, p. 308
30. Agawa, *op. cit*, p. 380

Footnotes to Chapter 3

1. Tameichi Hara, *Japanese Destroyer Captain*, p. 34
2. Gordon Prange, *At Dawn We Slept*, p. 300
3. Hiroyuki Agawa, *Reluctant Admiral*, p. 130
4. Prange, *op. cit*, p. 280
5. *Ibid*, p. 344
6. *Ibid*, p. 573
7. John Costello, *The Pacific War*, p. 319
8. Mitsuo Fuchida & Masatake Okumiya, *Midway*, pp. 197-98
9. Hara, *op. cit*, p. 256

Notes to Chapter 4

1. Tamiechi Hara, *Japanese Destroyer Captain*, p. 44
2. *Ibid*, p. 97
3. Paul Dull, *The Imperial Japanese Navy*, p. 190
4. Lawrence Cortesi, *Bloody Friday off Guadalcanal*, p. 19

5. Jack Coggins, *The Campaign For Guadalcanal*, p. 156
6. Hara, *op. cit*, p. 161
7. *Ibid*, p. 164
8. *Ibid*, p. 165
9. Cortesi, *op. cit*, p. 301

Notes to Chapter 5

1. A. Frank Reel, *The Case of General Yamashita*, p. 56
2. *Ibid*, p. 57
3. *Ibid*, p. 58
4. A.J. Barker, *Yamashita*, p. 16
5. *Ibid*, pp. 31-32
6. *Ibid*, p. 33
7. *Ibid*, p. 33
8. *Ibid*, p. 41
9. Arthur Swinson, *Defeat In Malaya*, p. 17
10. *Ibid*, pp. 12-13
11. *Ibid*, p. 39
12. *Ibid*, p. 74
13. Barker, *op. cit*, p. 68
16. Winston Churchill, *The Hinge Of Fate*, p. 53
15. Swinson, *op. cit*, p. 135
16. Noel Barber, *A Sinister Twilight*, pp. 216-17
17. Swinson, *op. cit*, p. 140
18. Barker, *op. cit*, p. 87
19. Stanley L. Falk, *Seventy Days To Singapore*, p. 257
20. Barker, *op. cit*, p. 104
21. *Ibid*, p. 113
22. Stanley Falk, *Liberation Of The Philippines*, p. 62
23. Barker, *op. cit*, p. 122
24. Lawrence Taylor, *A Trial Of Generals*, p. 98
25. Barker, *op. cit*, pp. 137-138
26. *Ibid*, p. 144

26. *Ibid*, p. 146
28. A. Frank Reel, *op. cit*, p. 173
29. *Ibid*, p. 241

Notes to Chapter 6

1. Hiroyuki Agawa, *The Reluctant Admiral*, p. 346
2. *Ibid*, p. 388
3. William Y'Blood, *Red Sun Setting*, p. 66
4. S.E. Smith, ed., *The United States Navy In World War II*, p. 864
5. *Ibid*, p. 864
6. *Ibid*, p. 864
7. *Ibid*, p. 864
8. Donald MacIntyre, *Leyte Gulf, Armada In The Pacific*, p. 127
9. *Ibid*, p. 150
10. Tameichi Hara, *Japanese Destroyer Captain*, p. 270

Bibliography to Introduction

1. BENEDICT, Ruth, *The Chrysanthemum and the Sword*. New American Library, New York, 1967.
2. COSTELLO, John, *The Pacific War*. Wade Publishers, Inc., New York, 1981.
3. DYESS, Lt. Col. William E., *The Dyess Story*. G.P. Putnam's Sons, New York, 1944.
4. FALK, Stanley, *Bataan: The March of Death*. Modern Library Editions, New York, 1962.
5. HAYASHI, Saburo, *Kogun: The Japanese Army in the Pacific War*. The Marine Corps Association, Quantico, Va., 1959.
6. IENAGA, Saburo, *The Pacific War*. Pantheon Books, New York, 1978.
7. KNOX, Donald, *Death March*. Harcourt, Brace, Jovanovich, New York, 1981.
8. MANCHESTER, William, *American Caesar*. Little, Brown and Co., Boston, 1978.
9. MORTON, Louis, *The Fall of the Philippines*. Office of the Chief of Military History, Washington, D.C., 1953.
10. PFANNES, C. and SALAMONE, V., *The Great Commanders of World War II, Volume III, The Americans*. Zebra Books, New York, 1981.
11. RUTHERFORD, Ward, *Fall of the Philippines*. Ballantine Books, New York, 1971.
12. TAYLOR, Lawrence, A Trial of Generals. Icarus Press, South Bend, Ind., 1981.
13. TOLAND, John, *But Not In Shame*. Random House, New York, 1961.
14. WAINWRIGHT, General Jonathan M., *General Wainwright's Story*. Doubleday & Co., New York, 1946.

Bibliography to Chapter 1

1. BERGAMINI, David, *Japan's Imperial Conspiracy*. Pocket Books, New York, 1972.
2. BROWNE, Courtney, *Tojo: The Last Banzai*. Paperback Library Inc., New York, 1967.
3. COLLIER, Basil, *The War in The Far East 1941-1945*. William Morrow & Co., New York, 1969.
4. COOX, Alvin, *Tojo*. Ballantine Books, New York, 1975.
5. DULL, Paul, *A Battle History of the Imperial Japanese Navy*. Naval Institute Press, Annapolis, 1978.
6. FAIRBANK, John K., et. al, *East Asia: Tradition and Transformation*. Houghton Mifflin Co., Boston, 1973.
7. FEIS, Herbert, *The Road to Pearl Harbor*. Atheneum, New York, 1963.
8. HAYASHI, Saburo, *Kogun: The Japanese Army in the Pacific War*. The Marine Corps Association, Quantico, Va., 1959.
9. IENAGA, Saburo, *The Pacific War*. Pantheon Books, New York, 1978.
10. MORISON, Samuel E., *The Two-Ocean War*. Little Brown and Co., Boston, 1963.
11. MORTON, Louis, *Strategy and Command: The First Two Years*. Office of the Chief of Military History, Wash. D.C., 1962.
12. MOSLEY, Leonard, *Hirohito*. Prentice-Hall Inc, Englewood Cliffs, N.J., 1966.
13. PFANNES, C., & SALAMONE, V., *The Great Commanders of WW II-The British*. Zebra Books, New York, 1981.
14. POTTER, E.B., & NIMITZ, Chester, *The Great Sea War*. Prentice-Hall Inc., Englewood Cliffs, N.J., 1960.
15. TOLAND, John, *The Rising Sun*. Random House,

New York, 1970.
16. WINTON, John, *War In The Pacific*. Mayflower Books Inc., New York, 1978.

Bibliography to Chapter 2

1. AGAWA, Hiroyuki, *The Reluctant Admiral*. Kodansha International Ltd., Tokyo, 1979.
2. BUELL, Thomas B., *The Quiet Warrior*. Little, Brown & Co., Boston, 1974.
3. CARVER, Field Marshal Sir Michael, ed., *The War Lords*. Little Brown & Co., Boston, 1976.
4. COLLIER, Basil, *The War In The Far East 1941-1945*. William Morrow & Co., New York, 1969.
5. COOK, Charles, *The Battle Of Cape Esperance*. Thomas Y. Corwell Co., New York, 1968.
6. d'ALBAS, Andrew, *Death Of A Navy*. The Devin-Adair Co., New York, 1957.
7. DULL, Paul S., *A Battle History Of The Imperial Japanese Navy 1941-1945*. Naval Institute Press, Annapolis, 1978.
8. FEIS, Herbert, *The Road To Pearl Harbor*. Atheneum, New York, 1963.
9. FUCHIDA, Mitsuo & OKUMIYA, Masatake, *Midway—The Battle That Doomed Japan*. Naval Institute Press, Annapolis, 1955.
10. Gill, G. *The Royal Australian Navy 1942–1945*, Australian War Memorial, Canberra, 1968.
11. HALSEY, William F. & BRYANN, J., *Admiral Halsey's Story*. McGraw Hill, New York, 1947.
12. Hoehling, A.A., *The Lexington Goes Down*. Prentice Hall, New Jersey, 1971.
13. HOUGH, Frank, LUDWIG, Verle, & SHAW, Henry, *Pearl Harbor To Guadalcanal*. U.S. Marine Corps, Washington, D.C., 1900.

14. HOYT, Edwin, *Blue Skies And Blood*. Paul S. Eriksson Inc., New York, 1975.
15. ITO, Masanori, *The End Of The Imperial Japanese Navy*. W.W. Norton, New York, 1956.
16. JOHNSTON, Stanley, *Queen Of The Flat Tops*. E.P. Dutton, New York, 1942.
17. LORD, Walter, *Day of Infamy*. Henry Holt & Co., New York, 1957.
18. LORD, Walter, *Incredible Victory*. Harper & Row, New York, 1967.
19. LINDSTROM, John, The First South Pacific Campaign. Naval Institute Press, Annapolis, 1976.
20. MILLER, John, *Guadalcanal: The First Offensive*. Department Of The Army, Washington, D.C., 1949.
21. MILLOT, Bernard, *The Battle Of The Coral Sea*. Naval Institute Press, Annapolis, 1974.
22. MORRISON, Samuel, *History Of United States Naval Operations In WW II Vol. III—The Rising Sun In The Pacific*. Little, Brown & Co., Boston, 1948.
23. MORRISON, Samuel, *History Of United States Naval Operations in WW II Vol. IV—Coral Sea, Midway & Submarine Actions*. Little, Brown & Co., Boston, 1949.
24. MORRISON, Samuel, *History Of United States Naval Operations In WW II Vol. V—The Struggle For Guadalcanal*. Little, Brown & Co., Boston, 1949.
25. POTTER, John D., *Yamamoto*. The Viking Press, New York, 1965.
26. POTTER, E.B., ed., & NIMITZ, Chester, *The Great Sea War*. Prentice Hall Inc., New Jersey, 1960.
27. POTTER, E.B., *NIMITZ*. Naval Institute Press, Annapolis, 1976.
28. ROSKILL, S.W., *The War At Sea—Vol. II*. Her Majesty's Stationery Office, London, 1956.
29. SMITH, S.F., ed., *The United States Navy In World War II*. William Morrow & Co., New York, 1966.
30. TOLAND, John, *But Not In Shame*. Random House, New York, 1961.
31. TOLAND, John, *The Rising Sun*. Random House, New York, 1970.

32. TULEJA, Thaddeus V., *Climax At Midway*. J.M. Dent & Sons Ltd., London, 1960.

Bibliography to Chapter 3

1. AGAWA, Hiroyuki, *The Reluctant Admiral*. Kodanska International, Tokyo, 1979.
2. COGGINS, Jack, *The Campaign For Guadalcanal*. Doubleday & Co., New York, 1972.
3. COLLIER, Basil, *The War In The Far East 1941-1945*. William Morrow & Co., New York, 1969.
4. Costello, John, *The Pacific War*. Rawson Wade Publishers, New York, 1981.
5. DULL, Paul, *A Battle History of the Imperial Japanese Navy*. Naval Institute Press, Annapolis, 1978.
6. FUCHIDA, M., & OKUMIYA, M., *Midway*. Naval Institute Press, Annapolis, 1955.
7. HARA, Tameichi, *Japanese Destroyer Captain*. Ballantine Books, New York, 1961.
8. HOYT, Edwin, *To The Marianas*. Van Nostrand Reinhold Co., New York, 1980.
9. HUMBLE, Richard, *Japanese High Seas Fleet*. Ballantine Books, New York, 1973.
10. LORD, Walter, *Day of Infamy*. Henry Holt & Co., New York, 1957.
11. LORD, Walter, *Incredible Victory*. Harper & Row, New York, 1967.
12. MORISON, Samuel E., *The Two-Ocean War*. Atlantic Little Brown, Boston, 1963.
13. PRANGE, Gordon, *At Dawn We Slept*. McGraw Hill, New York, 1981.
14. ROHWER, J. & HUMMELCHEN, C., *Chronology of the War At Sea Vol I*. Arco Publishing, New York, 1972.
15. SALMAGGI, C. & PALLAVISINI, A., *2,194 Days Of War*. Windward, London, 1977.

16. SILVERSTONE, Paul, *U.S. Warships of World War II*. Doubleday & Co., New York, 1965.
17. SMITH, S.E., ed., *The United States Navy In World War II*. William Morrow & Co., New York, 1966.
18. TOLAND, John, *But Not In Shame*. Random House, New York, 1961.
19. TOLAND, John, *The Rising Sun*. Random House, New York, 1970.
20. WATTS, A.J., *Japanese Warships of World War II*. Ian Allen, London, 1966.
21. WATTS, A.J., & GORDON, B.G., *The Imperial Japanese Navy*. Doubleday & Co., New York, 1971.
22. WINTON, John, *War In The Pacific*. Mayflower Books, New York, 1978.
23. *U.S. Strategic Bombing Survey-Interrogation of Japanese Officials*. U.S. Government Printing Office, Wash., D.C., 1947.

Bibliography to Chapter 4

1. AGAWA, Hiroyuki, *The Reluctant Admiral*. Kodansha International, Tokyo, 1979.
2. COGGINS, Jack, *The Campaign For Guadalcanal*. Doubleday & Co., Garden City, 1972.
3. CORTESI, Lawrence, *Bloody Friday Off Guadalcanal*. Zebra Books, New York, 1981.
4. COSTELLO, John, The Pacific War. Rawson Wade Publishers, New York, 1981.
5. DULL, Paul, *The Imperial Japanese Navy*. Naval Institute Press, Annapolis, 1978.
6. FUCHIDA, M., & OKUMUYO, M., *Midway*. Naval Institute Press, Annapolis, 1955.
7. HARA, Tamiechi, *Japanese Destroyer Captain*. Ballantine Books Inc., New York, 1961.
8. HOYT, Edwin, *Guadalcanal*. Stein & Day, New York, 1981.

9. HUMBLE, Richard, *Japanese High Seas Fleet*. Ballantine Books Inc., New York, 1973.
10. KENT, Graeme, *Guadalcanal—Island Ordeal*. Ballantine Books, N.Y., 1971.
11. LECKIE, Robert, *Challenge For The Pacific*. Doubleday & Co., Garden City, 1965.
12. MORISON, Samuel E., *The Two Ocean War*. Atlantic Little Brown & Co., Boston, 1963.
13. MORRIS, C. & CAVE, H., *The Fighten'est Ship*. Zenger Publishing, Washington, D.C., 1944.
14. ROWHER, J. & HUMMELCHEN, J., *Chronology of the War At Sea—Vol. I*. Arco Publishing, New York, 1974.
15. SALMAGGI, C. & PALLAVISINI, A., *2,194 Days Of War*. Windward, London, 1977.
16. SILVERSTONE, Paul, *U.S. Warships of World War II*. Doubleday & Co., Garden City, 1965.
17. SMITH, S.E., ed., *The United States Navy In World War II*. William Morrow & Co., New York, 1966.
18. SMITH, Stan, *The Navy At Guadalcanal*. Lancer Books, New York, 1963.
19. THOMAS, David, *The Battle Of The Java Sea*. Stein & Day, New York, 1968.
20. TOLAND, John, *The Rising Sun*. Random House, New York, 1970.
21. VAN OOSTEN, F.F., *The Battle Of The Java Sea*. Ian Allen, London, 1976.
22. WATTS, A.J., & GORDON, B.G., *The Imperial Japanese Navy*. Doubleday & Co., Garden City, 1971.
23. WATTS, A.J., *Japanese Warships Of World War II*. Ian Allen, London, 1966.
24. WINTON, John, *The War In The Pacific*. Mayflower Books, New York, 1978.

Bibliography to Chapter 5

1. BARBER, Noel, *A Sinister Twilight*. Houghton Mifflin Co., Boston, 1968.
2. BARBEY, Daniel E., *MacArthur's Amphibious Navy*. United States Naval Institute, Annapolis, 1969.
3. BARKER, A.J., *Yamashita*. Ballantine Books, New York, 1973.
4. BERGAMINI, David, *Japan's Imperial Conspiracy*. Pocket Books, New York, 1971.
5. CANNON, M. Hamlin, *Leyte: The Return To The Philippines*. Office of the Chief of Military History, Dept. of the Army, Wash., 1954.
6. CHURCHILL, Winston, *The Hinge of Fate*. Houghton Mifflin Co., Boston, 1950.
7. COSTELLO, John, *The Pacific War*. Rawson Wade Publishers, New York, 1981.
8. FALK, Stanley, *Decision At Leyte*. W.W. Norton & Co., New York, 1966.
9. FALK, Stanley, *Liberation Of The Philippines*. Ballantine Books, New York, 1971.
10. FALK, Stanley, *Seventy Days To Singapore*. G.P. Putnam's Sons, New York, 1975.
11. HAYASHI, K. & COOX, A. *Kogun: The Japanese Army In The Pacific War*. The Marine Corps Association, Quantico, Va., 1959.
12. IENAGA, Saburo, *The Pacific War*. Pantheon Books, New York, 1978.
13. KIRBY, S. Woodburn et. al., *The War Against Japan Volume I*. Her Majesty's Stationery Office, London, 1957.
14. KRUEGER, Gen. Walter, *From Down Under To Nippon*. Combat Forces Press, Wash., D.C., 1953.
15. MANCHESTER, William *American Caesar*. Little, Brown & Co., Boston, 1978.

16. MORISON, Samuel E., *History Of United States Naval Operations in World War II—Volume XII: Leyte*. Little, Brown & Co., Boston, 1958.
17. REEL, A. Frank, *The Case Of General Yamashita*. Octogon Books, New York, 1971.
18. SASTRI, K.N.V. & BHARGAWA, K.D., *Official History of the Indian Armed Forces In the Second World War 1939-45: Campaigns In South-East Asia*. Orient Longmans, 1960.
19. SMITH, Robert, *Triumph In The Philippines*. Department of the Army, Wash, D.C., 1963.
20. SWINSON, Arthur, *Defeat In Malaya*. Ballantine Books, New York, 1969.
21. TAYLOR, Lawrence, *A Trial Of Generals*. Icarus Press, South Bend, Ind., 1981.
22. TOLAND, John, *But Not In Shame*. Random House, New York, 1961.
23. TOLAND, John, *The Rising Sun*. Random House, New York, 1970.
24. WIGMORE, Lionel, *The Japanese Thrust*. Australian War Memorial, Canberra, 1957.

Bibliography to Chapter 6

1. AGAWA, Hiroyuki, *The Reluctant Admiral*. Kodansha International, Tokyo, 1979.
2. CORTESI, Lawrence, *Valor Off Samar*. Zebra Books, New York, 1980.
3. CORTESI, Lawrence, *Pacific Breakthrough*. Zebra Books, New York, 1981.
4. COSTELLO, John, *The Pacific War*. Rawson Wade Publishers, New York, 1981.
5. DULL, Paul, *The Imperial Japanese Navy*. Naval Institute Press, Annapolis, 1978.
6. HALSEY, W. & BRYANN, J., *Admiral Halsey's Story*. Curtis Publishing Co., New York, 1947.

7. HARA, Tameichi, *Japanese Destroyer Captain*. Ballantine Books, New York, 1961.
8. HOYT, Edwin, *To The Marianas*. Van Nostrand Reinhold Co., New York, 1980.
9. HOYT, Edwin, *Guadalcanal*. Stein & Day, New York, 1981.
10. HOYT, Edwin, *The Battle For Leyte Gulf*. Weybright & Talley, New York, 1972.
11. HOYT, Edwin, *How They Won The War In The Pacific*. Weybright & Talley, New York, 1970.
12. HUMBLE, Richard, *Japanese High Seas Fleet*. Ballantine Books, New York, 1973.
13. MACINTYRE, Donald, *Leyte Gulf, Armada In The Pacific*. Ballantine Books, New York, 1969.
14. MORISON, Samuel, *The Two Ocean War*. Atlantic, Little Brown, Boston, 1963.
15. PRANGE, Gordon, *At Dawn We Slept*. McGraw Hill, New York, 1981.
16. REYNOLDS, Clark, *The Fast Carriers*. McGraw Hill, New York, 1968.
17. ROHWER, J., & HUMMELCHEN, G., *Chronology Of The War At Sea, Vol, II*. Arco Publishing, New York, 1974.
18. SALMAGGI, C., & PALLAVISINI, A., *2,194 Days of War*. Windward, London, 1977.
19. SMITH, S.E., ed., *The United States Navy In World War II*. William Morrow & Co., New York, 1966.
20. VAN OOSTEN, F.C., *The Battle Of The Java Sea*. Ian Allan, London, 1976.
21. WATTS, A.J., *Japanese Warships Of World War II*. Ian Allan, London, 1966.
22. WATTS, A.J. & GORDON, B.G., *The Imperial Japanese Navy*. Doubleday & Co., New York, 1971.
23. WINTON, John, *War In The Pacific*. Mayflower Books, New York, 1978.
24. WOODWARD, C. Van, *The Battle For Leyte Gulf*. MacMillan & Co., New York, 1947.
25. Y'BLOOD, William, *Red Sun Setting*. Naval Institute Press, Annapolis, 1981.

26. YOUNG, Peter, ed., *Atlas Of The Second World War*. G.P. Putnam's Sons., New York, 1974.
27. *U.S. Strategic Bombing Survey-Interrogation of Japanese Officials*. U.S. Government Printing Office, Wash., D.C., 1947.

A SPECTACULAR NEW ADULT WESTERN SERIES BY PAUL LEDD

SHELTER #1: PRISONER OF REVENGE (598, $1.95)
After seven years in prison for a crime he didn't commit, exconfederate soldier, Shelter Dorsett, was free and plotting his revenge on the "friends" who had used him in their scheme and left him the blame.

SHELTER #2: HANGING MOON (637, $1.95)
In search of a double-crossing death battalion sergeant, Shelter heads across the Arizona territory—with lucious Drusilla, who is pure gold. So is the cargo beneath the wagon's floorboads!

SHELTER #3: CHAIN GANG KILL (658, $1.95)
Shelter finds himself "wanted" by a member of the death battalion who double-crossed him seven years before *and* by a fiery wench. Bound by lust, Shelter aims to please; burning with vengeance, he seeks to kill!

SHELTER #4: CHINA DOLL (682, $1.95)
The closer the *Drake* sails to San Francisco, the closer Shelter is to the target of his revenge—until he discovers the woman hiding below deck whose captivating powers steer him off course.

SHELTER #9: APACHE TRAIL (956, $2.25)
Shelter tracks down a sharp-shooting traitor, while a tempting lady almost makes him miss his target!

SHELTER #10: MASSACRE MOUNTAIN (972, $2.25)
A pistol-packin' lady suspects Shell is her enemy—and her gun isn't the only thing that goes off!

Available wherever paperbacks are sold, or order direct from the Publisher. Send cover price plus 50¢ per copy for mailing and handling to Zebra Books, 475 Park Avenue South, New York, N.Y. 10016. DO NOT SEND CASH.

THE GUNN SERIES BY JORY SHERMAN

GUNN #1: DAWN OF REVENGE (594, $1.95)
Accused of killing his wife, William Gunnison changes his name to Gunn and begins his fight for revenge. He'll kill, maim, turn the west blood red—until he finds the men who murdered his wife.

GUNN #2: MEXICAN SHOWDOWN (628, $1.95)
When Gunn rode into the town of Cuchillo, he didn't know the rules. But when he walked into Paula's Cantina, he knew he'd learn them.

GUNN #3: DEATH'S HEAD TRAIL (648, $1.95)
With his hands on his holster and his eyes on the sumptuous Angela Larkin, Gunn goes off hot—on his enemy's trail.

GUNN #4: BLOOD JUSTICE (670, $1.95)
Gunn is enticed into playing a round with a ruthless gambling scoundrel—and playing around with the scoundrel's estranged wife!

GUNN #8: APACHE ARROWS (791, $2.25)
Gunn gets more than he bargained for when he rides in with pistols cocked to save a beautiful settler woman from ruthless Apache renegades.

GUNN #9: BOOTHILL BOUNTY (830, $2.25)
When Gunn receives a desperate plea for help from the sumptuous Trilla, he's quick to respond—because he knows she'll make it worth his while!

GUNN #10: HARD BULLETS (896, $2.25)
The disappearance of a gunsmith and a wagon full of ammo sparks suspicion in the gunsmith's daughter. She thinks Gunn was involved, and she's up-in-arms!

GUNN #11: TRIAL BY SIXGUN (918, $2.25)
Gunn offers help to a pistol-whipped gambler and his well-endowed daughter—only to find that he'll have to lay more on the table than his cards!

GUNN #12: THE WIDOW-MAKER (987, $2.25)
Gunn offers to help the lovely ladies of Luna Creek when the ruthless Widow-maker gang kills off their husbands. It's hard work, but the rewards are mounting!

Available wherever paperbacks are sold, or order direct from the Publisher. Send cover price plus 50¢ per copy for mailing and handling to Zebra Books, 475 Park Avenue South, New York, N.Y. 10016. DO NOT SEND CASH.

THE CONTINUING BOLT SERIES
BY CORT MARTIN

BOLT #3: SHOWDOWN AT BLACK MESA (812, $2.25)
Wanted for bank robbery and murder, Bolt returns to Black Mesa to rescue beautiful Belle Wilkins. Bounty hunters and a cut-throat cattle baron make it a challenge for him just to stay alive!

BOLT #4: THE GUNS OF TAOS (873, $2.25)
When a dying man warns Bolt to get out of Taos or meet with the same fate, hard living—and loving—Bolt doesn't take the threat lightly!

BOLT #5: SHOOTOUT AT SANTA FE (943, $2.25)
While tracking down the murderers of a U.S. Marshal, Bolt befriend's the dead man's pretty young daughter. And along the way, he teaches her the facts of life—and then some!

BOLT #6: TOMBSTONE HONEYPOT (1009, $2.25)
In Tombstone, Bolt meets up with luscious Honey Carberry who tricks him into her beehive. But Bolt has a stinger of his own!

Available wherever paperbacks are sold, or order direct from the Publisher. Send cover price plus 50¢ per copy for mailing and handling to Zebra Books, 475 Park Avenue South, New York, N.Y. 10016. DO NOT SEND CASH.

BESTSELLING BLOCKBUSTERS FROM ZEBRA . . .

EXTRATERRESTRIAL (1033, $2.95)
by Julian Shock
From millions of light years away—they came. And the earth would never be the same. They were peaceful, harmless, friendly. But, *they were not one of us* . . .

SPY GAME (1038, $2.95)
by John McNeil
When a Russian microcomputer is hooked into the Vulcan war games system, U.S. military secrets are beamed straight into the Soviet Union. And if someone hits the right joystick, killer rockets will turn a video joy game into a deadly SPY GAME!

SHUTTLE (951, $3.25)
by David C. Onley
A giant hypersonic jet—with the shuttle *Columbia* clasped to its back—climbs into the sky. Neither craft will reach its destination. One will never return. . . .

MOON LAKE (1004, $2.95)
by Stephan Gresham
Slowly, silently, fear began to grow on Moon Lake. And from the murky depths, an almost human face took form. Its red eyes glowed, its evil breath chilled the air—and it claimed the innocent in a terrifying nightmare of unspeakable horror!

Available wherever paperbacks are sold, or order directly from the Publisher. Send cover price plus 50¢ per copy for mailing and handling to Zebra Books, 475 Park Avenue South, New York, N. Y. 10016. DO NOT SEND CASH.